Whiskey Mountain

Whiskey Mountain Series

Something To Talk About

Something To Think About

Something To Believe In

Something To Live For

Something To Love

Something To Talk About

Whiskey Mountain Book 1

Samantha Baca

Copyright © 2022 by Samantha Baca.

Cover Design: Oh So Novel

<u>One</u>

Maggie

"Welcome to Spill The Beans, I'll be right with you," I called over my shoulder as I finished the last few sentences on my recent blog post. I made sure to save the document before I minimized the window and closed my laptop.

My stomach flip-flopped as I headed over to the front counter and recognized the grumpy man waiting impatiently at the cash register. It wasn't his obnoxiously tall, muscular frame that gave him away, nor was it the jet-black hair that was perfectly trimmed and fell neatly into place. It was the piercing green eyes that locked on me and pulled me into the abyss as I stood in front of him. Every single time I looked at him, I could feel myself slipping deeper into their depths.

He looked tired but not tired enough to neglect the thin goatee that dotted his jawline. Apparently, his priorities included grooming and not sleep—not that I was one to judge. I was almost late this morning because I took an extra five minutes to shave my legs even though it was the dead of winter in Montana and no one would see them. But still—it made me feel better.

"Good morning," I greeted in my usual chipper tone. "What can I get you? We have a few specials if you'd like to hear them." I knew that he didn't, but I offered anyway.

He raised a brow and tapped his debit card on the counter. I let out a heavy sigh and pulled my mouth to the side.

"Are you sure I can't convince you to try something new? Just this once?" I asked, pressing my hands in front of me while giving him the best puppy dog eyes I had.

"No, thank you."

I waited a few seconds to see if he would change his mind, even though I knew he wouldn't. While I didn't know Owen Crawford very well, I knew that he drank his coffee black and shot down every recommendation I had ever suggested to help liven it up.

"Okay," I replied casually. "Anything else this morning?"

"No."

"Not even a muffin? I just baked a fresh batch of *banana nut*," I offered.

I wasn't sure it was possible, but his brows rose even higher on his forehead, disappearing into his hairline.

"Is that supposed to mean something?" he questioned, his voice containing a hint of amusement.

"What?" I asked, looking over my shoulder as I prepared his coffee in a to-go cup.

"The way you said *banana nut*, it felt like there was some hidden message I was supposed to pick up on."

I snapped the lid onto his cup and slid it across the counter to him.

"Oh," I stammered, wiping my now sweaty palms on the front of my jeans. "I just thought, you know, it was a good choice because you're a man."

"And it's a *manly muffin?*"

"Not per se…."

"The other muffins are too feminine for me?" He bent slightly and looked into the case. "Is the double chocolate chunk muffin not a manly choice?"

"Just forget I said anything," I laughed, waving my hand in the air. I reached forward to take his card as he pulled it away.

The hint of a smile curled up the corners of his plump lips, making my insides feel all mushy. He was staring at me, giving me his undivided attention while I was squirming to get away. Owen NEVER paid this much attention to me, and it was now apparent that my body had no idea how to handle it. I was sweaty and twitchy and pretty sure I might explode from the adrenaline that started pumping through me as I scrambled to talk my way out of this one.

"No way, I want to know what you were insinuating." He smiled. An honest, genuine smile that crinkled the corners of his eyes.

Gosh, he was so good-looking. Older but not too old. Hair that begged to have my hands run through it. Biceps that could easily lift me and toss me over his shoulder as he paraded me down the hallway to my bed.

"I wasn't," I lied, retracting my hand and lowering it to my side while trying to force the inappropriate daydream out of my head. Man, I desperately needed to get laid. But since I was single and Whiskey Mountain was a small town with no prospects, it really meant that I needed a night alone with a bottle of wine and my vibrating rose.

His eyes locked on me, and for a moment, I felt like I was going to get consumed in the thick green forest. *Had I ever seen anyone with such dark green eyes before? They were hypnotizing, and I wanted to get lost.*

"What's so special about the banana nut?" His voice was softer now, all hints of mocking me gone.

I took a deep breath and pulled my shoulders back. He wasn't going to let this go, so I had no choice but to tell him.

"Fine," I sighed. "Bananas contain potassium, magnesium, and B vitamins, which increase the body's overall energy levels. They also contain the bromelain enzyme." I lowered my eyes and looked away.

"And that's supposed to mean what? What does the bromelain enzyme do?"

I felt my neck flame with heat as it rushed to my cheeks. While I had good intentions for recommending it, I never imagined having to explain it out loud. When people came here for a date, I could get by with making my subtle suggestions to the guys, and that was the end of it.

"It helps improve blood flow and increases libido," I rushed out, then tried to cover my last few words with a cough behind my fist.

His brows were back up, drastically high again, as he took in my words.

He licked his lips, and I found myself following the trail of wetness that his tongue left across them. Then he leaned in closer and whispered.

"So, you're telling me that you think that I should have a banana nut muffin this morning because *you're* worried about *my* libido?"

I was suddenly on fire and took a step back. His words shot straight through my body, spreading heat along the way.

"Umm…."

I shook my head, trying to clear the word *libido* from my head. Something about how he said it made it sound so dirty and arousing. *Libido…. Libido… Li… Bi… Do.*

"Maggie?" he asked, pulling me out of my fog.

"Sorry, what?"

He chuckled and tapped his debit card again.

"I was just saying that I'll go ahead and take a muffin," he said, extending his card to me. Before I could grab it, he pulled it back again, our fingers brushing against each other in the process. "Better yet, why don't you make it two."

"Two?" I choked out, finally taking his card.

"Yeah, I wouldn't want my *libido* to suffer this morning."

My heart thumped wildly in my chest as I rang him up, then went to grab his muffins. He thanked me, and for the first time since he'd started coming in two months ago, he smiled at me as he left. TWO smiles in one day? Something was definitely amiss in the universe.

I leaned back against the counter, allowing it to hold me steady as my knees wobbled beneath me.

Men like him didn't exist in Whiskey Mountain, which was why all the women had been going crazy since he arrived. Now I understood what all of the fuss was about.

After I gathered myself again, I went back to the table in the corner that had the best view and started a new blog post. Spill The Beans wasn't just the name of my adorable coffee shop but also the blog I ran that focused on relationship advice. Not that I was an expert of any sort, but if there was anyone who loved love, it was me.

Two

Owen

I sat at my desk, peeling back the wrapper on the muffin. I purposely tried to avoid getting to know people in town since I wasn't planning on staying in Whiskey Mountain very long. Just long enough to do my job, then return home to New York City.

But there was something about Maggie—I finally stopped long enough to read the name tag that was conveniently right above her right breast—that drew me in this morning. Maybe it was that I was too tired to dart in and out of the coffee shop like I normally did, or perhaps it was how flustered she got when she started rambling on about the damn muffins. Then again, maybe I was so used to interacting with people and the constant buzz in NYC that I actually craved talking to someone this morning.

My first meeting of the day had been rescheduled, which gave me the opportunity to google whether or not bananas were supposed to improve male libido. Sure enough, they were a great natural option, and so was pineapple. And after a lengthy search and plenty of rabbit holes later, I also found that if I ate enough pineapple, it would make my cum taste better too. Not that I had anyone to try that out on.

I was single and planned to stay that way. Relationships weren't my thing. Committing to someone who would just turn around and break every promise they'd ever made—as well as your heart—kept me guarded and ready to run the second a woman looked at me a certain way. Trust me—we all knew the look. If you hadn't seen it yourself in person, it was in every chick flick I had ever seen, almost like it was some sort of how-to guide that taught girls how to master it.

I chewed the last bite of muffin and wiped my face with the napkin. No matter how hard I tried, I still couldn't get Maggie out of my head. The way her short hair fell into her eyes when she bashfully looked away, or her full lips that begged to be kissed. She was bite-sized compared to my tall stature, but that didn't stop me from imagining her wrapped around my waist as I showed her that I didn't need a damn muffin to help my libido. Her blue eyes were like kryptonite and had me going crazy.

Once I was done eating, I cleared the trash from my desk and got started with my day. My first meeting this morning was supposed to be with the planning committee to discuss the proposals I had come up with for revitalizing the old, run-down strip mall that sat just within city limits. I knew that I had been chosen for this project because of the recent work that I had done in Fallen Oaks, which was the next small town over.

I had already drafted several proposals that included different options for the committee to discuss. The best option, in my opinion, was for them to knock down the current structure and rebuild. But if I'd learned anything from working in small towns, it was that the locals were rarely ever supportive of destroying an existing establishment and starting over.

There was something refreshing and invigorating about starting fresh and building something new. Being able to make it exactly what you wanted without any restrictions. Not having to worry about what problems might be hiding, waiting to come out like dirty little secrets. That's how I would handle things, but unfortunately, my job entailed that I discuss all of the options available and then figure out which one worked best for everyone involved.

By mid-day, I had rescheduled meetings and set up appointments to look at some additional land that the mayor wanted to discuss. It had been sitting vacant for years, and after I discussed some of the work I had done in Fallen Oaks, we agreed that it might be worth looking into ways to develop the land to create more business for the neighboring towns.

I looked out my office window and smiled at the people walking past, huddling close together to avoid the cold while they rushed into the next shop. It was a small building—roughly the size of my office in New York—with one bathroom, a small room in the back that I was currently using as a conference room for meetings, and the space up front where I'd set up my desk. After working in Fallen Oaks, I knew that it was important to come across as approachable when people came to my office, even if I kept my distance from everyone everywhere else.

This was the second strip mall in Whiskey Mountain, the other one being the property I was supposed to discuss this morning before the meeting was canceled. There were roughly fifteen shops that spanned the length of Main Street. Each one faced the street, and the back of the building was for parking. My office was set up between a cozy-looking book shop and a gift shop that got a lot of traffic. I was also only a few spaces down from Spill The Beans, which I convinced myself was why I stopped by there every morning for my coffee fix. It wasn't that I couldn't just make my own damn coffee—it was as basic as coffee could be.

But Maggie, on the other hand, was anything but basic, and I found myself wanting an excuse to see her more often. My mind knew better than to allow myself to get to know a woman like her, but damn if my body didn't get the same message. The problem was, women like Maggie weren't into no-strings-attached hook-ups, and unfortunately, that's all that I had in me anymore.

Three

Maggie

I sat down at my desk and opened my emails, ready to answer the ones that had come in today while I was working at the coffee shop. Since we were only open until three, it gave me plenty of time to respond to reader emails as part of my weekly *Ask Mags* section, which focused on relationship and love advice.

I sipped my tea and brought my knees up against my chest as I read the first one.

Ask Mags,

I recently found out that my boyfriend has been talking to another woman. He insists that she's just a friend, but I feel like there's more to it. He hides his phone from me, and the other day lied and said he was talking to his mom. I knew he was lying because I had just gotten off the phone with her. What should I do? I don't feel like I can trust him anymore.

-- Confused in Montana

I sucked in a deep breath, cracked my knuckles, and dove in.

Dear Confused in Montana,

I'm sorry to hear that; I can imagine how frustrating and disheartening that must have been to find out. I think there are many things happening here that need to be considered. First, your boyfriend is talking to another woman who he insists is just a friend. If you're unsure whether to believe him, I would sit down and talk to him. If she really is a friend, then maybe the three of you can go do something together so you can get to know her. I understand that he was wrong for not telling you about her, but I think the lines of communication are closed on both ends. Do you think there's a reason he's so closed off and doesn't want to tell you that he's talking to her?

Is it possible that he feels you might not be supportive or that you could be jealous of her? I wouldn't jump to the worst conclusion right away, but I do think that you owe it to yourself to have an honest conversation with him. If you're still unsure and unable to trust him, then maybe it's best to re-examine your relationship and see if you can move forward. A relationship without trust isn't healthy and won't last long. Best of luck, and please let me know how it goes.

I pressed send and leaned back against the kitchen chair. While I didn't enjoy these types of emails, I never ignored them because everyone deserved an opportunity to discuss whatever was going on in their lives. And even if this relationship didn't work out for them, I knew in my heart that they were destined to find love. We all were. Some of us just took longer than others....

But, that also didn't mean that my eyes didn't light up and my heart didn't swell when I got the sweet ones about trying to find love, like the next one.

Ask Mags,

Help! I recently started a new job, and my coworker is soooo cute! But every time he tries to talk to me, I clam up and walk away. I can't help it! He makes me shy, and I can't think of anything logical to say. I don't want to mess things up with him by looking like I'm stupid. You have to help me! Show me the way!

--Twitterpated and Confused

I giggled as my fingers began moving swiftly across the keyboard.

Dear Twitterpated and Confused,

This is an excellent thing! I'm so excited for you! But don't worry, those feelings are normal and we've all been there at some point or another.

The next time you see him, try to initiate a conversation. Keep it short and straightforward, and maybe practice saying it in your head ahead of time, that way you don't freeze by trying to come up with something on the spot. It can be as simple as—"hey, it looks cloudy. I wonder if it's going to rain." Once he starts talking, focus on what he says—not what his mouth looks like as he speaks.

Soon, you'll find that the conversation gets easier, and then you can see about asking him out. Start with a casual, easy-going date so you're both comfortable and no one feels the need to impress each other. I always like to suggest coffee dates, and as you probably know—I happen to have the CUTEST coffee shop where you guys can meet! I promise I won't spill the beans, *but I'll probably be standing behind the counter, squealing for joy for you! Also, if you do come to the shop, be sure to try the lavender latte. It's a calming mix of lavender, chamomile, and honey—and it's delicious! The perfect combination for those first date jitters.*

I answered a few more emails, then shut off my computer. It was early in the day, and I was surprisingly caught up. After the holidays, things usually slowed down for me. Tourists were no longer flocking to Whiskey Mountain to rent a snowy cabin to spend Christmas. Instead, they were all back at home, trying to keep those New Year's resolutions they set a few months ago. Which speaking of, I had started to let slide.

I pulled my hair into a ponytail, struggling with a few pieces that were too short to go in right. I hated my hair too long because it got in my way, but at the same time, I hated it being too short because I was constantly putting it up, which got harder the shorter it was.

The weather app on my phone showed that it was as cold outside as it looked, but that wasn't going to stop me. I was born and raised in Montana, so I was already used to the cold weather. I put on my shoes, grabbed my phone, popped an earbud in my ear, and headed out for a run.

I wasn't one of those people who listened to music while I ran. Nope, I was one of those women who listened to audiobooks and purposely chose the smuttiest one that I could find. Nothing helped me get those extra few steps in like a woman panting heavily in my ear as some devilishly handsome man pushed her over the edge as she climaxed.

My feet pounded the pavement as I sprinted through town, watching out for pedestrians as I breezed past them on the sidewalk. It wasn't my favorite place to run, but the trail I preferred was covered in ice, leaving few choices for me today.

Just as I was about to slow down to avoid an elderly man coming out of a shop, a door swung open and hit me in the face as I ran into it.

"Son of a bitch!" I yelled, bouncing back as I watched the stars dancing in front of my face.

"Oh my God!" a deep voice muttered. "Are you okay?"

I held my fingers to the bridge of my nose, trying to stop the bleeding as I felt the warm liquid drip from my face.

"I'm bleeding," I stammered, unable to lift my head enough to see who was talking to me. Not that I needed to, I would recognize that voice anywhere.

Suddenly he moved, towering over me as his eyes cautiously looked me over, checking for other injuries. His height gave him an advantage so he didn't have to strain to see me, which made me feel ridiculously small.

"What the hell were you doing running here anyways?" he asked, looking around and leading me to the side by my elbow so we were out of the way. He grabbed the travel pack of tissues the old lady handed him before shuffling into the store. He fished a few out and gave them to me. "Is someone trying to hurt you? Were you being followed?"

I sat on the bench outside the bookstore and narrowed my eyes as he kneeled in front of me. I held the tissue tightly to my nose and pinched it. His gray button-up shirt wrapped snuggly around his broad chest, and the rolled-up sleeves showed off tattoos I hadn't seen before.

"Why would someone be trying to hurt me?" I asked dumbly.

"Because you were running like a mad woman down the sidewalk."

He looked at me like it was an obvious answer, then frowned when I let my head fall back and laughed.

"I do not run like a mad woman."

"Normal people don't run down sidewalks."

"There was nowhere else to run." I pulled the tissue away, thankful that it looked like a minor nosebleed that was already starting to slow down.

He continued to study me intently as he stood and folded his arms over his chest. The way he looked right now reminded me of a business casual Superman, and that sent weird tingles between my thighs. Suddenly, I remembered the audiobook that was still playing in my ear. I pulled my phone out, turned it off, and shoved the earbud into my pocket.

He was about to say something but stopped short when the audiobook decided to play through my phone speaker instead of the earbud that I had thought I had turned off.

"Do you like it when I fuck you from behind?" a deep voice asked, followed by a moaning *yes* from a breathy woman. My cheeks flamed with embarrassment as I fumbled with my phone, trying to turn the book off. My fingers were clumsy as they tried to unlock the screen and press the volume button down.

"Take it, Ava," he groaned. "Take this huge coc—"

I stabbed at the screen repeatedly until it finally stopped.

He covered his mouth with his hand and looked away while I refused to make eye contact with him. Nothing, and I mean *NOTHING* this embarrassing had ever happened to me before.

"So, um…" He rubbed his lips together while he continued to look the other way. He shoved his hands into his trouser pockets and rocked back on his heels.

Was this as uncomfortable for him as it was for me?

The way he was now grinning made me think that he somehow enjoyed seeing me embarrassed.

"Do you think he had a banana nut muffin for breakfast?" he asked coolly.

I finally allowed my eyes to lift and found his as they danced with delight.

"Because maybe you were right." He shrugged. "She sure seemed to be a fan either way."

I inhaled slowly and gripped the bench beneath me. This was officially the worst day ever.

"I'm going to go," I blurted out and pushed up to a standing position, only I wasn't quite steady enough to get up that fast after getting hit in the face by a door.

I stumbled and extended my arm to brace myself when I felt his arm wrap around my waist and hold me steady.

"Why don't you come inside for a bit and rest?" he offered.

I looked up, realizing I was standing between the bookstore and his new office.

There was a new sign that had been put up that read *Advantage Realty Group* above the red door. I wasn't sure it was the best color to use for a company that's been proposing tearing down one of Whiskey Mountain's oldest strip malls, but who was I to judge?

My door was hot pink with polka dots. Red could also be a color of love, not just aggression.

"I need to get home," I objected, smelling the scent of his cologne as he stood next to me.

"I don't think that's the best idea right now. I'm happy to take you home later when you're ready."

My brows rose with what he said. A few seconds later, he realized the accidental innuendo and cleared his throat.

"I meant I could drive you to your house and drop you off. Make sure you got inside okay without running into any more doors."

"You hit me with one; I didn't run into it."

I let him lead me to the entrance of his office, knowing he was right. I wasn't in any condition to walk home on my own right now.

"In all fairness, I never expected anyone to come flying down the sidewalk like some serial killer was on their heels."

"Are you saying that I run fast?" I asked, looking up at him with a cheeky smile.

"No, I'm saying that you were running like a crazy person. Like Phoebe, from Friends."

"Who?"

He stopped walking and stared at me in disbelief.

"You don't know who Phoebe is?"

"Nope." I pulled my mouth into a thin line and offered a small smile.

"How old are you?" he asked, wincing as he rubbed the back of his neck.

"Twenty-two."

I couldn't hear what he said, but I was pretty sure he had muttered a curse word under his breath.

"Why, how old are you?"

"Too old," he sighed, then went back to leading me inside.

Something changed with him, and his fun, flirty side quickly disappeared and went back to the grumpy, standoffish side I was used to.

"I really should get home," I said, pulling away. "I need to go check on Leroy." I was lying through my teeth—Leroy was fine and didn't need me to rush back, given I had just left him less than an hour ago. But Owen didn't need to know that, and I was desperate for an excuse to escape.

His fingers gripped my elbow again and turned me back toward the door.

"Who is Leroy? I can see if someone else can go check on him, but I really think you need to stay here for a little bit until you can walk right."

My legs felt like Jell-O, but I was willing to run on wobbly legs like Bambi to avoid having to be around grumpy Owen. I firmly believed in people absorbing each other's energy, which meant I tried to hang out with positive, fun people like me and avoid the energies that would bring mine down.

"It's fine; I'll be okay. Thank you, though."

"Maggie, who is Leroy? I can go check on him. Just tell me where to find him, and I'll go real quick."

I smiled and turned to face him.

"He's under my bed. Probably wearing my bra on his head."

He pulled his head back and furrowed his brow.

"Is he your boyfriend?"

I could see the wheels in his head turning as he tried to figure out why a man would be under my bed, wearing my bra as a hat.

"No, but he would make a pretty decent one."

He waited me out and started tapping his foot impatiently.

"He's my pet turtle," I laughed. "Though if I don't get home soon, he'll probably eat my underwear again."

"Do I even want to know?" he asked, rubbing his hand across his strong jaw with a raised brow.

"He can't always see what's food and what's not. Last time he mistook my green lace panties for lettuce and chewed a hole right through the crotc—"

"I get the picture." He held up a hand to stop me from continuing.

"Okay. Why don't I drive you home and make sure you're okay before Leroy eats more of your belongings?"

I wanted to say no. I wanted to convince him that I was fine getting home on my own. I've never needed anyone before, so it was a struggle to admit that I needed someone now.

Before I could object, my knees buckled, and I felt myself in his arms again.

"Okay," I breathed, no longer determined to fight him. "If you're sure you don't mind."

"It would be my pleasure."

His fingers gently trailed down my back before he planted his hand firmly on my lower back and guided me toward his car.

<u>Four</u>

Owen

"Leroy," she called, bending down and looking under the kitchen table as she walked the short distance between the kitchen and living room.

I closed the door behind us, making sure Leroy didn't try to escape.

"Leroy Mitchell Elwood, get your little green butt out here right now."

She picked up a shirt from the arm of the couch and leaned over to look at the floor as she continued to search for the turtle.

I stayed put, not willing to randomly invite myself further into her house to find a lost reptile. My only reason for even being here right now was to make sure she didn't fall and get hurt after getting hit in the face with the door. I still felt terrible about it, but who in their right mind runs down a busy sidewalk with plenty of doors that could swing open?

I heard her voice carry as she went through the rest of the house, calling his name.

As I glanced down to check my watch, a glimpse of something moving caught the corner of my eye and made me jump.

"Son of a bitch!" I exclaimed, moving back as Maggie headed back down the hallway.

She looked at me in surprise before looking down to see what had startled me.

"Leroy," she sighed, walking over and plucking the red lace panties from his head. She quickly pushed them into her pocket and then picked him up. "You know you're not supposed to escape."

I watched as she walked over to a wooden terrarium set up by the floor-to-ceiling window in the kitchen. There wasn't a dining table or chairs, so I assumed she ate most of her meals on the couch and reserved the space for Leroy's cage.

"How did he escape?" I asked, joining her as she sat him down in the terrarium. At first glance, it looked to be in great condition, though when she squatted down to adjust the bottom, I noticed where the two pieces of wood had come apart, and he had pushed his way through.

"He knows that if he pushes hard enough, he can squeeze through this opening. I've been meaning to get a glass one, but I have to find someone to go with me since it's too big for me to bring back on my own without dropping it."

"Have you had Leroy long?"

She shook her head, grabbed a handful of lettuce from the fridge, and then dropped it into his food bowl.

"Only a few weeks. My neighbor got him for her kids, but he scared her daughter, so she asked if I could take him. One look at those beautiful eyes, and I couldn't say no. I'm a sucker." She shrugged and looked adoringly at her turtle. "But unfortunately, her kids were a little rough with the cage, and as you can see, it broke. I haven't had a chance to get a new one, and honestly, he seems to prefer roaming the house anyway."

"Well, if you need help, I'm happy to go with you."

She tilted her head and eyed me curiously.

"Why are you being nice to me?"

I pulled my head back in response. I knew I had never engaged her much in conversation, aside from this morning, but had I been mean to her? I hated the thought that my avoiding people had come across that way.

When I failed to come up with a response to her question, she waved dismissively and started talking again.

"It's okay, I have a friend who should be back in town soon. He has a truck, so I can ask him to drive me over and help me set it up."

I knew I had no right to feel jealous, but I did. And that stupid feeling had my mouth moving faster than my brain could keep up.

"It's not a problem. I can take you now if you want."

"Don't you need to get back to work?"

I glanced at my watch. I still had two hours left and a ton of work I needed to finish before my meetings tomorrow.

"Nope, I'm fine," I lied. "Grab your stuff, and I'll meet you in the car."

Before she could object, I turned and walked out the door, letting out a heavy breath once I was alone.

What the fuck was I thinking?

Ten minutes later, she was climbing in and buckling her seatbelt.

"Where did you want to go?" I asked, starting the engine.

"There's a pet store just outside of town that has the one that I want. But really, we don't have to go if it's out of your way. I can wait."

Her fingers twitched as if ready to unbuckle herself and jump out of the car.

"It's fine, I really don't mind. What's the name of it?"

"Cool Cats. It's my friend's pet shop, and she's kinda—*out there*," she laughed. "I don't know how to explain it, but she's always been obsessed with the prohibition era, so she named her shop Cool Cats, and it's got a speakeasy type of vibe. You can't see into the shop, there's no sign out front, and there's a password to get in."

"You're kidding?" I turned to face her as I headed down the street. That might've been the coolest thing I've heard since arriving in Whiskey Mountain.

"Nope. She loves it, and the people in town enjoy it too. Just something fun and different."

"Sounds like it," I smiled. "I can't wait to check it out."

We drove in silence for a few minutes while she went online to get the password. Apparently, there was a riddle that you had to solve before gaining access to the store webpage. Once you were in, you could place orders online or get the password to visit the store.

"Today's password is All Hail The Tipsy Tail."

I laughed and looked at her.

"Does that mean that there will be drunk cats there, too?"

"Na," she giggled. "Only cool cats and kittens."

I loved how her face lit up with happiness and wondered if she was always this way. I had yet to see her grumpy or in a bad mood, but then again, I hadn't spent much time around her.

"How's your nose feel?" I asked as we headed to Fallen Oaks.

"It's better. I took some Tylenol before we left, but I should have thought to grab an ice pack too. I imagine I'll have a beautiful bruise that I'll have to explain tomorrow. It's a good thing I'm off."

"I'm really sorry," I apologized again. "I feel terrible for hitting you with the door. If I would have known that you were running…."

"It's okay, really. It's not like you could see me. I think your door is the only one on the strip that doesn't have a glass pane."

"I might have to request one now."

"Or I'll just avoid running by your office," she laughed. "Usually, I'm on the trail behind the strip, but it's still covered in ice from the last freeze we had."

The weather hadn't been as bad as I had imagined, though I was also used to winter in New York City. I'm not sure what I was expecting, but something along the lines of extreme blizzards and snow piles that were over four feet tall came to mind.

Soon we were pulling up to an unmarked building with blacked-out windows. I put the car in park and looked over at her with as much seriousness as I could muster.

"If you brought me here to kill me…."

I watched as her lips curled up into a smile as she unbuckled.

"There's only one way to find out."

<u>Five</u>

Maggie

"All hail the tipsy tail," I said into the speaker box outside.

We waited a few seconds, then pulled the door open once we heard the buzz.

I led Owen down the steps toward the entrance, trying not to laugh at how nervous he seemed. If he thought I was going to kill him, I couldn't imagine how he would react once we were inside the store.

His footsteps fell heavily behind mine and stopped as we reached the door. I looked over my shoulder and smiled as I opened the door and stepped aside to let him go first.

"Nope," he shook his head. "Ladies first."

"Are you still worried that I'm trying to kill you?" I laughed and waited for him to go.

"No, but *if* someone wants to kill us, it seems fitting that you should lead the way since this was all your idea.

"We don't kill people," Ramona said as she walked around the corner to greet us. "The wild animals prefer that they're alive so they can hunt them."

Her hazel eyes sparkled with mischief as the parrot on her shoulder squawked *hunt them, kill them.*

"That's enough, Pablo," she scolded, popping a treat into the bird's mouth. "We don't want to scare off our new friend."

I laughed and walked inside, waiting for Owen to join us.

"Ramona, this is Owen. Owen, this is Ramona, and that's Pablo. He has a foul mouth and knows more curse words than a drunk sailor."

"Cocksucker," Pablo squawked and bounced to Ramona's other shoulder. "Pussy eater damn shithead."

"That's enough," Ramona tsked and lifted her finger to transfer him to his cage.

"Sorry," she apologized, extending her hand to Owen. "It's nice to meet you."

"You too." He shook her hand and looked around the store. "I can't believe this is down here; you'd never know from the looks of it outside."

She smiled proudly, letting it stretch across her cheeks.

I excused myself to go look at the new terrariums she mentioned she had when I texted her earlier to let her know that we were on our way. I listened as she told Owen the story about how this building had been in her family for generations and how it once served as a speakeasy during the prohibition.

There were a handful of options to choose from when it came to picking the perfect setup for Leroy. I crouched down and looked over the different bags of substrate to line the bottom of the enclosure. I already picked out a basking lamp as well as a few ceramic heat emitters and made sure to grab a UVB light since it was still too cold to allow Leroy to spend time outside until it warmed up. I grabbed plenty of bags of substrate that was chemical-free topsoil, leaves, and moss and did the math to make sure I had plenty for him to have room to burrow.

It was fun picking out the accessories that would go into his house. Since Leroy was still technically a baby, I read that he needed food at least every 24 hours and made sure to add a plate that would make it easier to eat his food without consuming any of the substrate. In all fairness, he had been wandering aimlessly through my apartment for a few days since I got him and ate holes in my panties, so this was already a step in the right direction.

I was adding the last few things to my cart when I heard Ramona and Owen talking. I leaned up on my tiptoes, trying to hear them better without knocking anything over.

"You haven't read it yet?!" Ramona exclaimed. "You have no idea what you're missing! It's literally the best advice column out there. Maggie *LOVES* love, and it shows every time she writes about it."

"I don't do a lot of reading," Owen replied lightly.

"It's so worth it. Maggie answers reader questions every day in her *Ask Mags* section, but then she also writes blog posts where she reflects on love and relationships. It's so heartwarming, and on occasion, she dives into the good stuff and we get *just the tip*—if you know what I mean...."

"Just the tip," Pablo squawked repeatedly. "Just the tip."

I pressed the palm of my head and closed my eyes. She was not seriously telling Owen about my blog!

Not that I was ashamed of it, but after spending time with Owen, it made me feel a little nervous about what he would say about it.

"She's also known as the town matchmaker. She's helped sooo many people get over their nerves and find their soul mate," she gushed. "It's really amazing. I'm still waiting for her to find her one true love. God knows she deserves it and is holding out for the real thing this time. After what that asshole did to her—"

I jumped away, her words making me want to flee. In the process, I knocked over a shelf of fish food, drawing their attention to where I was now trying to hide.

"Fucking shit," I muttered quietly. Or so I thought.

"Fucking shit. Fucking shit. Shit on a cracker. Shit on Poly. Poly wants a fucking cracker."

"Everything alright?" Owen asked, rounding the corner and taking in the mess I'd made.

I nodded and scrambled to pick up the boxes as quickly as possible. He bent down and helped, though I could tell his body was way more relaxed than mine. His fingers weren't struggling to hold onto the boxes as he put them back; instead, they gripped each one firmly, and I found myself staring inappropriately.

"You sure you're okay?" he whispered, doing the raised brow thing again.

Why was his cocked eyebrow so sexy?

"Yeah, I wasn't paying attention and bumped the shelf."

Ramona was up front, on the phone with a customer, while Pablo continued with his obscenities.

"What's with the bird?" Owen asked, nodding in his direction.

"He was dropped off with a note that said they couldn't care for him anymore. Ramona took him in but hasn't decided if she's going to keep him for herself or allow someone to adopt him. Obviously, it would take the right people and not a family with kids," I laughed. "For now, they keep each other company, and I think she's gotten used to his random outbursts. The other day, I was talking to her on the phone and heard him tell her to get him a shot of whiskey. Apparently, his previous owner also liked to indulge."

"Sounds like it," Owen laughed, putting the last box on the shelf.

I grabbed the last few things I needed and went up front to pay. I wanted to ask Ramona why she told Owen about the blog but knew I couldn't without sounding weird about it. I've never had a problem with people knowing what I write about until now, but I've also never had to worry about the prospect of dating anyone in town. Until now.

<u>Six</u>

Owen

After I dropped Maggie off and helped her set up Leroy's terrarium, I headed back to the office to finish the work that I needed to get done. While I knew I had a long night ahead of me, I didn't regret spending time with her, which was a bit unnerving to me. The last thing that I needed was to get close to anyone in town—especially Maggie.

I couldn't help but play Ramona's words over and over in my head about how Maggie deserved to find her one true love after what that asshole did to her. Unfortunately, I wasn't given any details about what happened because that was the moment Maggie decided to throw fish food across the store like it was confetti.

I wanted to ask Maggie about it on the way back but knew that it wasn't my place. Not only that, I didn't want to give off the wrong impression and allow her to think that I was interested in getting to know her that well. Granted I wanted to, but there was no way that I could allow myself to act on it, especially now that I knew that Maggie *loved* love.

My computer dinged with another email, forcing me back to reality and away from thoughts of the woman who had been on my mind all damn day. I replied to the email, closed it out, and went back to printing the reports I had asked my friend in Fallen Oaks to send over. I knew there was still a lot of indecisiveness over what to do with the abandoned strip mall, and my goal was to show them the growth that Fallen Oaks was seeing after revitalizing one of their own.

As I stood by the printer and waited, I thought back to being in Maggie's house, searching for Leroy again once we got back. He was probably the best escape artist I had seen and this time was found chewing through another pair of underwear he had stolen from a laundry basket in her bedroom. I had no idea how many pairs of panties she had already gone through, but I had a feeling this turtle was going to be more expensive than she thought at this rate.

Once the pages were printed, I sat down at my desk and stacked them in a pile with the rest of the items I needed for tomorrow morning. I opened a new browser window on my computer and meant to type in *Fallen Oaks Tourism*, but instead found *Spill The Beans* in the search bar as I hit enter.

I promised myself that I would just take a quick glance at the blog Ramona told me about—just to satisfy my curiosity so I could get back to work. But the next thing I knew, it had been over an hour, my coffee was cold, and I was fully invested in *Just The Tip*.

Just The Tip,

My boyfriend has no idea how to make me come during sex. I wanted to bring a toy into the bedroom with us, but he said it was rude and made him feel like he couldn't satisfy me.

Honestly—he can't. But what am I supposed to do? He won't take my advice when I try to tell him what I like, and I can't keep sending him for sugar and flour just to get a few minutes alone with my vibrator. What do I do?

-- Buzzing and Frustrated

Dear Buzzing and Frustrated,

I can imagine just how frustrating that is. I think you deserve to get what you want out of your relationship, and that means in the bedroom. Have you thought about going to one of those Deliciously Pink parties? They have ones for couples, and a trained professional talks about different toy options and how to use them as a couple. He may not know that toys can be just as fun for him as they are for you. I would sit down and talk to him first, but if he's still not interested, then maybe it's time to consider whether you'll be satisfied by staying in this relationship.

One of the most essential components of any relationship is being able to feel loved and trusting your partner. If you can't openly discuss what you want with him, he may not be the one. Hopefully, he'll take a step back and listen to what you're asking for. Just make sure to do it at the right time—as in not in the bedroom, during sex, or before you think you might have sex. He's going to be more likely to shut down and not hear what you're saying during these times.

And, if all else fails, send him over to Spill The Beans to grab you a lavender latte while you get your buzz on! There's no shame in bringing toys into the bedroom; always remember that.

I swallowed hard and adjusted the tie that suddenly felt too tight around my neck. This was a different side to Maggie that I honestly hadn't expected to see. I tried to force myself to close the window and get to work, but once again, I found myself clicking on the next one.

Just The Tip,

I had a sex dream last night, and it's FREAKING me out.

It's not just the fact that it wasn't about my boyfriend, but that it was HIS DAD instead. I could feel everything he did to me in my dream as he pounded into me and made me come multiple times. It was an amazing dream, and I was so disappointed when I woke up.

But that's not the only problem. Not only do I feel guilty about fantasizing about my boyfriend's dad, but I'm also embarrassed that I'm disappointed that he got me off so well in a dream, yet his son can't give me an orgasm to save his life.

What do I do? I can't pretend that the dream didn't happen— nor do I want to! But I also can't just break up with my current boyfriend and go ask his dad to rail me. Am I a horrible person?

-- Dream Slut

Dear Dream Slut,

Can I just start by saying I don't love this name for you? Fantasizing about someone in your dreams is an action by your subconscious and is no different than having a dream about   going off and murdering a bunch of people because they ate the last donut. You wouldn't wake up and continue to obsess over such a random—and made-up—act of violence, now would you? Though, I would personally probably still obsess over the donuts because, well, donuts.

But that's not what you asked for my help with, so I'll get to the point. You're not a slut for dreaming of your boyfriend's dad. Our brains are tricky, and who knows why your subconscious chose him to put into the sex dream, but it sounds like it was an amazing one. Maybe you had recently interacted with him, or something reminded you of him, and that's why he popped up in dreamland. Either way, it doesn't sound like you're usually sitting around obsessing over dirty thoughts with him, so I wouldn't put too much concern into it.

Now, onto the bigger issue. You've said that you woke up feeling frustrated that your boyfriend doesn't get you off.

That's a problem that a lot of women face—and men, if you're reading this—LISTEN UP.

It takes a lot more to get a woman to climax than it does for men. It's not as simple as just stroking a cock for a few minutes to get the job done. Our bodies are made differently, and our minds play a huge role in whether or not we're able to get to the big O.

Sometimes we're in the mood and can get there relatively quickly with direct pressure on our clit. Other times, we're too busy making a to-do list for the weekend or trying to remember what items we need to add to our grocery list. It isn't that we don't want it; we just sometimes struggle to get out of our heads.

I recommend discussing this with your boyfriend and seeing what changes you guys can make. Does he try to get you off? Is he using a touch that you enjoy? Maybe you can try having him talk dirty to you if you're not able to get your head clear while he's touching you. Or even better, maybe show him what you like and touch yourself while he watches. It can be incredibly arousing to watch your partner masturbate.

If those things don't work and you're still obsessing over his father, maybe ask him if he thinks his dad would be interested in a threesome. Totally kidding—unless you think he'd be into it— then I say go for it.

Keep me posted, dream slut.

I didn't know that it was possible to feel so aroused by reading Maggie answer sex questions in a damn blog, but the way my trousers were suddenly snug against my cock proved that it was. Frustrated, I pushed my chair away and took a trip to the bathroom.

SOMETHING TO TALK ABOUT

<u>S</u>even

Maggie

"How is Leroy adjusting to his new home?" Ramona asked as I pushed my phone between my ear and neck to hold it in place while I loaded clothes into the washer.

"He seems to like it," I said, looking over my shoulder to see him trying to ram it open with no luck. "Though I think he much prefers to be out roaming my apartment and eating my underwear."

"How many pairs has he devoured?" She laughed, and I knew she thoroughly enjoyed hearing the stories of Leroy and his crazy antics from the moment I adopted him.

"Seven," I sighed. I tossed in the last few garments and closed the lid.

"How did he get ahold of that many? Do you just have underwear lying all over your house?"

"No. I recently went shopping and bought all new underwear after my breakup with Samuel. It was my gift to myself for walking away from such a toxic relationship. I just got them on Sunday, then Liz brought Leroy over that night, and everything has been hectic and chaotic ever since. I didn't have a chance to pick the bag up off the floor by my dresser, and he's been sneaking in and stealing them. Every time I finally remember, something else happens, and I get distracted."

Ramona laughed louder, encouraging a loud squawking laugh from Pablo.

"It's not funny," I whined. "By Wednesday, I finally remembered and picked them up off the floor. But then I put them in the hamper, and he found a way to pull them through the holes to get them out. He's obsessed."

"Is it just panties?"

"Pretty much, though I did catch him wearing one of my new bras on his head the other day. But I think it fell on his head when he was rummaging through the bag, trying to get to the good stuff."

"I've never seen an animal so obsessed with eating clothes than Leroy. I wonder why?"

"Probably because he knows how expensive they were. My name isn't Victoria, and it's no secret that I over-indulged in buying more than I needed. I even bought a few new pieces of sexy lingerie, though Lord knows I'll only be wearing them for myself."

"Don't say that." Her voice softened, and I could tell that mentioning my pending doom of singledom had dampened the conversation.

"It's true." I sat down on the couch and pulled off the lid of the Ben and Jerry's pint I had opened last night. "My only true love is Chunky Monkey because that's what I'm going to be if I don't stop eating ice cream for dinner every night."

"You're not chunky, though I think you're onto something with the monkey and bananas." She laughed, and I knew what she was getting at.

"You read my recent blog post," I giggled, lifting the spoon to my lips and allowing the cold metal to sting for a second before taking a bite.

"I sure did. Who knew that there were that many foods that could have sexual benefits? I swear, I'm going to start eating better."

"Why? It's not like you and Daniel don't have a great sex life. God knows I hear about it often enough."

"Dan's the man. Dan's the man. Do it alllll nigghhttt. Dan's the big man."

I choked on the next spoonful of ice cream as I tried to hold in my laughter at Pablo's outburst.

"Dan give it to you how you like it. Dan has a big coc—"

"Okay, that's enough out of you, bird," Ramona mumbled something else before I heard the metal cage shut and shuffling on the other line. "Sorry, he overhears way too much."

"So, Dan's the man?" I smiled cheekily, taking another bite.

"Most of the time. But that doesn't mean that I skip over *Just The Tip*. I don't know what makes you more popular in town, your incredibly sweet blog posts about love and romance, or the down and dirty details you get into in the *hidden* part of the column."

"It's not so hidden if people can find it."

Sometimes I hated that it was so easy for them to locate it. Just a few clicks on the menu, and they'd find the ominous link at the bottom. I should have taken Ramona's lead and gone with a speakeasy vibe that required a password to access it. Oh well, it was too late to worry about that now.

"Apparently so is the g-spot, not like I would know."

"Still no luck with that?"

"Nope. And I asked Dan about going to one of those classes with the sex toys, but he immediately rejected the idea. I think he thinks we're fine because I have an occasional orgasm, but I'm not gonna lie—sometimes I want to punch him in the balls when he comes and I don't."

I pressed my lips together to keep from laughing.

"Okay," she sighed. "I know. I'm being dramatic. It's every time."

I tipped my head back and let it out. She quickly joined in, and I remembered why having a rowdy best friend was the best therapy I could have.

"Well, it's not like I would know what they're like either," I said quietly, depositing the empty container into the trash before adding *Chunky Monkey* to my shopping list on the fridge.

"It'll happen soon enough. Don't stress about it."

"I'm twenty-two, Ramona. Twenty. Two."

"Relax, it's not like you're turning forty and still a virgin," she laughed. "You're still young; you just haven't met the right guy to share that with."

"The older I get, the harder it will be to find someone willing to take it. I'm going to have to be like one of those homeless people on the corner with a sign begging for money. But instead, it's going to be me begging them to take my virginity."

"That's not going to happen."

"It could."

"If you stood outside with a sign advertising that you wanted to have sex, you'd have all of Whiskey Mountain lined up, as well as all of Montana. Trust me—guys have no problem taking a girl up on her offer to have sex."

"I know," I exhaled slowly. "That's not the problem, and we both know it."

"Yeah, we do. It's not just having sex that you want. It's finding someone worthy of earning it from you. Someone who you're in love with."

We sat quietly for a few minutes, letting the words float in the air around us.

"See, it's never going to happen. I can help others work through their problems and find their happily ever afters, but I can't even find a nice guy worth dating myself. It's hopeless."

"It's not hopeless."

I felt my shoulders tense and hated that I was now out of ice cream. It was too late to run out and get some now. Everything in town had closed an hour ago, and I wasn't willing to drive a few hours out of the way for it. At least I was off tomorrow, so I could lay in bed and wallow in self-pity for a bit before forcing myself to get up and go for a run.

My fingers reached up and gingerly touched the bruise on my nose. Maybe I wouldn't run through the strip mall tomorrow. But then again, maybe I could run into Owen. Not literally, of course; that was a little painful.

My mind had drifted to thoughts of him and our afternoon spent working on putting the terrarium together for Leroy. He had even been kind enough to stop by the market so I could grab a few groceries before he dropped me off. It had been nice to see him laughing and more relaxed than he usually was when he came in for his daily black coffee. When I first met him, I thought he was just some arrogant ass from NYC and couldn't wait for him to leave town. But now, I was second-guessing my opinion of him. I couldn't help but wonder who Owen really was and if I'd get another chance to get to know him.

Eight

Owen

The next few days were busy, but thankfully the meetings had gone smoothly. I had met with the mayor, the city council, and the planning committee to discuss the options for the current strip mall that I had been brought in for, as well as a few vacant pieces of land that Mayor Landing inquired about.

Saturday morning, I got up early and headed out to run a handful of errands. Besides grocery shopping, I desperately needed to wash my truck to get the mud splatters off from the recent storm. Usually, I made coffee at home on the weekend, but since I was officially out of that, I found myself walking into Spill The Beans as my nerves balled in my stomach.

There were a few people in line, so I took the opportunity to stand back and watch Maggie as she worked. Her brown hair was pulled into a ponytail that bounced lightly as she moved around behind the counter, working on orders. You could tell that she knew the locals because of how her blue eyes crinkled when she laughed at something they said.

I hated the way I felt drawn to her, constantly pulled into this world that I didn't belong in. I knew she was younger than me—though I didn't realize how young until a few days ago. Twelve years might not be a big deal to some people, but in my head, it was a huge fucking deal when it meant that a thirty-four-year-old was hitting on someone who was barely legal.

The line moved forward and her eyes lit up when she saw me. She gave me a small smile before tucking a strand of hair behind her ear that had fallen out of her ponytail. I could tell she was just as nervous to see me as I was to see her, though I didn't know why.

For me, I needed to make sure that when I talked to her, I did it with my head on straight and not with my dick. The last thing I wanted to do was lead her to think that I was interested in getting to know her, even if it made something deep inside me ache at the thought of never knowing who she really was.

I had spent the past few days convincing myself that I was simply infatuated with her because she was like a shiny new toy, and I wanted to play with it. Okay—her—I wanted to play with her.

Which was exactly why I should have avoided coming here this morning. There was a café just a few blocks away that served coffee that I could have gone to instead. Hell, I went there every now and then when I needed a caffeine fix and Spill The Beans was closed. But for whatever reason, I was stupid enough to convince myself to come here and believed that seeing her wouldn't have any impact on me.

My heart started racing, and before I knew it, I was next in line.

"You ready?" she asked, leaning forward over the counter as if she was calling over a scared puppy that was stranded on a busy highway with cars darting toward it.

"Yeah," I cleared my throat. "Sorry."

"No worries." She laughed, but it didn't meet her eyes the way it did a few minutes ago when she was talking to the older couple and promised to come by to try the huckleberry jam their daughter had made. "What can I get you?"

I could tell she was used to asking everyone because she shook her head and entered something into the computer.

"Sorry," she laughed again. "Coffee black." She looked up, and our eyes locked. "Anything else?"

"I um," I cleared my throat again, hating that it was suddenly so dry. "Actually, I thought I would try something new this morning."

What the hell? I didn't drink fancy coffee. What was I planning to order? I was going to sound like a dumbass for asking for something like—coffee with sugar, please. Look at me—could I be any more adventurous?

"Yeah?" She tilted her head and looked genuinely surprised.

I nodded but kept my mouth shut.

Don't look stupid. Don't look stupid.

"Okay," she spoke slowly, again like she was approaching a skittish dog. "Did you have something in mind?"

I opened my mouth to tell her never mind, and I would just do my usual, but snapped it shut.

"I thought maybe you might have a recommendation for me?"

Her eyes widened, showing me the most beautiful blue I had ever seen. The ocean had nothing on the radiant color looking at me.

"Is there anything you *don't* like? Honey? Cinnamon?"

I looked behind me, nervous that I was holding up the line but felt oddly comforted that there was no one behind me.

"I have no idea," I laughed nervously. "As you know, I don't experiment much with my drinks."

She laughed and reached across the counter to gently squeeze my hand.

"Don't worry; I think I have something you'll like."

She let go, and I immediately missed the warmth of her soft skin. I knew that I shouldn't, but I was also human, and it had been a long time since anyone had touched me aside from the men who shook my hand in the meetings yesterday. Oddly enough, the women already felt like we were "family" and insisted on hugging instead.

I stepped to the side and watched as she worked. She'd look over her shoulder every now and then, probably checking to make sure I hadn't darted out of the shop and changed my mind.

Whatever she was making smelled delicious, which was a good thing, given that I had already decided to commit to this stupid idea.

A few minutes later, I watched as she snapped a lid on a to-go cup and slid one of those protective sleeves on.

"Here you go," she said, extending it to me. "It's a flat white, which is simply espresso with steamed milk on top. Nothing too sweet or complicated."

She smiled proudly and watched as I took a sip.

I closed my eyes as the hot liquid touched my lips then moved on to grace my tastebuds.

She was right all along—this was delicious. Why hadn't I given in to allow her to make any suggestions before now?

Maybe I had just been too busy, or maybe it was because small-town women were different from the women in NYC. Back home, no one bothered to make recommendations or took the time to ask what you liked. You got in, ordered your drink, and got out of the way because there was a line a mile long and wrapped around the building. I had told myself the moment my plane landed in Montana that I needed to remember that people, in general, were different here, and Maggie was proving that right now.

"So," she asked nervously, watching me as I took another sip. "What do you think?"

"It's delicious," I admitted and lowered the cup from my mouth so she could hear me. "Thank you."

She giggled and looked away, but not before I noticed a slight blush creep up her neck and onto her cheeks.

I narrowed my eyes suspiciously, wondering if she was now making fun of me for my drink choice.

"Sorry," she laughed more and then pointed to my mouth. "You have a little foam mustache, and I can't stop staring at it. It's so cute that I just want to reach over and…."

Her words stopped suddenly, and while I was thankful that she hadn't continued her sentence, I also hated not knowing what it was. *Reach over and wipe it off with her fingers? Reach over and lick it off with her tongue? What did she want to do?*

"Thanks for telling me," I said with a chuckle and then wiped it away. "See, this is why I stick to black coffee." I winked to let her know that I was joking but then regretted it because it also felt like maybe I was flirting with her. And by the way her cheeks flushed even more, I knew she was thinking the same thing—I was flirting with her.

"How much do I owe you?" I asked abruptly, causing her to flinch slightly. I pulled my wallet out and kept my eyes on finding my debit card to avoid looking at her.

"Don't worry about it," she said quickly, putting her hand out to stop me. "It's on the house."

"No, really, I insist on paying."

"Thank you, but I refuse your payment. You finally gave in and allowed me to recommend something new, so it's my treat."

I knew how she was looking at me, even without lifting my eyes to see it. I could feel it in my body, and with any other woman, it would have been a clear sign for me to invite her back to my place. But this was Maggie. Twenty-two-year-old Maggie. Small-town Maggie who wanted to find true love. I didn't have to ask to know that she wasn't also no-strings-attached Maggie, which was why I tucked my wallet back into my pocket, muttered a quick thank you, and got the hell out of there.

Nine

Maggie

I woke up Sunday morning feeling tired and achy. I had tried to get a good night's sleep last night, but I was restless and had terrible dreams that Leroy had escaped his new home and ate my entire house. For some reason, it was believable enough that I got out of bed around 4:30 to make sure he hadn't devoured the living room like I had seen in my dream. After that, it took forever to fall asleep, leaving me feeling slightly grumpy this morning. Good thing it was Sunday, and Spill The Beans was closed today.

After making a quick stop in the bathroom, I padded down the hallway, rubbing the sleep from my eyes so I could see to start the coffee. Today was supposed to be my self-care day, which meant that I wasn't likely to change out of my flannel pajamas or comb my hair. Or at least that's what I told myself when I needed an excuse not to do it.

I loaded the Keurig and pressed start, anxious for that first drop of sweetness to hit my tongue. I loved coffee more than anyone I knew, which meant I treated myself to the good stuff at home.

While the sweet aroma filled the kitchen, I grabbed my laptop and sat on the couch. Running Spill The Beans was probably my favorite part of my life, and it never felt like a chore to read the emails that came in with people asking for advice. I glanced over at Leroy as he paced around his terrarium and wondered whether that was still true. Now that I had him, he might very well be my favorite thing.

I logged into my email and waited for the page to load with the new messages while I got up and fixed my coffee. I heard the distinctive ding as the emails came through and decided to make a quick bagel while I was up. Once I was done, I curled up on the couch and got settled. I pulled the TV tray close to me and opened the first email.

Ask Mags,

I'm not sure why I'm even writing to you, but I guess that's what a few fingers of whiskey does to some people. I know that I don't need help, but I'm also not sure what to do.

I like a woman that I just met, and I find myself feeling drawn to her in a way that I've never experienced with anyone else. The problem is that she's looking for a serious commitment, and I'm not a relationship or commitment type of guy. We're as opposite as opposite can be.

No matter how hard I try, I can't get her off my mind. How do I get over someone I was never supposed to allow myself to get attached to in the first place?

--Stupid In Montana

I took a sip of coffee and held the warm mug between my hands as I reread the email. There was something about the email that kept sending a dagger straight to my heart, but I couldn't figure out why.

I went to the next few emails and tried to focus on them, but it was pointless. My mind was still focused on the first one, and I knew that I couldn't move on until I'd at least tried to answer it. Only, I didn't know how to answer it because it sounded like they already knew that they didn't want to get involved with this person for whatever reason.

Dear Stupid In Montana,

You don't sound stupid to me. In fact, you sound like you know exactly what you want, even if you're struggling to allow yourself to have it. I know that you said this woman is looking for a serious commitment, and that's not something you're interested in. Still, I'm curious to know if you've had this conversation with her or if you're assuming that's what she's interested in.

I know a lot of people who have a general idea of what they want out of life, but that doesn't mean that they might want different things along the way. Take me, for example. When I was younger, I was convinced that I would be married and starting a family by the time I was twenty-three. Given that I'm single and already twenty-two, I'm going to say that I don't think this is a realistic goal after all. Does that mean that I've given up all hope for ever having the family that I want to have? No. It just means that my future looks different than I thought it did when I was younger.

Just because I want to be married and have a family someday doesn't mean that I would rule out dating anyone right now if they didn't share the same vision as me. Who knows what can change along the way, and more importantly, imagine what would happen if I missed out on meeting the person I was meant to be with by limiting myself so early on.

I don't know the reason why you're against commitment or being in a relationship, but I would like to encourage you to step back and consider whether those things are still as important to you as they once were. If not, maybe it's worth exploring what could be there with this woman you can't stop thinking about. Just saying that's how a lot of the great love stories start…

I pressed send and moved on to the next few emails while I ate my bagel. The morning was already starting to feel better now that I'd had some coffee and was doing what I loved most—helping others find love. I had just finished replying to all of the new emails when another one popped up in my inbox.

Ask Mags,

Unfortunately, I don't think it's that simple. See, I've been in committed relationships in the past and have seen firsthand how quickly you can get hurt. I've put myself out there, taken the steps to move forward, and was left at the alter as my bride-to-be ran off with the best man—aka my best friend.

This woman, she's light in the darkness. She's the good in a world filled with evil. She's everything I'm not and deserves better than I could ever give her.

I'm not destined for great love, and I wouldn't want her to miss out on hers by wasting her time on me.

--Stupid In Montana

My heart sank as I read the words on the screen. He had written back, which meant he was likely sitting somewhere, waiting for my reply.

This time, I decided to reply privately to him and not through the blog. He seemed like someone who could use a friend, and I didn't want him to stop talking to me if he thought I would publish all of it on the blog.

My fingers moved quickly across the keyboard, eager to reply.

It's Okay To Be Loved In Montana,

I took the liberty of changing your name for you. You're welcome (winking emoji). There's nothing stupid about your situation, and thank you for sharing some more of your story with me.

I understand how guarded you must feel after having your fiancé leave you on your wedding day with your best friend. I can't imagine the heartache that must have caused you. I hope you at least had the opportunity to indulge in some cake and drink the champagne. That sounds like how I would have handled it if it was me!

Going through a breakup like that would leave anyone guarded. I can empathize with why you don't want to get involved in another committed relationship, but I think you also owe it to yourself to try.

You're not someone who doesn't want love, you're someone who doesn't want to get hurt. And if you put yourself out there again, there's a chance it could happen. The only way to keep from feeling that pain again is to close yourself off and not allow anyone to get close to you.

I totally get the thought process and the desire to protect yourself, but I also want to remind you that not all women are like your ex. In fact, very few of them are.

If you're feeling chemistry with this other woman, I think you owe it to yourself to explore what those feelings are. You don't have to rush into anything. Take your time. Be honest with her, as well as with yourself. If it doesn't work out, then at least you can say that you tried. It's better to at least take a chance and know what it is than to be too afraid to go for it and constantly wonder what could have been.

I sighed heavily, pressed send, and then waited for a response that never came.

<u>Ten</u>

Owen

I continued staring at my laptop, reading the response that I had gotten back from Maggie this morning. I hadn't imagined that she would reply to my email, but then again, I hadn't meant to send one to begin with.

Last night had been rough, and I had handled it the best way I knew how at the time—whiskey.

Between seeing Maggie at Spill The Beans yesterday, then getting a call from Sebastian—my former best friend—I was feeling a little more than slightly off-kilter. It wasn't the first time he'd tried to call me in the fourteen months since he'd run off with my fiancé on my wedding day. But it was the first time I had listened to the voicemail he left after I'd refused to answer.

"Owen, please call me. I want to explain what happened. We didn't mean to hurt you. It wasn't supposed to happen this way."

I pressed delete before he could continue and then blocked the new number he had called me from. I was usually a rather forgiving person, but even I had boundaries, and they both had crossed them.

When I'd emailed Spill The Beans blog, I assumed it would be lost in the depths of darkness on the internet or sent to the spam filter. Never in a million years did I think that Maggie would think my pathetic email was worth responding to. Which just went to show what kind of person she really was.

You're not someone who doesn't want love, you're someone who doesn't want to get hurt. And if you put yourself out there again, there's a chance it could happen. The only way to keep from feeling that pain again is to close yourself off and not allow anyone to get close to you.

Her words had sent an anchor right through my heart and wedged itself there. She was spot on, as always. Just like her, I'd once had the same dream of one day having a family and the happily ever after, but I'd been jaded ever since Brittany walked out on me. She was supposed to be the love of my life, the one I'd chosen to be my forever. Aside from the anger I felt from her betrayal, I'd also harbored a large amount of bitterness with myself for not seeing before then that she didn't love me the same way I loved her. That might have been what hurt the most—that I was so blinded by the idea of having what I thought I always wanted that I didn't actually see what was in front of me.

I totally get the thought process and the desire to protect yourself, but I also want to remind you that not all women are like your ex. In fact, very few of them are.

I knew that Maggie was right; not all women were the same as Brittany. But that didn't help me let my guard down any when it came to thoughts about Maggie. Even if she didn't want a committed relationship right now—despite what Ramona told me when Maggie wasn't around—that didn't mean that she was someone I should try to start something with.

For one, she was much too young for me. Twelve years to be exact. Maybe it wouldn't be such a big deal if she was older, but she was still technically a kid as far as knowing what she wanted out of life.

By that afternoon, I had considered replying to her email but didn't know what to say. Everything that I typed out was just as quickly deleted. I didn't want to acknowledge that she was right because once I allowed that thought to fester in my head, I knew that it would be even harder to keep my distance from her.

So instead, I changed clothes and went for a quick run, making sure to avoid any pedestrians on Main Street.

The cold air felt good against my face as I pushed myself to run faster. If I could burn off some of this energy, then I would be in a better head space the next time I went into Spill The Beans. Granted, I could just stop going there, but to be completely honest, the coffee wasn't nearly as good at the café. Maggie had really done me in yesterday with the concoction that she made me, and now I knew that I wouldn't be as content with plain black coffee anymore.

It wasn't that it was Maggie's fault—though technically it was—but it was almost like she had some sort of magic and kept me locked under a spell. A deliciously flavored coffee spell.

I turned the corner, allowing my body to slow for a brief moment as I kept along the side of the mountain. It wasn't that high up the hill but was one of the few trails I had found that didn't have a thick layer of ice. Even though I still stood by my statement that she looked like crazy Phoebe from Friends when she ran, I now understood why she had avoided the other trails after seeing them this morning.

I was lost in thought as I ran, not bothering to look up at the person heading my way until they were right in front of me and we were about to collide.

"Hey, watch it," a woman shouted, moving to the side before she plowed into me.

I looked around, noticing that I was running down the middle of the trail instead of off to the side, so there was room for her to pass.

She gave me a dirty look, then kept going.

My heart thumped wildly in my chest as I bent over and tried to catch my breath. I had my hands on my knees, feeling like my lungs were about to explode when I heard footsteps approaching me.

"You alright there?" Maggie asked, coming to a stop beside me.

"Yeah," I panted, standing upright, so I didn't look like a total spaz. Hell, if I could barely handle running in the cold, how would I possibly think that I could handle a woman like Maggie? Her age definitely showed as she bounced in place in front of me, keeping her heart rate up before she took off running again.

"I take it you don't get out here and run much?" she asked, her voice sweet and the perfect pitch to make my dick twitch in my pants. *Traitor.*

"I used to run a lot in New York City," I panted, trying not to show my struggle. I placed my hands on my hips, hoping my broad frame would help me look manlier than I felt.

"Well, Whiskey Mountain is a lot different. I'm sure you're used to running on flat ground back home, not the incline you decided to go up today."

She nodded behind me so I turned and saw what she was talking about. I had been so lost in thought that I hadn't noticed the change in the trail as it climbed the side of the mountain.

"Fuck," I muttered, running a hand down my face. "Honestly, I was a little distracted and hadn't paid attention."

She smiled and tucked a strand of wispy brown hair behind her ear.

"I'm finishing up if you want to run down with me," she offered, eyeing me cautiously as if she was worried that I was going to pass out in front of her. "Unless you're a glutton for punishment and want to keep going up."

"Did you go all the way up?" I asked, pointing to the steep incline behind her.

"Yeah, but I'm used to this trail. It's one of the few that rarely gets covered in ice because the sun constantly melts it."

I nodded, unsure of what to say. Of course she could handle this stupid trail. Her body was sculpted to perfection, and her ass filled out the skintight workout pants that looked like they were painted to her body.

"So, do you wanna do it together?" She raised her brows and waited for my answer.

I felt my head spinning, wondering how she could possibly know that I wanted to fuck her. Was it the thick, hard rod that was threatening to poke out of my gray sweatpants? Or did I have the words *I wanna fuck you* written on my head?

"Are you sure you're okay?" She tilted her head to the side and placed her hands on her hips as her eyes narrowed at me.

"Oh, yeah," I sighed and tried to shake it off. "Sorry. What did you ask?"

If she was really propositioning me on the side of a mountain, I needed to know for sure. If not, I was pretty sure I was about to see a bright yellow light calling me home and that this was just some bizarre hallucination to comfort me before death pulled me in.

"I asked if you wanted to finish your run with me," she said slowly, as if I was stupid. Which, by the way—I was. "Unless you were determined on finishing the run up, then back down. It's up to you."

"The run," I mumbled, spitting words out of my mouth before I could think about them. "You want to run with me, not do me on the side of the mountain."

I shook my head, forcing the stupidity out. When I looked up at her, her blue eyes danced with mischief, and I knew that she had heard everything I'd meant to keep in my head.

"Yeah, we should make our way back down."

"Okay," she said softly. "Whenever you're ready."

My body already felt tired, so the thought of running back down the mountain sounded terrible, but it wasn't like we could just stay up here all day. It was already midday, but soon the sun would start to set, and I couldn't imagine anyone would want to get stranded out here willingly.

"You can go ahead of me," I offered, not wanting her to watch me.

"It's okay, I don't mind bringing up the rear." She winked playfully.

"Is that code for you want to check out my ass?" I joked, walking beside her as she led the way down.

"I mean, I can't say I won't look if that's what you're asking."

"You're such a pervert." I winked, instantly regretting that I was flirting with her again when I saw her reaction to it.

"What can I say? It's the sweatpants. Every guy knows that you don't wear gray sweatpants unless you want women to check you out. Heck, even guys."

I turned to look at her, wondering what the hell she was talking about.

"Am I going to regret asking you what that's supposed to mean?" I asked, picking up my pace as she lightly started to jog. I knew that she was easing into it for me, and while I hated it, I also appreciated it.

"Oh, come on, *everyone* knows about it! It's in all of the romance books, in magazines—it's not a secret!"

"Is this like the whole banana and increased libido thing?"

She studied me for a moment, then shrugged.

"Guess you'll have to look it up and find out for yourself." She gave me a coy smile and then took off running down the mountain, giving me the perfect view of her ass as I involuntarily chased after it.

Eleven

Maggie

The run down the mountain was a lot more enjoyable, and I was thankful to see that Owen seemed to be doing better than he was when I first found him. In the two months since he'd been in Whiskey Mountain, I hadn't seen him running on any of the trails, so it didn't surprise me that he was blindsided by the steep incline on this one.

If you weren't from around here, it was easy to miss because you didn't see how intense it got until you were already halfway up the hill. Personally, I loved it because it pushed me when I really needed it—and today, I definitely needed it.

"You doing okay?" I asked as we slowed at the bottom of the hill and stepped to the side so we were off the trail. I took a long drink of water and focused on him as his breathing evened out.

"Yeah, thanks."

He seemed a little winded still, but I could tell he didn't want to be the center of attention right now, so I looked away and gave him a few minutes.

"Do you do this often?" he asked, nodding to the hill behind us.

"Not all of the time. I tend to stick to the flat trails that run behind the strip mall, but this one is my favorite when I need to clear my head or after I've over-indulged and need to work off some of the calories." I laughed but didn't miss it when his eyes roamed over my body.

He didn't say anything but did move his eyes away from my tits. *So, he's a boob guy. Good thing I have plenty to offer in that department.*

I looked up at the sky, admiring the colors changing as the sun started to set.

"Do you have dinner plans?" I blurted out, startling both of us.

"Dinner plans?"

"Yeah, you know—like sitting down and having dinner with someone? Or going somewhere to eat?"

"No…." There was an uneasiness in his voice that matched the tension tightening his shoulders.

"Well, how about we go grab a bite to eat?" I suggested, trying to keep my voice as neutral as possible so I didn't scare him off. He was sending mixed signals left and right, and I had no idea what to think. First, he ogled my body like it was the first time he'd ever seen boobs, and now he was acting like I had offended his people by asking to share a meal. "I'll pay," I added, trying to keep my smile from getting too big.

"Thanks, but…." He scrubbed a hand down the thin hair that dotted his jaw. "I don't think it's a good idea."

"Relax," I laughed. "It's not a date; you don't have to be so nervous."

He eyed me suspiciously.

"I just thought because we were both done with our run, and neither of us have eaten dinner, that maybe we could go somewhere together. Sometimes it gets boring eating by yourself." I tried to keep any hints of sadness out of my voice but failed. "Plus, I owe you for all of your help with Leroy the other day."

I rocked back on my heels and held my hands in front of me, holding the water bottle.

He waited me out, the decision warring through his brain while he struggled to decide. Finally, he sighed heavily and let his shoulders fall.

"Did you have somewhere in mind?"

I clapped my hands excitedly and let out a slight squeal.

"Yay! I know the perfect place!"

I couldn't tell if he was as excited about it as I was or if he was simply trying to pacify me, but he followed me nonetheless until we got to the now empty parking lot. I had thought about asking him if he wanted to ride over together, but given how he had reacted to my dinner invite, I didn't want to overdo it.

He followed me to Main Street, and we were both lucky to find parking on the street, which was rare and unusual. I should have known then that this wouldn't turn out how I thought it would.

When we got out and walked up to the door of La Salsa, there was a sign on the front that it was closed to a pipe bursting earlier in the day.

I frowned and stared at it, disappointed that I wasn't going to get my chips and salsa fix tonight after all. I had run my ass off, and that was supposed to be my treat, along with a refreshingly cold margarita.

"Damn it," I muttered, rubbing the back of my neck.

"Is there somewhere else you want to go instead?" Owen asked, though he kept staring at the sign and not at me.

"I don't know. It's getting late, and everything in town will be closed soon." I folded my arms over my chest and tried not to sound too whiney. "I really wanted their tacos."

He arched a brow and finally turned to look at me.

"Tacos?"

"They have THE BEST tacos. They're deliciously mouthwatering, and I earned them, along with a margarita."

He rubbed his lips together and then turned to look at me.

"I can make tacos."

"What?" I felt the grin spread quickly across my face. For sure, I thought he would run the first chance he got, but here he was, offering to cook.

"I know how to make tacos. We can stop by the market before they close and grab the stuff we need. I don't mind cooking."

"Who are you, and what have you done with the *real Owen*?" I teased, bumping my elbow against his.

"This is the *real* Owen," he laughed.

"The real Owen seemed reluctant to have dinner with me tonight, and now he's offering to cook for me. Just seems a bit off, that's all." I smiled up at him as we walked back to our cars.

"Well, for the record, the real Owen loves to cook and rarely does so anymore. Plus, you seemed so disappointed; I couldn't look at that sad puppy look on your face for another second."

My heart fluttered inside my chest, and I had to remind it that this wasn't anything to get excited about. Owen was just being friendly; it didn't mean he was interested in me.

"So, do you want to go to the market with me so you can pick out your margaritas? I don't know if you want super fruity or regular." He shrugged, and I could tell that he was back to feeling nervous.

"Sounds good. I'll follow you over."

He nodded and then got into his truck while I climbed into mine. Tonight was going to be fun; I could almost guarantee it.

<u>Twelve</u>

Owen

Shopping with Maggie was more fun than I would have imagined. Her face lit up as we ventured down the candy aisle, and I watched as she tossed a few bags of chocolate into her cart. I had insisted on buying the stuff to make dinner, but she had quickly objected and informed me that she was paying.

I took the liberty to pick out the meat and fixings while she perused the alcohol section and grabbed stuff to make margaritas. Granted, there were bottles of premade ones, but she made a sour face and told me that only crazy people drank those.

Once we had everything we needed—along with some items that we didn't—we checked out, and I loaded the groceries into her vehicle.

"Did you want to come to my place?" she offered after I stuffed the last bag in the backseat on the floor.

"Sure." I shoved my hands into my pockets and remembered the comments she had made earlier about wearing these damn sweats. Suddenly, her eyes trailed down at the movement and locked onto my crotch.

I knew I should have looked away or moved, but I didn't. For a fraction of a second, I enjoyed standing there, knowing she was just as attracted to me as I was to her. Even though I couldn't act on it, it was reassuring to see that it was mutual.

"Okay," she said, shaking her head and clearing her throat. "You can follow me if you don't remember where my house is."

"I remember."

My voice was thick as my cock hardened. Her thick lashes fluttered as she looked up at me.

"I'll see you there in a few minutes."

Her voice was soft and whispery, making me wonder what she would sound like in the middle of an orgasm. Would she be one of those girls who were shy and quiet, or would she be loud and vocal, screaming my name as I pleasured her?

I quickly adjusted myself once I was in my truck and followed her the short distance to her house. Once there, I helped her carry the groceries in and followed her lead on where to put them.

"Pans are in there," she said and pointed as we walked through the kitchen. "Spices are in the cabinet next to the stove. Help yourself to whatever you need, and I'll be back to help in a few minutes."

She smiled, then rushed down the hall and slipped into the bathroom.

I grabbed the stuff that I needed and got started.

It had been a while since I had anyone to cook for, and I had gotten so busy with work that I rarely took the time to do it for myself.

While the beef cooked in the pan, I took the time to finely chop an onion and tossed some in with the meat while keeping the rest to the side for salsa. I loved fresh ingredients and was surprised by what I was able to find at the market this time of year. In New York, we had access to a lot more than I imagined a small town in rural Montana would have.

While the meat was cooking, I prepared the salsa and then put it in the fridge to keep it cold. Maggie insisted that she was good with just tacos, chips, and salsa; therefore, we didn't grab anything for the sides. I knew that tacos were plenty for me, though I might have been thinking about another type of taco— as well as thinking with my dick—when we were discussing it.

The bathroom door opened, then Maggie padded down the carpeted hallway into the living room. She bent down to check on Leroy before joining me in the kitchen.

"I chopped up some lettuce for the tacos and put some aside for Leroy," I said, pointing to the plate I had made for him while she was cleaning up.

"Thank you, that was very thoughtful of you."

She took the lettuce and placed it in his terrarium, giving him a soft pat on the shell.

"Okay, what can I help with?" she asked, wiping her hands on the shorts she was wearing.

Was she trying to kill me?

I thought she looked amazing in the running gear she had on earlier, but this was even more erection-inducing.

It was the middle of winter and freezing outside, though her house was a little warmer than normal, so I could understand her wearing the flimsy shorts. I tried to convince myself that she was only wearing them because it was toasty in here and not because she was trying to seduce me.

"Owen?"

I turned my head and found her watching me with a slight smirk on her face.

"Yeah?"

"I asked what I could help with." She grinned, and I knew that she knew what she was doing to me.

You could sit on my face and let me eat the taco that I really want.

"Umm," I stuttered, turning my focus to the stove as I stirred the meat that was just about done. "I think I've got it all covered. Dinner should be ready in a few minutes."

"Okay. I'll make us some margaritas then."

She moved around me, making the air smell like coconuts.

I turned the burner for the meat down to warm and grabbed another pan to fry the tortillas. My goal was to stay in my area and not venture into hers, but when I turned to get the oil from the cabinet, my chest collided with her head.

My hands reached out to brace her, feeling the curves of her body against mine.

"Sorry," she laughed. "I was trying to get the glasses out of the cabinet."

"Here, let me."

I knew that in order to do it, I had to let her go, yet my fingers dug deeper into her skin. I could swear that I heard a soft moan escape her lips when I did.

She was fire, and I was about to get burned.

I cleared my throat and stepped to the side as I avoided looking at her.

"Which ones?" I asked once I had the cabinet opened.

"The short ones with the blue rims. They're my favorite."

Blue was my favorite too—like the color of her eyes. Though I didn't love the blue balls I was getting from being around her.

I grabbed the glasses and set them down on the counter, too afraid that I might accidentally drop them if our hands brushed against each other.

"There you go," I grumbled, then quickly turned the other way and checked on the meat that didn't need to be checked on.

Maggie made her way over to the fridge and began filling a pitcher with ice. Once she was on the other side of the kitchen, I grabbed the oil and started frying the tortillas.

Everything smelled delicious, and my stomach growled in anticipation. I stacked the tortillas on a paper towel to soak up the excess grease and then grabbed the fixings and salsa from the fridge. Everything was set out and ready to go by the time she finished mixing the margaritas.

She smiled and took another sip before walking over and handing me a small cup with liquid in it.

"Try it and let me know if it needs more tequila?" she asked, lifting it toward me.

I took a small sip, but it wasn't enough to determine whether or not it needed more alcohol. Instead, I lied and said that it was fine. I didn't know how much she had put in the pitcher already, but I didn't want either of us to get drunk tonight. Hell, I wasn't even planning on having a drink, but it felt like it would be rude to decline now that she'd already prepared a glass for me with salt on the rim and a lime wedge.

"Dinner's ready," I said, handing the cup back to her.

"Perfect timing," she replied happily as she set the empty cup in the sink. "We can sit on the couch since I don't have an actual table to eat at."

"Sounds good."

We fixed our plates and then sat down. Maggie pulled the coffee table closer to us, then lifted the top that extended into a table for us to eat on.

"Very nice." I nodded and scooted closer to make sure I didn't drop any food on the rug beneath us.

"Thanks. I don't have people over often, so I've never needed a lot of furniture. Then I got Leroy, and he took up any extra space I had," she laughed. "But this works for me, and the couch is my favorite place to sit anyway, so I can't complain."

"I don't have a lot of furniture either. Just what came with the house when I rented it. I haven't had a need to buy anything else."

"Is it weird?" she asked around a bite of taco. "This is amazing, by the way."

She closed her eyes and chewed, moaning not so subtly anymore.

"Is what weird?" I leaned forward and dipped a chip in salsa.

"Being away from your home for so long? Living in someone else's house and trying to make it yours. Does it get lonely?"

She wiped her mouth with a napkin and watched me as I thought about it.

"Honestly, it doesn't feel much different other than being surrounded by other people's stuff instead of my own. I miss my bed, but as far as being lonely, it's no different than it was when I was in the city."

Her head tilted to the side, and a frown fell on her face. She set her taco down and turned toward me, facing me head-on.

"That's so sad."

I shrugged and took a bite of my taco so I didn't have to say anything. It was sad, but she didn't need to know just how pathetic my life had been after Brittany and I broke up.

"Do you have a girlfriend back home?"

I shook my head and took another bite. I didn't want to have this conversation with her. Not right now. Not ever.

She continued to study me for a few seconds before she turned back to her food and took another bite. We ate in silence for a few minutes, leaving me thankful that she didn't keep pressing for information on why I was such a lonely loser.

Thirteen

Maggie

I was three margaritas in and had quickly learned that Owen didn't want to talk about anything involving his personal life. It felt like playing a game of twenty questions with him, yet almost everything was answered with quick, one-word responses that gave no insight into who he was.

"Do you want a refill?" I asked, nodding to his empty margarita glass clutched in his hand.

He shook his head.

"I'd better not, thanks."

"Okay." I got up, grabbed the pitcher from the counter, and set it down on the coffee table after refilling mine.

I had barely put any tequila in them when I made them, so it wasn't like we were going to get drunk anytime soon. On top of that, we were drinking out of my favorite tumblers, which were half the size of what we would have gotten at La Salsa.

"So, how long do you think you'll stay in Whiskey Mountain?" I asked, pulling the bottom of my shorts down so I didn't expose my ass as I shifted on the couch. I had my knee pulled up to my chest as I leaned into the cushion.

I had taken a quick shower when we got back and then realized I didn't have any clean clothes because, like a dummy, I'd forgotten to move the load I had washed earlier from the washer to the dryer. Granted, I had some clean clothes, but not much I felt comfortable wearing around Owen. I didn't want to look like a granny with my ratty t-shirts that I used to sleep in, which left me looking a bit slutty in booty pajama shorts in the dead of winter.

Granted, it was warm enough in the house to justify it since I'd started keeping the temperature higher in here for Leroy.

"I'm not sure. I'm still waiting for the planning committee and city council to vote on the proposed projects before we can get started, then I'll stick around to see them through. I'd say six months at a minimum, though I expect it to be closer to a year."

I felt somewhat relieved that he would be here for a little while, though I knew I didn't have a reason to be. It wasn't like he was going to start something up with me, nor did I want a casual fling. *Not that I wouldn't want him to fling me over his shoulder and slap my ass with that big, strong, manly hand that I had been admiring all night.*

"So, no girlfriend back home. Do you have a secret wife? Kids?" I wiggled my eyebrows playfully but noticed the way he tensed up at the word *wife*.

"Nope. Nothing."

"Is it something that you want?"

The question flew out of my mouth before I could stop it. I set my glass down and realized that maybe there was more tequila in the margaritas than I had thought. Suddenly, I felt less inhibited with Owen, and while that was thrilling for me, it felt like he was closing himself off even more.

"I used to think that was what I wanted, but things change. I'm not a committed relationship kind of guy. I'm not destined for great love."

He took a sip of his drink and looked away, but the words he'd just said hung in the air around me. Where had I heard that before?

Before I could think about it too much, his phone dinged on the coffee table. He picked it up and frowned before his fingers moved across the screen as he responded to the message.

I took another drink, allowing him the time to deal with whatever had his attention. Suddenly he lowered his phone to his lap and closed his eyes.

"I'm sorry, I need to go deal with something. Thank you for having me over."

He stood up and took his cup to the sink, rinsing it out before putting it in the dishwasher that he had insisted on helping me load earlier.

I followed him to the front door and stood back while he put on his coat and fished his keys out of the pocket. While I had had three margaritas, he had barely gotten halfway through his first one, so I didn't have to worry whether he was okay to drive.

"Thanks again," he said, leaning in for a hug.

I wasn't prepared or expecting it, which left my head tilted back at an awkward angle, allowing his mouth to brush against my throat. My heart beat wildly in my chest as his hot breath skimmed over the skin, leaving fire in its wake. I waited for him to realize and pull away, but instead, he pulled me closer and moved his lips against me, pressing firm kisses and making my clit tingle.

Instinctively, my hands moved up into his hair, holding his head in place while his tongue licked a trail from my jawline down to my collarbone.

He reached down and grabbed my ass, lifting me to his hips before pressing me against the door. I could feel the throbbing hard erection through his sweats and worked myself against it.

"Fuck," he groaned, kissing the other side of my neck and squeezing my ass harder.

I could feel the heat and wetness pooling between my legs. I hadn't been with a man before, but I'd also never felt this turned on by one before, either.

While I used to tell myself that I'd held out this long on having sex because I wanted to find someone who I was in love with to share my first time with, part of me now wondered if maybe I was just holding out for someone that I had insane chemistry with.

Owen had barely touched me, and I felt like I was on the verge of an orgasm. All he would have to do was—

Fuck… That. Right there. All he had to do was slide his fingers under my panties and rub my clit the way he was doing right now.

I dug my nails into his shoulders and bit down on my lip as I tried to keep from coming. He had barely touched me, and I was about to lose it.

There was no way he was this goo—

"Oh my God," I moaned against his neck as his fingers coaxed every last bit of orgasm out of me. My legs trembled as I panted heavily, thankful that he was still holding me up since I didn't trust my legs to do their job now.

"We shouldn't be doing this," he moaned in my ear before nipping it. "I'm too old for you."

"You're not."

"I am. You're still just a baby."

I could feel his dick pressing against my sensitive clit and wanted to give him as much pleasure as he'd just given me. Despite how nervous I felt about the actual sex part, I'd given plenty of hand jobs and blow jobs to know how to get a man off quickly.

"I'm twenty-two and know what I want." I reached down and grabbed his cock, moaning again at the heaviness in my hand. He wasn't just big—he was the biggest I had ever felt, and I wasn't sure if that was a good thing or a bad thing for someone's first time. Guess we were about to find out.

I pulled the front of his sweats down, along with his briefs, and felt the drop of precum on the tip of his dick as it popped free.

I stroked him slowly, trying to wrap my hand around his girth. He was huge. Massive. I wanted to drop to my knees and take him in my mouth, but I needed him to put me down first.

As I continued to work him in my hand, he planted kisses along my neck, dipping lower toward my chest. God, I wanted this so badly. With one hand, I reached up and tugged my shirt down, exposing one breast.

Picking up on what I wanted, he slid a finger inside the cup of my bra and pulled it down. Then he lowered his head and licked the hardened nipple before sliding it into his mouth and sucking.

I bucked against the wall, moaning as he sucked harder. This was heaven and hell at the same time as my body reacted to his every touch and geared up for another orgasm.

There was no doubt about it, I wanted Owen to fuck me, and I wanted it to happen now.

"Let's go to my room," I panted. "I want you to fuck me."

"We should stop," he mumbled as he worked the other side of my bra down and tortured my other nipple.

"No. I don't want to stop. I want you to fuck me. Now. Be my first."

My eyes were shut as I enjoyed every second of arousing pleasure until it suddenly stopped, and I realized what I had said.

I opened them slowly and found Owen's face hardened as he looked at me. He lowered me to the floor and stepped away, quickly tucking his cock back into his pants.

I pulled my bra and shirt back up, then covered my chest with my arms while I chewed on my lip.

"I, um…." I started but stopped when he held up his hand.

He let his head fall back and closed his eyes.

"First?" he asked, still not looking at me.

My heart was racing again, but this time for a different reason.

"It's not a big deal," I said quietly.

It felt like years before he turned and looked at me.

"I have to go."

I didn't have a chance to say anything before the door opened and slammed shut as he left.

Fourteen

Maggie

I stared at the front door for what felt like an eternity before picking my jaw up off the floor and turning the lock. It wasn't like I had expected Owen to come rushing back in and change his mind, but somehow locking the door made me feel more protected from the hurt he'd just inflicted.

My mind was going a mile a minute, trying to process what had just happened. My body was still humming from the incredible orgasm he'd given me with his fingers, but I hated that it still wanted more.

What do you even know? It's not like you know what it feels like or what you're missing out on by not having sex.

I forced the bitter thoughts away and checked in on Leroy before grabbing my phone that was ringing on the coffee table. I was hopeful that it was Owen calling but found Ramona's name on the caller ID instead.

Deciding that I needed company, I lifted Leroy out of his terrarium and then pressed the button to answer the call.

"Hey," I muttered, plopping down on the couch. Leroy trotted around in front of me, following the path of the light pink flowers on the rug that looked vaguely like berries. I knew he wasn't hungry, given he'd already devoured the food I had given him when Owen was here, but it was still cute to watch him try to eat the rug.

"What's wrong? You sound like someone peed in your Cheerios."

"Nothing," I lied. "What's up."

"Nope. You first. What happened?"

"It's nothing, really."

"You're such a terrible liar. And lucky for you, I have all night."

"Where's Daniel?"

"Out."

"Are you guys fighting again?"

"When aren't we?"

I leaned against the couch and pressed the phone closer to my ear, ready to be a good friend and lend her an ear. They'd had more fights lately, and she'd recently confided that they'd talked about separating. Ramona and Daniel met in high school and had been together ever since, but they both seemed to realize that maybe they'd drifted in different directions.

"I'm sorry. What was it about this time?"

"I asked him about taking a vacation this year, and we argued about where to go. I want to go hiking and explore some of the national parks before I'm too old and don't have the energy to do it. He wants to drink beer and live by the pool where hot girls flaunt around in bikinis."

"Men suck," I muttered, curling my feet underneath me as I pulled my knees to my chest.

"Yes they do. Now tell me what happened. Was it Samuel or Owen?"

"I haven't heard from Samuel since I told him it was over. He hasn't bothered to contact me, and I couldn't be happier."

"Okay," she sighed. "What happened with Owen?"

"I might've accidentally mentioned the *v-word* while we were…. You know."

She gasped on the other end, and I cringed.

"Vin Diesel?"

The laughter erupted out of me before I could stop it.

"No, you dork."

She laughed on the other end, automatically making me feel less stressed about it.

"So, did you guys…."

"No. We didn't get that far. Things were going well, and then I asked him to be my first while I was in the throes of passion."

"Wow."

I scrubbed a hand down my face and felt my face flush with embarrassment again.

"I'm so embarrassed."

"Why? You shouldn't be. If he was doing something that great to get you to come out and ask him to take your virginity, I don't think there was anything to be ashamed of."

I thought about how easily I'd been turned on and how he knew exactly where to touch me to get me off in record-breaking time.

"So, what happened," she asked gently.

"He freaked out and confirmed that I had said *first*. Then he stormed out, and I haven't heard anything from him since."

"Just give him time. Guys freak out easily, and you did say that he's older than you. It's probably been a while since he's talked to someone as *innocent* as you."

"I don't know. I think I'm chasing after something that isn't even a possibility," I admitted bitterly. "Every time I try to get to know him, he's always so guarded. Earlier, when I asked him to go to dinner, he looked like I'd ask him to go on a killing spree with me. I had to rush to reassure him that it *wasn't* a date and that I just wanted to say thanks for his help setting up Leroy's home the other day."

"Maybe he's just naturally shy with people?" she offered. "I mean, he's no Vin Diesel."

"What's your obsession with him anyway?" I laughed.

"He's sooo hot. Just saying, I would do a bunch of illegal shit and race cars just to hang out with him."

"You know that's just for the movies, right? It's not like he does that stuff in real life."

"Don't go ruining my fantasy," she scolded.

"Hey, at least one of us still has them."

I could hear rustling around and then heard Pablo yelling at the cat. *Pussy face. Here pussy pussy pussy.*

"Please tell me that Daniel didn't teach Pablo that," I giggled, imagining how she would explain that to her mother the next time she came to visit.

"Of course he did." She sighed heavily. "So, are you going to reach out to Owen and talk about what happened? I mean, it seems like there's a chemistry there that you both started to act on."

I shifted on the couch and kicked my legs out in front of me.

"I don't know. I honestly don't even know what I would say. It's not like I know him that well, and now I've dropped the V-word and scared him off."

"Maybe he just needs time. Don't write him off yet."

"When I finally got him to open up a little bit during dinner, I asked if he had a girlfriend, and he said no. I joked about him hiding a wife and kid back home, and he tensed up. Then he mentioned that he wasn't a commitment type of guy and that he wasn't—"

Suddenly I had a flashback to the email I had read earlier and realized that Owen had said the exact same thing as the person who wrote to Spill The Beans had said.

I'm not destined for great love.

"What?" Ramona asked, interrupting my train of thought.

"Hold on," I rushed out as I jumped up and grabbed my laptop.

I logged into my email and looked for the ones from *Stupid In Montana.*

My eyes scanned it quickly, looking for anything that might tell me whether it was Owen or not.

"Maggie, what's going on? You can't just leave me hanging!"

"Sorry," I said, scrolling to the bottom of the last email. "I think Owen emailed me."

"To apologize for being a chicken shit and walking out on you instead of taking your v-card? Or to invite you over for a ride on the hard-cock express?"

I pulled my head back and frowned.

"Ramona!" I shrieked, then laughed. "Do you always have to be so crass?"

"Hey, don't blame me. You know you were thinking the same thing. So did he?"

I shook my head, trying to figure out what she was saying, but I was still distracted by the email.

"Did he what?"

"Email you to apologize."

"No." I clicked on the first email and reread it. "I think he emailed the blog anonymously."

"What makes you think that?"

"When he was here, he told me that he wasn't destined for great love. Earlier today, I responded to an email that had come in late last night from someone asking for help but admitting that they didn't really want it."

"Okay…."

"In the email, he writes, *I'm not sure why I'm even writing to you, but I guess that's what a few fingers of whiskey does to some people. I know that I don't need help, but I'm also not sure what to do. I like a woman that I just met, and I find myself feeling drawn to her in a way that I've never experienced with anyone else. The problem is that she's looking for a serious commitment, and I'm not a relationship or commitment type of guy. We're as opposite as opposite can be. No matter how hard I try, I can't get her off my mind. How do I get over someone I was never supposed to allow myself to get attached to in the first place?*"

I paused to take a breath but felt a rush of excitement course through me. This had to be Owen; I just knew it.

"When I responded to his email, I talked to him about giving love a try, and he mentioned that he'd been hurt by his fiancé after she left him on their wedding day and ran off with the best man—who also happened to be his best friend. Then he replied, *this woman, she's light in the darkness. She's the good in a world filled with evil. She's everything I'm not and deserves better than I could ever give her. I'm not destined for great love, and I wouldn't want her to miss out on hers by wasting her time on me.* That's the same thing he told me tonight when I asked him about having a girlfriend."

"Maybe it is him," Ramona agreed. "It definitely sounds like it fits."

"Not only that, but he kept saying that we shouldn't do this when we were kissing. He kept saying how he was too old for me. It was like he was looking for every excuse he could find for why we shouldn't do anything."

"Because he's attracted to you but doesn't want to risk hurting you because he thinks you're looking for a commitment that he can't give you."

"I never told him that I was looking for a commitment."

The line got quiet on the other side then I heard a heavy sigh from Ramona.

"No, but I might have mentioned to him that you were looking for your one true love and that you deserved it after what Samuel did."

I pressed a hand to my forehead, completely forgetting about their conversation in Cool Cats the other day.

"Damn it."

"I'm so sorry," she apologized. "I didn't think about it when I said it. I was so proud of you and your blog that I was gushing about how much you love love and deserve to find it yourself."

"It's okay." I shrugged my shoulders and closed my laptop. "It's not like there was anything there, to begin with."

"I know I've already said it like a million times, but don't rule it out yet. You never know, maybe he just needed a few minutes to process the news."

"Yeah, maybe." I set my computer on the coffee table and watched Leroy head toward my bedroom, probably trying to find more underwear to eat. "I better get going, Leroy is on the loose, and I can't afford to keep buying new clothes."

It was a bullshit excuse to hang up, but I wasn't in the right frame of mind to talk about Owen anymore.

"Okay, I'll check in tomorrow, but if you need anything, you know where to find me."

"Up your ass," Pablo called out. "Up your ass."

The corners of my lips lifted into a brief smile at the rowdy bird, then I hung up and chased after Leroy before he got any ideas from Pablo.

Fifteen

Owen

Monday morning I woke up with a pounding headache from a lack of sleep and an overwhelming amount of regret that weighed a ton sitting on my shoulders. I attempted to stop by the café for my coffee to avoid seeing Maggie, but they were closed due to a family emergency that felt a bit too convenient. It was like the universe was laughing in my face, knowing that I would either give in and go to Spill The Beans or dig my heels in and end up with a migraine.

It wasn't that I didn't want to see Maggie, I did. I wanted to pick up right where we'd left off before she uttered those words that sent me flying through her door.

Did I feel like a total prick for how I handled it? Yes.

Did she deserve better than that? Yes.

But at the end of the day, I was trying to do what I thought was best for everyone involved, including her. She had her whole life in front of her and should have someone who could give her more than I could, especially for her first time.

I'd been sitting at my desk for over an hour, staring at the cup of coffee I'd attempted to make this morning. It tasted like shit. There was nothing special about it, but even the regular black coffee that I got from Spill The Beans tasted better than this. It wasn't that I didn't know how to make coffee—I'd been doing it since I was old enough to make it for my grandpa. But something about this cup tasted more bitter than it should.

I answered a few emails and then jumped on to the Zoom meeting I had with my office in NYC. I was the last one to join, which wasn't a big surprise given that I was moving slower than Leroy on a bad day.

"Alright, now that we're ready to start," Beverly said, pushing her glasses up her nose as she leaned in to read her computer screen. "Let's begin with an update on the Hudson Creek project."

She looked up and stared at the camera as Tim, a guy working out of our Idaho office, began talking about the progress of the development he'd been sent there to oversee. I tried to focus and pay attention, but every time I yawned, I found myself sinking a little lower in my chair.

Next up was an update from Ashley out of our main office. There were some budget details that didn't impact me, so I tuned her out and waited until Beverly moved on to the next person. I was thankful that I didn't have much that I needed to discuss and even more grateful that I was last on the agenda.

"I'm meeting with the mayor and city council tomorrow morning to discuss their decision on breaking ground on the vacant land between Whiskey Mountain and Fallen Oaks. I've also reached out to a referral that I had for local contractors in Fallen Oaks to see if they'd be on board for giving us a quote for the project."

"Sounds great," Beverly said with a smile. "Keep us updated on the final decision, and let me know if you need me to send someone to assist now that it's going to be a larger project than anticipated. I know we discussed you being in Whiskey Mountain for six months, but I imagine this project would extend beyond that. We can discuss options and whether you'd prefer to hand this off to an assistant once it's up and running so you can return to New York."

I smiled, but it didn't meet my eyes. The thought of leaving Whiskey Mountain was something that I had been thinking about nonstop from the moment my flight landed two months ago. Now that I'd been getting to know Maggie more, I felt this uncomfortable feeling in the pit of my stomach at the thought of leaving.

The meeting ended, and I was suddenly starving. It was already afternoon, so I locked my office and went in search of something to eat. I walked a few blocks down Main Street and popped into the deli on the corner. Even though they didn't serve coffee, they had a nice selection of energy drinks in the cooler by the register, so at least I could get some caffeine in me.

I placed my order and stood to the side while waiting for it. The place was busy, but that wasn't unusual. I'd realized that almost every place in Whiskey Mountain felt busy because there weren't that many places to go. But even then, it felt calm and relaxing, unlike the chaotic buzz I was used to in New York City.

No one here bumped into you and kept walking. They didn't look past you as they hurried by.

Instead, it was just like you'd see in those Hallmark movies where people stop to say hi as they pass you or invite you to join them if they see you sitting by yourself to eat. Things that I had never experienced before I came here.

As if proving a point, an elderly couple brushed by me as they headed out the door and stopped to apologize before asking how my day was going. I'd met them a few times at the town hall meetings and knew they were passionate about keeping the current strip mall intact instead of knocking it down.

"Take care; we'll see you at the next meeting," Trixie said with a smile as she allowed her husband to guide her out the door.

"You too; it was nice seeing you."

I smiled and held the door open for them before returning to my spot on the wall.

"Owen," a voice called from over the counter.

I turned to grab my order and almost bumped into another person as they tried to move to the side and out of the way.

"Sorry," I said, stepping back to make room for them.

"Hey," Ramona said, smiling once she noticed me.

"Hey. I almost didn't recognize you without Pablo," I laughed, remembering her from the pet store.

"Yeah, I can't take him many places with me unless I want a slew of curse words tossed around at innocent bystanders."

"That could be fun." I shrugged.

I'd never been a pet person—you know, the whole commitment thing apparently wasn't my thing—but I could see myself with a bird like Pablo. Something about him and his carefree attitude made me almost want to be him.

"A lot of the locals are used to him, but we get plenty of tourists that are not big fans of his potty mouth." She laughed, and I joined her.

"You grabbing something to eat?" she asked, looking over the counter at the guy who was still holding the bag with my to-go order.

"Yeah, just a quick bite. You?"

She nodded, and I noticed a change in how she looked at me. It was almost as if she'd gone from happy to see me to pity, though I didn't know why she would do that.

"Do you want to eat together?" she offered, lifting her brows hopefully.

I reached over and took my order so the guy could get back to work. While I wanted nothing more than to go back to my office and eat alone, something made me reconsider.

From what I could tell, Ramona knew Maggie pretty well, which meant that I might be able to check in to see how she was doing without having to tell her what I did. Though, if they were super close, then Ramona likely already knew what happened, which might be why she had given me that look.

She tilted her head and waited for my answer.

"Um, sure." I pressed my lips into a thin line, suddenly uncomfortable and unsure what to do.

She smiled as if sensing my discomfort and looked around the room.

"There's a table in the back. If you want to grab it, I'll meet you in a few minutes once my order is ready."

I nodded and then took off to grab the table. Once I was situated, I opened my energy drink and took a long sip, hoping the caffeine would give me some sort of magical powers to handle the conversation that I suddenly wanted to have with Ramona but knew that I shouldn't.

By the time she got her order and sat down, I'd already finished my drink and ran off to grab another.

I could tell she was trying to give me space before we started talking, and I appreciated that. We ate in silence, nearly finishing our sandwiches before I got the nerve to speak.

"I fucked up," I blurted out randomly, startling her as she held her spicy tuna wrap to her lips.

She lowered it to the plate on the table and then wiped her hands on the napkin.

"Like with your order? You didn't like the club sandwich?"

I shook my head, feeling stupid.

"Sometimes they don't get the bacon right, so it's not always my go-to. They have a delicious Cubano if you want to try that instead. Or this one is really good if you want to try a bite and see if you like it?" She lifted her food and extended it to me.

"No," I sighed, leaning back in the metal chair and tossing my napkin onto the table in front of me. "I fucked up with Maggie."

She was still holding her wrap in front of her when the realization hit. The way her hazel eyes narrowed slightly told me that she already knew what had happened between us.

"I don't know that she would want me talking about this with you," she said quietly before taking a bite and keeping her eyes on the table.

"I know," I admitted and ran a hand through my hair. "I feel like a complete idiot and don't know what to do."

She continued chewing, wiped her mouth, then spoke.

"Have you thought about reaching out to her?"

I shook my head.

"I've been trying to avoid her from the moment I first saw her." I grinned but not because it was funny. She'd been addicting the second I laid eyes on her, and I should have known from the start that she would be my undoing.

"I hate to tell you, but it's pretty hard to avoid anyone in Whiskey Mountain." I could tell that she was joking, but it was true.

"I know. I just feel terrible about what happened."

Ramona finished her wrap and then took a long drink of water as she watched me.

"Is it because of what happened or because of how you handled it?"

I cringed as I thought about my answer.

"Both."

That was a lie, but it was one that I needed to convince myself to believe. If I allowed my brain to think about how good she felt wrapped around my fingers as she climaxed, I would never walk away, and she would end up getting hurt in the process.

"Then talk to her and tell her that." Ramona pulled in a deep breath, then let her shoulders fall. "Look, I don't want to get in the middle of whatever this is between the two of you, but I feel like I have a small amount of responsibility here too. I should have never told you that Maggie was looking for her one true love. I get that it makes it sound like she's one of those clingy women who are so desperate for love that they jump into relationships without bothering to look first. That's not Maggie. She broke up with her last boyfriend because he was a douchebag who didn't deserve her." She locked eyes with me before continuing.

"He knew she was a virgin and constantly tried to make her feel guilty for not having sex with him. Trust me when I say that Maggie is not someone who does something unless she wants to. So, if she was close to having sex with you and asked you to be her first—it wasn't something that her last boyfriend ever earned, and they'd been together over six months. He wasn't the only guy she'd dated in the past year. Don't get me wrong, it's not like she's going out with guys left and right, but she does get her fair share of guys who are interested in her.

"The thing about Maggie is that she respects herself enough to know what she wants and what she doesn't. That's why she's so good with the advice she gives others. She doesn't encourage them to settle to be happy. She truly believes that you should create your own happiness and not rely on someone else to provide it for you. She's never needed a man for anything in her life. She runs a successful business and enjoys having her blog. *When* Maggie finds her one true love, she won't have to question it because it will be one of those experiences that make heaven and earth move. She deserves to have that, and I'm proud of her for waiting for it. God knows I should have."

She crumpled up her trash and collected mine before she stood up.

"I can't give you advice on what you should or shouldn't do, but what I can tell you is that if you're afraid to get to know her because you're afraid that she's going to fall in love with you, there are worse things that could happen. Being loved isn't a bad thing, and you should want that for yourself too, Owen. We all deserve it; some of us just have to fight harder for it than others. Do yourself a favor and have an honest conversation with her."

She offered a sympathetic smile before tossing our trash and heading out the door. I sat there for a few minutes, allowing the words to circle around in my head with no idea what to do with them.

Sixteen

Maggie

I'd been thankful for a busy Monday to keep me distracted from thinking about Owen, but after the final customer left, I found myself alone in the café with those stupid thoughts that hadn't shut up since he left last night.

Talking to Ramona had been somewhat helpful, though I didn't feel like I had any resolution after we hung up. I knew that she meant well and wanted things between Owen and me to have a chance, but I couldn't shake the thought that maybe this was the universe's way of stepping in and stopping things before I could get hurt.

Maybe I'd finally had enough of my fair share of shitty relationships that I was finally being spared.

I wiped down the counters and restocked the supplies for tomorrow morning before sitting down and turning on my computer. For once, I wasn't in the mood to answer emails about finding love or staying in it. I was bitter and sour from last night, which made it hard to focus on other people's problems.

As I waited for the new emails to finish populating, I heard the text message notification on my phone and picked it up.

Samuel: Hey beautiful, can I take you to dinner tonight?

My stomach curdled at the thought, and my fingers flew rapidly across my phone as I typed out my response.

Me: This number has been disconnected and is no longer in service.

A cheeky grin spread across my face as I slid my phone to the side and opened the first email. It wasn't too heavy, so I went ahead and replied to it, giving them the best advice I could.

An hour later, I'd worked through almost all of the emails when a new one popped up.

My heart hammered in my chest as I read the sender's name and found that it had been sent to the blog, not my personal email address.

Ask Mags,

It seems like I've found myself in a position where I need help again. This time I acted on my instincts and ended up hurting the woman I was trying to stay away from. It seems I can't avoid hurting her, no matter how hard I try.

I've made a fool of myself, and worse, I worry that I've caused her to feel unworthy of the attention and love she so clearly deserves. How do you go back in time and fix something that should have never happened?

--Stupid In Montana

I swallowed hard as the tears slid down my face. If I had any doubt before that this was Owen, this now confirmed it for me.

I knew that he freaked out last night when I asked him to be my first, but I didn't stop to think that he might actually regret it. That hit harder than I could've imagined.

Was it a mistake? If it was, then why did it feel so good?

I chewed my nail as I continued to stare at the email, debating whether to reply or not.

Last night was a night of heavy thinking, and even though I had enjoyed what happened between us, I found myself going back and forth on whether it was the right thing. Maybe Owen was right that we should have stopped and not let it happen to begin with.

I'd even gone as far as making a list of pros and cons of being with someone like Owen and frowned when I'd seen that there were more cons written on the paper than pros.

Pros:

Attractive

Good with his hands

Makes me feel good

Cons:

Lives in NY

No commitment

Doesn't open up

Older

Afraid to settle down

Has been hurt and has emotional scars

Doesn't want a committed relationship

Doesn't believe in true love

Refuses to commit

Okay, so maybe the commitment thing was a bit overkill, but I couldn't push it out of my head if I'd tried. And trust me, I've tried. The thought of not being with someone that made me feel so electrically charged when they'd touched me like Owen did made it hard to ignore. But I wasn't willing to allow myself to start something based purely on physical attraction, only to have my heart broken by it later.

I inhaled slowly as I steadied myself, then exhaled and began writing my response to his email.

Dear Stupid In Montana,

I'm sorry to hear that. It's hard to put yourself out there and then later feel like you regret what you did.

While you can't go back and fix something that's already happened, you can grow from the experience, which I think you have. You've acknowledged that your actions have had an impact on someone else, and you're more concerned with their happiness than your own. I know a lot of people who still aren't able to do that.

As far as worrying about making her feel unworthy unless you blatantly told her that she wasn't worthy, I wouldn't be too concerned about it. If she's smart, she'll know her worth without having to rely on anyone else to confirm it. Believe it or not, there are people who are able to hold their own in a relationship and don't need anyone else to be responsible for them. That's the beautiful thing about most relationships— you share things together. It's not a job or a duty. You don't have to constantly prioritize the other person's happiness over your own.

If you do decide to embark on a new relationship, you owe it to yourself to find out what makes you happy first. Don't ever rely on someone else to create your own happiness, and don't allow anyone to make you feel responsible for theirs.

I pressed send and swallowed back the tears that threatened to burst free. Whether Owen knew I knew it was him emailing me or not didn't make a difference in how I responded. If anything, I hoped he knew so that it would save us from having an uncomfortable conversation the next time we saw each other. I imagined that wouldn't be anytime soon, given that he'd avoided me all day, and I had gotten a text message from a girl I went to school with, asking if Ramona was cheating on Daniel because she saw her having lunch with the hot new guy in town.

I knew Ramona would tell me about their lunch date when she was ready, but it still irritated me that I had to hear it through the grapevine of small-town gossip first.

I closed my email and shut my computer down before packing up for the day. While I usually enjoyed hanging out and people-watching until it got dark, I wasn't in the mood today. If anything, I was more eager to get home and spend some quality time with Leroy than risk running into Owen when he left for the day.

Seventeen

Owen

I had dated plenty of women to know that Maggie was pissed when I read her email response. I hadn't put my name in the emails when I'd sent them, and thanks to sending them through the blog, it allowed me to post under an anonymous profile. But somehow, deep inside, I felt like she knew it was me.

Hell, it would be hard for her *not* to know that it was me. It wasn't like I had tried to be secretive when I'd sent the recent email, and it basically spelled out what had happened. But I was desperate and wanted to clear the air between us, yet I was too scared to go see her in person.

I knew that I owed it to her to have the conversation face to face, but I didn't trust myself not to try to touch her again. It was like she was an addiction, and I didn't want to succumb.

After talking to Ramona, I knew that she was right about Maggie. She didn't have to tell me how strong and independent she was; I could see it every time I talked to her. From her taking control of getting Leroy set up in his new terrarium to how she navigated leading me back down the trail after I'd gotten myself winded, she never once asked for help. She didn't need to, just like she didn't need me.

When I'd realized I had been wrong about her all along, I'd started to see Maggie differently. She wasn't this young, love-sick, hormonal teenager that was going to turn clingy and require me to do everything for her. She was funny, mature, and successful and genuinely enjoyed my company.

I had been a dick to her by putting her in a box that she never belonged in, to begin with. When I heard that she *loved* love, it instantly put every wall up that I could. Love was the last thing I needed, and a relationship was even further off the table, given that I wasn't staying in Whiskey Mountain.

But something about Maggie changed the way I'd started thinking, and I hated that I suddenly felt so open to the idea of so many things.

Even though I was still much too old for her, it didn't feel like it when we were together. Honestly, she was a lot more mature than most girls her age. Or maybe I just remembered twenty-two-year-olds differently from when I was that age and was obsessed with bedding as many of them as possible.

Maggie didn't act childish, nor did she act her age. If anything, it felt like she was closer to my age. When we talked on our way back from Cool Cats, it was effortless conversation and flowed so easily. Just like it did last night during dinner—after I finally loosened up enough to talk to her.

I had been such an idiot and hadn't realized what I was doing until it was too late. Maggie wasn't someone that I needed to avoid—I was someone she probably should have avoided. I had no idea what I was doing and was so afraid of love that I was willing to push away the first person to take a genuine interest in me. I couldn't remember the last time anyone had asked me questions that they actually wanted an answer to, nor could I remember the last time anyone took the time to talk to me about things that weren't superficial, like the weather.

Ramona was right, Maggie was something special, and I was the dumbass who didn't see it until it was too late.

I grabbed a beer out of the fridge, sat on the couch, and turned on my laptop.

Ask Mags,

It's refreshing to hear your take on relationships, and I admit, I've never given much thought to what would make me happy.

You see, from a young age, I've always been responsible for other people's happiness. My mother was a drug addict, and I was the only one who didn't walk away from her when she tried to get clean. Her happiness fell on me, and if I messed up, she would relapse. There was never anyone else around to show me another way. The only male role model I've had in my life was my grandfather, who was my best friend until he died from a stroke. He taught me to love and take care of my mother, even during the times when I felt she didn't deserve it.

Growing up with a mother who constantly needed me to take care of her, I found myself dating women who needed the same. I was always responsible for everyone else's happiness, which started to feel like a burden, and I resented them for it. I was drowning in the weight of everything that I tried to carry by myself with no one to help.

I was elated when I'd finally found someone who didn't need me to take care of them. I knew then that I'd found my one true love. It was such a rush to know that I could love them freely without having to worry about creating their happiness or sacrificing my own. I was thirty-two, and finally over all of the drama of dating in my twenties.

But then things changed, and I realized it wasn't as easy as I'd thought. You see, she wasn't happy, and it was my fault. I had dropped the ball and didn't stop to take care of her like I had everyone else. I expected too much from her, and in the end, she left me for someone that made her happier than I could.

This is all that I've ever known when it comes to relationships of any kind. They're one-sided, and I'm always the one who is responsible for making sure things work. It's a heavy weight to carry and has left me guarded against starting any new relationships because I'm still exhausted from the ones I've had.

But when you mentioned that relationships shouldn't be a job or a duty and that both people should share in taking care of it, that meant something to me and made me realize that I've been stuck in toxic relationships my entire life and have never known what a healthy one looks like until now.

Granted, I'm not in a relationship with this woman, but that doesn't mean I don't see the possibility now that I've stepped back and examined things.

I believe she can be happy on her own, but part of me wonders if she could be happier with me. I don't know if I know how to love the way she needs me to, but for once, I know that I want to try.

I don't want to be a victim to love anymore. I'm so tired of feeling unworthy of it, and now that I've seen the light in this woman, I don't want to let her go.

Do you think there's a chance she'll let me make it up to her? I know that I'm not responsible for her happiness, but I would like to get to know her if she'd let me because that would make me happy.

Stupid In Montana

Eighteen

Maggie

My eyes burned from crying. Between the recent email from Owen, the slew of unwanted text messages from Samuel, and the chewed-up panties that I'd found Leroy eating in the laundry room, I was at the end of my rope.

I knew better than to let him roam too freely in the house and had completely forgotten to close the laundry room door before I took him out of his terrarium. I also knew that he could pull clothes out of the holes in the hamper, hence how he got my favorite pair of panties.

They weren't sexy or anything special, but they were the softest ones I owned and felt like heaven against my body. They were what I called my "comfties," aka comfort panties. And now they were crotchless with tiny little gnawed through holes all over the place.

Ramona had called a few times, but I'd been cranky and sent her to voicemail. She didn't bother to leave a message, which meant she would call back again. Today was the most Mondayest Monday ever, and I couldn't wait for it to be over.

I checked on Leroy as I passed by to grab the laundry from the dryer, making sure he didn't have any underwear stuck in his shell after he'd tried to crawl through one of the smaller holes he'd made. Right as I'd finished pulling the clean clothes out, I heard the doorbell.

I grunted and headed to the couch, not bothering to go to the door. Whoever was there could leave since I wasn't up for company and hadn't invited anyone over. My parents lived out of state and never just dropped in. I didn't have any friends other than Ramona, and she knew better than to just show up when I was in a bad mood. Besides, she was supposed to be working tonight. That left Owen and Samuel—both of which I didn't want to see.

The TV was on, but the sound turned down as a commercial played. I pulled out a pair of leggings, folded them, then set them on the coffee table as I grabbed another pair. The doorbell rang again, so I ignored it. If it was an emergency, they could go to one of the neighbor's houses.

I kept working through the pile of clothes, relieved that whoever it was seemed to have left because the ringing had stopped. Then suddenly, I saw movement outside the window behind the couch and tossed the clothes on my lap to the floor.

Startled, I jumped up and clutched a hand to my chest.

I lived in small-town Montana where the crime rate was pretty much non-existent, so it wasn't like I had any freaking clue what to do with an intruder outside.

I stood there stupidly staring at the back door as the handle rattled.

"Maggie! Open up!"

I tilted my head to the side and listened again.

"Open up, or I'm going to break a window and come in."

Finally recognizing the voice, I rolled my eyes and opened the back door. Rain came pelting in, spraying me in the face with the gush of wind that whipped by.

"What the hell are you doing?" I demanded as Ramona came in, soaking wet and dripping on the rug.

I closed the door and locked it behind her before reaching into the laundry basket and tossing her a towel.

"You haven't been answering your phone, and you wouldn't answer your door," she replied as her teeth chattered.

"I didn't feel like talking."

I kept my hands on my hips, glaring at her.

"You could have been dead." She shivered again, looking like a frozen popsicle in the middle of my living room.

"Here, put this on," I offered and handed her a clean hoodie.

She turned around and pulled hers off, along with her soaked shirt, and slipped it on.

"Thank you."

I plopped down on the couch and nodded for her to sit in the chair across from me. She sat on the edge, trying not to get it wet.

"What are you really doing here?"

"I came to check on you."

"I'm fine," I lied.

"You've been crying."

"So."

"You're not fine."

"Okay," I sighed with a shrug. "Maybe not right now, but I will be. I've been through worse, this too shall pass."

"I saw the recent Spill The Beans post," she said softly. "Have you talked to him?"

"Not outside of the emails you saw. He replied to mine, but I haven't done anything with it yet."

She leaned back in the chair and waited patiently, not forcing me to say anything more.

Finally, she got up and walked into the kitchen. I turned to see her opening one of the drawers and rummaging around.

"What are you doing?" I asked.

"Looking for the takeout menu from that place you like."

"Which one?"

"The one with the chips and salsa." She pulled out a stack of menus and sorted through them. "There it is! Okay, what do you want from La Salsa?"

I sunk back against the cushion.

"I think they're still closed."

"We won't know unless we try. Now, what do you want, and I'll call in an order."

"You don't have to do that."

"Stop it," she hissed. "I'm here for the night, and we're going to eat tacos and talk through this. So again, what do you want?"

"I'll do the taco trio with guacamole, queso, and an order of chips and salsa."

"Got it," she said, then turned and lifted her phone to her ear.

I had waited for her to give me the bad news that they were still closed. It just seemed fitting that I wouldn't get my La Salsa craving satisfied two nights in a row.

I was still wallowing in self-pity when Ramona came back into the living room and sat down.

"It'll be here in twenty minutes."

My eyes widened in surprise while my stomach growled.

"Wow, I thought for sure they'd still be closed."

"It looks like good things are bound to happen." She gave me a cheeky grin, and I knew there was more that she wasn't telling me.

"Mmmhmm."

I eyed her suspiciously but turned my attention to Leroy before I could give her the fifth degree. He was making a hacking noise from his terrarium, and I knew he would soon be throwing up my underwear, just like he always did.

"Is he okay?" Ramona asked, leaning forward to see him.

"Yeah, he ate my comfties. He'll be fine."

She turned from looking at him to me in disbelief.

"No! He ate your comfort panties?!"

I nodded, feeling the tears sting my eyes again.

"I'm sorry, I know how much they meant to you."

"It's okay. They were just underwear."

"They were the best underwear and will be remembered."

I felt the rumble in my chest as I laughed. It felt good, and I hated that I'd spent so much of my time and energy tonight on being sad and depressed. What had I just told Owen? That he needed to be responsible for his own happiness and not rely on anyone else. Why wasn't I doing the same?

Just because I had been embarrassed and felt a little rejected last night didn't mean I couldn't still be happy. It wasn't like Owen, and I were even dating. We'd just barely started talking, and then things got wildly out of hand when he touched me. It wasn't like this was some relationship I'd invested a lot of time and energy into, so why was I letting it take so much out of me? I was better than this, and I sure as hell was stronger than this.

But there was something different about Owen. Something that I desperately wanted to explore, and now it was gone. Maybe I felt so heartbroken about what happened because, for once, I'd felt something with him that I'd never felt with anyone else, and that gave me hope that maybe he was the real thing. Even if it felt like it was hard to get him to let me in, part of me knew that it would be so rewarding once he did.

"So, are you ready to talk yet, or do you want to wait until you have some tacos in you?" Ramona asked as she studied me from across the room.

"There really isn't anything to talk about. I liked him, but he doesn't feel the same way. He's too old for me and didn't want anything to happen to begin with. We got caught up in the moment, and it was a mistake. But we weren't dating, so I don't know why I'm so hung up on it."

"Maybe because you actually cared for him," she offered softly.

"How do you even like someone that you don't know?" I laughed, realizing how stupid I sounded. "I barely got to know him. I think I was just more obsessed with the idea of who he is than who he really is. I still have no idea what's beneath the layers of barriers he has up, and I don't think I ever will."

"You can like someone without having to know everything about them. There's this strange thing called chemistry— you might've heard about it. Anyway, it's where people just connect—they click in a way they've never clicked with anyone else. And when they do, it's indescribable."

"Chemistry is overrated," I joked as I got up to answer the door. It didn't feel like twenty minutes, but my stomach was excited, nonetheless.

I pulled the door open and frowned.

"You're not La Salsa," I answered dumbly.

"Nope," Daniel said, letting the *p* pop. He held a duffle bag in one hand and a fabric tote bag in the other. He looked past me to where Ramona was sitting with her chin tucked to her chest. "I brought the stuff you asked for."

"Thank you." She didn't look up as she answered him.

I felt awkward standing there, unsure of what to do. He extended the items to me, so I took them and tried to force a smile.

"I know this is what you asked for," he said quietly. "But this isn't what I want. My phone is on if you change your mind and want to talk about it."

She remained quiet and looked out the door she had come in through earlier. I offered a crooked smile and shut the door as he turned around and left.

I walked over, set the bags on the floor beside her, and then took a seat on the edge of the wooden coffee table.

"Okay, your turn to talk. What was that about?"

Her lip quivered as she tried to blink away the tears.

"I left Daniel."

Nineteen

Owen

Two days had passed by without me giving in and going to Spill The Beans for my daily caffeine fix. Instead, the corner market and café had gotten used to me, and I could tell that people around town were already starting to gossip. Last I'd overheard, Ramona was leaving her boyfriend of three years for the sexy new silver fox in town, aka me.

After that rumor, I'd spent a few minutes longer than usual studying myself in the mirror this morning for any traces of gray hair. Not that I was opposed to going gray—I just knew for a fact that I didn't have a single gray hair on my body.

I'd waited patiently for Maggie to reply to my email, but her response never came. I knew at that point that she knew it was me and assumed that Ramona had spoken to her as well. It wasn't like I had any place to be upset about what happened—I was the one who had been holding her at an arm's distance to keep her from getting too close. And look where that got me.

I sat numbly through the day's meetings and tried my best to appear lively when I had my last phone call of the day with the planning committee to discuss their decision about the strip mall. After a unanimous vote, the current strip mall would stay intact, and we would move forward with renovating it and turning it into new shopping and dining options.

It was already after two, and I knew Spill The Beans would be closing soon. Maggie usually kept it open until three, but the past few days, she'd closed earlier and skipped out instead of sitting by the window and writing like she'd done since I first moved here. I hadn't noticed how much I'd been watching her without realizing it until things changed. Suddenly, I knew more about her habits and routines, which made her changing them up feel more directed at avoiding me.

Without giving it much thought, I grabbed my keys and phone from the table and rushed out of the office, determined to talk to her. I had no idea what to say but knew that I owed it to her to say something. Anything was better than nothing at this point. While I thought I was getting what I wanted by pushing her away, I realized that *not* talking to her was more agonizing than allowing myself to get to know her. It didn't mean that we had to sleep together or start anything serious, I just wanted to explore the connection that I'd felt with her because it was unlike anything I'd ever felt before. Unlike most guys her age, it wasn't just about sex. While that was great and all, Maggie could ask me to wait a year before we did anything, and I would because there was more to her than that, and I wanted every single part of her.

When I got to Spill The Beans, I was relieved to see that the lights and the open sign were still turned on. My hand gripped the handle to open it but stopped when I spotted Maggie sitting at one of the tables, across from a guy who was looking at her like she was the most incredible thing he'd ever seen. *Not that I could blame him.*

He reached over and held her hands, tilting his head to the side as he said something that made her giggle. I didn't have to be close to see the blush that traveled up her neck and spread across her cheeks from the words he'd said.

I pulled my hand away and stepped back. Ramona had said something along the lines of Maggie having a lot of prospects. I was stupid for not thinking someone might be lined up and ready to swoop in before I could talk to her. Again, she owed me nothing and had every right to speak to whomever she wanted. It wasn't like we were dating, so I had absolutely no claim to her, even though I suddenly wished I did.

Staring for a few seconds too long, I finally stepped back and walked away with my head hung in defeat. While I wanted to allow myself to slip into a poor me pity party, I knew that wasn't an option. I needed to be stronger than this. Maggie was just a woman who wasn't in my league, no big deal. Nothing to feel like the world was crumbling around me over.

It was better this way. I could walk away from everything and not have to worry about hurting her in the long run when my work here was over, and I returned to the city. Maggie could find someone to fall in love with who was her age and could give her what she needed. That person wasn't me, and this was exactly how things should be. I was stupid for allowing myself to think that there was anything between Maggie and me other than some explosive chemistry when we touched.

Once back in my office, I closed the door and took a deep breath. I needed to get focused and remember why I was here to begin with.

Van Halen played loudly on my laptop speakers as I cranked through the paperwork to get the ball rolling on the strip mall. I was already ahead of where I needed to be, but that didn't stop me. Something had shifted inside of me, and I felt more driven and determined than ever to see this project through to the end, even if that meant that I would be in Whiskey Mountain longer than anticipated and would have to see Maggie flaunting around her new relationship.

While I had no idea if she was in a relationship, I would still have to see her with someone that wasn't me. The thought of knowing that he was touching her the way I wanted to did nothing to soothe the fire that had been burning in me all afternoon. By four, I had nothing left to work on, so I called it a day and changed into running gear. I'd opted for the gray sweats this morning, hoping that I might run into Maggie, but now I didn't care. It didn't matter anyway.

I grabbed my phone, keys, and earbuds from my desk and headed out the door. There was still at least another hour before the sun started to set, and I had energy to burn.

Twenty

Maggie

"I'm so sorry, Dylan," I said sympathetically as I held onto his hands. "I knew you guys were having some trouble, but I didn't think it was that bad. You should have called me sooner."

He shrugged his shoulders and leaned back in the chair, allowing our hands to fall on the table between us.

"I just feel stupid that I didn't see it sooner. I knew she wasn't that busy and felt like she was making excuses not to see me. I really thought I was being a good boyfriend by surprising her in Fallen Oaks. Guess the joke was on me."

"Stop. She's the only one to blame here. You did nothing wrong."

"I shouldn't have started dating her again, to begin with. It's like I never learn my lesson."

"It's hard to move on when we feel a connection to someone." I pulled my lips into a thin line. "You loved her and weren't ready to give up on that yet."

"No, but I should have listened. You and Ramona told me she wasn't good enough for me, and you were right."

"I don't think we said those words, but yes, we do believe that you deserve better."

Dylan had been one of my best friends since he moved here four years ago. Ramona and I took him in and adopted him as our brother. When he first started dating Kim a year ago, we stayed quiet and prayed that she had changed from the girl we knew in high school. After they broke up the first time, we thought he'd surely learned his lesson. But then Kim pulled the same act she'd used on her other boyfriends, and he took her back.

While I didn't initially want to be the one to come out and tell him that I thought she was cheating on him, I now regretted it. I hated to see him hurting the way he was over someone who didn't respect him and was probably already crawling into bed with the next guy.

"I think I'm just destined to be single for a while. Every relationship I've been in has ended with them cheating on me, and that has to mean something."

I reached over and squeezed his hand again, waiting until his eyes caught mine.

"It means that you haven't found the right person yet. These failed relationships are nothing other than a guide to show you what you deserve and to teach you to appreciate the wonderful parts of a real relationship, so you know what it looks like when you see it. You're only twenty-two; you have plenty of time to find that person for you."

"So," he shifted in his seat and looked around. "What's going on with you? Has Samuel come crawling back yet?"

I crossed my leg over my knee under the table and grunted.

"He doesn't get the message. I've asked him to stop texting and calling me well over a hundred times, and he just doesn't get it."

"Oh, he gets it. He's just determined to squeeze his way back into your life."

"Why do you say that?" I furrowed my brow at the smile plastered across his face.

"Because he's an asshole, and you have something he wants."

"I do?" My eyebrow arched high on my forehead.

"Obviously. You know every guy wants to be able to say that they took *it*. He's no exception. He's hoping that you'll take him back and give him a second chance so he can try again."

I pulled my head back in disgust and scoffed.

"That's both stupid and gross."

"Trust me—I know men my age. He'll stop coming around once he knows that someone else got it. Until then, it's like a challenge, and he wants to win. All men do."

I shook my head but knew that he was right.

"No, not *all* men," I muttered quietly and looked out the window.

"Is there someone new that I don't know about?" he asked, leaning forward with interest. He twirled his finger in the air at me. "I sense new gossip that you're holding out on me."

"No," I waved him off. "I was just saying in general."

His eyes narrowed as he called my bullshit.

"Nope. You're lying. Spill it."

My eyes widened as the guilt etched across my face.

"I'm not lying, I don't know what you're talking about," I laughed nervously.

He gave me one quick cursory glance, then picked up his phone and began typing.

"What are you doing?" I asked, leaning forward to look at his screen before he pulled it closer to his chest and out of my sight.

"Getting the 411."

I rolled my eyes and leaned back in my chair. If he was checking the blog for info, he wasn't going to find anything helpful.

He set the phone down and placed his hands in front of him as he stared at me.

"You can tell me now or wait for Ramona to fill me in. Your choice."

I inhaled sharply, feeling slightly betrayed though I should have seen it coming.

"By the way, I don't need your truck anymore," I said randomly, trying to pull his attention to something else. Anything else.

"No? Why not? Did you decide on something else for Leroy?"

"I actually had someone else help me while you were gone."

He clapped a hand over his heart as if he'd been wounded.

"You went to someone else for help?" he gasped, playing the part of dramatic best friend perfectly.

"I didn't go to them; they just happened to be there and offered to take me."

His phone dinged and he picked it up, glancing at me before reading the message.

"Would that happen to be the new older guy in town that totally fucked up?"

He turned his phone to show me the message from Ramona.

Ramona: Owen—the sexy older guy handling the strip mall. Totally fucked up, and now Mags won't get out of her own way to allow something to happen between them.

I chewed my lip and kept quiet. Double betrayal.

"It's nothing. He helped me get the stuff I needed for Leroy, we had dinner once, then he found out that I was a virgin and booked it out of my apartment faster than a bolt of lightning. There's nothing more to it than that."

"Then why does Ramona think that you're getting in your own way?"

"Because she wants something to happen for me so badly that she can't see the truth of what's actually there."

"Which is what?"

"Nothing. Absolutely nothing. Unlike Samuel, Owen isn't interested in trying to take my virginity. He's so far off from being interested in me that he'd rather bolt out of my house than hear that I haven't had sex before. So see, not all guys are like Sam. Some of them don't even want that from me."

I sank down in my chair and pretended to listen as Dylan listed all of the reasons why I was wrong. It didn't matter; I knew deep down what the truth was.

<u>Twenty-One</u>

Owen

It was amazing how easily you could avoid someone in a small town if you really tried. Granted, I was down to a few slices of bread, some leftover pizza, and a questionable block of cheese, so I couldn't avoid going out for much longer. I needed to do some grocery shopping but knew that the chances of running into Maggie on a Saturday were fairly high given that she'd chosen to close the coffee shop today—not that I'd been by to notice.

I knew it was stupid and childish to avoid her, but it'd been a week since I'd run out of her apartment, and the longer we went without talking, the more awkward it felt. How was I supposed to look her in the eye after having my fingers deep inside of her and act like nothing had happened? Yet I had to do exactly that because the few times I've seen her in passing, she's been with the same guy I saw her in the coffee shop with.

Knowing I needed to get over myself, I grabbed my keys and headed to the store. It was busy with people filling the aisles, but nothing like what I was used to in New York City. I browsed casually, trying to convince myself that I was solely checking out the options so I could plan some meals to cook this week and that I wasn't purposely lingering around in the hopes of running into her.

It was like running hot and cold—I wanted to see Maggie, then I wanted to avoid her. At this point, I didn't know which end was up, and I hated that I felt as indecisive as a kid in a candy shop.

While I knew what I wanted, my head was struggling to convince my heart that it wasn't something I could have. Women like Maggie didn't belong with men like me, and it needed to stay that way. I had to remember that it was selfish to entertain ideas of us together because I was the one who would be walking away and breaking her heart in the process.

I wandered aimlessly down the rice and bean aisle, pushing my cart slowly as I scanned the different options.

"Find anything good?"

I looked up to find Mayor Landing beside me, looking at the shelf that held my attention.

"Um," I frowned and looked closer. "No idea."

She laughed and rested her hand on my shopping cart.

"How are you?" she asked, and I couldn't help but notice something different in her voice. It sounded motherly, which hit me in an odd way, given that my mother was never clean or sober enough to bother trying to be mine.

"Good. Just picking up some groceries. How are you?"

"Great, thank you. I'm helping plan my granddaughter's eighth birthday party and had to come for some last-minute supplies."

I smiled at the way her face lit up when she spoke about her family and then tried to push aside my discomfort of not knowing what that felt like.

I glanced in her cart and noticed an abundance of pink as it overflowed with streamers, balloons, and princess fairy wands.

"It's a princess tea party," she offered, looking down and laughing. "My husband has been groaning nonstop about how our house looks like Pepto-Bismol. He'll be glad once the party is over. My daughter and I felt bad about all of the girly stuff taking over his space that we're sending him to play golf on Sunday while we clean up."

"That sounds like a nice gesture; I'm sure he'll appreciate it."

"If there's anything he loves *almost* as much as his family, it's golf."

I laughed softly, having met him a few times, and knew this to be true from the handful of stories he'd told me.

"Well," she said with a sigh. "I need to finish up my errands before the day gets away from me. It was wonderful to see you."

"You too, take care, and I hope your granddaughter has a great party."

"Thank you. You're more than welcome to join us. It's Saturday at two. Just go down Townsend Drive, and you'll find it—it'll be the only house decked out in pink."

I smiled and nodded, not saying anything so I didn't accidentally commit myself. She gave a little wave and then took off down the aisle to finish shopping.

Deciding that I didn't need rice or beans, I pushed my cart down the aisle and around the corner to the next one when I stopped short to avoid hitting someone.

I didn't have to wait for her to whip around and show me her face to know it was Maggie. Her ass in the tight yoga pants was enough confirmation for me.

My mind raced as I tried to decide whether to pull back and go in the opposite direction before she could see me, but it was too late.

Her eyes widened when she saw me, and I could tell she had been avoiding me, just as I had been avoiding her.

"Hey," she whispered softly, her hands gripping the shopping cart handle tighter.

"Hi."

I stood there, frozen in place, as we stared at each other.

The seconds ticked by, sounding loud in my head as the blood rushed past my ears.

"How are you?" I finally rushed out before I could chicken out.

"Good."

I swallowed hard, forcing the rush of emotion back down. She wasn't as talkative as I remembered her being before, which made me even more nervous.

We continued to stand to the side of the aisle as other customers passed by. No one bothered to say anything, but that didn't mean there weren't curious glances and hushed whispers.

"I'm really sorry about what happened," I said quietly, leaning toward her so she could hear me.

"Don't be. It's fine."

My shoulders tightened, knowing that it was anything but fine. She wouldn't be this stiff and guarded toward me if it was. I'd hurt her, just like I wanted to avoid all along.

"Maggie," I sighed and ran my hand through my hair. "It's not fine, and I owe you an explanation."

"No, you don't. You were the one who told me that we should stop; I should have listened."

I pushed my cart to the side and took up the space beside her so I could talk without everyone else listening.

"Yes, I said that. But Maggie, that doesn't mean that I regret what happened. I've been stuck in my head trying to figure this thing out, and I still have no idea what any of it means. I'm completely lost and out of my element here. You're twelve years younger than me, and I don't want to take advantage of you. Not only that, you're—"

"A virgin. I get it," she snapped, looking sharply at me then around to make sure no one else heard her. "I was stupid for

132

letting anything happen as well. It wasn't just you. We both made a mistake. It won't happen again."

She reached for her cart as I stepped forward and blocked her. Trying to respect her space, I put my hand on the shopping cart to keep her from leaving.

"Despite everything telling me that I should leave you alone and walk away, I find that incredibly hard to do," I admitted.

She arched a brow and narrowed her eyes.

"There's no prize to be won, so feel free to move along."

I pulled my head back and frowned. What the hell was she talking about? Prize??

Then suddenly, it clicked.

I leaned forward, forcing her back against the shelf of canned goods behind her. I looked over my shoulder to make sure no one was watching as I gently placed my hand on her hip and whispered in her ear.

"Maggie, rest assured that I am not interested in *winning* anything, nor do I care whether you're a virgin. If you decided to go have sex with someone else, just to keep me from being able to say that I took that from you, be my guest. I'm not interested in this thing with you because I want to take your virginity. I'm interested in you. Who you are. What you like. And more importantly, because of how you make me feel when you're around me. So let me just make this abundantly clear—if given a chance with you, I will NOT initiate sex. That power is yours, Maggie. I respect the fuck out of you for knowing what you want and not giving that part of yourself to just anyone."

I pulled back slowly and allowed my hand to fall to my side. Her breathing had increased, and her pupils were dilated, matching what I imagined mine now looked like as well. I felt intense chemistry every time I touched her, and this was no exception.

"Owen, I can't," she started before I held up a hand and cut her off.

"I know that I hurt you, Maggie, and I'm sorry. I hate myself for causing you any kind of pain. But you can't deny that there's something between us. You feel it too, I can tell by the way you react when I touch you."

She leaned away from the shelf and straightened her back, taking a deep breath and slowly letting it out as she tried to compose herself.

"Yes, there may be something between us *physically*, but that's not enough for me."

My heart dropped.

"While I admit that I would love nothing more than to explore whatever this is between us, I can't allow myself to do that. At the end of the day, I'm still the same girl you were trying to avoid—the one who loves love and wants her happily ever after someday. It's not fair to me when I know it would be temporary."

"I know," I said softly, flexing my fingers to keep from reaching for her again. "But plenty of people have long-distance relationships."

My eyes locked onto hers, begging her to listen.

"I know, but that's not the real problem."

"Okay," I took a shuddered breath. "What's the problem? I know there's a way we can solve it."

She took a step back as if she needed more space from me to get her words out.

"At the end of the day, I'm still someone who is going to want more than what you're willing to give to me. I want someone I can spend forever with and be committed to."

"I'm not afraid of commitment," I said quickly. "I know that I thought I was, but you've made me realize that I felt that way because I didn't have anyone worth committing to."

She shook her head as tears welled in her eyes.

"I know that it was you emailing me. *Stupid In Montana.*"

I let my shoulders fall and looked away.

"I don't blame you for having a hard time committing, given what happened with your fiancé. On top of that, you had a childhood that required you to take care of your mother. You said it yourself that you've never been in a relationship with anyone that wasn't toxic. I get it, and I'm sorry you've had to go through all that."

I rubbed my lips together, feeling the anxiety bubbling to the surface.

"But I can't willingly look away and pretend I don't know any of this. My mother taught me to pay attention if someone shows you who they are. You've said countless times that you're not a commitment type of person and that you don't feel like you're destined for great love."

"I didn't know any better at the time," I whispered, hating where this was going.

"I know. But the moment something happened between us, you freaked out and left. You were scared that my being a virgin meant that I would automatically cling to you and that you would have to take care of me, even though I hadn't asked you to. You were so quick to flee because there was the possibility of commitment. I can't look past that, Owen. It's not fair to me, and honestly, it's not fair to you, either. We both deserve happiness, but I don't believe that it's going to come from each other. We're too different and want different things out of life."

I covered my mouth with my hand, then allowed my fingers to trail down the scruff that dotted my jaw.

"I wish you the best, Owen. I really do."

She smiled sadly and walked away.

Twenty-Two

Maggie

One Week Later

"There, yeah, that's it."

"Are you sure that's the right hole? It feels a little tight."

"It's supposed to be tight."

"This tight??"

"Yes, now push it in harder. All the way."

"Ouch!"

"Okay, I'm almost in."

"You're going to have to go deeper. I can't feel anything."

"That's not what a guy wants to hear."

"Funny," I laughed, wiggling my butt on the floor to scoot to the side as Dylan stood over me and tried to line up the top of the cage that we were helping Ramona build for Cool Cats.

"Okay, push down hard," Ramona directed with the instruction manual in front of her.

"I love how we're doing all of the hard work, and she gets to stand there and bark orders at us," I mumbled.

"Hey, *she* is buying you tacos and margaritas as soon as this damn thing is built."

"Did you really need to go all out and get the biggest setup they had?" Dylan asked, stepping back to look at his work.

It was over the top big and could easily house a hundred parakeets. For now, it was going to be Pablo's new home since Ramona and Daniel had officially split, and she was planning to convert the storage room at Cool Cats into a living space for herself. The building already had a bathroom and full kitchen in what she called the breakroom, even though there were no other employees for her to give a break to.

"I wanted him to have the best cage there was since he was being uprooted again. Poor guy hasn't had any real stability in the past six months, and I know that it stresses him out."

"So, have you decided to adopt him yourself?" I asked, moving the empty boxes out of the way so we could clean up and go get food.

"Yeah, he's grown on me, even with his foul mouth."

"Foul mouth. Foul mouth. Bad bird. Who's a naughty bird."

We all looked over and laughed at Pablo as he bounced around on the outside of his old cage.

After Ramona got him situated and made sure he couldn't escape, we piled into Dylan's car and headed to La Salsa.

I bobbed my head as the music played over the speakers while we waited for our waiter to return with our margaritas. A young kid passed by a few minutes later to drop off glasses of water, along with two baskets of chips and salsa. I wasted no time digging in and shoving one in my face when I looked up and saw Owen walk in.

My hand froze in front of my face, and my jaw dropped as I stared at him.

"What?" Ramona asked, then turned around and noticed him. "Oh."

"Have you guys talked since you ran into him at the supermarket last week?" Dylan asked quietly as all three of us continued to watch him.

I couldn't focus on anything other than how the army green sweater wrapped tightly around his chest as he slid into a booth across from a woman.

He was here on a date. He'd done what I told him to and moved on.

"No," I replied so quietly that they both leaned forward to hear me. "He hasn't been in for coffee, and I haven't seen him around town until now."

"Guess he got the message, loud and clear." Ramona frowned in his direction.

"It's what I wanted." I shrugged as if it didn't matter and popped the chip into my mouth.

Ramona and Dylan continued talking about Owen while I tried to wash my worries away with salsa. No matter how hard I tried, I couldn't quite shake the jealousy I felt whenever my eyes traveled in his direction.

It was stupid to be this upset over something I'd never had. Sure, he'd given me the best orgasm of my life, but that was no reason to obsess over him.

Dinner had carried on uneventfully, and I was thankful that the conversation had shifted from Owen to Ramona and Daniel's split. I hated to see either of my friends hurting, but I was pleasantly surprised by how well she was handling it. She'd laughed, and cried, and then laughed some more. I wasn't sure that she had technically processed everything yet, but it was nothing that her second margarita couldn't help.

"Okay, truth or dare," Dylan said around a mouthful of sopapilla.

"Come on, aren't we too old for this game?" I whined and popped a bite into my mouth.

"No. We're not too old. We're young and free and careless. And between the two of you, you're depressing, and we need to liven the night up. So pick one—truth or dare."

"I'm not playing," I shook my head.

"Fine, dare," Ramona said, jutting her chin out. "I could use a little adventure in my life these days."

Dylan wiped his hands on a napkin and then rubbed them together excitedly.

"Alright, I dare you to go over to the two guys sitting in the corner and ask one of them out."

Ramona lifted in her seat to get a good look at them.

"They're out of towners, I already checked." He gave her a pointed look.

"Fine," she tossed out, then got up and walked over.

I didn't bother to look back and see what she was doing because it just so happened to be that they were sitting at the table next to Owen's. I had a feeling that Dylan chose them on purpose because of where they were seated and wanted no part of it. I was also suspicious that Ramona only agreed to it so she could get closer to Owen and his date, given that she wasn't anywhere near ready to think about dating again already. They'd only been split up for a little over a week, and her wounds were still fresh.

I waited a few more minutes, then pulled my wallet out of my purse and tossed a few bills on the table.

"I hate to be a party pooper, but I'm going to head out," I said quickly. "Tell Ramona I'll call her later."

I darted out of the booth before he could stop me.

Twenty-Three

Owen

I knew it wouldn't take long before people started whispering and gossiping once I stepped foot in La Salsa. I hadn't expected that Maggie and Ramona would be there as well, either. I noticed that the same guy I'd been seeing her with was sitting with them too, but on the other side of the booth and not next to her.

I was halfway through my dinner meeting when I spied Ramona talking to the guys at the table next to me. She'd bent down to ask something, but her hazel eyes locked onto mine instead. I tried to look away but couldn't. There were so many questions I wanted to ask her.

Once she was finished getting one of the guy's phone numbers, she walked around and stopped in front of my table. I straightened my spine and forced a professional smile across my face.

"Fancy seeing you here," Ramona said, glancing between me and the woman across from me. I knew what she thought was going on. It was the same thing that had gotten under Maggie's skin and made her twitchy until she finally got up and fled out of the restaurant.

"You too," I said coolly. "Ramona, this is Bellamy Rhodes. She's starting a bed and breakfast in Fallen Oaks, so we're discussing some business opportunities. Bellamy, this is my friend Ramona. She owns Cool Cats, it's a—"

"You own Cool Cats?!" Bellamy shrieked, extending a hand out to Ramona.

"I do. It used to be a speakeasy that my grandpa owned, so I kept the same vibe and turned it into a pet shop."

"I've been there once, and it's amazing!"

I leaned back in my seat and let the two girls talk for a few minutes, thankful that I didn't have to bother explaining to Ramona who Bellamy was.

I was about to tell Ramona that we needed to get back to business when Bellamy's phone dinged.

"Sorry, I need to get going," she said, setting her phone down and reaching for her purse.

"Dinner is on me," I said, holding my hand up to stop her. "Thank you for meeting with me and sharing your experience. I appreciate it, and I'll be in touch as soon as I can set up a meeting with Mayor Landing."

"Sounds great, thank you. It was nice to meet you, Ramona."

Bellamy got up and left, her spot quickly filled by Ramona.

I was about to say something about needing to leave too, but she held her hand up and stopped me.

"I won't keep you here all night," she said as if reading my mind. "I just wanted to check to see how you're doing."

"I'm fine," I lied. She didn't need to know that I'd been miserable ever since I ran into Maggie at the grocery store. Nor did she need to know that I hadn't gone through half of the stuff I'd bought because I no longer had an appetite, hence the half-eaten plate of food that sat in front of me.

"You know she's just as depressed as you are," she said softly.

"I'm trying to give her what she wants."

"She doesn't know what she wants," a deep voice said behind me.

I looked up to find the guy I'd been seeing with Maggie standing there.

"Mind if I join you guys? It was getting pretty lonely at the table by myself."

"Be my guest." I extended my hand to the other side of the booth where Ramona was sitting.

"I'm Dylan, Maggie and Ramona's best friend," he said as he reached his hand out to me. "I'm the guy with the truck that was supposed to help her with Leroy's terrarium."

I nodded as it clicked into place.

"Well then, I guess you already know everything about me."

He shrugged nonchalantly.

"I know what I need to know."

"And what's that?" I asked, leaning back against the booth.

"That Maggie is head over heels in love with the idea of being in love, yet she won't get out of her own way to give this thing with you a chance. It's like now that she has the possibility of actually finding it, she's running scared in the opposite direction."

I chewed the inside of my cheek and folded my hands in front of me.

"I don't know what to do," I admitted. "She has it set in her head that it won't work between us. I know that it's my fault, I was the one who told her that I wasn't someone who wanted a commitment, and then I freaked out when she told me…."

"What do you want now?" Ramona asked.

"I want Maggie." It felt good to get it off my chest and say it out loud. "I don't know anything other than I can't stop thinking about her. I've never felt this way about anyone before, and it scares me, but the thing that keeps me up the most at night is the thought of not having her at all."

"So tell her that. Make her listen." Ramona smiled as if she had the answer to life's biggest problems.

"It's not that easy," I sighed. "She won't listen to me. She's already convinced herself that it won't work, that I won't be able to commit to her and give her what she needs. I literally have no idea how to prove to her that I can commit and that I'm in this for the long run. Between my past track record with relationships and living in NYC, it's kinda hard to show her that I'm willing to try."

"How long before you have to go back?" Dylan asked.

"Now that the Mayor wants to discuss additional projects, I expect to be here at least twelve months, if not longer."

"That's plenty of time to show someone you can commit to them," Dylan noted.

"But how? She won't give me a chance. Aside from buying a house to show her that I'm here for the long run, I'm out of ideas. And while real estate is a hobby of mine, I don't know that I'm ready for *that big* of a commitment right now."

"No, maybe nothing that drastic, but I have an idea," Ramona squealed with a mischievous grin.

Twenty-Four

Maggie

Ask Mags,

My girlfriend recently broke up with me because she's convinced I'm obsessed with sex. It's not like I'm sitting around watching porn twenty-four hours a day, but it wouldn't hurt for us to have it at least once a day. I have needs, and it feels like she's not bothering to meet them. What should I do? Also, I sent an email to Just The Tip, but it's gone unanswered for over a week.

--Dry and Lonely

My shoulders tightened, and then I responded.

Dear Dry and Lonely,

Have you ever stopped to consider whether her needs were being met instead of focusing on your own? It doesn't sound like it to me. And honestly, the whole 'men have needs' bullshit is getting old. Women have needs too. We need to feel loved. Wanted. Important. Respected. Valued. Cared for.

Are you making her feel those things? If the answer is no or I don't know, then you need to try harder. If she isn't in the mood to have sex with you when you want it, then you need to step back and ask yourself why. Have you recently neglected her and what she needs? Did you present it as something fun you could do together, or did you demand that she get you off because you needed to feel good?

Figure out how to be less selfish, and maybe she'll come around. If not, be sure to send her over to Spill The Beans. I'll gladly treat her to a latte and discuss the new sex toys out there that can surely get her off so good she won't ever want anyone else to do the job for her.

I knew that part of my sour mood was from seeing Owen at La Salsa last night, but there was also something about this email that reminded me of Samuel and made my blood boil. That right there was the reason that I had never moved forward with any of my relationships and had sex with the guys. It was ridiculous how immature and arrogant most of them were.

I moved to the next email as I sipped a hot mug of coffee and curled my toes between the couch cushions.

Ask Mags,

I've made a mistake and lost the only girl I've ever felt something with. I was stupid and allowed my bruised ego to stand in the way. Now she won't talk to me, and I'm at a loss for what to do. I don't want to move on and forget about her. That would be like refusing to look up at the beautiful night sky because you'd missed seeing a shooting star as it passed by.

But I don't want to force her into anything, either. I respect her, and if she's really decided that she's moving on, then I won't try to stop her. But the problem is that I don't know how to tell the difference between her being pissed off at me and her being done with me. I can't just walk away and risk getting a second chance with her if she changes her mind.

Please tell me what to do. I'm so lost.

-- About to lose the greatest thing ever

My throat tightened as I read the email, feeling the heaviness of the emotions that were poured into his words. Tears stung my eyes as I quickly tried to blink them away. I set my coffee cup down and began typing.

Dear About to lose the greatest thing ever,

I can feel the pain you're feeling through your email and can empathize with you. I'm sorry that you're feeling this way.

Unfortunately, there are plenty of things that can cause tension in relationships, but it sounds like you've already realized what it was and are ready to fix it if you can. While I don't know what happened, I'm still rooting for you to get the second chance you're so desperately seeking.

I can't tell you what to do—only you can decide that. But I can tell you that actions always speak louder than words. You can talk until you're blue in the face, but your actions will be what she actually hears. Don't be afraid to step out of your comfort zone and show her what she needs to see.

Wishing you all the best. Please let me know how it goes.

I pressed send and wiped away the stray tear that had slipped down my face. Deciding that I'd had enough for the day, I shut off my laptop and put it on the table.

Leroy was pacing in his terrarium, looking ready to blast through the side of it, so I picked him up and set him down on the rug so he could roam around for a bit. While I tried to make Sundays my self-care days, I hadn't been up for anything today and decided that it was as good of a day as any to start some spring cleaning. Sure there was still a heavy layer of ice that covered my patio furniture outside, but one could be hopeful that it would be coming soon.

I started in the bathroom, cleaning everything until it sparkled, then moved on to my bedroom, which was already fairly clean given that I hardly spent any time in it other than to sleep. I opened the blinds to let in some light while I changed the sheets and made the bed. When I went to toss the dirty linens in the hamper, I'd found Leroy wedged between the washer and dryer, trying to pull a pair of panties out of the bottom.

The depths of my depression had brought me to the low of not bothering to care that he was eating more of my underwear. It seemed he had an obsession that even I couldn't cure him of.

I picked him up and set him back in the living room after closing the door to the laundry room to keep him out. I finished sweeping and was getting ready to start mopping the kitchen floor when I heard the doorbell.

"Who's here?" I asked Leroy, not that he could answer me. But that hadn't stopped me from talking to him nonstop since I'd gotten him.

As I pulled the door open, I heard a familiar squawk and smiled.

"Panty eater cocksucker." Pablo bounced excitedly, though it was the person whose shoulder he was bouncing on that surprised me the most.

"What are you doing here?" I asked, gripping the side of the door to keep my legs from betraying me and giving out.

"I'm sorry for showing up without an invite, but I really need to talk to you. Can I come in?"

Owen's eyes locked onto mine, and for a moment, it felt like we were the only two people left on the planet. That was until Pablo started cursing again and repeating some lyrics from an Eminem song.

"Please," he whispered.

"Please, Maggie. I'm so lonely. Lonely and horny. Horny and lonely. Pattthhheeetttiiiccc," Pablo sang.

My brow arched, wondering what exactly had been said in front of the bird.

"Okay." I pulled my shoulders back and moved aside to let them in.

"Turtle! Turtle food!" Pablo squawked, then flew off Owen's shoulder and landed on the coffee table, where he paced back and forth, watching Leroy.

"Is he going to try to eat him?" Owen asked with concern.

"No, he's fine." I laughed and let my shoulders relax a bit. "Ramona has been bringing Pablo over when she's stayed with me, and they get along just fine. He says turtle food because he likes to watch Leroy eat."

"Oh, okay." He closed the door behind him and shrugged off his jacket.

"Speaking of which, why do you have Pablo?" I asked, spinning around to face him. I hadn't anticipated how quickly he'd crossed the room until his hands gripped my hips to keep me from falling into him.

"Well, that was one of the things that I wanted to talk to you about."

I swallowed hard, feeling the tingle up my spine that I got when something terrible happened.

"Is Ramona okay? Did something happen?"

"No," Owen rushed out, his fingers still burning into my skin. "Ramona is fine."

I slowly blew out the breath I'd been holding and waited for him to continue.

"I have Pablo because I decided to adopt him."

My jaw dropped open as I looked from him to the bird that had hopped down onto the floor.

"What?"

He nodded and looked past me to the pets.

"Why would you do that?"

He smiled softly, his breathing calming me as I tried to figure out what was happening. Ramona loved Pablo and had just said last night that she wasn't going to adopt him out to anyone. Why the sudden change?

"I talked with Ramona and Dylan last night after you left La Salsa."

I wasn't sure if he'd seen me but should have known they would talk to him after I left.

"I asked for their help, and the next thing I knew, I was at Cool Cats, loading some ridiculously huge cage into Dylan's truck and bringing Pablo home with me."

"Okay," I paused. "I don't understand. Why did you take Pablo home? What's going on?" I could hear the panic and uncertainty in my voice, and I hated it.

"Because, Maggie, I needed something to show you that I'm not afraid of commitment. You said my actions would speak louder than words, so I wanted to show you that I could be what you wanted. I'm not sure if you know this or not, but African grey parrots have an extremely long lifespan—somewhere around sixty to eighty years. They are also highly social birds and rely on the stability of having one owner. That means that Pablo and I will be together for the rest of his life or mine—I'm not sure which of us is going to go first at this point."

He laughed nervously, and I could tell that this conversation still made him slightly uncomfortable, even though he was the one to bring it up.

"I've spent a lot of time online researching the best care to make sure I don't mess this up. I'm all in with Pablo and want to give him the best home I can."

"What about when you go back to New York?" I asked dumbly. I had plenty of questions, none of which were ready to come out yet.

"I have at least a year in Whiskey Mountain, maybe longer. After that, I'll talk to my office and discuss options." He shrugged.

"What does that mean?" I leaned closer, hanging on to his every word.

"It means that I've found a reason to stay in Whiskey Mountain, and there are a lot of small towns close by that I can work on developing."

"Pablo's one lucky bird," I said weakly when I felt Owen's hand gently touch my shoulder.

I wanted to give in and allow myself to fall into his embrace, but I couldn't.

"He is, but that's not why I'm considering staying here."

"No?" My voice was so quiet that I barely heard the words come out.

"Maggie, I know I messed up before, and I'm sorry. But I can't walk away from you, no matter how hard I try. There are a million reasons why this thing between us might not work, but I'm only looking for one reason for us to move forward and explore whatever this is. I'm not asking you to rush into anything with me, but I would love a second chance to pick up where things were going before."

I felt my cheeks flush as I remembered where we had left things before he walked out.

"I don't mean that exactly," he rushed to assure me. "I mean, I'm not saying I wouldn't enjoy doing it again, but I'm not pushing you to give me a second chance just so we can have sex. I wasn't lying when I said I would wait forever, Maggie. I will never force you to do anything you don't want."

My stomach felt swishy as my heart hammered against my chest. Was this really happening right now?

"I don't know, Owen," I sighed, taking a step back so I could get some fresh air that wasn't filled with the scent of his cologne. "What if it doesn't work out?"

"What if it does?"

I rubbed my lips together as my mind went a mile a minute. Deciding that I'd had enough thinking, I leaned forward and wrapped my arms around his neck before lifting my lips to his.

There was no hesitancy on his end as his mouth crashed over mine and parted, welcoming my tongue to explore.

Just like before, I felt my body come alive from his touch. Suddenly, I needed more. I pulled his head down, trying to get him closer to me even though we were already as close as we could get.

He reached down and lifted me to his hips before setting me down on the edge of the island. We kept kissing while his hands roamed over my back and grazed my butt.

Everything was alive and on fire as heat spread across my skin from his fingers.

I pulled away, panting for air, as he nudged my head to the side and kissed along my neck. I moaned helplessly as the warmth spread between my legs.

I knew it was a big step for Owen to adopt a bird and that he'd done that to show me that he wasn't afraid of commitment. When I'd gone back and forth in my head on the reasons to be with him versus the reasons we shouldn't be together, I couldn't help but focus on how I felt with him. It wasn't just that he was able to give me a mind-blowing orgasm with little effort, but now I realized that I felt safe and comfortable with him, as if I belonged in his arms.

His hands continued to roam along my back and sides but stayed away from the areas I wanted him to touch the most. I scooted closer and tried to rub myself against him, but he chuckled and pulled away.

My chest heaved as I watched him step back and study me before licking his lips. *Fuck, I was going to come just from watching him do that.*

"Maggie, Maggie, Maggie," he tsked, pulling his lip between his teeth.

"I want more," I panted, letting my legs slightly part.

His green eyes sparkled in the light as they danced with delight at how needy I'd suddenly become. Then he slowly rolled his sleeves up, one at a time, and I couldn't think of anything other than those strong hands touching my body and making me come again.

"I would love to give you more, Maggie, but I need something from you first."

My mind blanked as I thought about how I'd give him whatever he wanted right now. Blow job? Done. Keys to my house? You got it. Just make me come, and I'd do anything he'd ask.

"Okay," I whispered.

"I need you to tell me that you want to be with me and give this a chance. Not sex, Maggie, but be with me in a committed relationship. No other guys. No other girls. Just us."

"No sex?" I asked weakly.

"Not right away," he chuckled, then rubbed the side of his thumb gently across my cheek. "Trust me, we will wait until the right time. When you're ready."

"I'm ready," I offered excitedly.

"There's no rush, Maggie. I can make you feel plenty good without sex. But I need that commitment from you first. So, what do you say?"

I leaned back on my hands and pretended to think about it.

"Are you asking me to be your girlfriend?"

He nodded and gave me a panty-dropping smile.

"Okay," I shrugged, then giggled when he leaned in and tickled my sides until I squealed.

Twenty-Five

Owen

I stared at Maggie as she lay on the bed, her brown hair fanned out beneath her as her sparkling blue eyes watched me. The moment she'd agreed to be my girlfriend, I'd tossed her over my shoulder and carried her to the bedroom, ready to give her exactly what she'd been not so subtly asking for.

I did stop to ensure that Leroy and Pablo were fine, but Maggie smacked my ass and told me not to worry about them, so I didn't.

I stood in front of her, slowly undressing from the waist up as she focused on my every move. While I wanted nothing more than to be inside of her, I wasn't planning to do that until I knew for absolute certainty that she was ready. Whether that be tonight or a year from now, it didn't matter to me.

"You're killing me over here," she said as she rested against a pile of pillows.

"Eager are we?"

"A little," she giggled as her hand trailed up her thigh.

"Don't even think about it," I warned, nodding to her hand that was now hovering above her pussy. "I get to bring that orgasm out of you tonight."

"Well then, hurry up."

I tossed my shirt to the floor, then kicked off my jeans. Wearing just my briefs, I climbed beside her on the bed. She glanced down at the bulge and her face flushed.

"We're not rushing into anything tonight," I reminded her and brushed a strand of hair off her face.

"It's not like I haven't done other stuff," she said quietly. "I've done everything but sex. So, you know, I'm not a *total virgin.*"

I nodded and leaned in, brushing my forehead against her cheek as I pushed her head to the side. I knew how much it turned her on when I kissed her neck, so I wanted to start there first.

A soft whimper escaped her lips as my tongue licked along her skin. She adjusted herself, allowing me more access as I trailed kisses down her collarbone and across her chest. My fingers skimmed along her thigh, slowly inching up toward her pussy.

Her chest rose and fell heavily as she panted while I pulled her t-shirt up and over her head. I was surprised that she wasn't wearing a bra underneath. My mouth eagerly moved across her breasts, pulling a hardened nipple and sucking it.

"Ohhh," she groaned and dug her nails into the sheets.

Focusing on how her body reacted to me, I laid my palm flat against her and gently rubbed the lace fabric over her slit. I could already feel how wet she was through the thin material and couldn't wait to feel her again as I slid it to the side and slipped a finger inside.

"Owen," she panted, bucking her hips off the bed.

I let go of one nipple, then pulled the other into my mouth and sucked hard while I eased another finger in. She was so fucking tight and wet that I felt like I was going to explode in my briefs. My erection strained against my stomach, and I shifted to give myself a little relief.

Knowing she was close to coming, I released her nipple and slid down her body, planting quick kisses over her abdomen before stopping at her pussy. I looked up to find her watching me as she bit her hand.

"Don't you dare keep those noises from me," I warned. "I want to hear every single sound you make, baby. You're about to come for me, and I want to hear it."

She nodded and dropped her hand as I hooked the thin straps of her thong under my thumbs and removed them. Tossing them aside, I licked my lips and got an up-close look at her beautiful pussy dripping with need. Locking eyes with her again, I lowered my head between her legs and licked.

A sharp exhale filled the air around us as her head fell back against the pillows. I smiled and continued to torture her with my tongue as I flicked her clit before taking it into my mouth and sucking while my fingers continued to fuck her.

"Fuuuccckkk," she cried out, pressing her thighs together as her orgasm crashed over her.

I kept my pace and waited until I felt the last spasm before I let go. I slowly rolled off her and wiped my mouth, loving how she looked post-orgasm.

"That was amazing," she sighed, rolling over to look at me. "But as your *girlfriend*, I'm entitled to take care of *that*." She nodded to the rock-hard erection in my briefs.

"We don't need to worry about that right now," I said softly. The last thing that I wanted was for her to feel like sex stuff was obligatory. If I made her come, it was because I wanted to. Not because I expected something in return.

"Oh please," she laughed and rolled over, her hand squeezing my dick. "I know you don't think you're going to come in here, sporting the biggest hard-on I've ever seen and not let me play with it."

A cocky grin spread across my face.

"You don't have to," I assured her.

"I know. I want to."

She squeezed closer to me, and I wrapped my arm around her shoulders as I laid on my back and allowed her hands to roam over my briefs. Her every touch felt amazing, but I was about to come if she didn't stop soon. As if sensing my need, she stopped and pulled my briefs down, allowing my cock to spring free.

Tossing them to the side, she grabbed me between her hands and slowly stroked me.

I let out a hiss between my teeth and found myself gripping the back of her head as she lowered her mouth and took me inside of it.

"Maggie," I moaned helplessly.

I wanted to tell her to stop, that she didn't owe me anything, but the way she worked her tongue and teeth over me told me that she wanted to do this. Not only that, she wasn't lying about having done it before.

Her hands worked the length that didn't fit in her mouth, even after I'd touched the back of her throat. On occasion, she'd reach back and caress my balls, sending me nearly over the edge. I was going to come soon at this rate.

She sucked harder and faster, forcing my balls to tighten beneath me.

"Maggie," I warned. "I'm going to come."

She locked even tighter around me and kept going until I exploded and shot ropes of cum down her throat.

Once my body stopped jerking, she slowly pulled away and wiped her mouth.

I panted as I tried to think of something to say, but when she laid down and cuddled next to me, I didn't bother. Her fingers curled into the hair on my chest while I held her, and for once, everything felt like it was perfect.

Twenty-Six

Maggie

"It's been two weeks, and you guys still haven't had sex?" Ramona asked in disbelief as she sat across from me at Spill The Beans. We'd already closed for the day, but she hung around for a cup of coffee and to catch up on girl talk.

"He said he's waiting until he knows I'm ready."

"Have you told him that you are? Hell, I'm getting blue balls from waiting this long," she joked and sipped her latte.

"I've told him, but it's usually when we're already doing other stuff, so I don't think he trusts it. I think he thinks that I'm just lost in the moment and that I'll regret it later."

"That's way too much thinking." She wrinkled her nose.

"Tell me about it."

"So do something to show him that's not the case."

"Like what?" I sipped mine and then took a bite of the apple crumble muffin I'd saved for myself this morning.

"You guys have another date tonight, right?"

"Yeah."

"Your place or his?"

"Mine."

"Okay, so put on some of your sluttiest lingerie and then surprise him with it as soon as he gets there. That way, you can let him know you're ready before anything happens."

"I can't do that," I said sadly. My shoulders slumped with disappointment.

"Why not?" She frowned.

"Because Leroy ate my last pair of sexy undies."

"What is it with that damn turtle and underwear?"

"I have no idea. But I'm officially out of sexy ones."

Ramona's phone dinged with a new text message, so I popped another bite of muffin into my mouth and waited for her to be done. She was grinning ear to ear, and I knew she must be talking to a new guy. So much for waiting a while before moving on from Daniel.

"Where were we?" she asked, then her brows rose when she remembered. "Oh yeah, what about the new ones you just bought?"

"He ate those too."

"How? Haven't you learned not to leave them on the floor?"

I laughed and felt the blush spread across my cheeks.

"Yeah, but it wasn't my fault. Owen came over and started kissing me, and I forgot that they were in the basket of clothes I was working on putting away when he got there. Leroy took advantage of pulling them out of the pile while Owen and I were in the bathroom."

"Bathroom?" She raised her brows and wiggled them.

"He had been out for a run and passed by my house to say hi. I offered to make him dinner, and he said he wanted to clean up first. One thing led to another, and he went down on me in the shower."

"You dirty, dirty girl."

"Actually, I was the clean one," I giggled.

"Okay, then let's go buy you some new lingerie for tonight." She got up and gave me a pointed look while she waited for me.

Two hours and fifty different outfits later, I was standing in front of the full-length mirror in my bedroom, regretting my choice.

Ramona and the sales lady convinced me this would look hot and make Owen crazy, so I got it. Now I couldn't help but feel nervous and insecure as I stared at the see-through black lace that barely covered my breasts and the matching thong that rode up my ass.

Before I could change my mind, the doorbell rang. I tossed on the robe that I'd bought to go with it and padded down the hallway to the door.

Leroy was secured in his terrarium, away from the bag of other lingerie I'd decided to purchase as well. I had washed the set for tonight but hadn't bothered with the others yet.

I opened the door and took him in as he held out a dozen roses to me.

"Thank you," I said softly, taking them from him and smelling them. "They're beautiful."

"You're beautiful." He leaned in and kissed my cheek.

I waited for him to come in before I closed the door and locked it. My palms started to feel sweaty as the realization of what I was about to do hit me.

"So," I said nervously. "I have something I want to show you."

"Oh yeah?" His crooked brow still did something to me.

I ignored the heat spreading between my legs and forced my fingers to work the tie on my robe. Once it was undone, I slowly opened it, trying to look sexier than I felt as I stood before him in the skimpy lingerie.

His Adam's apple bobbed in his throat as he swallowed. I felt the heat of his gaze as his eyes traveled over my body, taking in every single inch.

"I like it," he said, his voice gruff.

"Tonight is the night," I replied steadily.

"Okay." He took two steps and was right in front of me as his fingers trailed over the thin lace of the bra.

"Okay?" I couldn't believe he was finally agreeing to give me what I wanted.

"If you feel like you're ready, we can have sex."

"I'm ready. Now. Right now." I nodded to the bedroom. "I've already ordered a pizza, so we don't have to worry about dinner. We can eat when we're done. I also tipped them twenty dollars to just leave it on the doorstep and not bother us with ringing the doorbell."

I watched as he struggled to fight back his laughter.

"I don't want anything to get in the way of this happening," I added.

"Noted."

"Okay," I breathed out. The only problem was that now I didn't know what to do with myself.

"Would you like me to take over?" he asked as he rocked back on his heels and shoved his hands in his pockets.

I nodded, suddenly worrying that maybe I'd bitten off more than I could chew.

As if noticing my discomfort—which was blatantly obvious— he reached out and gently stroked my cheek.

"Relax, baby. You're still in control, and nothing will happen if you don't want it to."

"Okay."

He pulled me close and wrapped his arms around my waist as his lips brushed against mine. And just like that, all of my worries melted away.

Once I knew that Owen wasn't going to talk me out of having sex with him, my nerves settled, and I was able to relax. We moved into the bedroom and made out for a while before he went down on me and gave me another mind-blowing orgasm.

I reached over to stroke him, but he gently pushed my hand away and held it.

"Do you still want to?" he asked softly, kissing behind my ear.

"Yes," I replied quickly. "I want to have sex with you, Owen."

A low growl slipped through his lips as he rolled over and pinned me to the bed.

"If at any time you want to stop, I need you to tell me. There's nothing wrong with not going all the way, okay?"

I nodded.

"And if it hurts, you have to tell me that as well. You're going to be super tight, and I might stretch you. But I don't want this to be painful, so I need you to be honest and let me know if it is."

I nodded again, wondering just how bad it was going to hurt.

Owen lifted his hips and pulled his briefs off, allowing the beast to spring free. Then he grabbed a condom from the dresser and rolled it over his length. I watched everything as it happened, trying to soak in every detail.

He rolled on top of me and lowered his mouth to mine as he slowly kissed me.

"We can stop at any time," he whispered.

My legs parted, allowing him access while he shifted and lined himself up at my entrance.

"Are you ready?"

I held my breath as I nodded.

"Say it, Maggie."

"I'm ready."

"Good girl," he whispered, then gently pushed inside.

I gasped at the intrusion, feeling a slight sting as his thick cock pushed through. He stopped and waited for me to adjust to him before inching in. It was the slowest motion, and the stinging stopped almost as quickly as it started.

I could see him struggling to control himself as he hovered above me. Once he was fully seated, I reached up and caressed his jaw. His arms looked huge as they flexed beside me, showing off the tattoos that I'd come to admire.

Gently, I rocked my hips to let him know that I was ready for more. He scrunched his face and bit down on his lip as I squeezed his cock with my pussy.

"Give me more, Owen," I coaxed. I couldn't imagine that anything else was going to be painful, and didn't want him to keep treating me like I was some delicate flower he was about to break.

His eyes searched mine, and then he nodded as he rocked into me, pushing himself even deeper.

"Ahhh," I cried out, scratching my nails down his back. He pumped faster, and soon we found a rhythm as our bodies moved against each other. My body felt wonderfully filled as he reached down and started to rub my clit.

My legs quivered as they fell to the sides to allow him complete access to my body. He lifted himself back and rested on his knees while keeping his cock still inside of me. His thumb caressed the heightened bundle of nerves as he watched his dick slide slowly in and out of me.

"This is perfection," he commented proudly. "Such perfection."

I could feel my orgasm building as he continued to rub faster and right as I was about to come, he slammed into me, sending a jolt of pleasure through me as I cried out his name. He kept pounding, not too hard but hard enough that I could hear the sound of his balls clapping against my ass. Then I felt him tighten above me as he shuddered and unloaded into the condom.

Once he was done, he pulled back slightly and studied my face to make sure I was okay.

"That was incredible," I assured him, gently stroking his cheek. "I can't wait to do it again."

"You're going to be the death of me," he chuckled, then laid his forehead against mine.

While I'd waited a long time to lose my virginity, I couldn't imagine waiting another second before I could feel Owen inside of me again.

Epilogue
Maggie
Three Months Later

"You're going to get a sunburn," Owen said as his shadow cast over me. I shielded my eyes with my hand and looked up to find him standing there with a bottle of sunscreen.

"Sit up, and I'll put some on you."

"Like you did with the massage oil the other night?" I teased but did as he asked.

It was unusually hot for May, and I'd decided to spend some time sunbathing in the backyard while Leroy got some sun. Except when I found out that Owen was coming home early from work today, I'd decided to go topless and wear my skimpiest bikini bottoms.

"I didn't hear any complaints after I massaged you. If anything, those moans begged me for more."

That was true, I had begged. But that wasn't unusual. It was like having sex with Owen unlocked some mysterious sex-fiend I couldn't contain when he was around. And now that he'd decided to take a permanent position in Whiskey Mountain, he was at my house often. So much so that I'd convinced him to move in with me and give up the rental home they'd initially put him in. There was more space at my place, so we spent most of our time there anyway.

"I would never complain about a massage. I just wasn't aware of the dick method."

"Well, my hands were a little busy with your shoulders, so it decided to jump in and get those hard-to-reach spots." He leaned close and whispered in my ear, "like your g-spot."

I had learned a lot about myself and what I liked in bed over the past three months, including that the g-spot very much existed and that some women are natural squirters. Ramona was now obsessed with learning as much as she could about it and was determined to find a guy who could do it for her.

"Feel free to massage that anytime you'd like," I offered, rolling over onto my back.

He stepped back and stared at my bare breasts as he squirted more lotion into the palm of his hand. I expected him to bend down and rub it on the same way he'd done my back, but instead, he kneeled beside me and slowly dripped it onto my body as if it were hot wax—which we had recently experimented with as well.

"I'll be massaging it here in a minute," he muttered, then spread the lotion across me, slowly focusing on my nipples as he traced circles around them.

"We don't have time; Ramona and Dylan will be here in half an hour."

"They can watch."

"I'm sure Ramona would," I laughed. "But I don't think I'm willing to listen to her obsess over your huge cock once she sees it."

"Fine," he sighed. "But in that case, you'd better put on more clothes before they get here."

He stood up and rubbed his hands together.

"Alright. I was just about cooked anyway."

He reached out a hand and helped me up. I wrapped my arms around his neck and pulled him into me for a kiss. Even after endless amounts of dirty, kinky sex, nothing made me feel better than the innocent kisses we shared together.

There was a lot of chemistry between us, but there was also this deep connection that neither of us had ever felt with anyone before. For the longest time, I'd been so afraid that I wouldn't find true love that I almost missed it when it was right in front of me the entire time.

Something To Talk About

Bonus Epilogue

Samantha Baca

Copyright © 2022 by Samantha Baca

Cover Design: Oh So Novel

<u>One</u>

Maggie

"I do not run like that," I laughed as I tucked my feet under Owen's butt.

It was the third time he'd shown me the clip from Friends where Phoebe and Rachel go running. The first time I'd watched it, Diet Coke came sputtering out of my nose as I laughed hysterically at her plowing into the horse.

"You do, and it's adorable."

"You said that you enjoyed running with me. Are you now saying you're embarrassed by me?"

He turned sideways and ran his hand up my leg, leaving goosebumps in its trail as it reached my thigh.

"I like running with you because I get to check out your ass in those tight pants you wear, and your breasts look amazing in that little sports bra."

His eyes darkened as he leaned forward and brushed a strand of hair from my face.

"And here I thought you were into physical fitness," I replied, my voice a little raspier than usual.

"Trust me, I'd like to physically fit this inside of you," he teased, grabbing my hand and rubbing it along his already hard cock.

"You're so bad," I giggled as he pulled me down onto the couch.

Once we had sex for the first time, we couldn't get enough of each other after that. I quickly went from a twenty-two-year-old virgin to a woman having sex multiple times a day—and I wasn't complaining. Though my neighbors did on occasion, but we quickly learned ways to keep me quiet when they were home in the middle of the day.

"You can't blame me when you're sitting there in panties that barely cover your ass and no bra under that tight tank top." He hooked a finger into the top of my panties and started to slide them down before his finger slipped into a hole.

"Leroy got these ones too?" he asked, studying the spot that had recently been attacked by a box turtle with a panty obsession.

"Unfortunately. He's nonstop; the second he sees them, he goes crazy. I've tried keeping him out of the laundry room, but he's taking advantage of the ones you fling around the house before you manhandle me in the bedroom and shower."

He arched a brow and pulled his bottom lip between his teeth.

"I'll buy you more," he promised, then slid them off and kissed my neck. "But I'm not going to stop ravishing you every chance I get."

"We might have to invest in stock since we go through so much."

"I'll add it to my to-do list," he groaned, slipping a finger inside as my legs fell to the side.

"Along with developing another strip mall in Whiskey Mountain and the new business you have going in Fallen Oaks."

He nipped at my neck, forcing a yelp out of my throat. I knew better than to talk about business right now, but I still couldn't believe that he'd officially moved in with me and given up his life in New York City. It was crazy, but he kept his word to his company that he would be the person to single-handedly manage the new business in Montana, which meant that he was busier than ever.

He pulled away and looked at me while his finger brushed slightly against my clit.

"Should I stop?" he asked, knowing damn well I didn't want him to.

I shook my head.

"Use your words, Maggie."

I licked my lips and felt the bulge in his pants as he pressed harder against me.

"No, sir."

"Good girl," he replied, knowing how much it turned me on.

He reached over and grabbed my panties that he'd tossed to the side, then pinned my hands together and bound them tightly.

"Did you just tie me up with my underwear?"

"Are you talking back to me?" He arched a brow, and I felt my insides quiver.

A sly smile spread across my face.

"Maybe. Whatcha gonna do about it?"

He pushed my hands higher above my head, undid his belt, and slid it through the hoops. I watched as he pulled it around the middle of the floor lamp tucked behind the coffee table and slid it through the panties wrapped around my wrists.

"Be a good girl, and don't pull. If you do, that lamp will come crashing down, and you'll be in trouble."

I nodded and tried not to giggle.

As much as I loved his dominant side, I knew that he was still a cuddly teddy bear underneath the layers of grumpiness I had to dig through when we first started to get to know each other.

He pulled away from me and turned his attention to the coffee table, which held the remnants of the takeout food we'd gotten earlier from La Salsa. Finally finding what he was looking for, he turned toward me with a devious grin.

I felt my center ache as he tore open a packet of honey with his teeth, the anticipation of what he was going to do with it driving me wild.

He squirted some out onto his finger, then slowly licked it off before popping his finger into his mouth and sucking.

It reminded me of how he'd licked whipped cream off of my breasts last week and how good he'd been at devouring the hot fudge he'd smeared all over my pussy when he said he wanted a sundae.

He climbed over me and pushed my legs apart again, holding them in place with his shoulders. Then he reached down and spread me with his fingers as he let the honey drip out of the packet and onto my clit.

"Fuuuccckkk," I cried, wanting him to touch me.

Slowly, he took his finger and smeared it along my lips, rubbing me along the way.

"Don't squirm, Maggie," he warned, kneeling in front of me as he gently pulled my hips to get my pussy lined up with his face and tossed the empty packet onto the coffee table. "We wouldn't want to get honey everywhere, now, would we?"

I couldn't find the words to say as his tongue caressed me, sending shivers up and down my spine. He nipped at me playfully, wanting a response.

"No," I moaned with my eyes closed. "It's sticky."

"So sticky," he agreed, holding my hips as he lowered his face deeper against my pussy. "It's going to take a lot of licking and sucking to get it off."

I moaned again, bucking as he slid his tongue between my folds.

He didn't ask me to speak anymore after that, which was great because I couldn't even tell you my name at that point. I was high on pleasure as he ate my pussy like it was his last meal.

Within minutes, I was coming against his face as he swallowed the spasms that ripped through me.

Something To Think About

Whiskey Mountain Book 2

Samantha Baca

Content Warning

Please note that this book may contain subject matter that may be bothersome for some readers. Please contact the author directly if you have any questions or need guidance before reading this book.

Suicide—mention of and with a secondary character. Not described in detail.

Mental health—touches on depression, anxiety, and suicide mentioned above.

<u>One</u>

Ramona

"I'll take the number three, hold the Pico de Gallo, and add a side of queso."

I rolled my eyes and shifted my weight while I waited for the guy in front of me to finish ordering. It wasn't just his tall 6'2 frame that irritated me; it was that there was zero fat on his lean, muscular body and that he had an ass so tight that you could crack a nut on it.

"Can I get a name for your order?" the girl behind the counter asked, her voice obnoxiously sweet and flirty.

"Preston."

My eye twitched as his deep voice rumbled across the air, sending a jolt to my stomach. It was the same stupid smooth tone that had all the women in Whiskey Mountain tossing their panties at him, except for me. Kind of like he thought he was God's gift to women or something. Spoiler alert—he wasn't.

He finally stepped to the side, took the number card the other girl handed him while batting her eyes, and got the hell out of my way.

"Hi, what can I get you?"

I narrowed my eyes at her, more than slightly miffed that her tone wasn't as cheerful with me as it was with him. *Well, excuse me for not being the symbol of a fucking sex God.*

"I'd like a number 5, extra sour cream, extra guacamole, and a side of queso."

I felt him watching me, his judgmental gaze speaking more than words could ever say.

"To drink?"

"Diet Coke." I hated Diet Coke and wanted a Root Beer float but having Mr. Perfect Body without an ounce of fat on his ridiculous body made me self-conscious, knowing he was criticizing what I had ordered.

The girl punched the information into the computer and then handed me my receipt with a fake smile that she probably used for everyone she didn't want to get laid by. Little did she know—I was a fucking fantastic lay. Her loss, not that I would do her, anyway.

I moved on and waited off to the side, as far away from him as possible, while they prepared my food. Maggie and Dylan were already here and waiting for me at a table tucked in the back of La Salsa. In the meantime, I was trying to shake off the sour mood I was in before I joined them. No need to ruin everyone else's day, too.

A few orders were up before mine, and then, finally, my number was called. I went to reach for the tray at the same time *Preston* did, pulling my hand away as quickly as possible when I realized we were about to touch.

"Excuse me, that's my order," I blurted out, placing a hand on my hip when he refused to let go of the tray.

"I don't think so. Yours has a deep-fried chimichanga and plenty of artery-clogging sides. This one is mine. Number 69—see?" He held the card up next to the receipt on the tray and waved it at me.

My eyes narrowed again, making me wish I had some sort of superpower to shoot laser beams out of them and light him on fire.

Being this close to him made me feel like I couldn't breathe. It wasn't just the cedary scent of his cologne that permeated the air around me; it was something deeper than that. Something that I didn't have the time to process—nor did I want to.

Before I could say anything or defend my food choices, he tossed me a wink before grabbing the tray and brushing past me, sending another spark through me.

What the fuck was that about?

I felt like an idiot for not hearing the number right the first time. Maybe I was just so hungry that I had imagined they'd called my number instead of his. It made sense that his would be ready before mine since he was in line in front of me, and I saw him still standing there before I almost stole his food.

I focused on pulling slow, calming breaths in through my nose and exhaling them through pursed lips while waiting for my food. My stomach growled again, reminding me I had skipped breakfast and was officially in the *danger zone*.

Finally, my order was up, so I grabbed the tray—double-checked that the number on the receipt matched the card I was holding—and headed to join Maggie and Dylan at the table.

I must have still been scowling by the time I sat down because they both stopped talking and stared at me.

"What?" I asked grumpily before pulling my chair closer to the table and popping a tortilla chip into my mouth. I couldn't tell if I was still just grumpy or if being hangry had taken over completely.

"Nothing," Maggie said, lifting her hands in front of her.

"Someone is hangry today," Dylan murmured to her from the side of his mouth, trying to keep me from hearing it.

"Shut up." I squirted some hot sauce onto my chimichanga and lifted it to take a bite when a perfectly buzzed cut head caught my attention from a few tables over. I lowered the food back to my plate and snarled.

"Uh oh." Dylan scooted away from the table as if he was afraid that I might flip it.

Maggie's eyes followed mine, the confusion not lasting long.

"Oh, come on, Ramona," she laughed. "Are you seriously that upset over Preston? He's just having lunch."

"It's not that he's here having lunch," I bit out. "It's that he's *everywhere*. It doesn't matter where I go or what I do—he's there."

"You know that's how living in a small-town works, right?" Maggie's smile was meant to disarm me, but it only fueled the fire raging inside me.

"Yeah, but he's not from *this one*. He's from Fallen Oaks and needs to go back to where he came from."

"Fallen Oaks is only a half hour from here—forty-five minutes, tops," Dylan said before ducking as I tossed a piece of napkin at his head.

"Whatever," I growled. "It doesn't matter where he came from. It matters that he doesn't need to be everywhere that I am. He's always slowing the lines down and causing delays because he's *so good-looking*." I rolled my eyes again, feeling completely childish for using such a mocking tone.

"Are you interested in him?" Maggie asked, her eyes dancing with delight.

"No."

"Are you sure? Because it seems like you might."

"NO," I repeated louder, drawing the attention of a few people close by, but thankfully not Preston. "YOU can love love, but that doesn't mean the rest of us have to."

"You're abnormally grumpy about love," Dylan commented, his eyebrows pulled together.

"Today would have been her and Daniel's anniversary." Maggie attempted to whisper behind her hand, but I could still hear her.

"Oh, shit."

"It's not a big deal," I lied. "We were together for three years. *I* broke up with *him*."

"Have you talked to him?" Maggie asked softly.

"Not since he called a few weeks ago to ask if I had one of his stupid PlayStation games."

"Why would you have it?" Maggie lifted her burrito to take a bite while she waited for my answer.

"Because he's Daniel and loses shit all the time. The same Daniel who refuses to take responsibility for anything and blames everyone else for the things that go wrong in his life."

"Yeah, but *you* moved out of the house. Why would he think that you would take his stuff? He's the one who kept the house and 90% of everything in it."

"Don't remind me," I said bitterly, sliding down lower in my chair. I poked at the chimichanga, suddenly not having the same appetite as I did when I first ordered the massive plate full of food.

"You're better off without him," Dylan said, locking eyes with me.

"I know," I sighed heavily. "Just when I was getting used to being single, this stupid date snuck up on me, and the gift I bought for him months before we broke up showed up at the store this morning. I had forgotten about it until I opened it up."

"What was it?" Maggie asked, looking down to check her phone.

"A collection of these exotic jerkies and assorted cheese and crackers. It was meant to go with the all-day gaming weekend I had planned for him—which should have been a sign that our relationship was doomed from the start if I focused only on *him* and what made him happy when I bought his gift."

"I'm sorry," Maggie apologized, her eyes softening.

"It's fine. I'm fine. Everything is fine."

I scooped a spoonful of guacamole out of the bowl and started smothering the chimichanga with it when I caught someone next to me out of the corner of my eye.

Preston tossed his trash in the trashcan before setting the basket and tray on top. He looked my way, gave me a devilish smile as if he knew how much it would get under my skin, then walked out the door.

My blood pressure rose a notch as I stabbed a giant piece of guac-covered chimichanga with my fork and shoved it into my mouth.

Two

Preston

"Why did you get a dog if you didn't have time to take care of it?" I asked my mom, patting the giant labradoodle's head as it panted heavily.

"Your dad was lonely, and I've been busy with work, so I thought it was a good idea." She shrugged and walked around the kitchen, looking for the spices she needed for the meatloaf.

"Why didn't you get a small lap dog? This thing is way too big for Dad and has too much energy. You need to take him for walks and get daily exercise."

"I've tried, but he doesn't want to get off the couch."

"The dog?"

"No, your dad."

I shook my head and laughed.

"Seriously, Mom. What were you thinking?"

"I don't know," she sighed, stopping what she was doing as she turned around and looked at me. "I thought if I got a big dog that was full of energy, it would keep your dad happy, and he wouldn't be so depressed anymore."

"He lost a job he's had for over thirty years, Mom. He's bound to be depressed for a while. Plus, I can't imagine how he feels knowing you're the only one bringing money into the house right now. He's a prideful man whose ego is taking one hell of a beating."

"I know. In hindsight, getting Rosco might not have been the best idea. But I was desperate, Preston. I wanted my husband back. I wanted to see the wrinkles around his lips as he smiled.

I wanted to hear him laugh again. I've missed all of it so much, and I was afraid I would lose him."

"I get it. I do. Have you told Kent about this?"

"No, and you better not before I can talk to him." She wagged her finger at me as she went back to working on the meatloaf.

"Fine, I won't tell him. But you better get around to it before he comes to town to visit and finds this behemoth of a creature eating your couch."

"I talked with him briefly the other day, and he mentioned he was busy helping with some B&B project. I don't think we'll see him for a couple of weeks."

"I don't know. I wouldn't count on it. It's not like Fallen Oaks is that long of a drive. And you know Kent, he likes to surprise people."

My mom turned around; her face twisted in an attempted smile.

"That's why I need your help."

"With what?" I asked, knowing it must be big because my mother *never* asked for help.

"Just a *little* favor." She held her fingers apart to show me how small it was.

"I have a feeling it's not little at all," I sighed, adjusting on the barstool I was sitting on as I braced myself for whatever she was about to ask for.

"I need you to take Rosco for a while."

"You're kidding me, right?"

"I wish I were, but now that I see you with him, it just seems like he's a better fit for you than he is for us."

"How long have you had him?"

"Two days."

"And you're not even going to give it a try first?"

"Who was I kidding, Preston?" She sighed and leaned against the counter. "You and I both know that your dad and I aren't cut out for a pet. Deep down, I guess I hoped you would come in here and tell me I was right and that I did the right thing for your dad by getting him a dog. But I could tell the moment you saw it that you didn't feel that way, and I guess it just made me realize how big of a mistake I made."

"Yeah, Mom. It's a dog—not a toy. It has actual needs, and you shouldn't have bought it without thinking about all of that first."

"I know, I know. I feel terrible. But I can't take him back to the place I got him, and I don't want to give him to just anyone. Even if you don't believe me, I love Rosco and want him to have a good home. Even if I can't give it to him."

"Is this why you invited me over?" I closed my eyes and pinched the bridge of my nose between my fingers.

This was all too much. I just came to check on my parents, maybe have a glass of my mom's famous sweet tea, and possibly score some meatloaf before I left now that I knew she was making my favorite meal.

I *didn't* expect to come by and leave as the proud new owner of some giant dog.

"Maybe…" Her voice teetered. "I know that it's a lot to ask, but I know you can handle it. You have that great big backyard he can run in. Plus, you work from home, so you'll be there to keep an eye on him. And not to make you feel bad, but it gives me a little satisfaction to know that you're not sitting there alone all the time, bored and lonely."

"I enjoy being alone," I said defiantly. "There's nothing wrong with being single."

"No, but you're almost—"

"Twenty-five? That's not old, Mom."

"I didn't say it was," she objected. "I just meant that I would like to see you find someone and settle down. Fall in love. Have a family."

"And a dog?"

My lips curled into a smile as the dog thumped its tail against the wooden floor.

I tried to look away and pretend that I wasn't affected by this damn dog, but once its beady brown eyes locked on mine, I couldn't.

Three

Ramona

"Yes, I've tried restarting the computer." I gritted my teeth, frustrated that this was the fourth IT support person I had spoken to who had no flipping idea what was happening with my computer. "It works for a little bit and then crashes."

I pressed the palm of my hand against my forehead and closed my eyes. If I couldn't get my computer to work right, then I couldn't keep my business open since I wouldn't be able to process sales. But more importantly—I couldn't stalk Maggie's blog page for more *Just The Tip* posts. I was single, but that didn't mean that I wasn't keeping up on all the sexual advice she gave there or that I didn't submit a question or two myself every now and then.

I waited impatiently while the person on the other end of the phone did something on their side—for all I knew, they were Googling how to fix a computer. Everyone I talked to seemed to have no clue how to solve the problem and kept sending me to someone else because they didn't want to bother figuring it out.

The clock on the wall above my head ticked loudly, reminding me I needed to open Cool Cats soon. The nice thing about owning a pet store was that it was doubling as my house since I couldn't afford to get my own place right now.

When I first left Daniel, I stayed with Maggie for a few weeks while I worked on converting the storage room into a bedroom. It was a decent-sized room once I got all the big boxes out of it, and thankfully everything fit so I didn't have to rent a storage unit. Dylan and Maggie had come by and helped me convert the two single bathrooms into one large bathroom with a tub/shower combo and a decent-sized vanity with plenty of storage.

The kitchen was already set up from when my great-grandparents owned the building and ran a small restaurant with a speakeasy bar in the back. I had been using the space as a break room but decided to update the appliances and flooring once it became my new kitchen. It was now fully functional, and I could technically say that I worked from home.

After fifteen minutes of waiting for IT support to confirm they had no idea what was happening with my computer, I gave up and ended the phone call. Thankfully, I was able to go online from my phone and set up the password for today. Granted, it wasn't technically *needed,* and the only reason I even required a password to enter was to keep the speakeasy vibe alive. I loved hearing the stories passed down from generation to generation about our family's history and wanted to keep the fun part of it going.

I loved that aside from the locals, no one knew that Cool Cats existed just from looking at the building. I had been open long enough that everyone in Whiskey Mountain and Fallen Oaks knew that they would have to go online, solve a riddle, and then they would be given the password for the day. Once they had it, they could either place an order online or come into the store.

I wrote *Drunken Dogs on Broken Logs* on a piece of paper that I kept by the speaker, so I didn't have to constantly pull it up on my phone when people came by. Not that I had a ton of customers, but every now and then, I was surprised by a busy day.

It was just after nine, and the meteorologist on the TV mounted in the corner of the room was talking about a massive storm headed for Whiskey Mountain. It wasn't unusual to get bad weather here, but it was definitely sooner than we usually got it—especially with a storm of this magnitude. I turned up the volume and listened as he went on about the possibility of getting 10-15 inches of snow this weekend—if not more.

I couldn't remember the last time I'd seen 10-15 inches of anything—snow or cock. Hell, I was lucky even to get a full *six* with Daniel, and that was when I got his full attention and he wasn't focused on getting back to his damn video game.

I debated whether I needed to head out and get supplies now or if I could wait a few days. It wasn't like I would need much since it was just me, but since Cool Cats was in the middle of nowhere, that didn't leave me many options if I ran out of something.

While Cool Cats was technically in Fallen Oaks, it didn't matter. All of Montana was going to get walloped, and I was going to be shit out of luck if I didn't get to the store now. If I waited too long, I would either risk everyone beating me there and be faced with empty shelves, or I would get stuck in the storm and wouldn't be allowed back on the highway to get to Cool Cats until they got a plow out there to clear the roads. Since it was in a deserted spot located between two small towns, it wasn't ever a priority when they worked on clearing the streets because people didn't tend to pass through during bad weather unless they absolutely had to.

I pulled out my phone, logged into the site, and posted a note that we would open later today. I grabbed my keys and wallet, then locked up and headed to Super Seven, the only supermarket in Whiskey Mountain.

By the time I got there, the parking lot was full, and almost all the shopping carts were taken. I pulled my shoulders back and tried to remind myself that everyone was there because they all needed supplies as well. I smiled politely at an old man who was shuffling his way to the cart return after unloading his bags into his car.

I looked around, trying not to make him feel rushed as I kept my distance. He walked past and gave me a quick wave before climbing into the car parked at the curb with his wife inside. I inhaled deeply, ready to get this over with.

I headed to the cart corral and reached for the one he'd just left, my hand brushing against someone else's as they grabbed it too.

I didn't have to look up to see who it was because the electrical shock that zapped my skin from the touch of his hand on mine had already told me that it was Preston.

"Sorry," I muttered before I could stop myself. It was more out of habit than anything. I didn't *really* want to apologize to him since I had been there first, and like always, he was in my way again.

"No, I'm sorry. I didn't see you there. Go ahead. You can have it."

I eyed him suspiciously, wondering why he was being nice.

"Really. Take it."

There was an impatience in his tone that dug its way under my skin as he shoved a hand through his short black hair.

"Thanks, since I *was* waiting for it first."

His gray eyes scanned my face as if trying to figure something out.

Irritated from the feeling he elicited every time he was this close, I grabbed the cart, yanked it out of the corral, and shoved it in front of me.

He grinned that stupid grin that seemed to work for everyone but me.

I didn't bother to look back to see if he was still standing there, staring at me. I had stuff to get done, and it didn't involve him.

The aisles were busy, but thankfully, people were quick to grab what they needed and move on. No one was shopping for fun or dilly-dallying around and taking their time. They knew this storm was coming, and no one trusted the weather in Montana to come when they predicted it, so they wanted to be as prepared as possible since it could be on us at any moment.

I grabbed a family-sized pack of toilet paper and shoved it on the bottom rack of the shopping cart, then grabbed another—just in case. My cart was packed with canned goods, non-perishable items, and basic necessities. Okay, so maybe coffee, Cool Ranch Doritos, Milk Duds, and Hot Tamales weren't necessities for anyone else, but they were for me. Just because we were going to have a record-breaking storm hit didn't mean that I couldn't indulge in some of my favorite treats.

I was perusing the wine aisle, looking for the cheap brand that I liked. It wasn't that I was opposed to spending money on a good bottle, but if the power went out—like it was known to do with bad storms—I wanted to be able to open a bottle with a screw-on top instead of messing with trying to use a bottle opener in the dark.

The alcohol section was quieter than the rest of the store, so I didn't pay attention that someone was standing at the end of the aisle while I was squatting to retrieve a bottle of Moscato on the bottom shelf that had been shoved to the back. I reached a little further, trying not to fall, when I heard a chuckle.

I looked up to see Preston watching me, amusement etched on his face. I bit my tongue to keep from saying anything while he looked at the expensive bottles of whiskey. I didn't need his judgment right now with my cheap bottles of wine, just like I didn't need it the other day with my order at La Salsa.

The bottle was just within reach as I scooted closer, leaning to the side and brushing against Preston's leg. I hadn't noticed that he had moved toward me until I was practically pressed into his leg, trying to grab the damn wine. I was about to say something to him about giving me space when I heard a familiar voice from the other end of the aisle.

"Always a sucker for those cheap bottles," Daniel said, tsking as he walked over to where I was still crouched on the ground with my hand wrapped around it.

I thought about pulling it out and whipping it at his head, but I didn't want to waste the only bottle of Moscato they had.

My heart raced, having to face Daniel for the first time since we broke up. He'd called and texted a handful of times over the past six months, but I ignored almost every single one.

"Why don't you just grab one of the better bottles? I'll get it for you, my treat. I know how *hard* things must be with you trying to do this on your own right now." A smug grin was plastered on Daniel's face as he leaned against a pole at the end of the aisle and watched me.

I looked up at Preston, embarrassed that he was standing there, hearing all of this. But since he was already a part of it—whether he wanted to be or not—I decided to use what I had at my disposal right now, even if I would later regret it.

I pushed up to a standing position and leaned in so only he could hear me.

"Pretend to be my boyfriend, or I'll break this bottle and cut your internal organs out with its jagged edge," I threatened, looking up to meet his eyes.

He licked his lips and let the bottom catch between his teeth. I could tell he was trying to keep from laughing, which further irritated me.

"You know I would have gotten that for you, baby," he said sweetly, gently wrapping his hand around mine as he relieved me from my weapon. He put it in his cart and then wrapped one arm around my waist, making sure our bodies were angled so Daniel could see it.

"Sorry," Daniel said, clearing his throat. "I didn't know you were here with someone."

His apology lacked genuine emotion, and I was pretty sure it wasn't directed at me.

I felt Preston's fingers dig deeper into my hip before his hand slid possessively across my stomach as he pulled me closer. My body was on fire from his touch, my senses on overload.

What in the world was this? Why did his touch elicit such powerful responses from my body?

"We better get going, Firecracker. That storm is moving in quickly, and we don't want to get stuck in it."

My brain was mush at the moment, trying to process what he was saying as his hand slipped from my waist and his fingers brushed across my ass.

"Firecracker?" Daniel questioned with a smirk. He hated pet names, so I knew he was going to take this opportunity to tell Preston how stupid they were. "Let me guess; you call her that because of her fiery temper?"

My face flushed with embarrassment. It wasn't like it was a lie—Preston would know that given how I'd treated him the handful of times we'd interacted with each other.

"Na, I call her that because I love the way she lights up when she comes. The way her body is on fire, ready for me to send her over the edge. Reminds me of the Fourth of July, and I just can't get enough of it."

He winked at Daniel, whose jaw was hanging as he processed what Preston said.

"If you want to grab the lube, chocolate syrup, and whipped cream, I'll meet you at the register," Preston added, giving me a sharp slap on the ass before releasing his grip on me. "Gotta make the best out of being cooped up in the house during the storm," he added, looking Daniel directly in the eye.

"Yeah, sure." I had no idea what to say. My brain was in a fog, and my ass was still burning from his touch. There was also this new ache building between my thighs that made me acutely aware of how close Preston was as I pushed the cart down the aisle and headed for the frozen food section.

Once we were out of sight of Daniel, I pushed my cart to the side and spun around to face him. He was sporting a shit-eating grin on his face, and his shoulders pulled back like he was proud of himself.

"What in the hell was that?!" I hissed, my eyes nearly bulging out of my head.

"*That* was me saving *your* ass and avoiding a shanking on aisle 3."

"You didn't have to slap my ass."

"Did you want him to buy it or not?"

"Yes, but—"

He leaned in and wrapped one hand behind my head while the other cupped the side of my face. His mouth crashed down on mine in the most gentle yet hungry kiss I'd ever experienced. His lips moved eagerly as his tongue slid across my lips.

Reluctantly, they parted, allowing his tongue to dance with mine. I reached up and wrapped my arms around his neck, pulling him closer while trying to refrain from wrapping my legs around his waist and riding him on aisle 5.

My pussy ached with need, my panties already soaked as I panted against his mouth when he broke the kiss too soon.

I opened my eyes, trying to force myself to focus, but all I could concentrate on right now was kissing him again.

"You're welcome," he said cockily.

"What?" I panted, my breaths ragged and shallow. I tilted my head to the side and studied him.

"I can't promise seven orgasms, but I think we know for a fact that you'll have at least five tonight." His voice was louder than necessary. "Though I'm always up for a challenge."

I squinted my eyes, having no clue what was going on. Did he kiss me so hard that he sucked all the brain cells out of my body? Was that a thing?

"He's on the aisle over. I think he's trying to get you alone to talk to you."

Oh. Fuck.

"Sorry," I whispered, though I had no idea what I was apologizing for.

"If you want to keep this up, we need to leave together and look like a happy couple, which means you're going to have to refrain from threatening to kill me until *after* we leave."

"Fine," I sighed. "I'm pretty much done. What about you?"

"I just have a few things left to get. Want to meet at the registers in ten minutes?"

I nodded and waited for him to go ahead of me so I could take a deep breath and try to calm my nerves. Never in a million years would I have ever imagined that I would be kissing Preston in the aisle of a grocery store while trying to avoid my ex, but here we were.

<u>Four</u>

Preston

I barely made it to the house I was renting before the snow started falling. I still needed to get food and supplies for Rosco, but they didn't have much at the supermarket. Not only that, but I got super distracted by Ramona and her constant threat of bodily harm if I didn't pretend to be her boyfriend.

I didn't know her well—mainly because she always looked like she was ready to kill me whenever we were around each other, so it left little opportunity for friendly conversation. But I didn't have to know her well to know that her attitude was bigger than her 5'2 self. Between the way her eyes constantly narrowed when she looked at me and the frown that always graced her face, I couldn't imagine that we would ever be the *best of friends* before I left Whiskey Mountain.

Rosco ran around the kitchen, pacing beside me as if he expected I had something for him, which I didn't. He was still a puppy; my mom had gotten him at eight weeks, so it had only been a few days since he'd been separated from his mom and siblings. I could tell that we would have a lot of work ahead of us with learning obedience, given that he had chewed up a pair of my shoes while I was at the store.

"You sure have a lot of energy, don't you, boy?" I scratched the top of his head as he stretched his legs and then rolled over so I could rub his stomach. "That storm is moving in quickly, so I need to get to the store before they close. Otherwise, you won't have food for a few days."

He whimpered and pawed at my hand as I pulled away to stand up.

I had looked up pet stores in town and found that the only one close by was one called Cool Cats, and it was at least an hour from where I was staying, right on the border of Whiskey

Mountain and the neighboring small town, Fallen Oaks. The storm was going to get worse before it got better, and I didn't want to start Rosco on people food, so I needed to get going before I got stuck in it.

I grabbed my keys and thought about whether I should lock him up somewhere to keep him from destroying anything while I was gone, but it wasn't like I'd had time to puppy-proof the house. It didn't say online whether animals were allowed inside Cool Cats, only that you had to have a password to get in. Deciding that it was better to keep Rosco with me so I could keep an eye on him, I attached the leash to the collar my mom had got him and led him out to my truck.

He climbed in easily, needing only a tiny bit of help. Then he plopped down on the leather seat and closed his eyes while the seat warmer did its magic. I laughed and shook my head, wondering how I got myself into this position.

I had a big heart and was a sucker for cute animals— that's how I got here.

An hour later, I slowed down as I pulled up in front of an unmarked building. I leaned forward, squinting to look for a sign, but I couldn't see anything through the thick snow falling around me. I circled the building, looking for any sign that I was in the right place, but aside from one lonely vehicle in the parking lot, there wasn't much to go off of.

I knew that it was a huge risk to head out in the storm. But unfortunately, it was either brave it and trust that my truck could handle the weather to get me to the store and back or share the food I had picked up for myself with Rosco and start a bad habit that I wouldn't be able to break.

I got out of the truck and walked around to get him. The temperature had already dropped significantly, so there was no way I was going to leave him in the truck while I went inside to grab stuff. Hopefully it would be a quick and easy trip, then we would be home and warmed by the fire.

I walked to the call box and pressed the button, shoving my hands in my pockets to keep warm. I wasn't sure if Cool Cats was even open since everything else seemed to shut down early because of the weather. I was about to leave and head back to the truck when I heard a voice come over the speaker.

"Hello?"

"Hi. Sorry to bother you. I was looking for Cool Cats. It's a pet—"

"What's the password?"

I pulled the piece of torn-off paper out of my pocket and unfolded it.

"Drunken dogs on broken logs," I answered, taken aback by the person's inhospitable vibe. While I knew a password was required to enter, I was still shocked that this was considered a business, given how unfriendly they were acting.

There was a loud beeping noise, and then I heard the lock click. I pulled the door open and headed down the stairs, wondering if this was a legit pet shop or if it was some shady business where they murdered unsuspecting victims coming in for dog treats. Guess I was about to find out.

I rounded the corner with Rosco leading the way, trying to gain control over him on the leash.

"Slow down," I said, pulling it back. "You're going to take me down if you don't stop."

"Wouldn't be such a bad thing," a feisty voice answered, a pile of raven black hair piled loosely on her head. Something about the snark in Ramona's tone sent a chill throughout my body. I wasn't sure whether it was fear or excitement, but it was there, nonetheless.

"So, we're back to that again?" I teased, attempting to keep Rosco from jumping on her as she squatted in front of a shelf that she was stocking with fish food.

"Back to what?" She frowned, her hazel eyes catching in the light above us.

"You wanting to kill me."

"Maybe." She stood up and eyed me suspiciously before looking down at Rosco. "What are you doing here?"

"I came for supplies."

"Whose dog is this?"

"Mine."

"Are you sure you didn't steal it from someone?" she asked, folding her arms over her chest. The red and black flannel shirt she was wearing unbuttoned over a tight-fitting tank top did nothing to hide the curves I'd felt earlier when I wrapped my arm around her waist. I hadn't noticed it earlier, given it was hidden under a big, bulky winter jacket.

"Why would I steal someone's dog?"

"So you'd have an excuse to come see me."

"You're kidding me, right?" I laughed, wondering what in the world was going on inside of that head of hers.

"Not one bit."

"Look," I sighed, shoving a hand through my hair. "I didn't even know you worked here. I just googled pet shops in Whiskey Mountain, and this was the only one that came up."

"I don't just *work* here. I own the place. And it's convenient that you show up with a dog and *need supplies* a few hours after you were just groping me in the supermarket."

She took a step toward me, her features flawless as she narrowed those gorgeous hazel eyes at me. Again.

"You needed me to," I countered.

"You wanted to."

Now it was my turn to feel flustered because she wasn't lying. I had wanted to and might have taken advantage of the situation to get the point across to her asshole ex.

I stepped toward her, so close that our bodies were almost touching and I could feel the heat coming off hers.

"I did, and I would do it again in a heartbeat if you'd let me," I admitted, my voice low and gruff.

She licked her lips, making me want to capture one between my teeth.

Her mouth opened like she was going to say something, but Rosco chose that time to yank forward on the leash, slamming my body into hers. I wrapped an arm around her waist and spun her to the side so her back was up against the shelf, my leg pinned in between hers to keep us from falling.

"He has a lot of energy," I apologized.

"He needs to be trained."

"I'm planning on it."

We stood there staring at each other, neither of us moving apart as the heat of our bodies spread between us.

"What did you need?" she finally asked, but my brain was focused on how her lips looked as they moved and not the words that came out of them.

She arched an eyebrow in irritation when I didn't answer her.

"What?"

"From the store. What did you need from the store?" she clarified, pushing a hand against my chest to separate us.

I stepped back, giving her some space as I tried not to trip over Rosco's leash.

"I can help you grab what you need so you can get going," Ramona said, pushing away from the shelf and walking in front of me. "That storm is getting worse, and if you don't get back soon, you're going to get stranded. Since there's nothing within miles of here, we don't want that to happen, now do we?"

"Right." I shook my head to clear it. "My mom got him for my dad and didn't think about how much work a puppy this size would be. She's had him for two days and gave me what she was given by the lady she bought him from, which wasn't much. So, I need everything—food, a bed, treats, toys, and anything else you can think of that I might be forgetting."

"Okay, let's get started." Ramona clapped her hands and took off down the aisles as Rosco and I followed behind her. I couldn't tell if she was excited to shop for dog stuff or more excited to get it over with so she could get rid of us.

Five

Ramona

"Are you sure you don't want another bag of treats?" I asked, trying not to look into the golden eyes of the boy who was begging me for another one as I rang his dad up.

"No, I think we're fine. I want him to earn them and not just get them because he's cute."

"But he is cute," I objected, refraining from digging in the jar for another one.

He raised an eyebrow and tilted his head.

"Okay, fine." I sighed heavily and entered the last few things into the system. "Alright, your total is…"

I waited impatiently for it to pop up on the screen but was instead greeted by the spinning wheel of death.

"Everything okay?" he asked, leaning to the side to look at the screen. "Did I buy so much that I broke your register?"

"No, it just does this," I muttered, tapping the refresh button with my nail repeatedly, hoping it would force it to work.

"Do you want me to pay with cash instead?"

"No, because I don't have the exact total for you, and most likely, I won't have the right change. Besides, who is walking around with that much cash? I don't know the exact number, but I can tell you that you're around $250, at minimum."

I couldn't remember the last time someone came in and spent that much at Cool Cats, aside from my best friend, Maggie, who bought the most expensive terrarium so her panty-eating turtle couldn't escape anymore. But Preston had frowned when I showed him a decent-sized dog bed for Rosco and insisted on getting the bigger one with a thick layer of memory foam and was lined with sherpa.

"I'm not that worried about the change. I don't want to stress you out with your system not working."

"It never works these days," I grumbled, jabbing my finger harder on the screen. "I've been trying to get it fixed, but no one seems to know what's wrong with it."

"Mind if I come around and take a look?" he offered.

"You know about computers?" I tried to keep the sarcasm out of my voice, but it felt like regardless of what I said to him, it always came out super bitchy. I guess he just had that effect on me.

"I know a thing or two." His grin was smug, but I didn't have time to read too much into it if I wanted to get him out the door and on his way before he was stuck here.

"Be my guest."

I stepped back and made room for him to come around the counter. His brows pinched together as he studied the screen while moving the mouse that wouldn't work.

He pressed a few buttons and I thought for a minute that maybe he had fixed it when the screen refreshed and went to the payment window, but a few seconds later, everything went black, and it did the same thing it had been doing.

"Ugh," I groaned, tossing my head back. "I'm so tired of that stupid black screen of death."

"How long has it been doing this?" he asked, looking at me over his shoulder.

"I don't know. A week? Maybe two."

"Have you run any updates recently?"

I scrunched my face as I tried to remember the last time it updated.

"I think it did one a few weeks ago."

"Okay, that might be what's causing this. I can try to do a system restore if you know approximately when that was."

"It's okay, I don't want to keep you here longer than needed. You'll never get home if you don't leave soon. Why don't you take what you have, and we can figure out the payment details later?"

"I'm not leaving here without paying for my stuff."

"Well, that's going to be hard because I don't know how much you owe me. Plus, it's not like you're going to skip town and I'll never see you again. I mean, you're already everywhere I go as it is."

My face reddened as I realized what I'd just said out loud. The corners of his lips twitched as he tried to hide a smile.

"Just take this, and we'll deal with the payment part later."

I was desperate for him to leave, but for once, it didn't feel like it was because he was annoying me. Instead, I was feeling a little more friendly with him and that was an unsettling feeling that I needed to get rid of as much as I needed to get rid of him.

"Fine," he sighed as he pulled his wallet out and tossed three-hundred-dollar bills on the counter.

"Preston," I objected, but he lifted a finger and placed it over my lips to stop me.

"Thank you for staying open so I could grab what I needed," he said, letting his finger trail across my skin as it slid down my lip and brushed against my cheek. "Take that for what I owe you for the supplies."

"This is too much."

"Well then, consider the extra to be a tip."

"A tip? I'm not a waitress," I sniped.

"That's probably a good thing." His stupid cocky grin spread across his cheeks again.

"What's that supposed to mean?" I planted a hand firmly on my hip and glared at him.

"That I'm glad you don't have access to my food or drink because I'm pretty sure you would have tried to poison me by now."

The corners of my lips twitched as I refused to let him see me smile.

"But seriously, thank you for staying open and letting me get the things we needed. Sorry to keep you so late."

"No problem."

I helped him grab the bags he couldn't carry and followed him up the stairs. He set his down and opened the door, only to have it flung against the wall as a gust of wind and snow blew in our faces, nearly taking our breath away.

I lifted my arm to shield myself from it and looked around for his truck, but the entire parking lot was covered in snow, and we couldn't see more than a few feet in front of us.

"Um, where did you park?" I asked nervously.

"Right there, up front." He pointed to a spot nearby, but neither of us could see it. "Fuck."

Fuck was right. There was no way he was going anywhere in this weather which meant he was now stuck here with me.

<u>Six</u>

Preston

I knew that I didn't have much time before the storm rolled in, but I thought for sure that I had enough to get the stuff I needed for Rosco and get home before this happened. We stood there for a few seconds, staring in disbelief at the whiteout in front of us before I fumbled around, reaching for the door and pulling it closed.

When I turned around, Ramona was standing behind me, the bags on the floor by her side while she nervously chewed her nails.

"I'm sorry. I thought I would make it out before it got that bad."

"It's okay," she said, but I could tell her mind was elsewhere. Her tone was clipped but not drooling with anger like it usually was.

"Do you know when they'll be out to plow the road?" I asked, already knowing the answer. No one was going out in this anytime soon until it calmed down and was safe.

"It'll be days, maybe even weeks. This stretch doesn't get much attention as they focus on clearing the main streets in Whiskey Mountain and Fallen Oaks first. Until there's more developed out here, it'll continue to be a low priority like it always has been."

Her voice was calmer, and for once, she didn't look like she wanted to kill me, which was odd.

"I, um, I'm sorry. I didn't mean to keep you from getting out of here on time to make it home. I feel bad that you're stuck here too."

She shook her head, grabbed the bags, and headed back into the shop.

"I'm not stuck here," she said over her shoulder. "I live here."

"You live here?" I set the bags I was holding beside hers on the floor, out of the way.

"Yeah, there are rooms in the back that I converted from storage and office space to living space a few months ago."

"Well, good, now I don't feel as bad about you not being able to get home because of me. Though I am sorry that you're stuck with me for the foreseeable future."

She looked around the room, her eyes roaming the space as if she were looking for an answer to a question I didn't know.

"It's fine, but I don't have anywhere for you to stay. The rooms in the back aren't very big, but we can try to figure something out. Follow me."

She didn't smile as she took off walking, expecting me to follow her.

I knew this was unplanned and hated that I had put her on the spot to share her space with Rosco and me, but it wasn't like I had any other choice. There was no way I could find my truck right now, let alone drive it. And even if I could find it, we would freeze to death if we tried to use it for shelter until the storm passed. Staying with Ramona was the only option we had.

"This is the kitchen. There's food in the fridge that you can help yourself to and stuff in the cabinets. Just don't get into my Cool Ranch Doritos or Milk Duds," she warned, pointing a finger at me as she stood behind one of the folding chairs scattered around the small circular table. "I stocked up on coffee today, so there should be plenty to get us through until the roads are cleared."

"Don't worry, I'm not a coffee drinker. It's all yours. And I promise I won't touch your snacks."

She eyed me suspiciously before giving me a tour of the rest of the space. There was a small room with a desk that she said was currently being used as her office and then a much larger room that she had converted into a bedroom.

"I can see if I have a sleeping bag," she offered as she rummaged through the walk-in closet.

There was a lot happening in the bedroom, but surprisingly, it didn't feel cramped or cluttered. A queen-sized bed sat along one wall with a dresser across from it and a TV mounted above. There was a nightstand on one side of the bed, and a surprisingly elaborate cat tower on the other, which I assumed belonged to the cat sprawled out on the navy floral comforter.

Along the wall with the window was a dog bed on the floor and a glass enclosure tucked into the corner. I couldn't tell whether it was a snake or a lizard inside, but whatever it was looked like it relied on plenty of heat, given the setup she had on top. I squinted to try to see it but was distracted by the sounds of her groaning from the closet as she moved stuff around.

"Sorry, I don't know where I put the damn thing," she called from inside it. "I was in a rush to get moved in, and things got thrown wherever they would fit."

"You don't have to worry about finding one," I said, making sure my voice carried across the room to her.

"I don't have anything else to offer if not." She came out and planted her hands on her hips, looking hotter than hell, which made it hard for me to think straight.

"We could share the bed," I suggested, wondering if there was anything in here she could shank me with. "It looks big enough to fit both of us, plus the cat." I pointed to where it had rolled over and stretched out further.

Her eyebrows rose into her hairline.

"What?"

"Share the bed," I repeated, patting the edge of it. "It's plenty big enough for both of us."

"You want me to share *my* bed with *you*?"

"I don't see why not. There aren't any other options since we're stuck together until this storm passes, and you owe me."

I shoved my hands into my pockets and leaned against the bedpost while I watched the features on her face change.

"I owe you? For what?"

"Pretending to be your boyfriend. If I hadn't spent time putting on that charade for your ex, I would have had time to get to a pet store before the storm rolled in and wouldn't be stranded here with you."

Her eyes narrowed further as she chewed her bottom lip angrily.

"Bullshit."

"It's true." I shrugged and pushed off the bedpost, stepping toward her until we were almost toe to toe. "If I wasn't so busy making out with you on aisle 5, I would have gotten everything done and avoided all of this."

"I'm the only pet store in town. You wouldn't have gotten anything done until I got home."

"Maybe. But I don't think that's what you're really upset about."

"90% of what you say upsets me."

She was putting the wall up again and trying to push me away, but I didn't care because she was hot as fuck when she was like this.

"Is that so?"

"Yes."

"Then why did you kiss me earlier?"

"I didn't. You kissed me, remember?"

"You kissed me back."

"I was faking it. Making sure it looked believable."

"Na," I said, leaning closer to her so my breath brushed against her temple as I spoke softly in her ear. "I felt the way you kissed me and how your body reacted to me. That wasn't faking."

"Apparently, you don't know a damn thing about me." Her words were laced with anger, but I could feel her body pulling into mine. There was a gravitational force that neither of us could deny, even if we wanted to.

"I think you don't want me in your bed because you don't trust yourself next to me."

"Oh, please," she scoffed, refusing to look at me.

"Then what's the real problem?"

"The real problem is that it isn't big enough because Daisy sleeps there, too."

"Who's Daisy?" I asked, wondering if some guy was hanging out that I hadn't seen when she'd given me the tour. There were a few rooms that we passed but didn't go into, so it wouldn't be totally inconceivable.

I waited for her to tell me, but her cell phone started ringing instead. She snapped out of whatever trance she was in, stormed down the hall, and slammed the bathroom door after she retreated inside, leaving me alone in her bedroom.

<u>Seven</u>

Ramona

"Hey," I whispered, tucking myself into the corner of the bathroom so Preston couldn't hear me. Not that I imagined him to be standing outside, lurking by the restroom. But then again, I didn't know the guy, so who knew what he was into?

"Hey," Maggie answered cheerfully. "Just checking to make sure you're okay and that you were able to get what you needed before the storm hit. Are you home and safe?"

"Yeah, I'm fine," I muttered, chewing my nail as I tried to figure out how to get rid of Preston, even though it wasn't a realistic possibility right now.

"What's wrong?"

"Preston's here," I whispered, trying to keep my freak out to a minimum.

"Where?"

"At Cool Cats."

"Why?"

"He came by to get supplies for his dog, and now he's stranded here because of the stupid storm."

"He has a dog? Aww, what kind?"

"Maggie!" I exclaimed, gripping the phone tighter. "Can you focus, please?"

"I am, but I don't see what the problem is." She laughed and I hated how light-hearted she was about this right now. Things were about to explode around me, and my best friend didn't even care.

"The problem is that he is stuck here—at Cool Cats. I have to share a space with him for who knows how long!"

"You're a grown woman, Ramona. I think you can bottle up your hostility toward him for a few days and figure out how to be around him without trying to murder him."

"I don't know," I sighed heavily. "I don't think I can handle him being that close to me 24/7 for days—maybe weeks."

"Why not?"

"Because—he makes me feel all…" I couldn't bring myself to finish the sentence.

"Horny like you want to ride the hard-cock express?" she offered, giggling on the other side.

"Maggie!"

"Oh, how the tables have turned," she said with a laugh. "Wasn't that the same thing you told me a while ago?"

"Yes, but it's only funny when it's about someone other than me. Plus, you totally wanted to board Owen's hard-cock express."

"Why are you being so weird about this? You've had Dylan stay over with you a few times since you moved into Cool Cats. Why is it so different to let Preston stay there for a few days?"

Because I didn't kiss Dylan, nor did I fantasize about what he might do to me if we shared a bed.

"It's just different, that's all."

"Why?"

She really wasn't going to let go of this, and I knew I would eventually tell her about it anyway.

"Because he kissed me."

"What?!"

I pulled the phone away as she shrieked in my ear.

"Do you have to be so loud?"

"You kissed Preston and expected me to be quiet about it?"

"Correction—I didn't kiss him. He kissed me."

"I'm so confused," Maggie said.

You and me both, my friend.

"It was all part of the ruse in making Daniel think we were together."

"Daniel? How does he fit into this?"

I exhaled heavily and then decided to spill all of it so she could get caught up and I could figure out how to get out of this shit show I'd gotten myself into.

"I was at Super Seven getting what I needed for the storm and ran into Preston on the wine aisle. I was trying to get a bottle from the bottom shelf when Daniel popped up out of thin air. I very quietly threatened to rearrange Preston's organs with broken glass if he didn't agree to pretend to be my boyfriend. He obliged and took the assignment a little too literally."

"So he just kissed you right there, in the middle of the wine aisle?"

"No, he kissed me a few aisles over because he knew Daniel was waiting to talk to me."

"Well, it sounds like it was just a simple kiss, and you both knew what you were doing. Why is it stressing you out so much?"

"Because," I exhaled. "It wasn't *just* the kiss. It was the way his fingers felt against my skin and the way he slapped my ass. Those were feelings that I've never felt before, and I can't process what it is with him constantly in my space, making me feel all… I don't even know what the word is."

"Horny. The word is horny, Ramona."

"Shut up. No, it isn't."

"You can deny it all you want to, but you know I'm right. He sparked something deep inside you, and while you'd love to act like you still hate him, you really want him to fuck your brains out."

I chewed the inside of my lip while I studied my reflection in the mirror. Was that true? Did I want him to fuck my brains out?

I mean, I wouldn't say no if he asked because I was super intrigued to see what else he could do, given he already had me on edge, and yet he'd barely touched me.

"Are you still there?" Maggie asked.

"Yeah, sorry. I was just thinking."

"About fucking Preston? I figured."

"Ugh, you're the worst," I joked.

"I know. But you love me anyway."

"Most days."

"Every day."

"Eh."

"Go get laid so I can have my happy best friend back. This one has been super cranky for months now, and that vibrating rose isn't doing the trick anymore."

"I'm not going to go get laid. Trust me, that's the last thing that will be happening between us. Just because you have Owen to satisfy those needs doesn't mean the rest of us are that lucky."

"If you say so," she sing-songed.

"I better get going. I don't know where he's at or what he's doing, so I need to make sure he doesn't let Daisy out."

"Alright, well, if you need anything, call me. Given how strong the wind is, I'm sure we'll lose power soon. Don't forget to charge your phone before then."

"Will do. Call if you need anything too."

I hung up and shoved my phone in my pocket before bracing myself against the sink. My cheeks were flushed, and I couldn't shake the thought of Preston fucking me, which only enhanced the redness. I grabbed my makeup bag, brushed some powder on my face, and prayed for the best.

The truth was that I wasn't ready to deal with someone else being in my space right now—regardless of who it was. Running into Daniel had been unexpected, and even though we'd been broken up for months, I hadn't seen him more than a few times since then. Even though Whiskey Mountain was a small town, he stayed inside most days, playing video games and living off the unemployment money he was getting after he got laid off shortly after we broke up.

I technically lived in Fallen Oaks now and only went to Whiskey Mountain to see Maggie and Dylan. We went to restaurants that I knew Daniel hated, just to avoid running into him. I also spent a lot of time at Spill The Beans, knowing that the likelihood of him walking in for a cup of coffee was zilch since he preferred beer most days.

But seeing him at the store today made me feel off, and I couldn't put my finger on why. Did I still want to be with him? No. But at the same time, I hated his smug attitude about me not being able to do this on my own. Sure, I'd moved in with him shortly after we became a couple, but it wasn't like he had purchased the house of his dreams and we were building our lives together. He had inherited an old, beat-up, single-story house that his grandpa left him when he died.

It was up to Daniel to fix it up and make it into what he wanted, but he lacked both the determination and desire to do anything with it. I'd made several recommendations on projects we could do together, but each one was brushed off and dismissed because it was *his family's house*.

I knew that Daniel wasn't struggling to make ends meet right now, given that he didn't have a mortgage and his parents had given him a brand-new truck when he graduated. The truck had been used and abused over the years, but he didn't have a payment on that either. His unemployment money would be enough to support his weekly groceries and beer, allowing him to live the life of his dreams: staying home all day, drinking beer, and playing video games until he was drunk by dinner time.

I fixed the lopsided bun on top of my head, squared my shoulders, and lied to myself about how I could spend the next few days with Preston without feeling something toward him.

Whether that feeling was horny or murderous, I wasn't sure.

Eight

Preston

I was sitting on the floor, trying to get Rosco to sit, when Ramona walked in. I didn't want to intrude, even though we would be staying here for a little while. I knew that it was as much of a shock to her as it was to me, and the last thing I wanted to do was make her uncomfortable.

"Sit," I commanded, holding a sausage-shaped treat in one hand while using the other to push Rosco's butt down.

His tail wagged excitedly as he lunged for it and almost snatched it from my grip.

"You need to teach him hand signals," Ramona said, grabbing the bag of treats from the floor beside me. "If you're going to train him to be obedient, you should be able to give him a sign without speaking and have him do what you're asking. That means that you'll also need to take him to public places and continue his training in those environments."

She stood in front of him, held her hand out in front of her with her palm facing up, and then raised it in an upward motion toward her shoulder while saying sit.

I was about to laugh and tell her *good luck, he doesn't know how to do that*, but as if some magical being had possessed him, he fucking did as she asked and plopped his ass on the linoleum floor.

"What the actual fuck?" I muttered, scrubbing a hand down my face. "I've been working with him for fifteen minutes and then you come out and he does it on the first try?"

"Most likely, he was already being taught in his previous home."

"I doubt it. My mom barely wanted to take the time to teach me and my brother when we were growing up. I can't imagine her doing it with a dog."

"No," she laughed, the sound surprisingly pleasant to my ears because I didn't hear it often enough from her. "I meant the people she bought him from. I know a few people in Whiskey Mountain who do dog training, and I believe Laurelyn mentioned something about her labradoodle having puppies soon. I'm guessing that's where your mom got him, and if I know Laurelyn, she was training them as early as she could."

"You can train dogs that young?"

She shrugged and repeated the command, smiling when he sat for another treat.

"Sometimes. Most dogs can start learning commands around 8 weeks, but exposing them to it early doesn't hurt. As long as you keep their training brief—maybe 5 minutes at most, and give positive reinforcement at the end, it's pretty easy."

"Easy for *you*," I teased, pushing up off the floor and wiping my hands on my jeans. "He hasn't been out since I left the house. Is there somewhere I can take him without worrying that you'll lock the door and leave us stranded in the blizzard?"

She pursed her lips, but I could see the hint of a smile playing on them.

"I would never leave Rosco outside to get stranded in a blizzard."

"Just Rosco? What about me?"

"Eh." She shrugged and waved for us to follow her down the hall.

She opened a door and stepped to the side, allowing us to enter first.

"Woah." It was the only thing I could get out because words couldn't describe the room we'd just walked into. "What is all of this?"

"This is Cool Cat's Dreamland," she said wistfully, closing the door. "I had this idea to open a pet daycare/play area for dogs. People could bring them in to hang out and burn off some energy while they went to work. Last year I started adding on to the existing structure and was able to design exactly what I wanted. The property sits on a large piece of land that my family owns, so it was easy to expand some without jumping through a bunch of hoops. Things were going great, but then my ex and I broke up, and I had to halt the project."

The room was massive, with kennels on one side of the walls, each with its own dog bed and food and water bowls. The floor was concrete, which Rosco enjoyed sniffing as we walked around and took everything in. A small patch of artificial grass was by a door that I assumed led outside, though I had no idea.

"He can go on the grass," Ramona said, pointing at it. "It's small enough that I can wash it in the shower, which is what I do for Daisy."

I nodded and led him over to it, where he promptly lifted his leg and relieved himself.

"Who's Daisy?" I asked, remembering her mentioning her earlier before her phone rang and she ran off.

"Daisy is this cute little girl," she replied, lifting a small dog out of a bed in one of the kennels.

She cuddled her in her arms against her chest and snuggled her as she yawned. Once she was awake and licking her face, she brought her over and sat her down on the grass next to Rosco.

As soon as I saw that Daisy was missing one of her back legs, I immediately pulled Rosco's leash to steer him away so he didn't hurt her.

"He's fine," she said, waving me off as she stood and watched the dogs together.

"I don't want Rosco to hurt her."

"Her best friend is a Weimaraner. She's fine."

"But…" I stuttered, wondering if she was aware that her dog only had three legs because she sure as hell didn't seem like it.

"She only has three legs?" she finished for me. "I know. It doesn't bother her at all. When I first got Daisy, it was after she had been hit by a car and her back leg was amputated. Her owner didn't want the responsibility of caring for her and doing rehab, so I took her in. Believe it or not, I don't think she even realizes that she's missing that leg anymore. She's gotten so used to going about without it."

"How long ago did it happen?"

"Two years."

"Wow. You've done a great job rehabbing her."

"Thank you." She looked up at me from under her dark lashes. "It helped that it was her hind leg instead of one of her front legs since that's where most of their body weight is concentrated. Plus, she's a small dog, so it wasn't as problematic for her. I bring her in here a few times a day and make her play when I can't take her for walks due to the weather."

"That's really cool. If I lived close by, I would love a place like this to take Rosco during the day to work off some of his energy."

"It's not that far," she said, frowning.

"Not right now, but when I go home it will be."

"To Fallen Oaks?"

It was my turn to frown.

"No, to Atlanta."

Her eyebrows rose as if she didn't expect me to say that.

"Oh. Sorry, I guess I just assumed that you were still in Fallen Oaks with your family."

"I moved to Atlanta a year ago after I got my master's degree. Been there ever since."

"What is your degree in?" she asked, neither of us looking at each other as we watched the dogs walk around and take turns sniffing each other.

"Computer science."

Her head whipped up as she looked at me with a shocked expression.

"So that's why you asked about my computer!"

It wasn't a question but more of a realization.

I nodded and rocked back on my heels.

"Do you really think you can fix it?"

"I don't know. First, I would have to look at it to see what the problem is."

"Okay. How much do you charge because I will gladly pay whatever it is if you can make that stupid black screen stop appearing. It's killing me," she groaned.

"I don't want your money," I replied, rubbing my lips together.

Her eyes scanned my face, and her cheeks turned the faintest shade of red as if she was imagining what I might want.

"Okay…" She turned to face me and schooled her features. "What do you want instead?"

"I want to share your bed."

234

SOMETHING TO THINK ABOUT

<u>Nine</u>

Ramona

"Is this Vin Diesel on your screensaver?" Preston asked, looking up at me as I popped a Cool Ranch Dorito into my mouth.

I nodded and hoped he couldn't see the blush on my cheeks with the fluorescent lights in the kitchen. It was the only space big enough for us to sit and eat dinner without hanging out in the shop. Rosco was in the play yard with Daisy, even though it took a lot of convincing for Preston to trust that his dog wouldn't eat mine. Once I showed him the cameras I had set up, he finally relaxed and agreed to come and have dinner.

"Do I want to know why you have yourself photoshopped on Michelle Rodriguez's body?"

"Because I want to be Letty," I laughed, covering my mouth so chip crumbs didn't shoot out.

He pulled his brows together and frowned.

"You know… Letty? Dom's girlfriend?"

Nothing. Just a blank stare as if I were speaking a foreign language.

I grabbed my phone from the table and pulled up the original image from the movie where she was sitting on his lap in the garage. I turned it to face him, trying not to laugh when he squinted his eyes and leaned closer to see it.

"No clue who that is."

"What?! That's Dom Toretto and Letty from *The Fast and The Furious*!"

"Never seen it."

My eyes bulged as I looked at him and then back to my phone.

"How could you have *not* seen it? It's a classic!"

"*Rocky. Gone In Sixty Seconds. Terminator. Gladiator.*"

I scrunched my nose and set my phone back down on the table before grabbing another chip out of the bag.

"What are you listing? Popular movies in retirement homes?"

He narrowed his eyes at me briefly before focusing on my laptop again.

"No. *Those* are classics."

"Maybe if you're super old. How old are you anyway?"

"Old enough to appreciate the true classics."

"Agree to disagree," I sighed, the crunch of the chips loud in my ears as I chewed. "Dom was hotter than any of those guys."

"I don't check men out, so I guess I'll have to go with whatever you say."

"You can't tell me that Letty isn't hot," I countered, grabbing my phone again. "Just look at her!"

"So you pasted your face on her body so you could be like her or so you could have her man?"

I shrugged sheepishly, hating that he was getting a little too close to the truth.

"Both, I guess."

"Do you have leather pants?"

"No, I don't. Why?"

"Because if you did, I could have you put them on and then decide who looks hotter in them. The girl in front of me that I could take them off of, or some girl on the internet that I could care less about."

I swallowed hard, thankful that the chip I'd eaten had fully passed down my throat before it could get lodged in it with how dry it suddenly was.

I got up and grabbed a glass from the cabinet, filling it with ice-cold water from the fridge. Preston was flirting with me—there was no doubt about that. The real question was why…

The cold liquid felt good as I chugged it like I was stranded on a deserted island. He lifted his sandwich to his lips, took a bite, then set it down before wiping the crumbs away with his thumb. The whole thing felt oddly erotic to watch, which was weird given that he was making a plain turkey and cheese sandwich look so arousing.

I pressed the glass against the bar and refilled it, barely paying enough attention to move it before it spilled over. I continued to watch him as he ate, completely entranced by how sexy it all looked. That was one fucking lucky sandwich.

But then again, it had nothing to do with the sandwich. He could be eating a piece of celery and it would have the same effect on me. Maybe deep down, I wanted to be the celery. We weren't that different anyway, both of us long and slender and, as of right now, packed full of water.

I set the glass down with a heavy thud on the counter, grabbing Preston's attention for a few seconds before he returned to fixing my computer. My stomach felt sloshy, and I knew that it was because I had just drunk my weight in water.

"So, I think I figured out—"

The lights flickered as the wind howled outside. They had been doing so for about half an hour and I was just waiting for the power to finally go out.

"Well, I was going to say that I think I figured out what's wrong with your computer," Preston said. "But given that I don't know how much longer we'll have power, I don't want to risk it starting on it right now."

As if right on cue, there was a loud thud outside, and then everything around us went pitch black.

Ten

Preston

"It looks like a tree fell against the wall right by the door. It must have gotten knocked down by the wind," I said, coming inside and shaking the snow from my hair. Ramona had grabbed a few candles and had given me a flashlight when I offered to go check to see what had happened. I didn't get far before spotting the fallen tree and knew that was the source of the noise. The power going out at the same time was just a coincidence but not a surprise, given how long the lights had been flickering before it finally cut out.

"Was there any damage?" she asked, sitting in the same spot in the kitchen where I had left her.

"Not that I could tell, but then again, I could barely see the tree. The snow hasn't let up and I can't see more than a few inches in front of me."

"It's going to get cold in here soon," she said, getting up and taking her plate to the sink. "We should probably call it a night and get some sleep. Maybe the power will be back when we wake up."

"Okay."

We still hadn't discussed where I would sleep tonight or what to do with Rosco. He was a puppy, and this was technically our first night together, so I had no clue what to expect from him. While I had teased her about us sharing her bed, I didn't actually mean it and didn't want to make her uncomfortable.

"There's extra space on the floor in my room if you want to put Rosco's bed there. If not, I have a big crate in the play yard that we can bring inside for him. I think it's big enough to stuff his bed in. It's up to you and whatever you think he'll do better in."

"Honestly, I have no idea. I just got him today, so I don't know what he's used to sleeping in or how he'll do."

I hated that I couldn't see her face in the dim light from the candle.

"Maybe it's better to crate him then. That way, he'll have his bed but can't wander or pace if he gets anxious. We can add a blanket or two to make sure he has a place to hide if he wants to."

"Sounds good. If you tell me where it is, I can get him set up. Just point me in the direction of where you want us."

"Okay, I'll go with you to get it."

I followed her to the playroom and held the flashlight above her head to light the way.

"You can grab that one," she said, pointing to the large one in the corner. "It's not as heavy as it looks. I carry it by myself all the time."

"Is that going to fit in your room?" I asked, taking in how large it was.

She turned to face me, her nose scrunched up.

"Yeah, maybe not. I forgot how big it was."

"I thought you said you carry it by yourself all the time?" I teased, shining the light at her like a cop would.

"I do," she laughed. "But it's just around in here. I never take it out of this room unless I have to."

I patted Rosco's head as we stared at the crate and tried to figure out how to move it to her room.

"I don't think it's going to fit in your room," I said.

"Yeah, looking at it now, I don't think so either."

"It's pretty warm in here. I think he might be okay to stay in here tonight if you're okay with it?"

She looked around and then looked at me.

"I don't want Rosco to sleep in here alone. What if he gets scared or lonely?"

"He's a dog. I think he'll be just fine. It's not like we're throwing him outside and making him sleep in the snow."

"No, but he's just a baby. He's probably used to sleeping in the same bed with his mom and siblings. It's hard for dogs to be separated from their pack and then to force them into an environment where they don't know what's going on—"

"Umm, Ramona?" I interrupted, looking down into one of the kennels beside us.

"What? I know what I'm talking about. He's going to whine and cry all night. There's no way we can leave him alone. He needs a companion to feel safe."

"Like this one?"

I shone the flashlight into the crate to show her Rosco curled up in the bed with Daisy, snuggled up against each other.

"Oh my God!" she squealed, taking the flashlight from me and pointing it closer to get a better look. "Would you look at that?"

Daisy looked up at us, yawned, and then rested her head on Rosco's leg as she curled up between his legs. It was like he was the big spoon, and she was the little one.

"I've never seen Daisy act like that with another dog before. I think she loves him!"

"It sure looks like it."

"Well, I guess that problem is settled then. This room is well insulated, as that was my top priority, given how cold it gets here during the winter. On top of that, they have each other's body heat to stay warm and chose the fleece-lined bed. I think they're good."

"Alright, if you want to show me where you want me to sleep, I'll get out of your hair."

She whipped around, almost crashing into me as the light danced wildly between us. I grabbed the flashlight, holding it steady as my hand brushed against hers. I could feel the change in her the same way I had the other times we touched.

Her breathing quickened, the sound almost deafening in the room aside from my racing heartbeat.

"You can sleep in my room," she breathed out.

I couldn't help but pick up on something hidden in her words, probably because she didn't speak them with sarcasm like she usually did. There was a vulnerability there, one that I was eager to explore.

"You don't have to let me sleep in your bed, Ramona. I was just giving you a hard time."

"I can't remember the last time I had something hard."

"What?" I asked, not sure that I heard her correctly.

A slight gasp escaped her lips when she realized what she said. I felt my cheeks burn from the grin spreading across my face as I rocked back on my heels.

"What?" she repeated nervously, acting like she hadn't said what she had just said.

"Oh, nothing. You were just telling me how you haven't had anything hard in a long time, and I was about to ask if you wanted me to remedy that tonight," I teased, knowing it would rile her up as she denied it.

She stood there for a few minutes in stunned silence. Not that I was complaining because at least she wasn't threatening me. I placed my hand on her lower back and spun her around, guiding her out of the play yard and into the hallway leading to her bedroom. She didn't say anything the entire time. No snarky comebacks or remarks about how she would rather do anything *but me*, and I couldn't help but wonder if maybe my dirty mouth broke Ramona.

Eleven

Ramona

I can't remember the last time I had something hard.

Why the fuck did I say that?! Just because I had twisted Preston's words when he said he was giving me a hard time didn't mean that I wanted him to know that I was fantasizing about just how *hard* of a time he could give me.

Maybe I was lacking oxygen, and that's why I couldn't think straight right now. Was that a thing—a power outage related oxygen shortage? Because I was pretty sure that was what we were dealing with.

I allowed him to guide me back to my bedroom, unsure of what to do from there. I couldn't in good conscious give him a blanket and tell him to go find somewhere to sleep, but I also couldn't trust myself to sleep in the same bed next to him and keep my hands to myself. Since Daisy was now sleeping in the play yard with Rosco, that meant she wouldn't be crawling out of her bed to lick his face if he slept on the floor, but then again, I couldn't imagine asking him to sleep on the floor. Probably because deep down, I wanted him in my bed, even if I had been trying to convince him—and myself—that I didn't.

I had no idea what had gotten into me—it sure as hell wasn't Preston, but that was beside the point. Something about him made me feel different than anyone else ever had. It was like he had this magic spell over me, and I couldn't escape if I tried.

"So, about that enclosure in the corner," Preston said, shining the flashlight at it. "Is there anything in there?"

"Yes, that's Louie's home."

"And Louie is?"

We walked over to the cage together, and I peered in, trying to find him. He was good at camouflaging himself, to begin with, but with very little light, it made it even more difficult to spot him.

"He's my veiled chameleon." I pointed to the hanging branch toward the back, where he was hiding behind some leaves and fake plants. It was his favorite spot and close to the heat lamp, so I wasn't surprised to find him there.

Preston leaned in, brushing my arm in the process and sending a waft of his cologne into the air in front of me. I sucked in a deep breath, trying to keep my composure instead of jumping his bones as my legs tried to part for him involuntarily.

"So, what do we need to do for this little guy since there's no power for his heat lamp?"

I bet Preston doesn't have a little guy. I bet it's big and thick and can show a girl a good time.

I shook my head, trying to clear the fog so I could answer him.

"He should be fine for tonight. I cranked the heater up earlier in anticipation of the power going out so that when the temperature drops in here, it'll level out around the normal temperature. I also have some reptile heating pads in the store that I can use tomorrow if the power isn't back. For now, he's good. I sprayed his plants earlier so he has plenty of humidity, and he can go a little while without the UV light."

I reached around, trying not to touch him, and grabbed a blanket from beneath the cage on the shelf I used to store supplies.

"I also have this blanket that I wrap around the cage to keep some heat inside since it's right by the window. Thankfully the winters here are pretty predictable, so this isn't our first rodeo."

I lifted it to show him but was surprised when he grabbed the other end and helped me put it on.

"Alright, that should do it," I said, turning around and smacking right into his rock-hard chest.

Fuck. Me. Is everything about him hard?

His fingers lightly tickled my skin as they wrapped around me and held me in place.

I wanted to look up and ask him what he was doing. Demand that he stop whatever this game was that he was playing, but I couldn't. My mouth refused to work because my brain refused to generate the words it needed to do so. I had spent so long being angry and frustrated with him for existing, and now I was like a dog in heat and wanted nothing *but* Preston to touch me.

"Are you okay?" he asked, his voice low as his fingers trailed lightly over my skin.

While it was in the negative digits outside, I had been roasting from cranking the heater up and had stripped off the flannel shirt earlier, leaving me in just a tank top. This left easy access for him to leave goosebumps along my bare skin from his touch, sending me even further up the wall with desire.

"Yeah. I'm fine. We should sleep together."

My heart raced so fast that I could barely hear my thoughts past the rush of blood passing through my ears as my blood pressure skyrocketed.

Did I just ask him to sleep with me?

"Um, I mean. We should both sleep. At the same time. Not like together, together. I didn't mean it that way. Just in the same bed because the floor is hard. Not as hard as you. Or rather, how your chest was when I touched it a few minutes ago. That was hard. But I think everything about you is hard. I mean, I'm not insinuating that your cock is hard, too—shit! I mean, I hope it is. Not right now, because that might be weird. But in general. Like you know, when you're aroused? Fuck. Now it sounds like I think you can't get hard. I didn't mean it that way; I just meant that maybe you are hard when you want to be and that I'm not insinuating that you have erectile dysfunction or anything. I mean—"

"Ramona?"

"Yeah?"

"Stop talking."

I took a deep breath and held it to keep myself from rambling on again. I was actively aware that I was holding it so I didn't pass out because I didn't need to add any more humiliation to the mix tonight. The last thing I wanted to be was like one of those girls in the romance novels I read where they *finally let out the breath they didn't realize they were holding*. Who does that?

I felt the heat flame my cheeks as he stood in front of me, his fingers burning into my skin that was already on fire from humiliation. I had just gone on and on about Preston and whether or not he could get an erection. I knew I had suspicions earlier about oxygen deprivation related to power outages, but now I knew for sure that it had to be true. What else could explain the total moron that I had turned into since then?

"Which side do you prefer?" he asked, catching me off guard.

I tilted my head and studied his face, hoping it would give me a clue about what he was talking about. Was he asking which side I preferred to be fucked on? I was used to just lying on my back and faking it, so I didn't have much of a preference on sides. However, I was definitely curious about it now.

"Are you sure you're okay?" he asked again, this time lifting my chin with his fingers to bring my eyes back to his.

Something snapped inside of me, and without thinking, I reached up and wrapped my arms around his neck, pulling him into me for a kiss.

My lips roamed over his eagerly, the kiss deepening as he grabbed the back of my neck and held me there while he pressed harder against mine. I moaned into it, my body betraying me as I pulled myself up and wrapped my legs around his waist as I felt the ache start between my thighs. This man was pure fire and I wanted to feel his heat. Okay—cock. I wanted to feel his cock.

His big, strong hands slipped down, grazing my back before grabbing handfuls of ass and squeezing. I arched into his touch, desperate for more. My hips rocked against him, and I heard a low growl escape his throat as I brushed against his erection.

It was massive and impressive—just like I imagined it would be. How he used it was the more important question, but given that his hands and lips seemed to be experts in the pleasure department, I didn't have to worry that his cock would be disappointing.

Suddenly, he pulled away, breaking the kiss and leaving both of us panting.

"Are you sure you want to do this?" he asked, keeping his head away so I couldn't kiss him again without answering first.

"Yes. I do. Let's go." I rocked harder against him, practically trying to dry hump him if he would let me.

He chuckled and lowered me back to the floor.

"What's wrong?" I asked, not too proud to hide the disappointment in my voice. "Is it the whole hard thing I said a few minutes ago? Because I was totally wrong about that. Obviously." I pointed to the bulge in his jeans.

"No," he laughed. "But I'm glad I was able to prove your hypothesis."

Hypothesis? What the fuck was that? I was too horny right now for logical thoughts or big words.

I shook my head.

"Okay, then what's the problem?"

"I don't know." He sighed and scrubbed a hand down his face. "I guess it's that I don't want to rush into something that you might regret when you're thinking clearly."

"Why would I regret it?" I rushed out a little too eagerly.

If he knew how long it had been since I had sex with someone who was rocking as hard of a cock as he was through his jeans, he wouldn't worry about me having any regrets.

"Because you've been trying to shoot lasers out of your eyes and into my head since I met you. You've threatened to kill me several times and now you're practically trying to ride me through my jeans."

I inhaled deeply and took a step back, hoping to find some air that wasn't contaminated with his scent. Maybe it wasn't an oxygen-related power outage at all. Perhaps I was just stupid around him because he somehow sucked all the brain cells out of my head without trying.

"So?"

"So? I don't know, Ramona. I guess maybe I'm just not sure whether to trust that you won't stab me with something as you climax. I don't know where this change came from—not that I don't like it. I mean, it's better than worrying about you plotting my gruesome murder and feeding me to the wild animals outside. But this is the first time you've been friendly to me since I set foot in Whiskey Mountain, so I don't know where it's coming from."

"There aren't any wild animals to worry about." I rolled my eyes though he couldn't see.

I didn't want to get into the reasons why I was suddenly being nice to him because it meant that I would have to stop and process it myself, and I wasn't in the mood to do that. There was something about Preston that made me feel different than anyone had ever made me feel before, and I was worried that if I didn't stop and act on this right here, right now, then it would disappear just as quickly as it came about.

"Pretty sure I heard some howling when I went to check on the noise," he added to fill the silence between us.

I shrugged my shoulders though I wasn't sure he could see it.

"I just think that we shouldn't rush into this." His voice was soft, but his words felt like they cut through me with a knife.

I didn't date much growing up and got with Daniel our senior year in high school. We didn't make it official until a year later, but we were still a thing. He was the only long-term relationship I've ever had, and aside from a few random hook ups after we broke up, I didn't know what it felt like to be with anyone but him.

Daniel wasn't perfect, but when we first started dating, he looked at me like I hung the moon and stars. He gave me everything I could ever ask for before things began to decline. Even then, feeling the change between us as we drifted apart didn't hurt nearly as bad as getting rejected by Preston.

Twelve

Preston

To say that Ramona was pissed off would be an understatement. It wasn't just the silent treatment she gave me last night when we went to bed or the pillow she shoved in my face because she "couldn't see where my head was," AKA she didn't *mean to* try to smother me. It was the way I could feel her shooting those daggers through my head again in the dead of night and how I relied on her snoring to know that she wasn't getting ready to shank me in my sleep.

I slept like shit—probably because I was trying to do it with one eye open. Or maybe it was because it was hard for me to sleep at night in general. Insomnia always crept up on me, and last night was no different. I finally decided to stop fighting it and got up for the day around five in the morning.

The power was still out, and I didn't want to waste what battery I had left on my cell phone by playing on it, so I went into the store and hung out until Ramona woke up. I had noticed her stocking the shelves yesterday when I first got there and saw that there were still a few boxes she hadn't gotten to. Determined to make myself helpful and not like the villain she thought I was, I started unpacking them and filled the shelves.

I was in the groove, slinging boxes of fish food onto the display next to the fish tanks, belting out my rendition of All Out of Love by Air Supply, when she walked in and scared the shit out of me.

"Those don't go there," she said, pointing to the boxes I had thrown in the air, landing on the floor between us.

"Sorry. You startled me." I bent down and started gathering them while she stood over me, watching.

"Well, I wasn't expecting to hear karaoke in the store this early in the morning. Is that one of the songs on the playlist at the retirement home? Do they play it between showings of Rocky and Gladiator?" she teased. Or at least I thought she was teasing. The way her hazel eyes darkened made me suddenly unsure.

"Laugh all you want, but Air Supply is a legendary band, and All Out of Love hit the number two spot on the Billboard Hot 100 in February 1980. In addition, they've had 7 other songs make the list as well. It's a classic, just like the movies."

"You do realize that we're not in the 80s, right? Were you even born in the 80s, or do you just have some old man spirit trapped in your body?"

"No, I wasn't born in the 80s, but my parents taught me to appreciate music from across many decades and to broaden my horizons. Just because something is old doesn't mean that it loses its value. It's called being open-minded."

"There's also nothing wrong with appreciating things from *this* decade," she remarked, redoing the boxes of food I had already put on the shelf.

"You're right. Unfortunately, I don't care for much of the so-called music from this decade. I'd much rather listen to something with soul and meaning. If music from this decade contained even an *ounce* of that, I would be willing to give it a try."

She shook her head but said nothing as her shoulders tightened. I was getting to her again without even trying.

"So, do you have anything else you need unpacked?" I asked, trying to change the subject.

"I have more boxes in the back that I've been meaning to go through, but you don't have to do that."

"I don't mind, really. I like staying busy, and it's not like I have anywhere to go."

She narrowed her eyes at me and placed her hands firmly on her hips.

"Why are you being nice?"

"I'm not. I'm bored and cold. Moving around keeps my blood flowing and helps me stay warm. Plus, it helps pass the time. So, if you need help with stuff, stop being stubborn and let me do it."

"I'm not starting on anything until I've had breakfast. You can come eat or stay here and freeze your balls off. It's up to you, but this is the coldest room in the building."

I pursed my lips and debated whether to join her or not. She seemed just as grumpy as she was last night when we went to bed, and I wasn't sure what it would take to improve her mood. I mean, I had an idea, but I couldn't imagine that walking into the kitchen with my cock out was going to go over well, even if that's what she really wanted. Knowing my luck, she'd come at it with a butcher's knife, which was a risk I wasn't willing to take.

"Are you coming or not?" she asked over her shoulder as she turned on her heel and walked away.

Against my better judgment, I followed her.

Thirteen

Ramona

"There are bagels on the counter or some granola bars in the cabinet. Help yourself."

I reached up on my tiptoes and grabbed the box of Frosted Flakes cereal from the top shelf in the pantry. I wasn't big on breakfast and only ate it because I got super cranky when I skipped meals. While I preferred to eat cereal with milk, I didn't trust that the gallon I had in the fridge was still good since the power had been out for so long. It had been over twelve hours and it wouldn't be the first time that milk had given me a sour surprise, so I wasn't testing my luck today.

Preston grabbed a granola bar out of the box and then closed the cabinet while he stood there to eat it. I could tell he wasn't comfortable sitting at the table with me, and I couldn't blame him. I'd been a raging bitch since last night, but that's what being mortified did to me.

I couldn't remember the last time I'd made a move on a guy that wasn't reciprocated. Granted, he was into it at first, but he also ended it and ultimately rejected me. I thought that I would be more grown up and mature about how I would handle it *if* it ever happened to me, but I guess I didn't give myself credit for thinking I could land a guy like Preston in the first place.

"You're eating dry cereal?" he questioned, keeping from raising his eyebrows even though the judgment was still laced in his tone.

"I don't trust the milk."

"Why not eat something else? I can't imagine that it's that satisfying to eat dry cereal. It's gotta be all scratchy and hard to get down."

"Because I like cereal. If I like something, I eat it. I don't make a big deal about it or find stuff that I don't like as much just because it fits the situation."

He rubbed his lips together and then popped the last piece of granola bar into his mouth before tossing the wrapper into the trash.

I continued eating but hated that he was right. It wasn't satisfying at all, and my mouth was dry. Typically, I would wash it down with my morning coffee, but given that we didn't have power still, it wasn't like I could make any.

"This sucks," I muttered under my breath, pushing the container away from me.

"What does?"

"Nothing."

My mood was getting sourer by the minute, and I didn't want to keep making myself a bigger bitch than I already was.

"What sucks, Ramona?" he pressed, crossing an ankle over the other as he casually leaned against the counter.

"That the power is out. That I don't trust that the milk is still good. That I can't even make coffee. That it's fucking colder than a witch's tit in here."

His lips curled up at the last one.

"I can make you coffee," he offered.

I cocked my head and glared at him.

"And how exactly are you going to do that?" I asked, trying not to get my hopes up.

"Do you have a kettle?"

"Yeah…"

"Is your water heater gas or electric?"

"Gas, thank God. There's no way I could go days without a hot shower."

"Grab the kettle, and I'll start getting everything else ready."

He moved about the kitchen, looking at the basic coffee maker sitting on the counter like it was the most complicated thing he'd ever seen.

"I don't believe in buying expensive coffee makers when this works just fine," I said, handing the steel kettle to him.

"I agree. Basic is best." He took it and went to the sink, waiting a few seconds until the water was hot.

I was a sucker for super-hot showers and baths, so I kept the temperature set high which meant he would burn himself in a matter of seconds if he didn't remove his fingers from the stream.

Finally, he pulled away and lowered the kettle into the stream, filling it as the steam billowed from the top.

I stood back and watched as he added a few scoops of coffee grounds to the filter and then very slowly poured the hot water over them in a circular motion. It felt like a magic trick as the coffee machine gurgled to life and liquid gold began dripping into the carafe.

The smell filled the air, bringing a smile to my face as my spirits lifted. I knew that Preston was watching me and hated that he was the reason for my happiness.

"No fucking way! That's amazing!" I exclaimed, genuinely impressed with his ability to make me coffee. "Thank you."

"It's not a big deal." He shrugged and poured the last bit of water in before setting the kettle on the trivet by the stove.

"How did you learn to do that?"

"Growing up, my parents took us camping a few times a year. They believe in using the resources you have available and taught my brother and me at an early age how to do a lot of things."

"Like making coffee during a power outage," I said with a smile.

"It's really quite simple. The only thing the machine does is heat the water before it spreads it over the coffee grounds. I just did the work for it."

"Well, I'm still impressed and very thankful for the coffee. It may not be a honey lavender latte from Spill The Beans, but it's definitely better than nothing."

"Glad I could help."

"Have you been to Spill The Beans? I know you said you don't drink coffee, but you're seriously missing out. I don't know what it is about that latte, but it just calms me down and makes me feel amazing."

He shook his head and smiled.

"No, I haven't been."

"You really should try it. It's amazing and magical."

"That's probably because lavender counteracts the negative effects of coffee. You get the energy jolt from the coffee without having the jittery side effects of the caffeine."

I pulled my head back in shock.

"Excuse me? There are no negative effects of coffee."

"Not true," he said, shaking his head and folding his arms over his chest. "Coffee is a stimulant, and depending on the amount consumed, it can induce anxiety, restlessness, insomnia, and even impact things like elevated heart rate and blood pressure. By adding lavender, you're slightly counteracting some of the negatives with the positive effects of it."

"Oh yeah? Like what?"

I knew I was in a losing battle, given that Preston seemed to know so much about everything, but part of me wanted to hear him talk about it. It was fascinating in a weird sort of way.

"Well, lavender contains a compound called linalool. It creates a soothing effect on the body when consumed in either tea or coffee. It also stimulates activity in certain areas of the brain, and the calming aroma helps it secrete serotonin while decreasing cortisol levels. When combined with coffee or tea, it allows the caffeine to provide the energy boost that you want while also giving you the soothing effect you desire."

The coffee was finally done, and the drip had stopped, so I pulled the carafe out and filled a cup for myself since Preston didn't drink coffee. I grabbed some powdered creamer and a few packets of sugar out of the cabinet and added them in, all while trying to come up with a witty comeback to what he had said.

"What are you? Some sort of walking, talking encyclopedia?" I asked, lifting the cup to my lips and taking a sip. He didn't reply. Instead, he just winked at me, pushed off the counter, and walked out of the kitchen, leaving me alone with the best stupid cup of coffee I'd had at home in a long time.

<u>Fourteen</u>

Preston

"I'm not usually this big of a bitch," Ramona commented randomly as we put away the empty boxes that were broken down and ready to be recycled once the roads opened again.

"Okay." I wasn't sure what to say to that.

Had she been grumpy with me? Yes. Had she threatened bodily harm recently? Also, yes. But did I think she was a bitch? No. There was something about her that I couldn't figure out, but deep down, I knew that this whole mean girl front was just that—a facade.

"I just wanted you to know that I haven't *always* been this way, and I feel bad for taking it out on you when you've been kind enough to help me stock the store and make coffee this morning."

"It's not a big deal. Like I said, I don't mind helping."

"Yeah, but you don't have to."

"What else am I going to do? I'm stuck here until the storm passes through and the roads are cleared. There's no electricity. I looked around but didn't see any books to read. It leaves me with nothing to do but help out in here, and honestly, I like it."

"You like stocking shelves and doing inventory?" she questioned, twisting her body to see me.

"I do. I like staying busy and being active. I hate just sitting around all day."

"But don't you sit all day at work doing computer stuff?"

"Every now and then. But I also get to work from home, and I have a standing desk, so I don't have to sit that long. I also have a full gym set up at my house in Atlanta."

As much as I enjoyed being close to my family, I missed having my own space back home. It was a small house with a minimalistic design. The walls were still the same dull white color they were when I bought it, and I hadn't taken the time to hang any pictures or art. I had a few essential pieces of furniture, but most of my focus was on the gym. That was where I had splurged and dedicated all my focus.

"Do you like working from home?"

I nodded because I never knew how to answer that question when people asked it. It felt rude to say that I much preferred the silent solitude of an empty house than to sit around and pretend to be engaged in boring small talk with people I didn't even like.

"It works well for me," I replied, leaving it at that.

"I never thought I would have the opportunity to work from home, but it turned out it just took dumping my boyfriend and ending up homeless for it to happen. That was the kick in the pants I needed to make the renovations I had been putting off here for so long." She laughed.

"Was that the guy at the store?"

She nodded, her face falling some before she turned away from me.

"That's him. Daniel."

"How long were you guys together?"

She sighed heavily before answering.

"We dated off and on throughout high school, mostly our senior year. After graduation, we were still dating, but he didn't make it *official* until we moved in together. So, if you count from that point—which he always did—we were together for 3 years."

"When do you count from?"

She shrugged and sat down on a box we hadn't unpacked yet.

"I guess from the moment I thought he was my boyfriend in high school. We were one of those couples who were always on again, off again, that it was hard to tell if we were together or not. I stayed committed to him, even on our breaks, but he didn't do the same. I should have seen what he was doing then, but I put my blinders on because I had the *hottest* boy at Fallen Oaks High. But then again, so did a lot of other girls, and I just pretended that I didn't know about it."

"That sucks. I'm sorry."

"Don't be. It's all for the better. I'm past that part of my life and ready to move on."

"Are you, though?" I questioned, though the way she stood up and narrowed her eyes at me made me immediately reconsider.

"Why wouldn't I be?"

"I don't know. I guess it was just the way you reacted to running into him at the store. It seemed like you still cared about what he thought about you."

She stepped closer and pointed a finger at me.

"You don't have a clue what you're talking about. I'm over Daniel. Leaving him was the best thing I've ever done."

"Then why did you need a fake boyfriend?" I countered, stepping closer and closing the gap between us.

"Why does it matter?"

"Because it does. You can't say that you're over him and don't care what he thinks when you threatened to stab me if I didn't pretend to be your new boyfriend."

"It was a rash decision," she hissed out. "One that I later regretted."

"What part?"

"All of it?"

"Liar."

She pulled her head back, her nostrils flaring with anger.

"You're calling me a liar?"

"You bet your sweet ass I am. You didn't regret one second of it. Not the way I kissed you, and sure as hell not the way your body reacted when I touched your ass."

"I was caught off guard, and it made me all—"

"Horny?" I offered, placing my leg between hers as I pinned her against the wall.

"No," she bit out, her words strained with the lie.

"Okay," I said slowly, gently placing my hand on her hip and looking around before allowing myself to look into those dark hazel eyes. "If you regretted it so much, why did you kiss me last night and try to get me to sleep with you?"

She opened her mouth to speak but then snapped it shut.

"You want me as bad as I want you, Ramona. Don't try to deny it because it's written all over your body."

"It is not."

Her chest rose and fell heavily as she folded her arms over it.

"If I would have said yes last night, you wouldn't have stopped me from doing all of the dirty things you've been thinking about me doing to you."

"But you didn't. You turned me down, and now you're humiliating me again by bringing it up. There, are you happy?"

My eyes locked onto hers, reading the emotions flickering across her face as she struggled to hide them.

"I turned you down because I didn't want you to do something you would regret. If you were some girl that I met under different circumstances, I might have agreed to it. But given that I know that you're fresh off a breakup and having seen how you reacted to seeing Daniel, I don't trust that you're doing it for the right reasons, and I don't want to be the thing you regret."

She let her head fall back and closed her eyes.

"I'm very attracted to you—just so we're clear on that," I added, making sure she didn't think that I wasn't. "I don't want to be the guy you use to get over your ex."

She stood there for a few minutes, not speaking, while my hand refused to move from her body. I could tell there was something she wanted to say, and I wanted to give her the space she needed so she could.

Finally, her eyes opened and caught mine.

"I've spent most of my life trying to be what everyone wanted me to be and always feeling like I'm failing. Not only with my parents but with Daniel, too. When we broke up, he got to keep everything, and I was the one who had to start over and figure out how to make it on my own. I didn't have help from anyone but my friends and I wasn't sure I could do it because I had never been on my own before. When I ran into Daniel at the store, I panicked. The last thing he had told me when we broke up was that I would never find anyone who would put up with and tolerate me like he did, so I wanted to prove him wrong. I wanted to show him I could find someone, and you just happened to be there."

"He sounds like a real asshole."

She lifted a shoulder and let it fall with a sigh.

"He didn't use to be. He was the perfect boyfriend when we first started dating. Always complimenting me and showering me with affection. Over the years, it slowed down, and I assumed it was just because we had gotten so used to each other. I tried to keep the spark alive and asked him to try new things with me. I worried he didn't find me attractive anymore, so I started working out and went on crazy diets to lose weight. But in the end, nothing I did was good enough."

I shook my head, not wanting to believe what I was hearing.

"When I kissed you last night, it wasn't because I'm some pathetic, lonely girl looking to jump into another relationship. I felt something with you that I've never felt before, and for the first time in a long time, I was excited about it. I wanted to explore whatever it was and see if maybe I wasn't dead inside after all. But I'm sorry if I made you uncomfortable. That wasn't my intention, and I shouldn't have been shitty to you about it when you said no."

"I'm not going to lie, Ramona. You did make me feel uncomfortable."

Her face fell as she hurried to look away so I couldn't see the hurt in her eyes.

"It was incredibly uncomfortable going to bed last night with blue balls and trying to sleep knowing that you were only a few inches away from me, wearing those thin silky sleep shorts that barely covered your ass."

The thought of her plump cheeks peeking out of them last night flashed through my head, sending a reminder straight to my cock. I lowered my hand from her hip and grabbed hers, dropping it to the bulge in my jeans.

"This is what you do to me, Ramona," I growled in her ear. "You're far from pathetic, and I feel the same insane chemistry you're feeling. If you want to act on this and explore whatever it is, fine with me. But you need to know before we start anything that I'm not a relationship guy. I don't do commitment. Never have, never will."

"I don't want one either," she rushed out, pressing her hand harder against me.

"Good."

"Good."

"We're just two friends that want to fuck, nothing more?"

"Just two friends," she breathed heavily, rubbing me through my jeans.

"Now that that's settled," I said, reaching down, grabbing her ass, and lifting her to my hips. "Let's get started."

Fifteen

Ramona

Preston's fingers slipped between my folds as my back arched and I leaned into his lips as they trailed kisses along my neck. I hadn't expected to end up in bed together, but there was not a single thing that I regretted about it either.

All it took was a few dirty words about what he wanted to do to me, and I was stripping off my clothes in record time. I was beyond hot and bothered by him—I was full-on wet and ready to do everything he said.

He insisted that we go slow and refused to take his clothes off right away, but I wasn't about to complain about it when his fingers worked my clit over the way they were. He had only been touching me for a few minutes, and I already felt like I was going to come.

When was the last time a man had given me an orgasm?

I bit down on my lip and tried to keep from orgasming because I didn't want him to think I was some loser who could come from a single touch. I was already embarrassed that he knew about the details of my past with Daniel; I didn't need him to think I was also an unsatisfactory lover.

My breathing quickened, and I dug my nails into the sheets, trying not to give in and allow myself to tumble over the edge and succumb.

"Stop fighting it," he whispered in my ear, pressing his thumb against my clit and rubbing it while his fingers thrust inside. "Let go and come."

"I can't," I lied, squirming beneath him.

"Yes, you can. I can feel your body, Ramona. I know it's there. Give it to me. Now."

He lowered his mouth and pulled a nipple between his lips, sucking so hard that I yelped and arched my back. The change in position forced more friction against my clit, and I couldn't hold it any longer.

My hips bucked against his hand as I spiraled out of control, waves of pleasure washing over me as I pulsated against his fingers.

"Fuck. Fuck. FUCK!"

I panted, trying to catch my breath as I came down from the most incredible, mind-blowing orgasm I ever had.

"There, that's more like it," he said, lifting himself onto his elbow to look at me. "If we're going to do this, you can't hold back on me. I will make you come as many times as I want, Ramona. Come hell or high water—you're going to give them to me."

"It's not always that easy," I muttered, still trying to catch my breath. "I think you just got lucky with that one. I don't usually come easy. Well, technically, I don't usually come at all."

"What do you mean?" His brows pulled together.

"I can't remember the last time someone gave me an orgasm. Usually, my trusty rose gets the job done, and even then, it's starting to fail."

He rolled onto his back and scrubbed a hand down the scruff dotting his jaw.

"Please tell me you're kidding."

"About which part?" I started to pull the sheets up to cover my naked body, but he quickly reached over and stopped me.

"I don't think so. I'm not done admiring your body, nor am I done exploring it."

My cheeks burned as the heat rushed through them.

He rolled onto his side and studied my face as he chewed his lower lip.

"My favorite part was how wet you were for me, Ramona. I had no trouble sliding my fingers inside of your pussy. It was so warm and tight, ready to be fucked."

My breathing grew shallow as the ache between my thighs started again. I shifted positions, trying to make it go away.

"You're so fucking beautiful when you're turned on. I love the way you blush when I tell you all the dirty things I want to do to you. And I was right; you are a fucking firecracker, lighting up in the most glorious way as you come."

"It would be better if there were a lot less talking and a lot more action," I said, trying to steady myself enough to get the words out without letting him know just how desperate I was for him to fuck me right now.

"Is that so?"

His lips turned up into the sexiest smirk I'd ever seen.

"I'm starting to wonder if you're even as skilled and talented between the sheets as you pretend to be…"

He climbed off the bed and stood beside it, locking eyes with me and refusing to look away as he slowly undressed. He reached behind, pulling his shirt over his head before tossing it to the floor. I licked my lips, admiring the perfectly sculpted abs that I imagined were there all along.

I wanted to climb over, run my tongue along the ridges, and follow the trail of hair that dipped into the low-hung jeans that he was now taking off. He stood before me wearing nothing but a pair of snug-fitting black boxer briefs that were desperately trying to contain the erection trapped inside.

I looked back up at him, seeing the same desire on his face that I knew was on mine. He was holding a condom between his fingers, but I had been so distracted by his body that I never saw him grab it from his jeans.

He lifted it to his mouth and held it between his teeth while hooking his thumbs into the waistband of his briefs and pulling them down his muscular thighs.

Fuck. Me.

His cock sprung free, jutting up to his stomach as he opened the foil package and sheathed himself.

"You ready for me to prove myself to you?" he asked, his voice deeper than usual.

I was sitting on my knees at the edge of the bed, waiting impatiently for him to fuck me and put me out of my misery.

I nodded, smiling when he stroked himself while I watched.

"How do you want me?" I asked, licking my lips.

"That depends. What kind of orgasm do you want?"

I frowned.

"You mean there's more than one?"

He chuckled and ran a hand along his jaw.

"Lie on your back, legs lifted, and ankles behind your head."

My jaw dropped as I stared at him in disbelief.

"You want me to do what?"

"You heard me. Now go. I'm waiting."

I climbed back on wobbly legs and laid down in the center of the bed. I wasn't sure I was flexible enough to get my ankles behind my head, but I did my best. I hadn't been to yoga in a few weeks, so my body was tighter than usual.

I felt completely on display and didn't miss how his eyes zeroed in on my pussy. Instinctively, I started lowering my legs so I could close them, but he climbed up on the bed and stopped me.

"I don't think so," he growled before dipping his head between my legs and licking.

I gasped and let them fall to the sides again as he mercilessly tortured my clit with his tongue, nearly bringing me to another orgasm. I panted heavily, running my fingers through his short hair that I desperately wanted to pull.

"You taste as good as I thought you would," he replied coolly as he pulled away, leaving me throbbing with need.

"You can keep eating if you're not full yet," I teased, though I desperately wanted him to make me come again. That would be a first, and I really wanted to be able to say that I was one of those girls who had several orgasms in one night.

"Trust me; you'll come again soon."

I was about to object and tell him I couldn't come during sex, but before I could say anything, he lined himself up at my entrance and pushed inside.

There was a slight sting as he stretched me, but it was quickly replaced with the most incredibly full feeling I'd ever felt. I shifted beneath him, forcing him deeper inside.

He rocked slowly, letting me get used to him before he pulled out and slammed into me again.

"Fuck!" I cried out, digging my nails into his back as I bit my lip.

The angle he was fucking me at allowed him to rub against my clit in the most perfect way, but there was this other bundle of nerves deeper inside that he was hitting that made me feel like I was going to pass out and see stars from it.

He pulled out and slammed into me a few more times until he finally gave in and started pounding into me. I closed my eyes and arched my back slightly to get the angle I needed so he could keep hitting this new spot. I had no idea what it was, but it felt fantastic.

"Breathe," he said softly, leaning in close to whisper it in my ear before nipping my earlobe. "You need to keep breathing, deep, full breaths."

"Okay," I panted, trying to do as he said.

I hadn't realized that my breathing was so shallow or that I was holding my breath as I waited for an orgasm to build until he mentioned it.

His dick pounded harder into me as his thumb rubbed my clit, sending me into sensory overload as I tried to remember to take deeper breaths.

"Your pussy is so tight. I love how she squeezes my cock and milks it, taking everything I give her. It's going to feel so good when you come around me, your walls spasming so fucking hard as I pull every ounce of your orgasm out of you."

I whimpered, his words my kryptonite.

I'd never come during sex before and didn't expect it to happen so quickly. Before I could stop it, I was crashing over the edge, spasming around him just like he said I would. He continued to rub my clit with his thumb while his cock put pressure exactly where I needed it.

"Fuck! Fuck! FUUUCCCKKK!"

I closed my eyes and allowed my orgasm to consume me.

Sixteen

Preston

The lights had come back on during Ramona's climax, but it wasn't anything either of us stopped to notice. I couldn't get over how beautiful she looked as she came, and I tried desperately to push the thoughts out of my head about how I could watch that forever. The truth was that this was a simple friends-with-benefits arrangement, and nothing further was going to come out of it. Ramona agreed that she didn't want a relationship, and I wasn't willing to dive into the reasons why I couldn't be in one, even if I wanted to.

Her hair was fanned out across the bed, her lips red and swollen from biting them as she tried to fight letting go. I could tell she was close, and I wanted her to give in and let go sooner, but I also didn't know why she was holding back. Again, this was simply a friendly sex exchange, so I didn't need to get caught up in the emotional details. I was there to give her mind-blowing orgasms, and that was it.

I climbed off the bed and went to the bathroom to dispose of the condom, carefully holding the base of it to keep it from leaking out with how full it was. I knew that sex with Ramona would be different, but I hadn't expected her to be so fucking tight. Her pussy wrapped around my cock like they were made for each other, and drew out every last drop of cum when I finally exploded inside of her.

When I got back to the bedroom, she was wrapped in a sheet, looking into Louie's tank as she turned on the heat lamp for him.

"Everything okay?" I asked, standing beside her and not bothering to cover myself or my still semi-hard cock.

She glanced down and arched an eyebrow.

"I should be asking you that."

"I can usually go a few rounds before it goes down completely." I shrugged.

"A few rounds?" she questioned in disbelief.

"Mmm hmm."

"Oh my."

She pulled her lower lip between her teeth and clutched the sheet tighter to her chest.

"I was going to take a hot shower. Want to join me?" I offered.

"Ummm…."

I tilted my head and studied her.

"I've literally had my head between your thighs. Tasted your pussy. Felt your body as you came on my cock and fingers. There's nothing to be shy about," I said softly.

"I know, but that was before when the power was still off, and you couldn't see me."

I arched a brow but refused to admit to her that I had seen everything or that the lights had come on while we were having sex.

As if reading my mind, her face turned scarlet red. She reached up to cover it, forgetting about the sheet she was still holding against her body. It started to fall, but before she could recover it, I snatched it away and tossed it to the floor away from her.

"Preston!"

"I already told you, Ramona. You don't get to keep this away from me."

I pulled her into me and held her against my chest as her breathing evened out.

"Now, let's go get cleaned up so I can make you all dirty again later."

She giggled and let me lead her down the hall.

It only took a few minutes for the water to heat up, and then we were both standing inside, trying to keep our hands off each other. Just seeing Ramona naked and wet sent signals straight to my cock and made it hard again.

She immediately noticed and gave me a devious smile before lathering her hands with soap and dropping to her knees. I stood there with the water beating down on my back while she caressed my shaft and balls, cleaning me in a way that was addicting.

I leaned back slightly, allowing the water to run down my chest and wash the soap off for her. She grinned, and then once it was clean, she leaned forward and pulled me into her mouth.

I braced a hand against the tiled wall, trying to keep myself steady as my other hand wrapped tightly in her hair, pushing her head down further onto my cock. She opened her mouth further, taking me as far down her throat as possible while she worked the rest of my shaft with her fist.

"Fuck, Ramona," I moaned. "I'm gonna come."

She sucked harder, gripping the base tighter as she hollowed out her cheeks and continued. I could feel myself wavering on the edge as I tried to hold off. It felt so fucking good that I didn't want it to stop.

"I don't want to come down your throat," I panted. "Step back and let me come on your chest. I want to see my cum all over those gorgeous tits."

She gave me one last hard suck and then slowly pulled off, her mouth making a popping noise once the suction was broken. Then, without having to be asked, she leaned back and rested on her heels, pushing her breasts together as I jacked myself off and shot ropes of cum all over them.

It was the perfect image, and I wanted to lock it away in my memory forever. Once I was done, I extended my hand and helped her up. She locked eyes with me while she rubbed it all over herself, smearing my cum on her body.

<u>Seventeen</u>

Ramona

After we showered, I helped Preston check on the dogs and was pleasantly surprised to see Daisy and Rosco up and playing. He had found a ball and was rolling it around, bouncing around as he waited for her to try to take it from him. We refilled their food and gave them fresh water, then let them be since they were having fun and we needed to eat. We had already fucked three times, and my energy was dwindling.

While I thought it would be awkward to let myself hook up with Preston, I was pleasantly surprised that it hadn't been at all. He wasn't lying when he said he knew what he was doing in the bedroom and my body was still recovering from his touch. He'd made me come so many times in such a short period that I wasn't sure what I was going to do once this ended.

The power had stayed on for a few hours, so I was hopeful that it wouldn't go out again. I knew it would be days—if not weeks—before they cleared the roads out here, but as long as we had power, we were fine. While I had planned for supplies for myself for a few weeks, I hadn't accounted for having Preston there. But for now, we didn't have to worry about any of that.

"What do you want for lunch?" I asked, standing in front of a cabinet, going through the options.

He slid up behind me and wrapped his arms around my waist while planting kisses behind my ear and along my neck. He knew this was my weak spot and had fully been taking advantage ever since.

"You."

"I'm not lunch," I giggled, though I wouldn't necessarily be opposed to him eating me out again.

"Wanna bet? I've been craving a pussy sandwich."

"You just had one less than an hour ago."

"I know. I'm addicted and know what I want."

"You're crazy," I laughed, ignoring the wetness pooling in my panties again. "But unlike you, I actually need real food."

"Okay, how about this? We make you some lunch, and then I'll have mine while you eat yours?"

My eyes lit up as I spun around and looked into his. He was incredibly good-looking, and I couldn't get over how gorgeous he was when he was between my thighs.

"Fine," I sighed, pretending it was such a big inconvenience.

"Alright, let's make this quick," he said, smacking me on the ass. "I'm starving."

I laughed and made myself a quick peanut butter and jelly sandwich, thankful I had a new jar of jelly that hadn't been opened yet. As I was finishing up making it, he stood behind me and pulled the drawstring of my sweats, letting them fall and pool at my feet. I stepped out of them, trying to focus on grabbing the bag of chips I wanted while his fingers skimmed along my panty line.

I was already needy and aching for relief as I clenched my thighs together, trying to ignore it.

As if sensing my needs again, Preston spun me around, lifted me by the waist, and sat me on the counter. My sandwich and chips were right beside me as he nodded to them, made sure I had what I needed, and lowered himself between my thighs.

I closed my eyes and focused on the touch of his fingers as they feathered across my skin, leaving goosebumps in their wake. At that moment, I couldn't care about anything other than the glorious man between my legs.

I spread them further, inviting him in as I felt him chuckle against my thigh. I was totally lost in the moment when my cell phone rang on the counter beside me.

Now that we had power and I was able to charge my battery, I knew that I needed to take the call. That was the thing with living in a small town and being stranded in the middle of nowhere—if someone called to check on you, you better answer it.

I looked down at the caller ID and saw Maggie's name.

"It's my best friend, Maggie. I need to take this," I said, letting him know that he would have to wait a few minutes.

"Go for it."

He licked his lips and leaned forward, running his tongue along my slit through the lace fabric of my panties.

"Preston! I can't answer her call while you're doing *that*."

"Why not?"

"Because! It's…"

I couldn't think about what the word was that I was looking for because my brain was turning to mush as he plunged his tongue in deeper, the pull of the fabric brushing against my clit.

"It's hot as fuck?" he offered, pulling back slightly to look at me.

It stopped ringing as I missed the call, but I knew she would call back in a few seconds and keep going until she got me on the phone.

"What if she knows what you're doing?" I whispered loudly as my phone started ringing again.

"She won't."

"How do you know?"

"I don't." He shrugged. "I guess you'll just have to do your best to stay quiet so she doesn't hear you."

"You can't be serious."

My heart was racing, my palms starting to sweat.

His eyes landed on mine again and held my gaze as he slipped a finger under my panties and slipped it inside.

"You're so fucking wet right now, Ramona. You know you want to come. I want to give it to you. So, you can decide whether to tell her what you're really doing, but either way, I'm eating my lunch."

The call ended again, and I could only imagine how panicked Maggie was getting with me not answering. If I had power, that meant that her power had just come back on as well, so she knew that I should be able to answer my phone.

"She's not going to stop calling," he added, nodding to the phone in my hand as it started ringing again. "Better to just deal with it now. You handle that, and I'll handle this."

I lifted the phone to my ear and pressed the button to answer it.

"Hey," I said. My voice sounded strange, and I knew she would immediately pick up on it.

"Hey. What's going on? You sound different."

"Nothing," I lied. "What's up with you?"

I was trying to focus on what she was saying, but Preston's tongue darting in and out of my folds made it nearly impossible.

"You're lying. Are you being weird because you did something to Preston? Don't admit it over the phone—I can't lie in court if I'm called in!"

I leaned back, closed my eyes, and ran my fingers through his hair as he sucked my clit.

"No."

"No?"

"What's she saying?"

I slightly recognized the other voice but wasn't paying enough attention to notice that I had been put on speaker phone. A soft moan escaped my lips, forcing Preston's head out from between my thighs as he gave me a warning look and pressed his finger to his lips to shoosh me.

"She hasn't said much. She's acting weird like she's drunk or something," Maggie answered.

"I haven't heard her say she loves you, so I don't think she's drunk," Dylan said.

"I'm not drunk," I muttered, still not focused. "I'm fine."

As soon as I said that, Preston pressed his face in closer and sucked my clit while his fingers curled inside and rubbed the spot that had been driving me nuts all afternoon. I wasn't fine— not at all. I was about to have one of the most intense orgasms while on the phone with my two best friends.

"You don't sound fine," Maggie noted, still unconvinced. "I know you didn't want to have Preston there, but I don't get what's happening or why you're being so strange. Is he like a serial killer, and he's now holding you there against your will?"

"No. I'm fine. Good. Soooo good," I panted. My legs trembled as I tried to keep them open while Preston continued his torture. "So fucking goooood."

Just then, Preston nipped my clit, sending a jolt right through me.

"Ahhh!" I cried out.

"You have to be quiet, or I'm not going to let you come," he warned quietly.

"What was that?" Maggie asked, suddenly more concerned.

"Nothing, I just stubbed my toe."

"Oh. That sucks."

I was thankful that Maggie bought my bullshit excuse and didn't press any further.

"I don't know, that didn't sound like she stubbed her toe," Dylan commented. "Before that, she sounded like she was—"

"What?!" Maggie asked.

I wanted to jump in and object, but Preston had increased his pressure as he brought me painstakingly closer to the edge.

"I'm fine," I panted, trying to say something so Dylan would drop it and move on, but I knew they could hear it in my voice. "Really fine. On top of the world."

"Ramona—please tell me you're not doing what I think you're doing," Dylan groaned.

"What do you think she's doing?"

Just then, Preston sucked harder, sending me over the edge. I bit down on my hand and pushed the phone away from my ear to try to keep them from hearing as I hissed instead of moaning.

I spasmed around his fingers, letting them take every last bit of my orgasm from my spent body.

My chest rose and fell heavily as I tried to catch my breath. The other end of the line had gone so quiet that I wasn't sure if Maggie was still there. Preston stood up and wiped his mouth with the back of his hand, but it did nothing to remove the smirk he was wearing.

He helped me down and then left the room to give me privacy as I sat at the table and pressed the phone to my ear again.

"Are you still there?" I asked nervously.

"Oh yeah, I'm still here. And you're going to tell me everything," Maggie said, a hint of satisfaction in her tone.

"I don't know what you're talking about."

"Bullshit. Let's start with how you just let Preston get you off while you were on the phone with me and Dylan."

I covered my hand with my face.

"Did he hear everything?"

"No, he left the room once he guessed what was happening."

"Ugh," I groaned. "I'm never going to be able to look him in the eye again."

"It's okay. I think he's going to avoid you for a while anyway." She laughed, and I felt the corners of my lips turn up.

"It wasn't my fault," I said lightly.

"Yeah, I just hate it when an attractive man pins me down and forces me to come while I'm on the phone with my best friend."

"It really wasn't," I laughed. "I told him we couldn't do that while I was on the phone."

"And what did he say?"

"He said that I had to be quiet, or he wouldn't let me come."

"That's so fucking hot," Maggie squealed.

"I know!" I whispered, hoping he wasn't close by and hearing our conversation. "I didn't expect it either."

"We have so much catching up to do as soon as they clear the roads and get you out of there."

"Yeah, we do."

"Until then, I'll let you go so you can get back to wherever that was going. But now that I know that you're safe and alive, I won't call again until you tell me to. Let me know if you need anything, though it sounds like Preston is right on top of filling those needs," she joked.

"I'll call you later," I said, eager to find him and finish what he just started.

"Make good choices. But in case you don't, I just want to say that Maggie would be an adorable name for a little girl."

"That's not happening," I lied.

"Like hell it isn't. I'm just saying you guys are going to run out of condoms before the roads are clear, so make sure you're making smart choices unless you want to make me an aunt. I won't object to that."

I said goodbye and promised to call her later, but I couldn't stop worrying about what would happen if we ran out. The problem was that it wasn't really a matter of *if* but *when*.

Eighteen

Preston

I tried to busy myself with fixing Ramona's computer to keep from allowing the thoughts to intrude my mind the way they wanted to. The goal was to keep things between us limited as friends with benefits—simple fuck buddies—and not let the emotional side creep in. Emotions were the one thing that I couldn't handle and had kept locked away ever since the day my world had come crashing down around me. It tried to break me then, and I wouldn't risk allowing that pain to take me now. But the only way to avoid it was to not let Ramona close enough to risk it, to begin with.

She was messing around in the store, moving boxes of inventory that we hadn't gotten to before we had sex. Daisy and Rosco were running around, chasing her down every aisle and waiting for her to give in and give them another treat. So much for trying to keep Rosco on a strict diet like I had imagined. He'd consumed his weight in treats as we worked with him on obedience training. But as long as he was trainable and learned, that was all that mattered.

I was waiting for an update to finish loading when my phone rang. I glanced down and saw my mom's name on the caller ID.

"Hey, Mom."

"Hello. Just checking in now that the power is on. How are you and Rosco?"

"We're fine. How are you and Dad?"

"Good. We're used to these. Do you need anything? They're working on the roads, so we can probably get over there tomorrow since it's already getting late today. Don't want to chance driving on black ice once it all freezes over again tonight."

"No, thank you. I'm not at home."

"Where are you?"

I clicked my tongue against the roof of my mouth, not wanting to tell her that I had been stranded with Ramona because I knew she would automatically think there was something going on between us. Now that there was, I couldn't technically lie to her about it, but we definitely had different definitions of what this thing between Ramona and me was.

"I'm actually staying with a friend," I said breezily, hoping she didn't press any further.

"A friend? Who?"

"You don't know them." I looked around, trying to find Ramona.

"Preston Elijah Roberts," she warned. "You know damn well that you don't have any friends that I don't know about. Why don't you want to tell me where you're at?"

I sighed heavily, leaning back in the chair behind the counter, still unable to spot where Ramona had wandered off to in the store.

"I'm with Ramona Watkins."

There was a heavy pause on the other end of the line before an audible gasp escaped her lips.

"It's not what you think, Mom. I came by Cool Cats to get some supplies for Rosco—you know, the dog that was forced upon me at last minute? Anyway, I thought I could make it and get back before the storm hit, but I didn't."

"Is Rosco at your house by himself?"

"No, I brought him to the store with me because I didn't want to come home to him eating half of it while I was gone. He's made a friend with Ramona's dog, Daisy."

"It sounds like love is in the air over there," she said softly, something in her tone getting under my skin and making me squirm.

"Absolutely not," I bit out. "And it would be great if you pushed that thought out of your head before you start getting any other ideas."

"I was talking about Rosco and Daisy." She laughed. "But I am curious why you're so quick to react that way when you thought I was talking about you and Ramona. Did something happen there as well?"

"I don't have time for this, Mom. I'm glad you and Dad are safe. I'll check in once I'm home, but it'll probably be a few days before they get the roads out here cleared."

"More like a week or two."

My brows pinched together as I read the error message on the screen. That was not what I was expecting. I moved the mouse, clicked a few boxes, and opened a new window.

"Are you still there?" she asked, pulling my attention back to her.

"Yeah, sorry. I was working on Ramona's computer for her."

"That's nice of you," she practically sang, the joy in her voice unmistakable.

"It's nothing. We're stranded here, and I have time to look at it for her. Nothing more than that."

"Okay, honey. If you say so."

"That's exactly what I'm saying."

I could feel my blood pressure rising. My mom always knew the buttons to push to get under my skin.

"I didn't mean anything bad by it. I simply meant that it was nice that you were helping her. I'm sure she appreciates it. She's such a nice girl. It wouldn't hurt to get to know—"

"Don't," I warned.

"Okay, fine. I'll let you go but call if you need anything."

"Will do."

"Love you."

"Love you too, Mom."

I hung up and set my phone on the counter next to the computer. I closed my eyes and tried to force down the feelings that were bubbling to the surface, too raw to deal with right now.

"Hey, are you okay?" Ramona asked, coming around the corner with both dogs following behind her.

"Yeah, I'm fine." I cleared my throat and pulled her computer closer to me, using it as a shield. "Just running another update, and hopefully, I can get this fixed for you."

"Thank you. I appreciate it. I was going to go look at options for dinner. Anything in the canned food category that sounds good to you?"

"I'm good with whatever," I answered, refusing to look at her.

I could feel her eyes on me but kept my focus on the screen so I didn't have to see the hurt look on her face. It had only been a few days, and she had already managed to get to me, which wasn't something that I could afford to have happen right now.

Nineteen

Ramona

Preston had been acting weird ever since he talked to his mom a few days ago. I didn't bother to ask him about it because he continuously made it clear that our arrangement included physically pleasuring each other and nothing beyond that. But from what I had overheard of his conversation with her, it didn't sound too bad, just that he was stranded here with me until the roads were cleared.

While I could assume that his mom was hinting at something happening between us, I couldn't figure out why Preston had such a cold reaction to it. I mean, we were literally fucking like bunnies, so *something* was going on. But there was an uneasiness in his tone when he spoke to her, and the way his shoulders knotted with tension once he hung up that made me think there was something else going on.

Since we hadn't talked about it, my brain had jumped down several rabbit holes, wondering if Preston was truly bothered to be stuck there with me. It was probably my own insecurities that stemmed from my relationship with Daniel that had me feeling like I wasn't worthy of Preston's attention. Not only that, but since Preston made it abundantly clear that this was a no strings attached hookup, I felt myself wondering if it would even happen if we weren't stranded together.

I couldn't help but question whether the chemistry was really there between us or if I had been imagining it. The way he could be so affectionate with me while we were having sex was so different from how he interacted with me when we weren't. It was like hot and cold, two very different extremes, and I hated it.

It had been almost a week since the storm first hit, and I had been focused on the news reports to see if they were going to work the roads out here any time soon. I was on edge today and found myself praying that they would get to us ASAP so Preston could leave and be on his way. Maybe then I could clear my head and sort out the confusion that was constantly fogging my brain these days.

I leaned forward and turned up the volume on the TV, listening to the news anchor go on about how they were being forced to take a break from clearing the roads because another storm was rolling in.

"Ugh," I groaned, flopping back in the chair and shaking my head.

"What's wrong?" Preston asked, walking in and looking from me to the TV.

"They're not going to get the roads cleared because there's another storm moving in. Guess we're stuck together even longer now. I'm sure you're happy about that."

His jaw tightened as he pulled his shoulders back.

"What's that supposed to mean?"

I could feel the tension in the air between us.

"Nothing." I shook my head and got up, walking past him to the sink.

He grabbed my hand and stopped me. I froze, refusing to look at him even though I could feel his eyes boring into me.

"What's that supposed to mean, Ramona?"

I rubbed my lips together, still unable to answer him. I didn't mean to say it, and now there was no way to backtrack and pretend that I hadn't.

"Talk to me. Tell me what's going on. If you don't want Rosco and me here anymore, I can figure out a way to get out of your hair."

"It's not that," I said softly. "I just know that *you're* anxious to get out of here. That's all."

"Why do you say that?"

"Because you've been acting different lately. Ever since you talked to your mom."

I lowered my voice, ashamed to admit that I had overheard their conversation—or at least one side of it.

He sucked in a deep breath and slowly let it out as he pulled me against his chest and wrapped his arms around me.

"I'm sorry. Sometimes my mom gets in my head, and it messes me up. I didn't mean to take it out on you."

"You don't have to apologize. It's not like we're in a relationship or anything. We're just friends who are fucking, right?"

There was a hint of uncertainty in my voice that I hated. I didn't want him to worry that I was hoping this would turn into more, but I also couldn't deny that I hadn't imagined the *what-ifs*.

"Is that what you still want?"

"I don't know," I whispered, pressing my cheek against his chest so he couldn't see me. "The sex is pretty great, so I don't necessarily want to stop that."

"But…"

And there it was. The elephant in the room that we both had been trying to avoid.

"But I can't lie and say that I don't feel like there could be something more than just sex between us. I like you, Preston, and I enjoy spending time with you, even if we're being forced into it."

His body stiffened against me, and I could tell he didn't feel the same way.

"I'm sorry, Ramona. I can't do more than just sex. I'm not a relationship guy. We talked about that before any of this ever started."

"I know. I just thought maybe you might change your mind if you felt the same—"

"I can't," he snapped, letting go of me and storming out of the kitchen.

<u>Twenty</u>

Preston

I tried to force the hurt look on Ramona's face out of my head as I struggled to find a way to burn off the excess energy that was coursing through me. Okay, so it wasn't energy—it was anxiety, and it was about to consume me if I didn't do something about it.

I knew that I owed it to her to talk about what happened earlier and why I couldn't be in a relationship, but no matter how hard I tried, I couldn't bring myself to do it. Instead, I'd been hiding in the play area with Rosco and Daisy, throwing a Frisbee so he could at least burn off some of his actual energy while Daisy cuddled beside me.

Things had gotten hard and out of place quicker than I had expected. But at the same time, I never expected to get stuck here with Ramona, nor did I anticipate that we would end up in bed together. If anything, I would have assumed I would have to spend my time stealthily dodging and avoiding her since all I had ever seen was her violent side.

To make matters even worse, there was another storm rolling in, and they hadn't even had a chance to clear the roads out here yet. I'd considered packing Rosco up, putting my truck in four-wheel drive, and taking my chances, but part of me worried about leaving Ramona alone by herself. Who knew how long it would take them to clear the roads after the next storm hit, and even worse, what if another one came along before they could? She would run out of supplies before she would have a chance to get more and end up in a bad spot.

That was the other thing that kept nagging at the back of my brain was that while I was here and essentially keeping her company for the most part, I was also utilizing said resources, and we were going to run out even faster at this rate. I felt like I was stuck in a tough position, no matter how I looked at it.

Or maybe I was just grumpy because I hated that I was feeling something for Ramona and knew that I shouldn't. It wasn't fair to her to lead her on and make her think I could give her something I couldn't.

After two hours had passed, Rosco gave up on me and passed out on the comfy bed next to Daisy, leaving me no excuse to continue to hang out in there. I could, but I might as well write the words *pussy* on my forehead because that was what I was acting like by continuing to avoid Ramona.

I gave them both a quick pat and then closed the door behind me as I left. I wasn't sure where Ramona was, but it wasn't like the place was that big that we could easily avoid each other unless I just hung out in the store, which felt weird. I took a deep breath and tried to calm my nerves before I faced her.

Just then, my phone started ringing. Saved by the bell. I glanced down and saw my brother's name on the screen.

"Hey, Kent," I answered.

"Mom got a fucking dog?"

I bit back a laugh and just shook my head.

"Yeah, only now *I* have a fucking dog. But I can't complain because he really is cute."

"I don't even know who you are," he teased. "Anyway, I was calling to check on you guys and see how things are going. I heard Whiskey Mountain got hit pretty hard."

"I'm actually stuck at a pet shop in Fallen Oaks. I came to get supplies for Rosco and didn't make it out before the storm blew in. By the time I was heading out, I couldn't even find my truck in the parking lot, it was that bad."

"Shit, that sucks." He whistled through his teeth. "But I'm sure the company isn't bad."

"Mom told you?" I groaned. I hated when she gossiped, especially when I was the one she was talking about.

"That and I know that the only pet shop in Fallen Oaks is Cool Cats, so I figured that's where you're at. Be careful, though. Ramona can be intense."

"Yeah, I've witnessed that a handful of times already. She threatened to rearrange some vital organs a time or two."

"Sounds like her." He laughed, and I realized how much I missed talking to him.

"How are things in Fallen Oaks? Did you guys get walloped too?"

"We got a couple of feet, but they've already cleared the main roads, so it's business as usual."

"That must be nice. I can't say that I missed this."

"Yeah, but we have something that Atlanta could never have."

"And what's that?" I asked, leaning against the wall.

"Family. We miss you, man."

I sucked in a breath and held it for a few beats before I let it out.

"I miss you guys too."

"You know you can always come back."

"I know. But it's like I told Mom, I'll never know what I'm capable of if I don't spread my wings and fly. There's a whole world out there full of possibilities. I don't want to be tied down and forced inside the constraints of small-town life where everyone knows your business whether you want them to or not."

"I know," he sighed. "I'm just saying, maybe it wouldn't be bad to plant some roots, meet someone, and then go exploring the world together."

"Now you sound just like Mom."

"Well, that's because she gets her wisdom from me."

"I'm gonna tell her you said that. She won't invite you the next time she makes meatloaf."

"Sure she will. I'll be her favorite child again because her other one will have abandoned her."

"I'm not abandoning anyone. I just don't want to be tied down and responsible for anyone else."

My neck tensed as I said the words, and I could tell by the silence on the other end of the line that he was trying to give me a moment.

"What happened with Shelby wasn't your fault."

"I don't have time for this," I muttered, ready to end the call.

"You never have time for it because you choose to live in a state of avoidance instead of choosing to talk about it and work through your grief."

"There's nothing to talk about!" I yelled, my voice echoing off the walls. "Shelby wanted more than I could give her. She made ultimatums and demands, and when I didn't give in to them, she took her own life! I can't be responsible for that again, Kent. I loved her, but it still wasn't enough. I couldn't save her, and that kills me every single day. *That's* why I choose not to be in relationships and refuse to commit. It's not that I don't *want* that kind of life for myself; it's that I don't deserve to have it, and I'm not willing to risk having this happen again."

"You guys were young. She was sick. It's not going to be the same. You won't know unless you let yourself try to—"

"I have to go. Talk to you later."

I didn't wait for him to reply before I hung up and shoved my phone into my pocket.

<u>Twenty-One</u>

Ramona

I was jamming out to Cardi B while painting my toenails on the bed when Preston walked into the bedroom, looking angry and upset. I dipped the brush into the bottle and then spread some of the mint green polish across my nail while I tried to give him some space as he paced back and forth in front of me.

"Is everything alright?" I finally asked, putting the brush back into the bottle and tightening it. I waved my hand across my toes, trying to get the polish to dry faster while I waited for his crazy eyes to focus on me.

"I need to go running," he blurted out.

"I don't think that's a good idea. The other storm is already moving in, and we're supposed to get 6-8 inches tonight. Plus, it's already dark outside, and you don't know the area."

He rubbed a hand along the back of his neck and let his head fall forward.

"What's wrong?"

"Nothing," he lied, shaking his head. "I'm used to being able to work out at home and burn off energy when needed. I feel like I'm going crazy, and there's no way to release this build-up."

I chewed my lower lip, nervous to even suggest what I was about to. We hadn't had sex in a few days, nor had we talked about his comment earlier about how he couldn't do the whole relationship thing. I had given him his space while I locked myself in the bathroom and cried for twenty minutes straight. It was what worked for me, but clearly, he needed something else. Something more physical.

"I know a way you can release some of the tension," I offered quietly.

He looked up and his eyes scanned over my body before reaching my face.

"I don't know if that's a good idea."

"Maybe. But it's also not a terrible one either." I shrugged as if it didn't matter to me either way, even though my center was already starting to get needy just looking at him and remembering all the delicious things he had done to my body before.

He stared at me a bit longer without saying anything, making me nervous.

"Look, I'm not proposing that we *make love*. I won't even ask to cuddle after we're done. I'm just saying you need a release, and I wouldn't complain about having an orgasm or two right now. It's a win-win."

"What about what you said earlier?" he prodded, folding his arms over his chest.

"I won't lie and say that I don't like you, but my world isn't going to end over you not returning the same feelings."

Something flashed quickly across his face as his jaw tightened.

"I'm just saying, I know how to do this with no strings attached. I'm not worried that if we have sex that I'm going to fall head over heels in love with you, Preston. Hell, at this point, I'm starting to reconsider and might threaten to stab you again. Who knows."

The corners of his lips started turning up.

I tilted my head to the side and studied him.

"Oh, is that your thing? Does my violent talk turn you on?"

"You have no fucking idea," he growled, crossing the room and tackling me on the bed.

I laughed as he tickled my sides, making me squirm until my legs fell open and he inserted himself in between.

"Nothing changes, this is still just sex between two friends," he said, pinching my chin between his fingers. "Got it?"

"Got it."

"Good. Now if you're a good girl, I'll make you squirt like you've been dying to."

Twenty-Two

Preston

I was guessing when I said that Ramona would be a squirter, but the way she clenched around my finger as I worked her g-spot told me I was right. I placed the palm of my hand down firmly on her lower stomach, creating as much pressure as possible as I used a come-hither motion with my fingers to bring her to climax.

Curse words spilled over her plump, beautiful lips as she tried to fight coming but couldn't. In just a short time, I already knew Ramona's body better than I knew my own and could tell that she was on the verge. I took my time and made sure I focused on where she needed me so I could finally give her the orgasm she had been craving.

"That was fucking amazing," she breathed, resting her arm over her head.

I wanted to say *you're fucking amazing* but bit back the compliment before it could be misinterpreted.

"Now that I've had mine let's get you yours."

She rolled over, reached across me, and grabbed the condom from the nightstand. Her breasts hung in my face, inviting me to pull a nipple into my mouth. I reached up and pulled her on top of me, devouring her as if I couldn't get enough. She giggled and then arched her back as I sucked harder, bordering on pushing her to her limit.

I took the condom from her fingers and continued sucking, only stopping for a brief second to open it before resuming my torture on her again. I rushed to sheath myself before grabbing her hips and lowering her onto my throbbing cock.

We both gasped as I slid inside her, stilling momentarily as I allowed her to adjust to my size. I loved how tight she was and never got over how well she wrapped so snuggly around me, squeezing and milking every drop of cum out of me when I came.

"Do you want me to ride the frustration out of you, or do you want to take me from behind and work it out yourself?"

"Ride me for a few minutes, and then I'll take you from behind."

"Sounds good," she said softly, closing her eyes and letting her head fall back as she moved her hips in the perfect rhythm.

I wanted to be in the moment and enjoy having sex with Ramona, but I couldn't. My conversation with Kent was playing over and over in my head, and all I could think about was Shelby and how I failed to see how much she was suffering.

I pinched my eyes closed and grabbed her hips, stopping her from moving.

"What's wrong?" she asked, concern heavy in her voice.

"Nothing. Let's change positions."

"Okay."

She climbed off me and waited beside me for me to tell her how I wanted her. The problem was that I didn't know. Nothing felt right. While I wanted to have her face down, ass up so I could pound my stress away, I couldn't stand the thought of using her like that. I wanted to look into her eyes and connect with her as we—fuck…

I slammed my hand down on the bed, startling her as she jumped back. I didn't bother to look at her before climbing down and heading to the bathroom to deal with my own shit.

My heart was pounding loudly as I stared at my reflection in the mirror, hating the man staring back at me.

How the fuck did I get to this point?

Up until now, I never had a problem having sex with someone and walking away from it without any emotions involved. But this was different, and I didn't understand it.

It had been four years since Shelby committed suicide and four years since I stopped believing I could have the kind of life I always wanted when I was younger. Her death rocked me in a way that I never saw coming and changed something so deep inside that I lost a huge piece of who I was.

What Shelby wanted from me wasn't that different than what any woman wants from a relationship. Love. Companionship. A best friend. A family. A house to call home. The only problem was that I had barely turned twenty-one and wasn't ready to settle down. I wanted to be wild and free, to explore the world before I was tied down with kids and a mortgage. I asked her to come along with me and go on these adventures together, but she said that wasn't the kind of life she wanted.

On our one-year anniversary, she gave me an ultimatum. Either propose to her and buy a house in the next six months, or she was going to walk away. I hated being forced into doing something I didn't feel in my heart, but I also didn't want to lose the first girl I had fallen in love with.

I gave in, and we looked at a few houses, but I should have known that Shelby would have already had one picked out. Everything had to be her way or nothing at all. We signed the papers, and she was happy until she wasn't.

One ultimatum led to another, and soon, she wasn't the same girl I had fallen in love with anymore. She was so obsessed with fitting in with small-town life and having what she thought she was supposed to that she didn't care about anything else. At one point, I wasn't sure that she even loved *me* anymore, but more so the idea of having the perfect husband/father for her dream life.

After a while, I started putting my foot down on her requests and decided that I couldn't go through with marrying someone

I didn't know. When I sat down and broke off the engagement, she couldn't handle it. She threatened me with everything she could, but I ignored her and walked away. That was the last time I saw Shelby before she took her life in the house we were supposed to turn into our home.

Twenty-Three

Ramona

I sat in the bed, unsure of what to do. Sure, I had questioned whether I was good in bed after Daniel and I broke up, but I'd never had someone walk away during sex. This was a first, and it left me feeling rattled and insecure.

The clock on the wall ticked at an annoyingly slow pace while I waited for Preston to come back. After twenty minutes, I decided that I wasn't going to sit around and wait for him anymore, so I got up, got dressed, and made my way to the kitchen. I knew better than to eat through my emotions, but I also couldn't just punch him in the throat like I really wanted to.

It wasn't that I was afraid of him or feared the thought of being stuck here alone with him. It was that something had changed deep inside with how I felt about him, and it no longer felt right to want to punch him. And that pissed me off even more.

How dare he squirm his way through the deep layers I put up and work his way into my heart, only to turn around and try to break it.

I slapped some peanut butter onto a slice of bread and spread it aggressively with a butter knife before plunging it into the jelly and scooping some out.

"Why do I have a feeling that the peanut butter is me?" Preston teased from the doorway, casually leaning against the frame with his ankles crossed and arms folded over his chest.

I arched an eyebrow and glared at him from the side of my eye without giving him my full attention. I wasn't *technically* mad at him, but I was feeling vulnerable, and *that* made me angry. I set the knife down on the counter and put the sandwich together on a plate before grabbing the nearly empty bag of Cool Ranch Doritos from the cabinet.

We were going through supplies quicker than I had anticipated, but then again, I had only accounted for myself being stuck here and not having a whole other human to feed as well. The news said there would be a small break between storms, but they advised not going out if you didn't have to. Normally I wouldn't risk it, but running out of chips was literally a crisis that I couldn't afford right now.

"I know that you're mad at me, and you have every right to be," he said with a sigh, not bothering to move from his place. Probably because I was still standing close to the knife block and had a menacing look on my face as I angrily shoved the sandwich into my mouth and took a huge bite.

"I'm not mad," I bit out as I chewed. "I'm irritated. With you. And whatever the fuck that was in the bedroom a few minutes ago." I stopped and looked at my watch. "Or half an hour ago if we're keeping track."

He tipped his head back and exhaled heavily through his nose before pushing off the wall and heading toward me. I swallowed hard, trying to ignore how my body felt as he got closer and instead focused on the anger still billowing up inside. I needed it to keep fueling me right now because if I let my guard down even a little bit, I would fall even harder for him than I had already.

"I'm sorry that you're irritated. I don't blame you. And when you're ready, I'd like to explain what happened."

"Oh, I fucking know what happened," I growled. "Do you think you're the first guy who's walked away and not wanted to fuck me? Spoiler alert!! It happened all the time with Daniel. It's nothing new, I guess I just expected more from you since you *seemed* interested in the first place."

He closed the distance between us and took the sandwich from my hands before slapping it down on the counter beside us. My eyes widened with fury. He was lucky that it was just the sandwich and that he didn't mess with my chips. That would have been a war that he wasn't ready for.

"I didn't walk away because I didn't want to fuck you, Ramona. I would have loved nothing more than to be balls deep inside you, feeling that tight pussy grip my cock the way she loves to as I pounded it."

A bead of sweat dotted my brow as my temperature skyrocketed with his dirty words.

"I walked away because I couldn't stand the thought of using you for sex. Or treating you as if you were nothing to me just so I could get off and relieve some stress. That's why I walked away, Ramona. Because you deserve better than that."

"But I said it was okay," I objected, my mouth moving faster than my brain.

Don't sound so desperate, stupid.

"I know, but my head wasn't in the right place, and I couldn't bring myself to do it. Believe it or not, I've enjoyed spending time with you while we've been snowed in together. I've never once treated you as just some girl I'm fucking, even though that was the original plan—just friends with benefits. But I think we both know that this is more than that, even if we didn't plan for it to be."

He rubbed his thumb against my cheek as his body pressed harder against mine, pinning me against the counter.

"But I'm frustrated because no matter how much I want to feel those feelings with you, I can't. It's not something I can allow to happen, and I'm sorry for that. I don't want to hurt you by leading you on or making this into something more than it should be, but I also can't seem to keep myself from wanting to be around you. So, it's putting me in a complicated position where I don't know what to do. The only thing I do know is that I'm not willing to treat you like you're nothing more than a piece of ass to work my stress out with."

"When you put it like that, it makes it kinda hard to stay mad at you," I mumbled, chewing my lower lip.

"Well, I wouldn't blame you if you did. I acted like an asshole, and I'm sorry for that. I've had a lot weighing on my mind today, and I let it get the best of me."

I leaned into him and rested my head against his chest. His arms wrapped around me, holding me tightly.

"Can I ask you a question?" I mumbled, not wanting to lift my head to speak to him.

"Anything."

"What's the deal with you and commitment? I mean, I'm not asking you to be my boyfriend or anything, so don't freak out. I'm just curious why you're so against it."

His body stiffened beneath me, and I knew that he wasn't going to tell me.

"It's a long story," he finally said. "One that I don't want to get into right now. Why don't we go hang out and watch a movie or something?"

I decided not to keep pressing and gave in. We grabbed my sandwich, a handful of snacks, and some drinks, then crawled into bed to watch a romcom he picked, though I knew it was because he was trying to make me happy. For just a moment, I allowed myself to cuddle next to him and pretend as though we didn't have any cares in the world.

Twenty-Four

Preston

"Sit. Down. Stay." I did all of the same hand motions that Ramona did but Rosco looked at me like I was an idiot and refused to follow any of the commands.

"Why does he hate me?" I asked her, turning to see her working with Daisy on some light exercise. The dogs were going as stir-crazy as we were with not being able to go outside in almost two weeks.

Another big storm came on the heels of the first one, dropping another four feet of snow in the process. That wouldn't have been bad except that no one had been out on this stretch of road to clear it so we could get out. The temperatures rarely made it above freezing so nothing melted off either.

"He doesn't hate you." She laughed and stood beside me. "Sit."

She lifted her hand and made the same motion she had taught me, and sure enough, Rosco sat down for her.

"Good boy!"

I rolled my eyes and planted my hands on my hips as he took the treat from her fingers and wagged his tail excitedly.

"Okay, he's officially your dog now. He likes you better anyway," I joked.

"Well, he has spent a lot of time here recently, so I wouldn't be surprised if he thought this was his home."

"I'm going to have a hard time getting him situated when I finally go to mine, aren't I?"

She shrugged and tried not to laugh.

"I told my mom I didn't want a damn dog," I muttered. "He's going to eat my couch in retaliation because I took him away from Daisy."

"That I wouldn't doubt. They do seem to love each other." Ramona looked down at the dogs with a peaceful look on her face, like that of a mother seeing her child fall in love for the first time.

"Love is overrated."

My words slipped out before I could stop them, but thankfully, Ramona didn't say anything.

It had been six days since we'd discussed what happened in the bedroom. She hadn't tried to approach the topic of my fear of commitment since then, and I hadn't allowed anything physical to happen between us either. It was as if we'd drawn a line in the sand, and now both of us were scared to cross it. Instead, we just enjoyed our time together as friends, which seemed to be something neither of us minded.

"They really need some fresh air," Ramona said randomly, staring down at the pups who were looking back up at her. "I bet we could clear a path out front and let them out for a bit."

"Do you think the snow is blocking the door, though?"

"Only one way to find out." She grinned devilishly and winked.

I helped her get the pups leashed and followed her to the front door, refraining from laughing as she tried to force it open by throwing herself into it.

"Want me to try?" I offered, extending Rosco's leash to her.

"Be my guest."

It was already unlocked, but there was definitely a massive clump of snow blocking the door on the other side. I mimicked her, throwing my weight at it a few times until it finally budged. A gust of cold air whipped past us through the crack as I shoved myself into it until it finally opened enough so I could squeeze through. There was a shovel by the door, so I grabbed it and went out first, squeezing myself through the small opening and clearing the path for them to come out.

"It's freaking cold out here," Ramona complained, wrapping her arms tightly around her waist while gripping the leashes tightly. She'd recommended giving them a decent amount of leeway so they could stretch and explore without getting too far ahead of us and ending up in dangerous territory.

I offered to take Rosco from her, but she waved me off and said she had them. Since we were finally able to get outside, I took the time to clear a path from the door to the parking lot and cleared off the layers of snow from our cars. It was a lot of work, but the physical activity made it easy to ignore how blistering cold it was outside.

Ramona was walking the dogs in the path that I cleared, allowing them to stop and sniff the trees that lined the edge of the parking lot without getting too deep in snow since it would literally swallow Daisy whole. I cleared my truck and felt giddy and excited that I could finally see it again. Aside from the freezing temperatures, it seemed the worst of the storms had already hit, and I prayed that we wouldn't get any more snow so I could get back to my house and, even more important, back to reality.

I moved over to Ramona's car and started working on clearing the snow from around it. I was just about done making a path when she turned and scanned the area, trying to find me. I lifted my hand and waved, giving her a smile as I stepped to the side to brush the snow from the top of her car.

"Preston! Watch out!" she yelled, but it was too late.

I felt my ankle twist into an unnatural position as I rolled it and fell into a large pothole.

<u>Twenty-Five</u>

Ramona

"Keep the ice on it," I said, pushing the bag back over Preston's ankle.

"It hurts."

"I know. That's because it's swollen. It's like double the size of your other one. Now ice it."

"You're so bossy."

"You know it. Now stop arguing with me and do as I say."

I stood up and walked over to the shelf I had dedicated to medical stuff in my pantry. I leaned on my tiptoes, trying to find anything that could help. I had him resting in the kitchen with his foot propped up on a pillow on a chair across from him, but I knew that I needed to find something to wrap it with, or it was going to keep swelling.

He could walk on it—though not very well—so I didn't think it was broken. Definitely sprained, which was something I knew a thing or two about, given how clumsy Maggie was and all of the sprains I had helped her tend to throughout the years.

"I'm fine. You don't need to go through all this trouble," he said, shifting in his chair.

I turned to find him lifting the ice bag off his foot and scowling. He lowered his eyes and put it back, then looked away.

"I need to go to the store," I mumbled, closing the cabinet door and pulling my phone out of my pocket. Rosco and Daisy were hanging out with us in the kitchen, so I kept an eye out for them so I didn't trip as I typed out a text message to Maggie.

Me: Hey, do you remember what all we use when you sprain your ankle? I know you like soaking in an Epsom salt bath, but what else really helps? Tylenol? Ibuprofen? That wrap stuff?

I waited a few minutes for her to reply, knowing that her phone was likely already in her hands.

Maggie: What happened? How did you get hurt?

Me: It's not me. It's Preston.

Maggie: What kind of dirty sex moves were you guys doing that hurt him? Did he sprain his penis?

Me: No, Maggie. He didn't sprain his penis.

Me: We decided to take the dogs outside for some fresh air, and he stepped into a pothole while trying to clear the snow from my car.

Maggie: That's so nice of him!

Me: It is, but I need you to focus on the part I actually need help with. He twisted his ankle, and it's really swollen.

Maggie: Epsom salt

    Ibuprofen

    Reusable ice packs

    Flavored lube

    Compression wrap

Me: What is the flavored lube for?

Maggie: Because you're going to owe him one hell of a blow job for clearing all that snow for you and then another one to nurse him back to health.

Me: You're ridiculous. You know that, right?

Maggie: (shrugging emoji)

Maggie: Hey, while I have you, did you get the email that I sent?

Me: No, I haven't been online in a while. Preston is working on fixing my computer, and I didn't want to rush him. Apparently, it was really messed up, but he's almost done. Why?

Maggie: It's nothing that can't wait. But let's talk when you do read it, okay?

Me: Sounds good. I'm heading out to the store before the next storm moves in.

Maggie: Please be safe and let me know when you get there and back.

Me: I will.

I shoved my phone back into my pocket and then took the pups to the play area so they could rest and use the bathroom without bothering Preston while I was gone. I hadn't told him I was leaving yet, but it wasn't like he was in any position to stop me.

I made a pitstop in the bedroom and put on my heavy jacket, thick gloves, and snow boots, then ensured I had my phone, wallet, and keys in my pocket. I didn't need anything to slow me down and knew I had limited time to get there and back before it was too late. It was a gamble, but I was willing to go for it.

"Hey, I'm going to run out to the store real quick. Do you need anything while I'm there?" I asked as nonchalantly as possible.

His eyes whipped up, dark gray irises burning into me.

"You're not going out in that," he hissed, nodding to the TV where the local weatherman was pointing to a greenscreen illuminated with dark blue spots that indicated the storm that was rolling in.

"I don't have a choice, Preston. You need things for your ankle that I don't have here."

"My ankle is fine. There, problem solved."

I placed my hands on my hips and leveled him with a look.

"No, it's not. And we're almost out of other supplies that we need."

"Like what?"

"Umm, food. Toilet paper. Batteries. And you could do with an extra change or two of clothes so you don't have to keep lounging in my robe while you wait for your laundry to be done."

"Fine, I'm coming with you," he grunted, trying to push himself out of the chair.

I reached my hand out and stopped him.

"No, you're not. You need to rest. Keep your ankle elevated and ice it. I'll be back before you know it. If you think of anything else that you need, text me."

I didn't wait for him to answer before I turned and rushed out of the kitchen. I hated going out in this kind of weather, but right now, I didn't have a choice. I pulled my beanie down over my ears and lifted my scarf to cover my mouth as I pushed the door open and got whipped in the face with a frigid gust of wind.

I made sure the door closed behind me before I climbed into my car and headed into town, praying that the roads would be clear enough to get me there and back safely.

Twenty-Six

Preston

Ramona had been gone for an hour, and I anxiously waited for her to return so I knew she was safe. She had texted me when she got there and then again ten minutes later to ask me which brand of frozen pizza I preferred for dinner tonight.

I tried to keep myself calm and not freak out about her taking her sweet ass time at the store as if she had no worries in the world. Her computer was still sitting on the table where I had left it yesterday while it did some updates. Since I had nothing better to do and was trying to rest like she asked, I pulled it over and turned it on so I could fix it while she was out. It would be a nice surprise for her to come home and it be completely done.

I waited while it started up, smiling when her Vin Diesel wallpaper filled the screen. I cleaned up a lot on her computer and eliminated most of the programs that came up every time her computer started since she didn't need them. Once everything was finished loading, I opened a new browser window and was surprised when her email automatically opened on the screen.

I was about to click the button to minimize it when a message caught my attention.

From: askmags@spillthebeans.com

To: rwatkins@coolcats.com

Date: October 17, 2022, 5:47 am

Subject: Is this about you?

Hey! This email came into Spill The Beans, and every time I read it, it feels oddly familiar. I don't want to jump to

assumptions but read it and let me know if you think so too. Love you!

Dear Ask Mags,

I've read your blog for years, and you've always been able to help other people, so I thought maybe you could help me too. You see, I've been madly in love with my best friend for over a year now and have never had the courage to tell her.

Before, I couldn't because she was with this guy who never treated her right. They started dating off and on in high school, and before I could shoot my shot, they moved in together.

They broke up a few months ago, and I was trying to give her time before I rushed in and told her how I felt, but now she's shacked up with someone else during the worst storms to date in Montana. I feel like every time I try to build the courage up to tell her, something gets in my way.

I want her to be happy, and part of me thinks that I'm the person who can do that for her if I could just get the chance. I know she's not meant to be with the guy she's stuck with right now because she could barely stand him before this happened. But I heard them doing stuff the other day, and now I can't get it out of my head that maybe she's just getting with him because she needs rebound sex to get over her ex.

Should I assume that's all this is and keep waiting for the right time to tell her that I'm in love with her? Or am I risking losing my best friend by crossing that line with her?

Heartbroken and lonely in Montana

I read the email a second time and hated that it did, in fact, sound a little familiar. Ramona had talked about her best friends—Maggie and Dylan, a handful of times, but I never got the vibe from her that she felt anything more than friendship for Dylan, unlike what he seemed to be feeling in this email if it was him.

I closed it out and told myself that I would pretend that I hadn't seen it. It wasn't any of my business, and I shouldn't have read it, to begin with. Just as I was about to close the email, another one popped up from the same sender. There was no stopping me this time as I clicked on it immediately and read it.

From: askmags@spillthebeans.com

To: rwatkins@coolcats.com

Date: October 21, 2022, 11:18 am

Subject: Holy Shit. This is about you.

Did you know that Dylan was in love with you?!? It honestly never even crossed my mind, so I feel as blindsided by this as I'm sure you're going to, unless you already knew and never told me (you bitch!). Also, I wonder if he's sending the messages through Spill The Beans hoping you'll see them and know it's him. Maybe this way, he doesn't have to risk facing rejection if he tells you to your face. I don't know. What are you going to do?

Dear Ask Mags,

Do you know what's really unfair about the whole "friends with benefits" thing? When it's the wrong friend that they're having benefits with.

I'm so lost and don't know what to do. I've dated my share of women and have plenty of experience with relationships, but I've never been in the position of wanting someone who doesn't even know how I feel about them.

How do you cross that line and make them see you in a new light? Because I'll be honest, I feel like I'm invisible to her as anything other than a friend.

But the problem is that now that I know how I feel about her, I feel like her friendship isn't enough for me anymore. I want her love and companionship, and need to find a way to confess my true feelings to her.

She doesn't even know how amazing she is, and I want to be the one to show her. To tell her every day how much I love and adore her while helping her chase her dreams and build the life that she wants. I want to show her that with a little hard work and dedication, she can have the doggy daycare she's always wanted while being a successful, independent business owner.

I'm going out of my mind thinking about her being stuck in this storm with some guy who doesn't even know her, let alone deserves to have her attention. I need a way to get through to her, to show her with some grand gesture that I'm the man she needs. The one who will give her everything she could ever want and more.

More Than Friends In Montana

I exhaled heavily and pushed the computer away, regretting that I stooped so low and read her emails.

<u>Twenty-Seven</u>

Ramona

I had two carts stacked full of groceries and necessities to get us through a few more weeks of being cooped up together. Sure, Preston could technically leave and go home since I was able to get out and get to a store, but I hated the thought of him being at home by himself with a hurt ankle. I knew that his parents had moved to Whiskey Mountain a few years ago from our recent conversations; however, I didn't know whether or not they lived close enough to go by and help him if needed during the storm.

I had taken the liberty to grab some new clothes for Preston and guessed his size since I wasn't willing to text him and ask. He was already cranky enough that I was out at the store, so I didn't want to make it worse before I got home. I also stocked up on double the amount of Cool Ranch Doritos I might need, just in case.

The store was busy with everyone stocking up again before the next storm hit. It wasn't uncommon to get a lot of snow in the winter, but the amount we were getting right now definitely wasn't normal, and everyone was having a hard time preparing for it.

After I paid, a few of the teens who worked there helped me get it all loaded into my car, filling my trunk and most of the back seat and floor space. Once I was situated, I sent a text message to Maggie and one to Preston to let them know I was headed back.

The snow had started falling, but thankfully it wasn't thick enough to blind me as I drove through it. I made sure to stick to a safe speed limit and gripped the steering wheel tighter as I headed straight into a thick cloud of white.

I tried my best not to panic and used my voice commands to make a hands-free phone call.

"Hey, where are you?" Preston answered, his tone strained.

"I'm about a few miles away from the store, heading back, but I'm stuck in a whiteout and can't see anything around me."

"Fuck," he muttered quietly, but I could still hear it.

"Okay, stay on the phone with me and go as slow as you can, okay?"

"Okay," I replied, my lower lip trembling.

It felt like I was stuck in this alternate universe, unable to see anything around me and having no idea if I was even still on the road or if I'd veered off.

"Can you see anything around you?"

"No," I whispered, trying to keep from crying.

"Hey, it's going to be okay."

I nodded though he couldn't see me.

"What did you buy at the store?" he asked, changing the subject.

I gripped the steering wheel tighter and tried to focus on what he was asking.

"What?"

"What did you get at the store besides frozen pizza and Cool Ranch Doritos?"

"How did you know I got more Doritos?"

My cheeks stung from the cold as they attempted to smile. I had turned the heater up to full blast before I left the store, and warm air was blowing directly at me, but it wasn't enough to counter the freezing temperature around me.

"Because I saw that you were almost out, and I know how crazy you get about them."

"I do not get crazy!" I laughed and it felt good. My shoulders relaxed a tiny bit, but I maintained my death grip on the steering wheel.

"Yes, you do. You threatened to cut me when I asked for one the other night."

"Because you tried to take the whole bag!"

"How else was I supposed to know which one I wanted?"

"There weren't that many to choose from," I objected.

"Because you had already devoured them and didn't think to save any for me."

"I told you from the start that they were off-limits and mine."

"It would have been nice if I had known the chip rule before I got stuck with you," he teased. "I could have made sure to have plenty of my own."

"Why? What kind of chips would you have stocked up on?"

"Funyuns."

"What?! Out of all the chips, that's what you're going with?"

"Hell yeah, they're the best."

I scrunched my nose.

"Nope. No way. They're too oniony."

"That's the best part."

"Well, I wouldn't have kissed you if you smelled like an onion all the time, so I guess it's a good thing you didn't have them."

My insides felt squishy as I processed my words and wondered if he was doing the same thing based on the silence on the other end.

"I do have a toothbrush, you know," he said, his tone more relaxed now as well.

"It wouldn't have been enough," I joked, relieved that some of the thick snow around me was thinning out, and I could see the faint outline of the road ahead of me again. "I can see the road again."

"Good, that's really good."

I heard him breathe out a sigh of relief.

"Do you see any mile markers? I want to keep track of where you're at."

"I can't see them. They're already covered in a few inches of snow."

"Okay, that's alright. We'll just have to go based on how long you've been driving then."

"Yeah, but I haven't been doing the speed limit. The store is about half an hour away from Cool Cats, but it took me forty-five minutes to get out here earlier before the storm rolled in. My guess is it might be an hour or two before I make it home with the speed I'm going."

"It's okay. We'll just keep talking. Just stay on the phone with me so I know you're okay."

"Now who's the bossy one?" I joked.

Suddenly my tires hit a patch of ice at the same time that a strong gust of wind came out of nowhere. Instinctively, I grabbed the wheel and gripped it harder as I removed my foot from the accelerator. I tapped the brakes gently and tried to steer in the opposite direction of where I was skidding, but another gust of wind gave me another push.

"Shit!" I exclaimed, panic fully settling in.

"What's wrong?"

"I hit a patch of ice, and the wind keeps pushing me off the road. I'm losing control!"

"Stay calm and focus, Ramona. Don't slam on the brakes and try to steer away from the skid."

"I am. It's not working!"

Another massive gust of wind caught the car at the right angle, sending it spinning off the side of the road and straight into a telephone pole. I heard a loud thud before my head whipped back, and the airbag exploded in my face.

Twenty-Eight

Preston

"Ramona! Ramona!" I screamed into the phone, my body going ice cold when she didn't reply. All I could hear was the sound of her horn blaring after the car hit something hard then the line went dead as the call disconnected.

I got up, ignoring the pain that shot up and radiated through my leg. I could walk on it so it wasn't broken, which was all that mattered right now. I rushed as quickly as I could into her bedroom, grabbed my keys and wallet, then pulled on my coat before running out the door and into my truck.

I worked on clearing the snow as quickly as I could. I didn't need much—just enough to see in front of me so I could get to her before it was too late. Thoughts of Shelby floated through my head, and I felt this instant stabbing pain in my heart when I thought about losing Ramona. Needing someone to get me out of my head, I grabbed my phone from my pocket, found my brother's name, and pressed send.

"Hey, what's up?" he answered on the third ring.

"Tell me that I'm not an unlucky bastard who loses everyone he loves."

"What's going on?"

"I need to know that I'm not some source of bad luck and that I don't kill everything that I love."

"You haven't killed me…"

I could almost see the stupid smug smile on his face.

"Well, that's not the best starting point. That would mean that I love your ugly face."

"Which you do. And you haven't killed Mom. Or Dad."

"Okay."

I wrapped my fingers around the steering wheel and focused on the road as the snow blew heavily across the highway in front of me.

"You still haven't answered me. What's going on?"

"Ramona went to the store to get supplies and I was on the phone with her while she was heading back. She hit a whiteout and couldn't see anything around her for a few miles, then it cleared up, but she hit a patch of ice and a gust of wind forced her car off the side of the road."

"Oh, shit. Is she okay?"

"I don't know. I'm headed to go find her now."

"Why would she go out in this weather to begin with?"

"I twisted my ankle earlier, and she went out for supplies. Plus, we were almost out of food and other necessities."

"How did you twist your ankle?"

"I was shoveling snow from the parking lot while she took the dogs for a walk. I didn't see a pothole and fell in it."

"Why didn't you just take her to your house instead of letting her go to the store? You guys would have been better off there since they will have the roads cleared within a few hours."

I swallowed hard, the bile rising in my throat.

"I don't take women to my house. You know that."

"So you would rather let her risk her life to go get stuff you need instead of sucking it up and allowing her into your space?"

"It sounded like an okay idea at the time. In all fairness, I told her not to go and tried to go with her when she insisted."

"And now?"

"Now I worry that I've killed another woman that I've allowed myself to fall in love with."

A single tear slid down my cheek, and I didn't bother to brush it away as the cold sting burned my cheek.

"You didn't kill Shelby. You know that. And you didn't kill Ramona."

"We don't even know if she's okay. I tried calling her back several times, but it went to voicemail."

"That doesn't mean that she's dead."

I released a shaky breath and pushed my foot down on the accelerator, more desperate to get to her than ever.

"Shelby was sick, Preston. You remember her mother telling you that. She had suffered from depression for years and refused to get help. It also wasn't the first time that she tried to commit suicide. You were not responsible for her death."

"Then why does it feel like I lose everyone I love?"

There was a heavy pause.

"Wait, did you just say that you love Ramona?" he questioned, ignoring mine.

"Yeah," I sighed heavily. "I think I do."

"You think, or you know?"

"I gotta go," I said, distracted by the sound of a car horn blaring in the distance.

Twenty-Nine

Ramona

My head throbbed as I tried to lean back and get the airbag out of my face. I tried swatting at it, but it wouldn't budge, and I didn't have the energy to keep trying. It was freezing, and my body was having a hard enough time staying warm.

I reached around for my phone but couldn't find it. It must have flown across the seat with the impact of hitting the telephone pole. The call with Preston had disconnected, and since I couldn't reach it to call for help, I knew that I would have to hope that he had heard the accident and would call for me.

I didn't know how much time had passed, but I was getting tired, my eyelids fluttering closed no matter how hard I tried to keep them open. It was exhausting but resting felt much better than fighting to stay awake.

I couldn't feel my feet or anything else for that matter, the freezing temperature numbing me from the inside out. Not having any other choice, I closed my eyes and allowed myself to rest.

I knew it must have been a dream when I was floating on a raft in a shimmery blue pool, the warmth from the sun beating down on my perfectly tanned skin. I lifted my tropical drink to my lips, pulling in a refreshingly cold sip that tasted delicious.

There was music floating around me, some pop song with a fun dance beat. I swayed my hips from side to side, moving with it until suddenly there was this deep base sound that didn't match the tempo. I frowned, irritated with whoever was interrupting my good vibes and dance party.

"RAMONA!"

I tried to open my eyes, but they were too heavy.

"RAMONA!"

I could hear sirens in the distance as the cold came over my body again. I pushed as hard as I could to wake up, but nothing happened.

Thirty

Ramona

"She'll need to stay overnight for monitoring," the doctor said to Preston and me as he stood beside me, squeezing my hand. "We'll let her rest, but if she needs anything, just push the call button, and we'll be right in."

"Thank you," he said, smiling politely at her, then turning to me after she left. "Hey, how are you feeling?"

"Like shit," I answered honestly, wincing as I tried to sit up more in the hospital bed. "How did you find me?"

"I heard the car horn and followed the sound. Then I called 911, and they were able to get to you and bring you to the hospital. You gave all of us one hell of a scare."

"I'm sorry," I whispered, my throat parched. "I didn't mean to."

"I know."

"You're supposed to be off your ankle and resting it," I scolded, pointing to it as I took the cup of ice chips from him.

He pulled a seat over and placed it as close to the side of the bed as possible.

"I don't care about my ankle, Ramona. I care about you."

"I know, but you shouldn't have been driving with it injured. You don't have the strength that you need to do things like brake or climb up into that big ol' truck of yours."

"I couldn't give a fuck about any of that. When I heard you get in that accident, my heart stopped. I couldn't breathe. I was so terrified of losing you that nothing else mattered at that moment. Come hell or high water, I was going to get to you and save you because there's no way in hell that I could stand to lose you."

A tear slid down my cheek as I heard the emotion behind his words.

"Do you know the reason why I said I couldn't be in a committed relationship?"

I shook my head, too terrified to answer because I didn't want him to stop talking. He was finally opening up to me.

"I was engaged to someone who I loved very much. But she wanted things that I couldn't give her. She started to rely on me for her happiness and blamed me for her unhappiness. One day, I had enough and called off our engagement."

He stopped for a moment and lowered his head between his hands, his shoulders tensing up.

"She committed suicide after that."

"Oh my God," I gasped, clutching my hand to my heart. "Preston, I'm so sorry!"

"Thank you," he whispered. "I don't like talking about it because I don't like to relive that part of my life. For so long, I've carried the guilt of her death with me and have allowed it to consume my thoughts of happiness. I've been so focused on keeping myself detached from everyone that I didn't know what to do when I started to feel something for you. It scared the shit out of me because I didn't want to lose you too."

"I'm not going anywhere, Preston. I promise."

"I almost lost you today, Ramona. And that scared the shit out of me. I've never fought harder for anything before in my life. Not knowing whether you were alive or dead was what motivated me to push through my pain and fear and to get to you. I couldn't save Shelby, but I would die trying if it meant I could save you."

"I'm so sorry that I put you through all of this. I should have just stayed home and figured out a way to make do until it was safe to go to the store."

"Don't be. I hate that you were in an accident, but I also feel that it put everything in perspective for me. Feeling like I could lose you pushed me to realize I wasn't afraid of falling in love anymore because I was already there. Now I was afraid of losing it all and had something to fight for. You woke up a part of me that's been dead inside for four years."

"I don't know what to say," I stammered, overwhelmed with emotion.

"You don't have to say anything. Just know that I love you, and I'll go to the ends of the earth to prove it to you. I know I might have some competition, but I'm willing to go after what I want."

My brows pulled together in confusion.

"What are you talking about? What competition?"

His phone started ringing in his pocket. He pulled it out and slid his finger across the screen to answer it.

"I need to take this real quick, but you might want to talk to Maggie and check your emails."

Thirty-One

Preston

"Are you sure you guys have time to do that? I know you have a lot going on with the B&B." I leaned against the wall while my brother confirmed a few details with his friend.

"Yeah, we can get out there in a few weeks once the roads are clear. It shouldn't take more than a day or two," Kent said.

"Perfect. Just email me the invoice, and I'll get it paid."

"Na, it's on the house."

"No, it's not. You can't just come do work for me for free. Besides, it's for Ramona, not me."

"Sure we can. Someone finally broke the spell and made my brother fall in love again. There's no price to put on that. I'll check in later."

"Alright, thanks, man."

I didn't bother to argue with him because Kent was riding an emotional high right now, and I wasn't going to be the one to bring him down.

I waited for the doctor to finish up with Ramona before I went back into the room. I smiled as we passed each other, pulled the chair beside her bed, and sat down.

"What did he say?"

"He thinks I can go home tomorrow at the earliest, possibly Friday at the latest. They're waiting for a few more tests before he feels comfortable clearing me. Maggie said that Dylan is going over to Cool Cats to take care of the pups for us and lock up when he leaves."

"Did she say anything else about Dylan?" I asked nervously, not wanting to admit that I had read her emails, but I also wasn't going to start a new relationship built off of lies and mistrust.

She swallowed hard and folded her hands in her lap.

"She told me about the emails to Spill The Beans and read them to me over the phone."

I nodded and pressed my tongue to the roof of my mouth to keep from interrupting her as she continued.

"I'm guessing you saw the emails, and that's why you mentioned the whole *competition* thing earlier. But honestly, Preston, I had no idea that Dylan felt that way. It's never been on my radar, and he never indicated his feelings for me. It's totally one-sided, and I don't feel the same way about him. I love him as a friend, but that's it."

"Are you going to talk to him about it?"

"Yeah," she sighed sadly. "I need to. I just hope that it doesn't ruin our friendship."

"I think as long as you don't threaten him with any acts of violence, you'll be fine."

I winked playfully.

"Oh, don't worry. I save those for you," she teased, returning the wink.

I stepped out of the room to give her some privacy while she took another phone call from Maggie. Everyone was happy to hear that Ramona was okay and were either dropping by to see her or calling and blowing up her phone with text messages.

While she was busy, I took the time to reach out to the mayor to start discussing options regarding clearing the roads on that stretch of highway. This wasn't the first time that Ramona had been impacted by bad weather, but I wanted to make sure that it was the last. I also reached out to Maggie's boyfriend, Owen, who handled all the commercial realty in Whiskey Mountain, to talk about building in that area. If there were more businesses and housing options out there, maybe it would be given the same amount of attention as Whiskey Mountain when it came to road safety.

It felt good to get the ball rolling on stuff that would help Ramona, and I didn't bother to ignore the butterflies that were swarming in my stomach when I thought about having a future with Ramona.

Thirty-Two

Ramona

One Week Later

It took longer to get discharged from the hospital than I had wanted, but I was relieved that Dylan had stuck around Cool Cats to take care of the pets while I was away. I knew I still needed to sit down and talk with him, but I just wasn't ready yet.

Things had been chaotic ever since the accident, and I was still trying to get used to the fact that Preston had yet to leave my side. He'd been sleeping on a pull-out couch bed that looked anything but comfortable. I offered for him to sleep in the bed with me, but given that I had two broken ribs and a broken arm, he quickly declined.

By the time I got released and we made it to Cool Cats, Dylan had already left—no doubt avoiding me since I was with Preston. It was nice to be home and even more of a pleasant surprise that someone had arranged to have everything in my car delivered here before it was taken to a repair shop in Whiskey Mountain.

I walked around slowly, enjoying the feeling of being home as I made my way to the back to check on Daisy and Rosco. Preston led the way, making sure that he had hold of Rosco before I went in so he couldn't jump up on me. The pups were doing well, and I was thankful that Dylan had been able to come by and take care of everything.

We went to the bedroom, and I laughed at how Lily was spread across the bed as if she owned the place. She was the most independent cat I'd ever seen, and I could imagine she gave Dylan the cold shoulder while he was here since she never warmed up to anyone. I went over to check on Louie and smiled when I saw Lily climb down as soon as she saw Preston walk in. She leaned into him as she rubbed herself against his leg and purred.

Preston grinned before bending down to scoop her into his arms. I was surprised by their interaction, but then again, I shouldn't have been given how much time Preston had spent here recently. Aside from Daniel, Lily didn't really know anyone else, and even then, she never acted like she liked Daniel the way she was with Preston right now.

I dropped some food into Louie's tank and did a quick check to make sure he had everything he needed. The humidity level was perfect, and the UV light had been turned on so he didn't need anything from me at the moment.

I sat down on the bed and took a moment to catch my breath. I was still exhausted and couldn't wait to sleep in my own bed tonight.

"You doing okay?" Preston asked, standing in front of me and caressing my cheek with his thumb.

"Yeah, I'm just tired."

"You don't have to go today. You can wait a few days until you're feeling better."

"I think it's better to just go and get it over with. The sooner we talk about it, the sooner things will go back to normal."

"Are you sure?"

I nodded and let my shoulders fall with my exhale.

"Okay, well, I'm still driving you. I don't want you going on your own."

"You do know that someday I'll have to go back to being on my own again, right?"

He sat down beside me, the bed dipping with his weight.

"I know. But not yet. Not today. I'm not ready."

"Okay."

I leaned into him and let him hold me, his arms wrapping gently around me.

An hour later, I had showered and changed into clean clothes, which felt amazing. Preston helped me climb into his truck since I was still without a car. It turned out that it would cost more to fix the damage that was done in the accident than it would to just buy a new car. I filed the insurance claim and was waiting for them to process it while I shopped for the perfect vehicle.

We pulled up to La Salsa, and Preston quickly jumped out and rushed around to assist me. It was nice to be pampered, but I hated the pain that came with it. I still had some pain meds I could take if I needed them, but I wanted to be in a clear mindset when I talked to Dylan, so I decided to skip them.

I kissed Preston and sent him on his way while I went inside and looked for Dylan. I spotted him at the table in the corner where we always sat and made my way over.

"Hey," he said nervously, standing up and pulling at his freshly ironed button-down shirt.

"Hi." I reached up and pulled him in for a hug, making sure that he knew first and foremost that I didn't think any differently about him now that I knew how he felt about me. "Thanks for meeting me for lunch today."

"Thanks for the invite." He laughed tensely and then took the seat across from me as I sat down. "I hope you don't mind, but I already ordered for us. I thought it might help so you didn't have to stand in line. I got you a number 5, extra sour cream, extra guacamole, and a side of queso."

"That's perfect. I appreciate it."

"No problem." He rubbed his hands together and scanned the room, looking everywhere but at me.

I steadied myself and took a few deep breaths, hoping my energy would transfer to his and calm him down, but it didn't. I knew I promised Preston that I would save the physical acts of violence for him, but I couldn't deny that my fingers weren't itching to reach out and smack him around a time or two. Just to knock some sense into him.

"Okay, enough!" I blurted out, startling a lady at the table across from us. I smiled and gave her a slight wave before turning my attention to a red-faced Dylan. "I'm sorry, but you're driving me crazy with how anxious you are. You need to chill out and just relax."

"That's a lot easier said than done," he said tightly. "You didn't admit that you were in love with your best friend through some tequila-inspired emails to your other best friend's online dating advice blog."

"No, but I did threaten to stab a guy in the liquor aisle if he didn't pretend to be my boyfriend after running into my ex." I shrugged and watched the shock and humor roll across Dylan's face.

"You what?!"

I nodded and leaned back so the waiter could set our plates down.

"Yup. I was getting stuff before the first storm hit, and Daniel surprised me while I was shopping for wine. Preston ended up being there at the same time, so I threatened him and forced him to pretend to be my boyfriend."

"So, are things between you guys still pretend…" His voice trailed off as I saw the sadness creep over his face when I shook my head.

"No, that was only in the store while Daniel was there. We really did get stuck together at Cool Cats when the storm hit, and then things sort of just happened between us. There was this chemistry we couldn't fight, so we decided to give in and see what it was all about."

"Does he make you happy?"

"He does."

I didn't even hesitate to answer him because there was nothing I was more certain of than how much Preston made me happy.

"I'm sorry, Dylan. I had no idea how you felt."

"Don't be. It's my fault for not saying something sooner."

"How long have you known?" I asked cautiously, lifting a bite to my mouth while he thought about his answer.

"I don't know. I guess I've always been in love with you but never let myself think about it because you were with Daniel. Then when you guys broke up, I found myself feeling more protective over you, but it still didn't occur to me why. I think I finally figured it out when I *heard* you that night on the phone. Something snapped inside of me, and it wasn't that I didn't want to hear it because I was your friend, and it was inappropriate. I didn't want to hear it because I was furious that someone else was touching what should have been mine."

I kept eating, unsure of what to say to that. Thankfully, our waitress chose that moment to come check on us and see if we needed anything. She smiled at me before turning her attention to Dylan, shamelessly flirting with him as if I weren't sitting there. Once she left, I set my fork down and leaned in so only he could hear me.

"That girl was trying to take you back to her place! She didn't even care that I was sitting right here!"

"Eh, she's not my type."

I lowered my eyes and felt my shoulders fall. I looked around, needing something to distract myself from feeling guilty about not feeling the same about him.

"You're going to meet the right girl, Dylan. I promise."

"I know."

He reached over and squeezed my hand gently before changing the conversation to a new blog post he had seen on Spill The Beans. I leaned back and covered my mouth as I tried to keep from spitting out my food as I laughed. This was what I loved about Dylan, and I was thankful that it was still there for us.

Thirty-Three

Preston

I was anxious the entire ride home after picking Ramona up from lunch with Dylan. It wasn't that I was worried about her having lunch with her best friend, who had confessed he was in love with her. It was that I had an entire crew at her house, working on bringing Cool Cat's Dreamland to life, and hadn't told her.

Kent had gotten there a few minutes after I dropped Ramona off earlier, and by the time I got there, there were five trucks with guys geared up and ready to go to work. While working on her computer a few weeks ago, I found a design she'd created for what she wanted the Dreamland to look like. I asked her about it, and her face lit up as she talked about the different sections she wanted but never had the time or money to get it started.

I sent the blueprint to Kent and asked him how much it would cost and whether it would be doable. While she was in the hospital, we spent time going over the small details, and he confirmed that his crew could come out this weekend to get it done. With a handful of guys on the job, they could complete it in a few days.

When I left to go pick Ramona up, they were erecting walls and pouring a foundation for the room addition that she had mentioned but wasn't part of the original plan. She had told me recently that the only thing she wished she had was a living room with a fireplace and large floor-to-ceiling windows. If she had those things, it would be the perfect house-slash-work combo.

So, I took the initiative to ask Kent about adding an additional room off the back of the building and turning it into the living room she wanted. They were only doing the physical part of it, the interior decoration would still be up to her.

When we pulled up, she frowned when she spotted the trucks and leaned forward to get a glimpse of the guys working in the back.

"What in the world is going on?" she asked, pulling back when it hurt.

"It's a surprise."

I put the truck in park and helped her down before walking her to the back and holding her steady so she didn't fall. The snow and ice had been cleared, but I still didn't trust anything when it came to her safety. I might have been a bit overprotective, but I wasn't willing to see her get hurt again.

"Ramona, this is my brother, Kent. Kent, this is Ramona." I smiled as they shook hands, a puzzled expression still playing on her face.

"It's a pleasure to meet you. I've heard a lot about you," Kent said with a wink in my direction.

"What is all of this?"

Kent stepped to the side and extended his arm.

"Welcome to Cool Cat's Dreamland."

"What?" Her eyes bulged as she whipped around to look at me. "You're kidding me, right?"

"Nope." I shook my head. "It's all being built from your blueprint, but if you want to change anything, just tell Kent, and he'll make sure it's taken care of."

Her eyes filled with tears as she looked between us.

"I can't afford this," she whispered, nervously tucking a strand of hair behind her ear.

"You don't have to worry about that," I assured her.

"We're taking care of it," Kent added. "As well as the room addition."

"Room addition?" She raised her eyebrows.

"Follow me."

I grabbed her hand and gently led her to the other side, stopping a safe distance from where the guys were working.

"They're able to add on at the back of the building. So where your bedroom currently ends, there will be a living room on the other side. There's also an extra bathroom being added in as well as I know that was on your dream board. We'll go over the layout, but like I said, if you want to change anything, just tell us. We'll make it happen."

The guys continued working on pouring the footing while she stared on in disbelief.

"I can't believe you did this for me," she whispered.

"For us," I corrected, pulling her into me.

"Oh really?" she cocked an eyebrow.

"Yeah, I was thinking you could keep sharing your bed with me."

"We're back to that again?" she teased, using the words I'd thrown at her the first time I stepped into Cool Cats on me now.

"You bet your ass. Now are you going to share it with me or not?" I pulled her gently against me and lightly tickled her sides.

"Alright, I guess I'll share my bed with you. But only because you're going to be in it with me tonight anyway."

She wiggled her eyebrows playfully as I leaned in and captured her lips with mine.

Epilogue

Ramona

Nine Months Later

"Okay, I think everything is ready," I said nervously, stepping back to look at the banner we'd hung in front of the entrance to Cool Cats Dreamland.

Maggie and Dylan were already inside, getting the rest of the decorations set up for the grand opening.

"It looks great," Preston said, wrapping his arms around my waist.

"I can't believe this is finally happening. It's been a dream for so long, it's crazy to think that it's actually reality. Thank you for everything you did to get this going."

I turned and wrapped my arms around his neck.

"It was nothing."

He planted a kiss on my forehead, making me melt beneath his touch. That and it was the middle of summer and already hot as heck outside.

"It was definitely more than nothing. It was weather-related delays with the construction. A random lumber shortage. There was an influx of new businesses around us utilizing the same resources we needed. It was a heck of a lot, and I appreciate everything you did to pull it together."

"Don't forget everything *I* did," Kent teased as he brushed past us, carrying a tray full of baked goods. "I made the magic happen."

"Maybe with getting the place built, but we all know that I make the real magic happen where it matters," Preston joked, pulling me closer so I could feel his cock. Thank God it wasn't hard right now—there would be no way to explain *that* level of excitement to everyone when we opened the doors.

"Don't be gross," his mom scolded, smacking him upside the back of his head. "Everything looks great, sweetie. We're so happy for you!"

She pushed Preston out of the way and pulled me in for a hug.

I'd gotten to know his family over the past nine months and simply adored them. It was nice having everyone so close, but I still couldn't get over them constantly thanking me for bringing Preston home.

Shortly after we started the construction to remodel Cool Cats, I asked him to move in with me. It was a bold move, but I had never been more sure of anything before in my life. He said yes without even an ounce of hesitation and got to work selling his house in Atlanta. We took a trip out there after Thanksgiving, packed everything up, and moved into my place.

We quickly realized that we needed a little more room for both of us to live comfortably and added an office for him along with the new living room and extra bathroom. I also took the time to restructure things in the store and created a new storage system for excess inventory which helped us maximize the existing space so we could focus on the home side of it.

"Everything is set up inside," Maggie said, joining us in the store. "We can open the doors whenever you're ready."

"You're not going to make everyone have a password to get in?" Dylan asked, his brows frowning.

"I am. I just posted it a few minutes ago."

"Oooh, what is it?" Maggie asked, clapping her hands.

I think she loved the daily passwords more than anyone.

I was about to tell them when Preston turned and interrupted me.

"About that," he said, clearing his throat. "I changed it."

"You changed it? To what?"

"Why don't you go online and see for yourself?"

I eyed him suspiciously as I pulled my phone out of my pocket and pulled up the webpage. Things worked so smoothly, and everything ran faster now that I had 24/7 tech support in-house. I was beyond grateful for Preston giving my online store the upgrade it needed and for making everything easy to find.

I clicked on the link for the password of the day and felt Preston move in front of me.

"Okay, today's password has been updated to *Ramona will you marry*—" I stopped and covered my mouth, finding Preston in front of me on one knee with a ring box in his hand.

There were whispers as everyone oohed and ahhed, but I couldn't focus on anything other than the incredible man kneeling before me.

"Ramona, I love you more than life itself. You've awakened a part of me that I thought I would never feel again and have brightened even my darkest days. I can't imagine living without you by my side, so will you please marry me?"

I nodded my head as tears pooled down my cheeks.

"Yes! Yes, I'll marry you!"

He stood up and placed the ring on my finger before lifting me in the air and twirling me in his arms.

I was on cloud nine, feeling on top of the world. We smiled and hugged everyone as they came around to congratulate us. I didn't want to rush the moment but knew that we needed to open the doors soon before there was a huge line outside.

Preston had rallied with everyone in Whiskey Mountain and Fallen Oaks to make today's grand opening as massive as possible. There was even going to be press coverage, with a few of the local news channels coming by to do interviews and live videos.

"I just updated the password back to what you originally had it as," Preston said, pulling me into him once we had a minute to ourselves. "Toodles Poodles is the password for today." He raised his voice, making sure everyone heard as they all scattered to help out where needed.

I took a deep breath and pulled my shoulders back, ready to take the next step in my career.

"Okay, open the doors," I announced, squeezing Preston's hand as nerves shot through me again.

I was overwhelmed by the number of people that I knew who had come in and brought their fur babies to check out Dreamland. Maggie was situated at the desk, signing people up for reservations while I circulated throughout the room, saying hi and introducing myself to the people I didn't know.

With all of the new businesses that had recently popped up, there were a lot of faces I didn't recognize. We had people coming from all over Montana, buying houses and setting up shops in the new *booming* part of town. I was thankful for the jump in business but couldn't believe the long line of people flooding Maggie's table, all wanting their chance to bring their pets to Dreamland.

I took a moment and walked over to the corner of the room where Dylan was standing, leaning against the wall.

"Hey," he said, smiling at me and pulling me in for a hug. "Congratulations on the grand opening. It's incredible."

"Thank you, it really is. I can't believe it's actually happening."

I looked around the room in awe.

"And congratulations on the other thing, too," he said, clearing his throat.

"On my engagement?"

I softened my tone and turned to face him.

"Yeah, that. Congratulations on your engagement. Happy looks great on you."

"Thank you."

I slowly pulled a breath in and held it for a few seconds, trying to figure out what to say to him. Things hadn't been weird for us since we talked about everything right after he confessed he had feelings for me, so I wasn't sure whether this was him being jealous of me getting engaged to Preston because he still had feelings for me or if it was something else.

"You're going to find the right girl someday, Dylan. I just know she's out there waiting for you."

"Yeah, maybe."

I raised my eyebrows and pressed my lips together. I hated seeing him so down.

"She is. Be patient because it's going to happen for you."

"I doubt it," he said, shoving a hand through his hair. "All I seem to find is the *wrong* girl. I think I've pretty much made my way through the decent girls in Whiskey Mountain—the joys of living in a super small town." He laughed, but it was forced.

I turned and leaned against the wall next to him. There were even more people filling the space now, and soon, there wasn't going to be room for everyone to be in Dreamland.

"Hi! Sorry to interrupt you guys, but can you tell me where I can find Ramona Watkins?"

"That's me," I said, raising my hand and noticing the blush that flushed across the girl's pale cheeks.

"Oh, hi! Sorry, I'm new in town and haven't had a chance to meet many people yet. I own Cravings, the new restaurant across the street, and Preston had asked me to cater some of the appetizers for the grand opening."

"Yes! I'm sorry; there's been so much going on. I totally spaced your name."

"It's Calli."

She extended her hand to shake mine.

"It's nice to meet you, Calli. And thank you so much for helping out with the food."

"No problem. It's my pleasure. I just needed to see where you wanted me to set up."

I couldn't help but notice the way Calli and Dylan kept passing curious glances at each other, so I took it as a sign from the universe to help things along.

"I need to get in there and help sort out some scheduling conflicts," I lied, gently placing a hand on Dylan's shoulder and shoving him forward. "But my friend Dylan would be more than happy to help you get set up. There's space in the store, right across from the register. If you want to set up there, we'll make an announcement to let people know to come by and grab some food."

"Sounds perfect, thank you."

Calli smiled up at Dylan, tucking her curly blonde hair behind her ear as he guided her through the crowd of people and into the store.

"What was that all about?" Preston asked, joining me as I headed toward Maggie.

"Nothing," I said with a shrug. "Just helping someone else find their happily ever after now that I have mine."

Something To Believe In
Whiskey Mountain Book 3

Samantha Baca

Copyright © 2023 by Samantha Baca

Cover Design: Oh So Novel

Content Warning

This book contains language and storylines that may be bothersome for some readers and is intended for a mature audience. Sexual scenes may be shown in detail as well. The reader is encouraged to reach out to the author directly (authorsamanthabaca@gmail.com) if they would like to further discuss the content warning(s) for this book.

Please note the following items that come up briefly in the book:

Dementia (secondary character)

<u>One</u>

Dylan

My palms were sweaty as I waited in line, staring at the chalkboard menu hanging on the wall. I had been to Cravings once since it opened, but it was for their grand opening, and I didn't have to order anything because there were samples out for everyone to try.

Now that I was here as a paying customer, there was a lot of pressure to place a simple order without embarrassing myself in front of Calli, the owner. It wasn't that I was stupid and didn't know how to; it was that she was the hottest woman I had ever laid eyes on, and that made me a nervous wreck.

The line moved in front of me, putting me closer to being in the spotlight. I swallowed hard, pulling at the neck of my t-shirt that suddenly felt like it was choking me. It was hot outside, but the temperature rose to unbearable heights the moment her eyes caught mine. I was burning up and sweaty—two very unattractive qualities to showcase right now.

I tried not to stare as she stood behind the counter, tucking a loose strand of curly blonde hair behind her ear while she took the older man's order. She was so patient—and possibly oblivious—as he made passes at her, shamelessly flirting as his wife smacked his arm with her handbag.

It was hard not to laugh as the older couple trotted off, the woman still hitting him as he did his best to convince her he wasn't hitting on Calli. I'd known the Thompsons since I was a little boy, and the whole town knew how big of a flirt George was.

"Are you ready?" she asked, startling me as her blue eyes lit up.

I looked around to find that everyone in front of me had moved on and was either filling their cups or waiting for their food.

"Oh, yeah," I stammered, forcing my feet to move forward without face-planting in front of her. "Sorry, I wasn't paying attention."

"It's not a problem," she said sweetly, with a warm grin. "What can I get you?"

"I'll have you."

Her brows rose slightly in surprise, her lips pressed together as she tried to keep from laughing.

At least she found it humorous, while all I wanted to do was smack myself upside the head. *Why did I say that?*

"I'm sorry," I apologized, clearing my throat. "I'll have you."

She lifted her hand and covered her smile behind it, bubble gum pink nails catching my eye.

I took a deep breath and slowly released it, not trusting myself to speak to her. This was going even worse than I had imagined. I could talk to people all day, every day, but give me a beautiful woman I felt attracted to, and I was a bumbling mess.

"I don't know what's wrong with me," I muttered, shaking my head and lowering it. I was ready to turn around and get the hell out of there, vowing never to return.

"You probably have low blood sugar," Ramona said, sneaking up on me and putting her arm around my shoulders. Leave it to my best friend to swoop in and save the day. "It's late in the day, and you probably skipped breakfast if I know you."

I turned my head and looked at her, relief washing over me that she was there so I wouldn't keep embarrassing myself.

"I hate getting low blood sugar," Calli replied. "It's the worst, and I feel like I'm in this fog until they come back up."

"Right? It's such a pain. I can usually cure mine with a bag of Cool Ranch Doritos." Ramona laughed, but I knew how serious she was about her chips. It was nice of her to save me from myself, even if it was something as silly as low blood sugar—which I didn't get, but she did often. Way too often.

"Well, I only have a few minutes before I need to get back to Cool Cats. What do you recommend today, Calli?" Ramona gave my shoulder a quick squeeze before releasing me.

"The spicy tuna wrap is always good for hot days, but if you don't want fish, I would go with the chicken and waffles."

"Oooh, spicy tuna sounds delicious. Let me get two of those, please," Ramona said, looking at me. "Do you want one too? They have a club sandwich on the board as well, if you'd rather that."

I loved how well she knew me and that she could tell I was still freezing up around Calli.

"The club would be perfect. Thank you." I cleared my throat again and then forced myself to stop before Calli started to think I was sick or something.

"Is it together or separate?" Calli asked, her fingers hovering above the register keys.

"Together." Ramona smiled and slid her card across the counter.

"No, I've got it," I objected before Ramona's hand darted out and slapped mine as I tried to pull her card back.

Calli raised her eyebrows and studied us, waiting before trying to take the card.

"I've got it," Ramona confirmed through somewhat gritted teeth.

I narrowed my eyes at her, knowing she knew how much I hated it when she did that.

"You didn't need to buy me lunch," I said as soon as we walked away to fill our cups.

"I know. It's my treat."

"Well, thank you. I appreciate it. You know how I feel about you paying for stuff for me, though."

"Oh, whatever." She waved her hand dismissively as she filled her cup with root beer. "If you really wanted to repay me, you could grab a carton of vanilla ice cream and bring it over to Cool Cats so we can make floats. That would be heavenly. It's too freaking hot out for the middle of August."

"As much as I would love to, I have to get back to work. Raincheck?"

"Of course."

We waited to the side while they made our order. Ramona was making small talk, telling me something about Preston and their progress with training their dog, Rosco, but I couldn't focus because I couldn't take my eyes off Calli.

She had the most perfect smile that brightened her eyes and lit up her face. Everyone around her seemed happier, too. It was like she could change anyone's mood just by smiling.

I felt eyes on me and looked down to find Ramona watching me with a shit-eating grin spread across her cheeks. Apparently, even I was smiling just watching her.

"What?" I asked when she continued to stare without saying anything.

"Nothing." She shrugged.

"Liar."

A young, scrawny kid grabbed a tray and loaded our order, sitting it on the counter before calling Ramona's name.

"I was just thinking about how you've got it bad. So freaking bad." She laughed and walked off, leaving me standing there feeling like a complete love-sick teenager.

Two

Calli

"I cannot believe how busy we've been," Paisley said, sitting down across from me at the table.

The rush finally died shortly after Dylan and Ramona left, leaving us with a slow trickle until we closed at 3:30.

"I know, it's incredible. I wasn't sure what to expect when I first signed the lease on this building, but I can say it's going better than I ever imagined."

"I told you, have faith, and good things will come."

I smiled at my best friend, thankful she had followed me and my heart to Whiskey Mountain, Montana. Technically, we were right smack on the line between Whiskey Mountain and Fallen Oaks, two very small towns that were growing by the minute.

"I'm trying," I sighed heavily, leaning back against the chair. "It's a lot all at once."

"I know. But I'm here to help. Lean on me and we'll figure all of this out together."

I nodded, too tired to say anything more.

I'd had no plans to leave Miami before my mom was diagnosed with dementia and needed my help. I packed up everything and moved to Whiskey Mountain, bringing Paisley along with me with no clue what I was going to do until I got here.

It wasn't that I didn't want to be here; it was just that I had no idea what I was going to do. I was used to big city life, and going to a small town where I knew no one made it hard to take that initial jump and trust that I could handle starting over.

I had worked at an upscale restaurant in Miami, but it was nothing compared to owning and running my own—something I had always dreamed of. When I first got to Whiskey Mountain, I stopped to get coffee at this cute little shop called Spill The Beans. It was there that I learned that they were looking to develop the area that was currently deserted aside from a cute little pet shop. Lo-and-behold, there just so happened to be a vacant spot left, which was perfect for a restaurant.

I cashed in my 401K, made a wish on a star, and never looked back.

"Your mom seems to enjoy it," Paisley noted, glancing at my mom sitting at a table in the corner, people-watching.

"I think so, too. Her doctor said it was good for her to be as involved as she wanted. It makes me more comfortable having her here with me than worrying about her being alone at home. I'm hoping that if she's here every day—or most days of the week when I'm here — that it'll be familiar to her. Plus, she enjoys helping with the menu."

"It was a genius idea." Paisley laughed. "Changing the menu every day depending on her cravings has been fun for the locals. There's nothing else like it around here."

"She always loved cooking, and if I can keep part of that alive for her, I'm going to. Once I get someone hired to take over up front, I can get back to the kitchen and have her help me. I think she'll really love that."

I smiled and watched as she sipped her afternoon tea, a look of peace and tranquility etched on her face.

<u>Three</u>

Dylan

I wiped the sweat from my brow and climbed down the ladder, ready to be done for the day. The sun was hotter than the devil's playground, making my mounting headache worse. Add on the overwhelming smell of tar, and it was a recipe for a migraine.

The job went later today than it should have, but we had a new guy who didn't know shit about roofing, which was what had kept us going longer than usual. I opened the top of the giant jug of water and began chugging, tempted to dump the other half over my head to cool me off.

"Good work up there today," Curtis said, nodding up to where the rest of the guys were collecting their supplies and coming down.

"Thanks. Should have been finished hours ago."

"I know. He'll learn. Everyone has to start somewhere."

"Well, maybe have them start elsewhere during the summer months so the rest of us don't have to suffer," I joked, giving him a wink so he knew I was playing.

"Hell no. This is the ultimate test to see if they have what it takes. See what they're made of."

"I hate to break it to you, but he's not cut out for this." I jerked my head to the side where the new guy was bent over the gravel, heaving.

"Fuck," Curtis said, rubbing a hand down his face in frustration. "We have six more jobs to get done before the end of September. I needed him to work out."

He heaved louder, drawing the attention of a few of the guys. No one went over to check on him, having seen this a handful of times already. Some guys could handle the physical labor of roofing and others couldn't. It was always easy to spot those ones.

"I'll start on the other building tomorrow," I offered, pulling another drink in. "I can be there by 4. Have Soliz and Lowry meet me there and send the other guys to finish this one. We can crank these out quicker if we work early in the morning before it gets too hot."

"Thanks, Dylan. You're gonna have a ton of overtime this week."

I knew he couldn't afford to keep paying me the overtime I was accruing, and given that he was my dad's best friend, I also couldn't take advantage of it either.

"How about we forget about the overtime, and you give me two weeks off once this project is done?"

"If you can crank out the last six retail shops before our deadline, I'll give you a full month off."

I arched my eyebrow, always enjoying a good bet.

"Yeah?"

"Yup. But I can't give you any more help than what you already have."

"And I can work whatever hours I need to?"

"Whatever it takes to get the job done *right*."

"Ha," I scoffed. "Have I ever *not* done a job right? I'm the image of perfection, don't you remember?"

I felt the dimples in my cheeks deepen with my grin.

Curtis rolled his eyes and pretended he wasn't amused.

"Yeah, and you get your humbled charm from your dad."

We both laughed, then he went off to talk to the new guy while I collected my stuff and got the hell out of there. Tomorrow was going to be a long day, which meant that I needed to shower and hit the sack early tonight.

****

Morning came quicker than I would have liked, given that I slept like shit and could use a few more hours of sleep. Wanting to keep my end of the bargain up for Curtis meant I needed to get over it and get my ass to the job site.

I loved that there were no cars on the road, no one to get in my way as I started the day. The only downside was that most of the businesses in Whiskey Mountain didn't open until 9, which meant that I was stuck with a crappy cup of coffee from home for my caffeine fix. I could have grabbed some energy drinks after I left last night, but I was exhausted and just wanted to go home. Today, I regretted that decision tenfold.

It was amazing to see how much had been developed in the small stretch between Whiskey Mountain and Fallen Oaks in just the past year. After a dangerous blizzard stranded Ramona with no easy access to necessities, her fiancé rallied everyone together and got the ball rolling on developing this part of town.

Since then, several other shops had opened around her pet store, and business was booming. Cravings was still the only restaurant, but there were plans to bring in a coffee shop and an upscale steakhouse as soon as the construction was completed.

The portion that we were working on was right next to Cravings and would be a smaller strip mall on Main Street, plus the movie theater that was right beside it, at the end of the street. The town locals were excited about that, given that the closest movie theater was over an hour away.

I grabbed my supplies and carried them up with me, heading down for another load when Soliz and Lowry showed up. I had worked with them for so long that we gave each other a quick nod as a greeting, and all got to work. I grabbed my tool belt and was securing it around my waist when I saw the door to Cravings open.

"Hey, I thought I heard someone out here," Calli said, peeking around the door. It was still dark out, only a few streetlights illuminating her features.

"Sorry if we bothered you. I didn't think anyone would be here this early."

"Nope, you didn't. I'm used to being aware of my surroundings and investigating every noise I hear after living in a big city." She laughed, pushing the door open and resting her shoulder against it as her arms folded across her chest. "So, what are you doing here so early?"

I nodded to the roof where the other guys were and then looked at her.

"We're working on the roofs on this side of the strip mall. I was hoping we'd get here before anyone opened so we could crank out the loud parts and not disrupt business."

She leaned forward and looked up before looking back at me.

"I didn't know you were a roofer."

"One of the best," I said with a cheesy grin and a wink. My palms started to sweat, and I suddenly felt all twitchy again.

"Well, I won't keep you so you can get started. I'll be here if you need water or coffee or anything. Just come on in."

"Thank you, I appreciate that. Why are you here so early?"

She yawned and tried to hide it behind her hand.

"My mom wanted biscuits and gravy this morning, so I came in early to get a head start on the food prep for the day. Everything she's talked about since last night has been a combination of breakfast foods, so that's what today's menu will be focused on. I'm going to be making some pastries, too. Stop by and try one if you'd like. I'll be sure to make those lemon blueberry donuts you like so much."

My cheeks flushed as she chewed her lower lip. She was right—I fucking loved those donuts. She had made them for the grand opening at Cool Cats when Ramona expanded and added a pet daycare, but I didn't expect her to notice.

"I'll be sure to come by to grab one in a bit. I brought coffee from home—"

She scrunched her nose in the most adorable way.

"What?" I asked playfully, a laugh floating off of my lips. "What's that face for?"

"What kind of coffee did you make?"

"I don't know. Black? It was that instant coffee you get in the can and add it to hot water."

"Noooo," she cried out, her face twisted in disgust. "That's not real coffee!"

"You sound just like my friend, Maggie. She takes coffee pretty seriously, too."

"Maggie from Spill The Beans?"

I nodded, feeling guilty for leaving the guys to work without me while I talked to Calli. But nothing could have torn me away from her now that I had her alone and could finally get actual words out of my mouth.

"The one and only," I confirmed.

"Well, Maggie is right. That's not real coffee. Now I can't make the incredible lattes that she makes, but I can make you a decent cup of coffee. Do you have a few minutes to come inside?"

I looked up at the roof, wondering how much the guys were going to hate me.

"I'll send you with coffee for them too. You'll be their new favorite once they taste my cold brew."

"Yeah, sure. I've got a few minutes," I said, forcing my feet to move and my heart to stop racing.

Four

Calli

"So, what do you think?" I pressed my fingers together in front of me and watched as Dylan took a sip.

His dark hair was buzzed and begged for me to run my hands over it. I imagined it was to keep him cool while working in the summer heat, but it also just looked incredible on him. Not that I was checking him out or anything.

"That's delicious," he said, setting his glass down and swiping his tongue over his upper lip to catch the tiny drops of the vanilla sweet cream cold foam. "That might be the best iced coffee I've ever had—don't tell Maggie I said that."

I giggled and shook my head.

"It will be our secret."

I couldn't help but look away as a rush of heat brushed across my cheeks. There were plenty of things I wanted to be *our secret*. But now wasn't the time to think those kinds of thoughts about him.

"Do you want 2 more to go for your friends?" I asked, grabbing the pitcher from the counter.

"Sure, that would be great. Thank you."

I smiled and prepared their drinks, thankful I had a few moments alone with Dylan without the rush of customers keeping me distracted.

I lined up the drinks, wiped them down after adding the foam, and then set them in a drink tray to make it easier for him to get them up there.

"How much do I owe you?" he asked, reaching for his wallet.

"Nothing." I held my hands up to stop him. "There's no charge."

He pulled his head back and frowned, wallet in hand, ready to pay.

"I'm not taking these for free. Please tell me how much they are."

I tugged my lip between my teeth, trying to force some of the nervous energy out of me. Only it wasn't just nervous energy but more of an excited energy, and I worried that if I didn't do something to keep myself busy, I would jump over the counter and kiss him.

"They're free." I shrugged.

"No, they're not. Please let me pay."

"I can't do that."

"And why not?"

"Because I don't sell cold brew. I sell basic coffee, like the kind you can make at home." I scrunched my face the same way I had when he told me what he had made.

"You don't sell this?"

I shook my head.

"Then why did you make it for me?"

"I couldn't stand the thought of you drinking that crap from home." I laughed, covering my mouth before I accidentally snorted.

"The same crap you serve to customers here?" he teased, his voice going sexily lower.

I nodded.

"Well, thank you for the drink. You didn't have to make one for the guys, too. I feel bad now that you won't let me pay you."

"It wasn't a problem at all. Plus, I knew you would need something to bribe them with since you took forever to get up there. I didn't want you to get picked on." I winked playfully.

"Eh, I've been around those guys so long that they know better. But seriously, thanks again. And if you ever need help with anything or have any roof-related issues—just let me know."

"I think I'm good there," I laughed. "Now, if you said you could fix a leaky pipe, that would be a different story."

I expected him to laugh and say something like—*yeah, no can do*. Instead, he gave me a smirk that made my insides melt.

"I'll be done around 4 today. If you need me before then, just let me know. Otherwise, I'll be back around then."

He winked and carried the drink tray tucked into his side before letting the door close behind him. I sagged against the counter, feeling the tingles spread through me and light my body on fire.

Five

Dylan

I'd never been more excited to work on a leaky pipe than I was to fix Calli's. The day dragged on, my excitement to see her overriding everything else. Being around Calli was like going to Disneyland and having no lines to wait in. Not that I was comparing her to a ride—though I also wouldn't mind riding her either.

I shook my head to clear the dirty thoughts as I packed up the last of my tools and carried them down to my truck. I gave a quick wave to the guys as they took off, then gave myself a pep-talk before heading inside.

Cravings was already empty, having closed a few minutes ago. I smiled at the employees who were cleaning up and scanned the room, looking for Calli. I didn't want anyone to think I was *that guy* who came in after they were closed and still expected to be served. I knew a few of the young kids who worked there, but the rest were all new faces.

"Can I help you?"

I spun around, startled by the girl behind me. She was young, around Calli's age, if I had to guess, with emerald green eyes and jet-black hair that made them look even more fierce.

"Hi, um, I'm looking for Calli." I cleared my throat, hating that it had taken over as a new nervous tick every time I said her name.

"She's in the office, back by the kitchen. You can go on back." She nodded, then gave me a smile that made me curious to know what Calli might have said to her about me.

I smacked my lips together, trying to play it cool but looking like a doofus instead. I refrained from showing my embarrassment as

I headed through the double doors into the kitchen. There was a radio playing music from the back of the room, and if I stopped moving, I could hear the faint sound of someone singing.

Not just anyone, Calli. And she wasn't just singing. She was singing a note so beautiful that even the angels in heaven would weep over it.

I made my way toward the office, not wanting to interrupt her. I could listen to her sing all day, every day. Hell, I would be ecstatic to sit down and record her singing just so I could use it as my daily playlist while working. It would make work a lot more pleasant, and the days would fly by just hearing the beautiful tone of her voice.

I paused by the door, waiting a few seconds before knocking as I listened to her sing along with Adele. Goosebumps spread across my skin quicker than lightning, my heart beating wildly in my chest as I soaked in every word that came out of her mouth.

"She's a good singer, isn't she?"

My head whipped around, startled again. I leaned forward a bit to read her name tag so at least I would know who the heck it was that kept sneaking up on me.

"Wonderful," I said quietly, hoping Calli couldn't hear us.

"I always told her she belonged on stage with her own music label, but she never believed me." Paisley stood next to me, smiling so big that it stretched across her cheeks.

"Have you known each other long?" I asked, keeping my voice low.

"Since we were babies. We grew up together."

"Wow. That's pretty awesome."

"Yeah, she's more like a sister to me than anything. I lost my mom when I was little, so her mom has always been like a second mom to me. She took me in and raised me right alongside Calli. Never complained about it a day in her life."

I smiled softly, eager to hear more about Calli's life.

"But you can't stand out here all day," Paisley said, shaking her head. "If you want to get that girl, you're gonna have to try harder."

"I—" I snapped my mouth shut. "That's not what I'm here for."

She raised an eyebrow while her mouth pulled to the side in a mischievous grin.

"No?"

I shook my head, trying to force the logical thoughts loose so they would float down and come out of my mouth.

"Calli asked me to fix her pipes. She's leaking."

Paisley's eyebrows shot higher on her forehead as her lips pressed into a thin line to keep from laughing.

Fuck. Why did I say that?

My mind was constantly mush whenever Calli was involved. I cleared my throat again and started over.

"I apologize. I meant to say that *they're* leaking. She has a leak somewhere, and I'm here to fix her. It. *Fix it.*" I swallowed hard, my throat uncomfortably dry.

I suddenly wished that the earth would just open and swallow me.

"I thought I heard voices," Calli said, peeking around the door. "Did I hear you say that I'm leaking?"

She gave me a cheeky grin, grabbed her water bottle from behind her, and came out.

"I say a lot of stupid shit lately," I mumbled, running a hand through my hair, remembering that I needed to shave my head again soon.

"Eh, we all do. Don't worry about it. How about we deal with the pipes in the bathroom for now, and we can worry about whatever leaks I have later?"

Calli tossed a wink over her shoulder as she led the way, but I couldn't help but pick up the flirty undertone in her words.

"You two have fun," Paisley called.

The hall was brightly lit with sconces adorning the walls next to framed family pictures. I wanted to stop and look but didn't want to be rude to Calli since she had asked for help with plumbing. I turned my head forward to focus but caught a glimpse of a photo that made me stop in my tracks.

I grinned as I looked at a faded portrait in an antique-looking frame of a toddler girl wearing a chef hat and apron, her face painted red with spaghetti sauce as she proudly held handfuls of noodles in each hand. Her grin was contagious, and I felt a tug at my heart as I realized it was Calli.

She stood next to me, smiling at the photo, but I could feel some tension coming from her.

"I was three," she said softly. "I told my mom I wanted to be a chef, so she got me the outfit. I wore it proudly every time I cooked. My dad was such a trickster and loved playing practical jokes. It was his idea to grab the giant balls of spaghetti to see how much I could hold at one time. There was sauce and noodles everywhere, but my parents didn't care. They just laughed and snapped photos."

"Sounds like a fun childhood."

"It was the best. I miss those days." Her voice cracked as her shoulders stiffened. "My dad was the best. I miss him every single day."

I opened my mouth to ask her what happened but closed it when I remembered I had a way of making an ass out of myself around her. As if sensing my discomfort and curiosity, she answered my unspoken question for me.

"He passed last year from a heart attack, which I'm sure you already heard about since he and my mom had lived here for a few years before it happened. Completely unexpected and no history of heart problems in our family."

"I'm so sorry for your loss."

"Thank you. It was hard on my family but hit my mom the worst. She was diagnosed with early-onset dementia shortly after it happened. It's progressed quickly. That's why I decided to move here, so I could take care of her."

My heart melted seeing the love in her eyes for her family.

"Anyway, you didn't ask to get bombarded with sad stories, so let's move on," she said with a forced laugh, turning away so I couldn't see the sadness flashing across her face.

Without thinking, I grabbed her elbow, gently turning her back to face me. Her breath caught in her throat as I pulled her against me, meaning to offer a sympathetic hug but not realizing the amount of chemistry pulling between us the second I touched her.

"I would gladly stand here for hours listening to you tell me the story behind each of these photos," I said softly, inhaling the light scent of jasmine that floated between us.

She licked her lips and looked up at me, something changing in her eyes as her breasts pushed slightly into my chest.

"There you go. That's what I'm talking about. You gotta work for it," Paisley said, startling me for the third time.

Calli immediately pulled back, breaking the connection between us.

"That's not—" I started before she cut me off.

"I know, I know. *That's not what I'm doing.*" She rolled her eyes playfully while balancing a basket of wrapped silverware on her hip. "Just be sure to take some time fixing that leak. Her pipes are *really tight,* if you know what I mean. A little bit of lube should have her up and running again."

"Paisley!" Calli hissed, her cheeks flushing a beautiful shade of red.

"What?" Paisley shrugged and grinned like the cat who ate the canary before returning to the dining area and leaving us alone again.

"I'm so sorry about that," Calli murmured, covering her face.

"Don't worry about it. Fixing pipes is my specialty."

I watched as another wave of crimson washed over her as she picked up on the innuendo I had been brave enough to put down.

<u>Six</u>

Calli

Watching the muscles move in Dylan's back as he leaned in and dipped his head under the sink sent waves of heat through my core. I wasn't sure if it was from all the sexual innuendos that had been flying around before he got started or if it was because those same innuendos made me think of the only time I had ever watched porn in my life. It was Paisley's idea, and the quality was as terrible as the acting, but it had a plumber, and he was definitely there to fix a different set of pipes.

I leaned against the wall out of his way and watched, trying to push down the desire to rush over and jump on him. He was a person—not a piece of meat. However, he would be one satisfying piece of meat if I said so myself.

He pulled out and wiped the sweat from his brow with the bottom of his shirt, revealing the most perfect and glorious abs I had ever seen. How was that even possible? I wanted to reach out and drag my nails along the ridges.

"Sorry," he mumbled, as if the sight of his hot, sweaty body was something to apologize for.

"Don't be."

"It gets hot working in small spaces."

"I bet it does," Paisley called from the hallway, but I wasn't sure that Dylan had heard her.

"You can take your shirt off," I offered, immediately second-guessing it.

He gave me a lopsided grin as he climbed up and stood across from me.

"Do you want me to take my shirt off?"

"She does," Paisley answered for me, this time grabbing Dylan's attention.

Instead of being irritated with our little eavesdropping friend, he seemed to find it amusing.

He lifted a brow, silently asking again.

"It's whatever makes you comfortable. You're hot with or without it."

I pressed the palm of my hand to my forehead.

"I mean, it's going to be hot either way. The air conditioning doesn't work back here, and I haven't been able to get anyone out to look at it."

"What's wrong with it?" he asked, tipping his head back to look at the vent.

"I'm not sure. It's a new building, so you would think everything would work fine, but here we are." I shrugged.

"I'll look at it before I go. If I can't figure it out, I'll call my friend to come look at it."

"Oh no, it's okay. You're already doing more than enough with fixing this." I pointed dumbly to the sink.

"It's not a big deal. Besides, he should have made sure it was working in the first place."

"Why's that?"

"Because he owns the company that did the heating and cooling for this building."

"Your friend is Maverick?" I asked, feeling stupid.

He had been around a lot when we were first getting everything set up, and Paisley had practically been drooling over him ever since. We hadn't seen him around town much, but she was nonetheless obsessed with him.

"The one and only."

Before I could say anything more, Paisley came flying around the corner, a flush of heat in her cheeks.

"Did someone say Maverick?"

Dylan gave me a curious look before giving Paisley a smug smile.

"Maybe. Why? Were you listening to our conversation or something?" he teased.

Paisley was one of the kindest people I'd ever known, but she was also the straight-shooter, never turn down a dare kind of girl as well.

"Just making sure you're getting the job done," she replied, tilting her head to the side and making the hair piled on top of her head flop with it.

"Which one?"

"Touché. You got me there. But back to the pressing matter at hand—did someone mention Maverick?"

"I was telling Dylan that it's hot in here because the AC isn't working right. He said he'll look at it, and if he can't fix it, he'll call Maverick to come out."

"No."

Paisley's features changed, her tone more stern.

"You don't want me to look at it?" Dylan asked, folding his arms over his chest.

"I mean, I didn't say that," she stammered. "It's just that you've already taken so much time fixing the sink and taking care of

Calli's pipes that it would be rude to tie up your time by having you look at the AC. I think we should just leave it be for now."

"You mean until Maverick comes back?" Dylan questioned, the dimples in his cheeks more prominent with the grin spreading across them.

"Is he coming back? Did he say that? When?"

"You're being strange," I said, eyeing her suspiciously. "What did you do?"

"Nothing." She shook her head, but her eyes told me she was lying.

"Paisley Marie…"

"Ugh, you sound just like Mom," she groaned, leaning against the door frame. "I didn't do anything."

Dylan and I both pinned her with a look but said nothing.

"Fine. I *might have* messed with the vent and shoved a towel up there to block the flow."

"Paisley!" I scolded, desperately trying to hold back my laughter.

"What? You're about to get your pipes fixed. Can't I get some service of my own?"

"You're ridiculous," I laughed, shaking my head.

"You know, you could just ask Maverick for his number," Dylan offered, still grinning.

"I haven't seen him around since he finished up here," she said, pressing her lips into a scowl.

"He's in Fallen Oaks working on a project there, but he'll be back in a few weeks to start the next phase of this development."

"A *few weeks?* That's going to take forever," Paisley groaned, letting her head hang forward.

I heard a heavy sigh from Dylan and looked up to find his fingers flying over the screen of his phone before pressing it to his ear.

"What are you doing?" I asked, an odd excitement flooding through me as he looked at me and his eyes locked on mine.

"Hey, Mav."

"No. Fucking. Way." Paisley's voice was barely above a whisper, but I could see the shock on her face as she watched Dylan.

"Nothing much, just here fixing a leaky pipe at Cravings. Tell your guys to pay better attention next time."

I couldn't hear what was being said on the other end of the line, but Dylan's smirk told me they talked shit to each other often.

"Well, I'm still here at Cravings, and I think you owe Calli and Paisley dinner for your guys fucking up on the job. They're new to town, and you don't want to make a poor impression, do you?"

I started waving my hands no in front of me, but Paisley quickly swatted them away while she hung onto every word Dylan said.

"When are you back in Whiskey Mountain?" He waited a moment while Maverick responded. "Friday? Okay, let me see."

He held the phone away from his face as he looked between Paisley and me.

"Are you ladies free for dinner on Friday?"

"Yes," Paisley squeaked, the excitement almost consuming her.

"Oh, no, I don't think I should be ther—"

"I thought the four of us could go to La Salsa," Dylan said as if reading my mind about not wanting to be a third wheel with Paisley and Maverick.

"Oh. Um. Okay, sure," I stammered as Paisley's nails dug into my hand.

Dylan winked at me, then turned away to continue his conversation while I slapped Paisley's hand away.

"Enough with that, Edward Scissorhands," I scolded, rubbing the skin where her nails had been.

"Sorry! I didn't mean to. I just got so excited!"

"Well then, I feel bad for Maverick if you guys end up in bed together," I teased, knowing it would spur her on.

"I've never had anyone complain yet." She winked.

"Me. I just complained," I joked, following her out of the bathroom to give Dylan time to finish whatever else he had to do. I didn't want to hover, and more importantly, I needed a moment to catch my breath and accept the fact that I was going out with Dylan on Friday night. Whether or not it was supposed to be a date didn't matter because the way he had been looking at me sure made it feel like it was one.

Seven

Dylan

"Why am I so fucking nervous?" I muttered, adjusting the collar of my polo shirt that I put on because I felt the need to dress up for dinner with Calli tonight. It wasn't technically a date since Maverick and Paisley would be there, but that didn't damper the thoughts of needing to impress her anyway.

I glanced at the clock, knowing I needed to get out the door before I was late. Again, it wasn't a date, but it would be rude to show up after the girls got there, given that I was the one who had set this whole thing up.

When I pulled into the parking lot of La Salsa, I found Maverick's truck and took the spot next to it. I didn't know what car Calli and Paisley would be in or whether they would even come together. I would have been nervous that they wouldn't have shown up, except that Paisley had practically squeezed the life out of me to say thank you after I hung up with Maverick.

I walked inside and spotted Maverick leaning against a wall, checking something on his phone. I looked around, hoping that we had beaten the girls.

"They're not here yet," Maverick said, not looking up as his fingers flew across the screen. He finished and then shoved it into his pocket.

"Cool," I breathed out and nodded, shoving my hands in my pockets to keep from fidgeting.

"So, wanna tell me what this is all about before they get here?" His lips turned into a grin, telling me he already knew.

That was Maverick, though. He had an uncanny ability to read people and immediately know what they were thinking. It was also the reason he kept his distance from most women and held his stance against serious relationships. His business was booming, and he didn't have the time for commitment or drama—which, according to him, went hand-in-hand.

"I just thought it would be nice to hang out and have dinner." I shrugged, looking away so he couldn't see the truth in my eyes.

"Which one are you trying to get with?

I could feel his gray eyes penetrating the back of my head as I scanned the room, avoiding the question.

"Given that I've been around both, I would put my money on Calli. I could be wrong, but I'm pretty sure you're not going after Paisley. But if you are, I'll admit that she's probably going to be more than you can handle." He chuckled lightly.

"Isn't that the truth?" I laughed. "She's a fireball. And speaking of which, here they come now."

I nodded to the parking lot, where both girls were climbing out of the back of a car that was dropping them off. Calli looked incredible in a light pink soft, flowy sundress while Paisley was rocking a pair of cutoff jean shorts and a low-cut black lace tank top. I knew from my conversations with Calli that they were best friends, though they couldn't be more different.

"So, am I here for moral support, or what's the game plan?" he asked as they approached the door.

"I have no fucking clue." I tried forcing a smile as they walked through the door, Calli's eyes lighting up the second she spotted me.

"Hey!" she said happily, pulling me in for a hug.

I tried to ignore what was happening in my jeans as she pressed her breasts against my chest, squeezing me tightly.

I could hear Maverick start to laugh before quickly covering it with a cough.

Calli pulled back, her cheeks slightly flushed as she stepped away and smoothed down the front of her dress.

"Sorry, we had a drink before we came, and I tend to get a little *clingy* after a drink or two," she admitted sheepishly.

"Do I make you that nervous?" I asked playfully, keeping my voice low so I didn't embarrass her.

Before she could answer, Paisley spoke for her.

"You do. She thinks you're hot." Paisley chewed her lower lip, satisfaction etched on her face as Calli's face turned beet red.

"Stop pulling that lip between your teeth before I do it for you," Maverick said, nodding to Paisley before stepping behind her. He placed his hand on her lower back to guide her to the line so we could order food.

"Well, if that's the case, I might just bite it even harder," she quipped, giving him a flirty, playful look over her shoulder.

"It starts already," Calli said, walking beside me as we stood behind them. She grinned to let me know she was just teasing.

I waited as the girls placed their orders, nodding for Maverick to go next so I could pay for dinner. I had just been giving him crap about owing the girls dinner and wasn't really going to let him pay.

Once the girls were done, they grabbed their cups and went to the drink station to fill them while we placed our orders. I pulled out my wallet, ready to pay, when Maverick shoved my hand away and shook his head.

"I got it," he informed the girl at the register, who was obviously into him based on the stars in her eyes, like a lovesick puppy.

"Let me get it. It was my idea to do this," I insisted.

He pushed the card across the counter and turned to face me.

"No, it was my guys who messed up the job and you got stuck fixing it. Between the leaky faucet and the AC, I owe you all a meal for that."

I felt my cheeks burn from the smile that split them.

"What?" he asked, taking his card back from the girl after she ran it.

"It turns out that nothing was wrong with the AC. Paisley stuffed a towel up in the vent to block it so she could get you to come back out. The leaky faucet was an easy fix. Don't worry about it."

He shook his head and grinned, looking over to where the girls were watching us from a booth in the corner. Each of them was on opposite sides, which meant that I would sit next to Calli, and Maverick would be next to Paisley. I swallowed hard, my throat suddenly parched as I thought about being in such close proximity to her.

"I'm in for it with her, aren't I?" he questioned, taking the plastic number for our order and heading to the drink station.

"Guess you made quite the impression."

"So it seems." He laughed and filled his cup with ice water while I tried to figure out how I was going to stay cool and not make a complete ass out of myself tonight.

Eight

Calli

I lifted the taco to my mouth, trying desperately to take a bite without making a mess. The last thing I wanted was to embarrass myself in front of Dylan by wearing half of my food.

When I'd gotten ready for tonight, I had thrown on a pair of loose shorts and a tank top but was then forced to put on something *cuter* when Paisley showed up and instantly judged my outfit. My mom had agreed with her and even picked the dress that I was wearing. It was her favorite because it had tiny strawberries that were hard to see unless you were really staring at it.

I opted for a comfy pair of flip-flops but was outnumbered once again and had compromised with a pair of wedge sandals that had one strap around my ankle.

I felt nervous being around Dylan outside of work, and even though this wasn't a date, it still didn't feel any less like one. I wanted to get to know him, and maybe if we hung out enough, it would dull that heat that always seemed to blaze through my veins whenever he was around.

"How's your food?" he asked, his voice low while Paisley told Maverick a story about getting chased by a shark when we lived in Miami. She was definitely playing it up and being dramatic about how her life was in danger when, in reality, it was a baby sand shark that she almost killed when she nearly stepped on it. Thankfully, it got away, and neither was hurt in the encounter.

"It's delicious," I replied, wiping my mouth with a napkin as I swallowed my bite. "How's yours?"

He lifted his fajita, the savory aroma of onions and peppers making my mouth water.

"Have a bite," he offered, lifting it toward my lips.

They parted of their own free will, accepting the bite he offered.

I bit down, the taste exploding on my tongue. I closed my eyes as I chewed, a soft moan escaping my lips. I had been to La Salsa plenty of times since moving here, but I had yet to try the fajitas. Now I didn't know how I would ever go back to eating anything else.

My eyelids fluttered open, and I found his eyes locked on me, his jaw tight as he held the fajita in his hand.

"That was delicious," I said softly, lowering my eyes to my plate while the heat flooded my body.

I could tell he wanted to say something, but he didn't. Instead, he lowered his head and took a bite, not bothering to look up when Paisley asked another question that both of us had missed the first time.

"Do you remember that, Calli?" she asked, her tone a little louder to make sure I heard her this time.

"Remember what?"

"That time we went skiing in Aspen and almost got stranded on the mountain?"

"Ugh, that I do." I groaned, remembering the bitter cold that clung to us hours after we figured out our way back down the mountain. "I'll never go skiing with you again."

"Eh, we were fine." Paisley shrugged her shoulders and lifted her fork to her mouth. Everyone else had some sort of fried food on their plate except for her. She'd gone with the taco salad and opted out of the fried tortilla shell—which I'd informed her she was crazy for doing.

Unlike me, Paisley was one of those people who couldn't eat when it was hot outside. She'd settle for a salad and eat as light as she could to avoid feeling sick after. Me, I could eat the heartiest of meals any time of year, which was a trait I got from my mother. It was also why I constantly had to reconsider the menu options at Cravings because not everyone wanted a Salisbury steak and mashed potatoes while they were roasting in the sun.

The conversation continued about the skiing mishap, which turned into a story about Dylan and Maverick snowboarding years ago and wiping out. Maverick had walked away with a few broken ribs, while Dylan broke his leg and had to wear a cast for 12 weeks.

I felt my body start to relax as the night continued, and suddenly it was time to go.

Paisley pulled out her phone and started requesting an Uber when I felt Dylan's body shift next to mine.

"Shit," she muttered, chewing her lip again.

"What's wrong?" I asked.

"It's going to be at least half an hour before we can get a ride." She lowered her phone and looked up at me. "Do you want to call your mo—"

"No," I snapped, a little more aggressively than I meant to. "You know that it's not safe for her to drive this late at night."

"Ok." Paisley set her phone on the table and waited for me to tell her what I wanted to do.

"I can give you a ride home," Dylan offered, looking between us.

"Thank you, but I don't want you to go out of your way."

"There's nothing in Whiskey Mountain that is out of the way," he countered. "Besides, Chuck over there is one of the few Uber drivers I know in town, and he's tossing back his third beer. I don't think you should take one home tonight. Let me drive you guys."

"But we're on opposite sides of town. That would be a lot to ask of you."

"It's not a problem."

"I'm heading to Fallen Oaks," Maverick said. "So, I can take whoever is headed that way."

"That would be me," Paisley said, beaming up at him.

"Then it looks like you're stuck with me," Dylan said, bumping his shoulder with mine.

Stuck wasn't how I would have put it.

Nine

Dylan

My mouth had a way of talking itself into situations that my brain wasn't prepared for. Like when I first set up the double date tonight and now with driving Calli home. She sat beside me, bouncing her head and tapping her feet to the song on the radio while I tried to maintain my grip on the steering wheel with sweaty palms.

I pulled into her driveway and cut the engine. I didn't look over at her, just kept my eyes straight ahead with my hands still gripping the leather of the steering wheel while I tried to figure out what to say.

"Tonight was fun. Thank you," she said, breaking the silence for me.

She unbuckled her seatbelt and turned toward me, a loose curl bouncing free from her ponytail before she tucked it behind her ear. I wanted to reach over and do it for her, to feel the soft touch of her skin.

"Thank you for coming. It was fun to hang out for a bit."

I sounded like a robot, everything coming out like preprogrammed responses that lacked any emotion to them.

"I would invite you in, but my mom might be up and—"

"It's not a problem. Really," I blurted out.

She reached over and gently squeezed my hand, getting my attention before her eyes landed on mine.

"Maybe we can hang out again soon? Just the two of us?" she offered.

"Like a date?" I asked before I could stop myself.

Her lips twitched as a smile spread across her face.

"Do you want it to be a date?"

"Fuck yeah I do," I rushed out, feeling a warmth spread through me as her grin widened.

"Well, then, it's a date." She laughed, then let go of my hand as she leaned in and kissed my cheek. "Does tomorrow night work for you?"

I knew Saturday nights were reserved for hanging out with Ramona and Maggie, but I also didn't want to say no to Calli. It wasn't like the girls hadn't canceled on me before so they could hang out with their boyfriends instead, yet this left me feeling guilty. Way too guilty.

"I, um, I have this thing—" I started but stopped when my phone started ringing. The Bluetooth in my truck picked up, showing Maggie's name on the screen.

"Sorry," I apologized, reaching to press the button to decline the call.

"Don't be. It's totally fine. I gotta get inside to check on my mom, but call me tomorrow and we can figure out a day that works."

She passed a piece of paper she pulled from her purse to me and opened the door. I opened mine and rushed around to help her out, frustrated that I hadn't gotten there in time to open the door for her.

"Such a gentleman," she said, taking my hand as I guided her down.

I ignored the way her dress rode high on her thighs, inches of skin begging to be touched.

Once she was out, I leaned in for a hug, more used to doing it with Maggie and Ramona than actually expecting to give her one.

But she didn't seem to mind as she wrapped her arms around my neck and lifted on her tiptoes. Her lips gently brushed against mine, planting the softest kiss on them. I kissed her back, trying to reign in the urge to lower my hands to her ass and plunge my tongue inside her mouth.

She giggled as if knowing what I was thinking.

Her hand came around and cupped my face as she tilted her head and deepened the kiss. Her lips parted, inviting me in.

I groaned as my cock stiffened between us, desperate to get under her dress.

"I'll talk to you tomorrow," she said breathlessly as she pulled away and placed her hand on my chest as we separated.

"Tomorrow," I repeated, already missing the feel of her lips on mine.

She turned and walked to the door, throwing one last look over her shoulder as she chewed her lip and went inside.

I climbed into my truck and found the piece of paper she left with her phone number on it, then quickly programmed it into my phone so I didn't lose it.

I sent a quick text message, letting her know it was me. I set my phone down and started the truck when Maggie called again. I pressed the accept button and backed out of the driveway so I didn't look like a weirdo for hanging out there.

"Hey," I said, my tone reflecting the high I currently felt.

"Hey, you," she replied with a laugh. "Someone is in a good mood tonight. What's going on?"

"Nothing," I lied, pulling up to a stop sign.

"Didn't he have that double date tonight?" Ramona offered, her voice further away than Maggie's, which meant I was on speakerphone.

"That's right!" Maggie squealed. "How was it? Did you fall in love?"

"Stop it," Ramona scolded playfully. "Not everyone *loves love* the way you do. Plus, how could he fall in love tonight when he was already head over heels in love with her *before* they went out?"

"I'm hanging up," I joked.

"No, you're not," Maggie said. "You love us, and you know it."

"There's a whole lot of the word *love* floating around tonight. You know it makes me get all itchy when I hear it."

"Oh, whatever. Knock it off or I'm going to hack into Maggie's blog and tell the world how much you love love and that you're in love with Calli."

I knew that Ramona was likely playing, but then again, there was a good chance she wasn't. Her fiancé was also a technology God, so there wasn't anything I wouldn't put past her at this point.

"Was there a reason for this call, or was it just to harass me?" I asked, turning on my signal to turn onto Main Street.

"Of course there was," Maggie laughed. "We wanted to see if you wanted to do lunch tomorrow instead of dinner. I'm heading out of town for a few days with Owen, and Ramona needs to do inventory."

"Yeah, lunch works."

I breathed a sigh of relief that I could meet up with Calli tomorrow night, after all, without having to cancel on my friends.

"Perfect! How about Whiskey's at 11?" Maggie asked. "We can go for brunch."

"I'll be there," I replied at the same time that Ramona confirmed she would be there too. There would be bacon and mimosas—two of the easiest ways to summon Ramona somewhere if you didn't have Cool Ranch Doritos.

I ended the call and headed home, desperate to talk to Calli again.

Ten

Calli

Mom was already asleep when I got home, so I made my way quietly to the kitchen and made a cup of chamomile tea. I was still wound up from that kiss with Dylan and needed something to help calm me so I could sleep tonight.

I knew his mouth would be magical just from how his full lips moved when he talked, but I never imagined they would leave me so breathless and desperate for more. I was a lady, so I had walked away and said goodnight, but part of me wanted to be like one of those girls in the romance books I read. They would have hiked up their dress and bent over the hood of the car as they got fucked into oblivion. Lucky bitches.

The tea kettle whistled at the same time that my phone dinged with a new text message alert. I moved the kettle to a trivet and turned off the stove while my fingers quickly raced across the screen to unlock it.

Unknown: Hey, this is Dylan. I saved your number in my phone.

Unknown: Thank you again for tonight. It was fun.

My cheeks split as I quickly added his contact info to my phone and texted him back.

Me: I saved yours too.

Me: Thank you for inviting me. Can't wait to see you again soon!

The text messages he had sent were from fifteen minutes ago, so I didn't expect him to be on his phone or to respond right away to mine. I poured the water into a mug, letting the tea steep when I heard the ding again.

Dylan: My plans for tomorrow changed, and I'm now free tomorrow night if you still wanted to hang out. If not, that's cool too.

Me: Tomorrow night is perfect. Is there anything you'd like to do?

Dylan: I'm up for whatever as long as I get to spend time with you.

I placed a hand over my heart as it fluttered in my chest.

Me: I was going to say the same thing.

Dylan: How about dinner? I can make a reservation somewhere if you'd like. We don't have a ton of fine dining options in Whiskey Mountain, but there are a few in Fallen Oaks if that's not too far for you.

I chewed my lip nervously, debating whether or not to be so bold.

Fuck it.

Me: Dinner sounds great, but I'd really rather do something lowkey instead, if that's okay?

Dylan: Absolutely.

Me: I don't want to be too forward, but since it's hard to cook for you here without having an extra guest during our date, I thought maybe I could cook for you at your house.

Me: You can say no. I don't want to make you uncomfortable.

Me: I just haven't quite gotten used to small-town life and everyone watching what you do when you go out. I miss being able to just be me and not have to worry about being the talk of the town.

Dylan: You don't have to cook for me, Calli. I can try to cook, or we can order in.

Me: I love cooking. It's my stress reliever and cooking for people brings me a lot of joy.

Dylan: Can I at least buy the groceries?

I pulled the teabag out of the mug and set it on the saucer before taking a sip.

Me: Thank you, but I got it. I like to decide what I'm making while I'm at the store, so it would be hard to give you a list.

I waited a few minutes for him to reply. I knew he didn't want to let me do the cooking, but it was such a soothing thing for me.

Finally, he responded.

Dylan: Alright. But I'm getting the wine and dessert.

Me: Deal.

Dylan: See you at my house around 7?

Me: Text me the address, and I'll be there.

A few minutes later, one final text message came through with his address and a smiley emoji. I took the empty mug to the sink and headed to my bedroom, my brain racing a mile a minute as I thought about what I would make for dinner tomorrow night.

Eleven

Dylan

Whiskey's was already packed by the time I got there. Thankfully the girls beat me and had snagged one of the last tables in the back.

"Sorry, there was an accident on Main Street," I explained, bending down to hug each of them. "Did you guys already order?"

I figured they would have, given that Ramona gets hangry quickly.

"We did. And we took the liberty of ordering for you, too," Ramona replied with a smile.

"How do you know what I want?" I pulled out the chair and sat down between them.

"Because you always get the same thing and have never once ordered anything different," Maggie said with a laugh. "French toast with a side of bacon and sourdough toast."

I grinned and nodded my head. She was right; I never deviated once I found something I liked.

"So, how was last night?" Maggie asked, immediately jumping in.

"It was fine," I replied, lowering my head as I adjusted the seat beneath me while avoiding their curious looks.

"Just fine?" Ramona pressed.

"Yeah." I shrugged.

"You had dinner with Calli, and it was *just fine*?" Her eyes narrowed as she waited for me to give in and elaborate.

That was the difference between Maggie and Ramona. Maggie was kinder and would back off until I was ready to talk about something, whereas Ramona would stab me if I didn't speak fast enough for her liking.

"It wasn't just Calli and me, remember? Maverick and Paisley were there too. It wasn't a date, just dinner with friends. I drove Calli home last night. It wasn't a big deal."

My cheeks flushed with heat as I remembered our kiss and I knew that I had just given myself away. Ramona and Maggie's eyebrows shot up as they studied me, wondering what I was withholding.

"Spill it," Ramona demanded, pointing a finger at me as a waitress arrived with our food. She set the plates down and promised to be back in a few minutes with the mimosas the girls had ordered. Once she was out of earshot, Ramona pressed harder. "Now."

I sighed heavily, feeling my shoulders rise and fall with my breath.

"Fine. She asked to hang out again and we have a *date* tonight."

"A date?!" Maggie squealed, clapping her hands excitedly. "Dyl! I'm so excited and happy for you!"

"Thanks," I said quietly, trying to avoid drawing more attention to our table.

The waitress returned with three mimosas, then scurried off to another table that was waiting to place their order.

"Nope. That's not all of it," Ramona said, her nostrils slightly flaring.

She had her food now, so she could technically eat and calm the fury raging inside, but that still didn't stop me from scanning the room for a bag of Cool Ranch Doritos. Usually, I could toss one her way and then run while she was distracted.

"Is there more?" Maggie asked with a tinge of hope in her voice.

I glared at Ramona and then turned to Maggie.

"We might have kissed."

I closed my eyes as Maggie squealed and Ramona fisted the air, talking about how she knew it.

We got a few looks from people at the other tables, but they turned and minded their own business when they saw it was just us. Apparently, this was the type of behavior the people in Whiskey Mountain expected of me and my friends.

"Oh my gosh!! I can't believe it! When are you going to see her again?" Maggie asked, still clapping excitedly.

"Tonight. She's coming to my place to cook dinner since she's living with her mom."

"You're letting her cook for you on your first official date?" Ramona questioned, brows pulled together as her breakfast burrito hung inches from her mouth.

"I offered to take her to dinner. To go somewhere where we had to make a reservation. Hell, I even offered to go to Fallen Oaks for dinner. But she didn't want to do any of that. She said that she just wanted to stay in and that she wanted to cook."

"You should treat her. It's the first date," Ramona continued.

"I agree, but I'm also listening to her and trying to make this about what *she* wants. I told her I'll take care of the wine and dessert."

"Do you know what she's making?" Maggie asked.

"No, she hasn't told me. I offered to buy the groceries, but she said no because she likes to pick stuff while she's at the store and figure out dinner there."

"Then how will you know what kind of wine to get if you don't know what you're having?" Ramona took a bite and then wiped her mouth while waiting for a response.

"I was planning to get a bottle of red and a bottle of white. Then I should be covered regardless of what she makes."

"What about dessert?" Ramona attempted to cover her mouth as she spoke but it was too full, so the words came out kind of muffled.

"I haven't decided yet."

I felt Maggie's eyes on me and knew she was up to something.

"What about banana nut muffins?" she offered. "I can whip up a batch so you have some fresh ones for tonight. Or I can call the store and see if there's any left, but I don't want you to take something that has been sitting out for a few hours."

"I'm good, but thank you."

"Oh, come on! They would be the *perfect* dessert for tonight! And did you know they have health benefits—especially for the guys? They increase—"

"Maggie, I'm begging you to stop right there. I appreciate you trying to help, but the last thing that I need for my date tonight is to remember that you made a dessert that can improve my stamina."

She shrugged and pressed her lips together.

"I'm just saying it's never hurt anyone. Owen doesn't complain—"

"Nope. None of that. I'm trying to eat my breakfast before Ramona calls dibs on it, so no more talking about food and their sexual benefits, please."

Maggie tipped her head back and laughed while Ramona blatantly eyed my plate. I stabbed a piece of French toast with my fork just to make sure she didn't get any more ideas.

Twelve

Calli

A wave of blonde curls clouded my vision as I bent over, picking up the cucumber I had dropped. I still had no idea what I was making for dinner, but I had to figure it out and fast because I was expected at Dylan's house in half an hour.

I put the rogue vegetable back in its bin and rounded the corner. It was freaking hot outside, so I didn't want to make anything heavy, but then again, making a simple salad didn't exactly scream *romantic date*.

I chewed my nail as I roamed the produce section, looking for anything that called out and gave me ideas. But instead of a vegetable calling to me, Paisley did instead.

"You look lost," she commented, her brows pulling together as she watched me lower my hand from my mouth.

"I'm trying to figure out what to make for dinner tonight."

"Frozen pizza. There. Done. Problem solved."

I rolled my eyes and shook my head.

"I'm not taking a frozen pizza," I laughed, walking along the other side of the produce section, disappointed with the quality.

"Taking? Where are you going?"

I chewed my lip nervously, picking up an eggplant and studying it before putting it down and turning to look at her.

"I'm making dinner at Dylan's tonight."

"You're making dinner?"

"Yeah, it's our first date," I answered sheepishly.

"He's making you cook on your first date?" she asked in disbelief.

"He's not making me do anything. He offered to take me to dinner, somewhere nice with reservations. But I asked him if we could stay in and have dinner at his place. I love cooking, and I think it will be nice to hang out and not have to worry about nosey people watching us."

She folded her arms over her chest, her shopping basket jutting out oddly at her side.

"What?" I laughed nervously and walked over to the fruit section. This wasn't helpful unless I was going to make a fruit salad, but I needed the distraction from her right now.

"What exactly are you planning to do that you don't want people seeing?" She wiggled her eyebrows suggestively.

"Nothing," I laughed again, but it sounded more fake this time because it was. I would be lying if I said that I hadn't been thinking about *all* the things that might happen at Dylan's house tonight.

"Let me guess, you're gonna play it off tomorrow as *nothing happened; it was just an innocent kiss*, and then withhold all of the dirty details from me."

"We technically already kissed," I said, grinning.

"When?!"

"Last night when he took me home. But it really was just a kiss, nothing more."

"I can tell that you wanted it to be, though."

"Me and him both," I laughed. "I could feel *everything* through my dress, and even though he tried to hide it, it was still there and *very obvious*."

"So then, is tonight going to be… you know? Wink, wink."

"I don't know," I giggled. "It's not like it's premeditated or anything."

"Well, all I can say is that if you hold his balls the way you're holding those plums, you have nothing to worry about."

I gasped and looked down at the plums I was cradling in my hand, conveniently right between my boobs.

"Oh my God!" I shrieked, dropping them back into their section. "What is wrong with me?"

"Relax." She laughed, locking her arm into mine. "You always make a killer Caprese pasta salad. Why not make that with some grilled chicken?"

"Have I ever told you how much I love you?" I looked up at her, batting my eyes.

"Yes, and I know you'll love me even more if I help you shop. So let's go."

Paisley and I scampered off to grab the stuff I needed for dinner, rushing to make it to Dylan's on time.

By the time I got there, I was a few minutes late, but he didn't seem to mind when he opened the door and insisted on taking the grocery bags from me.

I was nervous being at his house, but the second that I walked in, all of that faded away when I smelled the soft scent of vanilla floating through the air. He set the groceries on the kitchen island, then took my hand and gave me a tour of the house.

It was nice and the complete opposite of what I imagined a "bachelor pad" to look like. Instead of mess and clutter everywhere, each room was clean and organized, with paintings on the walls and framed family photos in the hallway.

We made our way back to the kitchen, and I could tell he didn't want to let go of my hand any more than I wanted him to.

"What can I help with?" he asked, looking incredibly delicious in a gray graphic t-shirt with cargo shorts. He was the perfect combination of comfy and sexy, though I wasn't sure he knew it. Most guys were super cocky when they knew they were attractive, but Dylan wasn't one of them.

"Do you have a grill?" I asked, looking up at him as I pulled stuff out of the bag.

"I do."

"Do you know how to use it?" I teased, remembering that he said he wasn't a good cook.

"That's pretty much the only thing I know how to use." He laughed.

"Perfect. Can you grill these without burning them" I arched an eyebrow as I held them out to him, refusing to hand them over until he agreed.

"Yes, I can grill them without burning them."

He took the package from me and then scrunched his face.

"Do you have a backup plan, though? Just in case?"

I opened my mouth to tell him not to worry about it but caught the wink he gave me and shook my head instead.

"Alright, Grill Master. Go do your thing so I can do mine," I teased.

"Holler if you need anything," he called on his way out the sliding glass door to the grill outback.

I nodded and took a deep breath, trying to shake off the nerves so *I* didn't end up being the one who ruined dinner.

Thirteen

Dylan

"You had one job," she teased, covering her mouth to keep from laughing as we stared at the black chicken on the grill.

"I know," I groaned, sliding a hand down my face.

"How did it happen?" She giggled. "I've never met anyone who's burned food on a grill."

"I have. I grew up with a guy who could burn anything. Wanted to be a chef when he grew up."

"Aww. So, what happened? Did he learn to cook and go on to be a chef?"

I turned to look at her and shook my head.

"The opposite. He became a firefighter. Probably a useful skill since he still catches everything on fire."

"Oh my God!" Her hands flew up to her mouth to hide her laughter as a snort erupted. "You're kidding, right?"

"Nope. True story. He lives in Beaumont Creek now. Still a terrible cook, but a decent firefighter," I joked, remembering that I needed to check in and see how Jones was doing. The last time I talked to him, he had caught cinnamon rolls on fire at the fire station.

"Wow. That's crazy. Poor guy."

I nodded and poked the chicken with a fork. It wasn't just burnt—it was burned to a crisp, and it was hard to tell what it was supposed to be.

Now it wasn't technically my fault that I burned it. I had been grilling since I was a teenager and my dad trusted me not to set the backyard on fire. But I had never had to grill while watching a beautiful woman cook inside my kitchen.

Things were going fine for a bit as I watched Calli move around as if she had been in my kitchen a thousand times. It was when she reached up to grab something out of the cabinet, and her sundress rose so high I could almost see her ass cheeks that did me in.

I shook my head and cleared it, trying to get out of the trance she had me in so I *didn't* burn the food. But then after I flipped the chicken, she bent over the sink, washing something in the colander she had found, and I was a goner.

Her dress rode up again, this time giving me that glimpse of her ass that I so desperately wanted. Given the amount of skin I saw without any panty lines, I assumed she was wearing a thong. I couldn't look away if I tried, my cock hardening almost instantly.

"Well, we have pasta salad and bread," Calli said, interrupting the train of thought that was leading into dangerous territory.

"Sounds perfect."

"There's no protein," she laughed, "but I think we'll make do without it. Are you ready to eat?"

She looked up at me, her blue eyes sparkling under her thick dark lashes.

"I'm more than ready to eat," I said, noticing the curious glance she gave me before heading inside.

I hadn't meant for it to come out that way, but then again, I hadn't meant to think about eating her when I answered.

We sat at the kitchen table, and Calli filled two bowls with the pasta salad before placing a basket of bread between us. I poured the wine while she finished getting everything ready, then we dove in.

The food was amazing but dull compared to the woman sitting across from me. Every time she talked, I watched her face light up, her lips plump and beautiful with each word she spoke. I didn't say much, just let her keep talking because I was mesmerized by her.

We finished dinner and then moved to the living room, sitting close enough on the couch where I could feel the heat coming from her body but far enough apart that I was able to refrain from reaching over and touching her.

"Do you want to watch a movie?" I asked. "Or we can play a game. I have a lot of board games. You can take your pick."

I snapped my mouth shut to keep from rambling again. I was nervous, and I knew she could tell.

"Well, while I love a good movie, I think it would be fun to play a game. What are the options?"

She grinned, and I smiled back, relaxing a little.

I got up and walked to the entertainment center to read them to her.

"We've got Monopoly, Scrabble, Clue, Battleship, and Twister."

Her grin widened as she leaned forward, mischief dancing on her face.

"Twister. Definitely gotta go with Twister."

"You sure?" I asked before taking it off the shelf. She was wearing a dress, and I could only imagine what would happen if we found ourselves in a tangled mess on the floor.

"Oh, I'm sure."

I pressed my lips together to keep from saying anything stupid and grabbed the game.

Since she was my guest and it was her idea to play Twister, I let her spin first.

"Right foot red," she announced, handing me the spinner while she put her foot on the red circle closest to the edge.

I flicked the spinner and watched as it spun around, landing in a spot that would put me in a hell of a predicament.

"Left hand blue." I offered an apologetic smile as I stood beside her and bent down, placing my left hand on the blue space beside her foot. My head was so close to her ass that I had to resist the urge to lean over and bite it.

Just a little nip. That was all that I needed.

She took the spinner and waited for it to land on her next move.

"Left hand yellow."

Her cheeks flushed as she handed me the spinner before leaning across and bending over to put her left hand on the yellow circle. Her ass popped right up in front of my face as she did.

Don't bite it.

I placed the spinner on the floor and used my right hand to spin it.

"Right foot red." *Fuck. How the hell was I supposed to play this game without thinking about all of the positions we could do it in?*

I stood up as much as I could, still keeping my left hand on the blue circle while trying to get my right foot on one of the red circles. I somehow maneuvered, but not without lining my pelvis up against her ass.

My cock stiffened right away, and the small gasp that escaped her throat confirmed that she felt it.

"We can stop if you want," I offered, not wanting her to be uncomfortable.

"Why? Are you afraid I'll win?" she asked, taking the spinner from me and placing it on the floor. She spun with her one free hand, and we watched as it stopped.

"Right hand blue," she said quietly.

She passed it back to me, then moved herself to get in position to have her right hand on the blue circle while her left stayed on the yellow. She was bent over even further, her dress riding dangerously high as her ass pressed harder into my groin.

I inhaled slowly and deeply, praying that the oxygen would rush back to my brain. I wasn't sure if it was just me that felt this game taking a sudden sexual twist, but I didn't want to be an ass and overstep if she hadn't intended for it to turn this way.

Right as I was about to spin, her phone rang.

I stilled momentarily, not wanting to knock her over if she needed to go get it. Her body had tensed almost immediately when she heard it.

"Do you want to get that?" I asked.

"I probably should. That's my mom's ringtone. I have it set to something different so I know when she calls."

I stepped back, extending my hand to help her up. She took it and smiled, tucking a strand of hair behind her ear after it popped out of her ponytail.

Wanting to give her some space, I went to the kitchen and filled a glass with ice water to cool me off while she talked to her mom.

Fourteen
Calli

Who knew their mom could be an accidental cock-block?

Things had started getting pretty hot and heavy with Dylan and me as we played Twister. I could feel the way his body reacted to mine every time we touched. There was a chemistry there that was almost as palpable as the cock that poked me in the butt when I bent over to put my hand on the blue circle.

I knew there was a good chance that playing the game while wearing a dress would result in some heavy foreplay, if not sex, but I was fully on board with it. Dylan seemed slightly relieved when my mom called and interrupted us, so maybe it was for the better. I could tell he was interested in me, but I didn't want to make him uncomfortable if we took things too fast.

I finished the phone call and assured my mom I would be home later. Paisley was hanging out there tonight so I didn't have to worry about Mom, but that didn't mean she wouldn't call me repeatedly to see where I was.

"Sorry about that," I apologized, setting my phone down on the coffee table as I sat beside Dylan on the couch. "My mom freaks out sometimes if she doesn't remember where I'm at."

"Don't apologize. She should always come first. How's she doing?"

I shrugged, letting a heavy breath out.

"She's okay I guess. When I first moved out here, she had just been diagnosed, and it was really mild. But she's struggling a lot lately with remembering things that happen. She's comfortable being at home where things feel familiar, but when I take her to the restaurant with me, sometimes she freaks out because she doesn't remember where she is. She has no idea that I moved here and opened a restaurant or that she helps me run the kitchen."

"That has to be hard," he said softly, his hand gently brushing mine.

"It is. But I think the hardest part is when she asks for my dad. It breaks my heart every single time and I don't have it in me to tell her he died. I re-live the grief and heartbreak every time we have the conversation. Her doctor said not to tell her he's dead, but she gets so obsessive about where he is that she has a panic attack, and I have no choice but to tell her."

My eyes filled with tears as I blinked quickly to force them away.

Dylan reached over and pulled me into his side, wrapping a protective arm around my shoulder.

"I'm sorry, this is so embarrassing," I muttered against his chest as he passed me a tissue.

I wiped my eyes and blew my nose, hating that I was falling apart on our first date.

"There's nothing embarrassing about you being human and having emotions, Calli."

"No, but I'm sitting here getting snot all over your shirt. There's nothing sexy about that," I snorted.

He pulled away slightly, and I was mortified that he was checking his shirt to look for said snot trails.

His eyes roamed my features, taking me in from head to toe as I found comfort in their earthy brown depths.

"You could wear a clown costume, and I would still think you're sexy."

I pulled my head back, slightly taken aback by his statement.

"What?" I laughed, my stomach shaking as it started to consume me. "You think clowns are sexy?"

"Not all clowns. But you as a clown? Fuck yeah."

"You mean like me wearing nothing but a red nose, right?"

"I'll take all of it, Calli. The red nose. Giant shoes. Shit, you could pull a rabbit out of your ass, and I would be both impressed and probably turned on because I got to see your ass."

I laughed so hard my stomach hurt.

"I might know a few tricks, but I can guarantee that I will not be pulling any rabbits out of my ass."

Not even the vibrating kind.

He reached over and pulled me closer, nestling my head under his chin as I laid on his chest.

"While I would love to see what tricks you've got, my point is that there's nothing about you that I wouldn't find sexy. I'm glad that you feel comfortable enough around me to let your walls down and be vulnerable. Taking care of someone who needs your help is a lot, and I admire how you've stepped up for your mom. You're an amazing woman, Calli. Someone to admire, not be embarrassed about."

I tipped my head up and looked at him, wondering how in the world I'd found someone as sweet as him.

Fifteen

Dylan

Dinner with Calli went better than I imagined, mainly because I had expected to make a fool of myself and scare her off before we even had dessert. We talked for a bit, had a little more wine, ate chocolate-covered strawberries on the deck while watching for shooting stars, and flirted shamelessly. It was the perfect night and I couldn't wait to see her again.

The week passed by at a mind-numbingly slow pace, each day dragging on worse than the one before. We were finishing up the rest of the shopping center, so I didn't get to see Calli much, given that her section was already complete and we were moving to the other side. Not only that, but Cravings had gotten a fresh wave of new customers which resulted in a constant line out the door.

We'd texted a few times once we were home and winding down from the day, but it wasn't the same as seeing her and watching her face as her features changed with every story she told. If she didn't own a successful restaurant, I would have thought she would be the perfect storyteller for kids because she was always so animated when she spoke, and it was impossible not to watch her.

I packed up my stuff and was glad to call it a day. It was Friday, which was the start of the weekend for most, but for me, it was date night with Calli.

She'd been stressed this week with her mom not doing as well as she had been before. I suggested doing something at her house, but she was worried that I would be uncomfortable spending our time together with her mom. I informed her that she was being silly and confirmed that I would be over at 6:30, the time her mother ate dinner every night.

I rushed home and showered before heading to the store to grab a few things to take to Calli's. My mom always taught me that it was rude to show up to dinner at someone's house empty-handed, but I didn't know what they were making, so it was hard to decide what to contribute.

I grabbed a bottle of sweet tea, knowing that Calli had mentioned it was her mom's favorite, and skipped the wine tonight. It was going to be another hot night, so I grabbed some ice cream cones and a fresh watermelon, remembering another of her mom's favorites.

When I got to her house, I balanced the shopping bag on one arm while I held onto the bouquets. I rang the doorbell, hoping I didn't startle her mom if she opened the door. Thankfully, Calli grabbed it instead, her eyes wide at the sight of the flowers.

"Dylan," she whispered, leaning around to see me past the massive bouquets.

"These are for you," I said, separating the ones I'd picked for her. "I wasn't sure what your favorite flower was, but I got these because they're vibrant and beautiful, just like you. I also added some calla lilies because they sounded like Calli." I shrugged and felt my cheeks prickle with embarrassment.

She lifted the flowers to her nose, breathing them in as she held the door open for me to come inside.

I expected the house to be less modernly decorated, given how old it was, but I was pleasantly surprised by the tile floors and gray walls. There were pops of color here and there with a random piece of art, but other than that, everything was clean and very minimalist.

"I got these for your mom," I said, following her into the kitchen and setting the bags down. "I remembered you saying that daisies were her favorite."

"They are my favorite," a voice behind me said.

I turned around to find Patti standing behind me. Seeing her and Calli together in the same room made my head spin with how much they looked alike.

"Thank you, Dylan. That was very kind of you." She leaned in for a hug and kissed my cheek as she took the flowers from me. "How are your parents?"

"They're doing well," I said, smiling. "It's nice to see you. Thank you for allowing me to join you ladies for dinner."

She smiled, and I saw the relief on Calli's face.

"I wasn't sure what to bring, so I grabbed a few things." I opened the grocery bag and began pulling stuff out. "I figured no matter what we're having, you can never go wrong with sweet tea. And since it's so hot outside, I grabbed some ice cream and watermelon to cool us off after dinner."

"That's so kind of you. Thank you." Calli's eyes started to water again, but she looked away before her mom noticed. "I'll take the ice cream to the freezer so it doesn't melt. Mom, do you want to fix everyone a glass of tea? Dinner should be ready in a few minutes."

"Of course, dear," Patti said, giving her daughter's hand a quick pat before walking to the cabinets next to the sink. Calli mouthed *thank you* as she walked past to take the ice cream to the deep freezer in the garage.

I was about to offer to help Patti when I saw her opening and closing all of the cabinet doors, sighing heavily in frustration. I stepped closer, unsure of what the problem was but not wanting to upset her.

"Can I help with anything?" I offered, my voice soft and gentle.

"I can't find a damn thing in this house anymore. I'm looking for the glasses with the blue geese at the bottom. Where's Charlie? He'll know what I'm talking about."

My words froze in my throat, unable to say anything.

"Dad's not here, Mom," Calli said, placing her arm around her mom's shoulders. "And we don't have the glasses with the blue geese anymore. You sold them when I was in kindergarten because you said they creeped you out."

Patti blinked her eyes a few times, seeming lost and disoriented.

"I did?"

"Yeah, but then you got the ones with pink hearts. You said they reminded you of Valentine's Day, which was also your and Dad's anniversary."

"Where is he? Is he coming home soon?"

"No, Mama. Daddy isn't coming home. Why don't I fix you a glass of sweet tea?"

She led her to the table in the dining room and pulled out a chair, helping her in before joining me in the kitchen again.

"I'm sorry about that," she apologized, opening the cabinet door before I reached up and closed it.

Her eyes snapped to mine, concern etched on her face.

I reached out and gently grabbed her waist, pulling her close to me.

"You do not get to apologize to me again tonight. Okay?"

She lowered her eyes, so I lifted her chin with my finger until she was looking at me again.

"I mean it, Calli. No more apologizing when you haven't done anything wrong. Nor has your mom. I'm here because I want to be, and I'm more than honored that you're letting me into this part of your life. I want to help; I just need you to tell me how. You're not in this alone, I promise."

Her lip trembled as she fought off the emotion that wanted to overcome her.

"Okay," she whispered. "Usually, she's better after we eat. She needs some time without being pushed into anything. I try not to bring up anything from the past which might upset her. Right now, she won't remember anything that's happened recently. So I let her guide the conversation and keep it as stress-free for her as possible."

"Got it," I replied softly. "You lead the way, and I'll follow. And Calli, if you need me to go, just say the word. I won't be offended by any means. I want to make your mom as comfortable as possible, and if my presence upsets her, I don't want to do that."

"Let's just see how it goes. I've learned that I never know what to expect, so I try to roll with the punches."

She smiled and leaned up to kiss my cheek. We both went about getting dinner ready while Patti sat at the dining room table sipping her sweet tea.

I helped Calli carry the dishes in and set them on the trivets on the table. Patti's eyes lit up when she noticed the casserole dish.

"Is that meatloaf?" she asked, leaning in and taking a deep breath.

"It is." Calli smiled down at her mom as she served some with mashed potatoes.

"Is it my birthday?" Patti asked, lifting her fork but stopping while she waited for an answer. "Charlie always makes me meatloaf for my birthday."

She smiled brightly; so much hope filled her eyes.

"Yes, Mama. He made you meatloaf for your birthday. We should eat before it gets cold." Calli's voice cracked, and I could hear the raw emotion in it.

Sixteen

Calli

"I'm sorry about tonight," I said, leaning back on the porch swing next to Dylan.

I knew tonight would be hard with my mother, but I hadn't imagined how difficult it would be. Having Dylan there seemed to help keep her spirits up after I had to give in and tell her that my dad had died. I wanted to ignore it and move past it like the doctor had advised me to, but when her anxiety spurred into a full-blown panic attack that he wasn't there, I had no choice.

"Please don't apologize. There's nothing to be sorry about. If anything, I'm sorry that I couldn't do more."

He gently squeezed my hand, the warmth of it comforting despite the hot summer air.

"You did plenty. Thank you."

My mom decided to call it a night a little while ago, but I waited until I knew that she was okay before stepping outside with Dylan. He'd been a champ through it all and gave us the space we needed to get her situated. Never once did he complain, though he didn't seem like the kind of guy who ever complained about much, to begin with.

"If you could have any superpower in the world, what would it be and why?" He turned to face me, his face illuminated under the gentle beam of the porch light.

"Hmm. I don't know." I laughed a little and gave it some serious thought. "What are my options?"

He leaned back and linked his fingers with mine before answering.

"Anything. Whatever your heart desires."

I tapped my finger to my chin, not missing the way his eyes followed my every movement.

"If I could have any superpower in the world, I would want the ability to read minds. Then I would know what people wanted without them having to tell me. Like my mom, I would be able to know what she was thinking, and maybe that would help me deal with her dementia better."

He smiled, but there was sadness lurking beneath it. I hated that I kept ruining the date by bringing everyone down. I shook my head, attempting to clear the dreary thoughts from it.

"Okay, your turn. What superpower would you want?"

"Easy," he said, not missing a beat. "I'd want to be invisible."

I raised my eyebrows and felt my lips curl up into a smile.

"Such a guy response," I teased. "Let me guess, that way you can spy on naked people?"

"Nope." He shook his head. "I want to be invisible so I can go around and do things for people without them knowing. Small acts of kindness that make their day better."

"Wow. I honestly wasn't expecting that," I admitted, pulling my head back.

"Don't get me wrong, I wouldn't mind checking out a hot naked girl, but I would never do that without her consent."

"You're such a nice guy." I leaned into him and bumped my shoulder against his.

"Thank you."

He turned to kiss my cheek at the same time I turned my head, our lips softly brushing against each other.

We both stilled for a moment, neither rushing to break the kiss.

My heart drummed in my chest, beating wildly out of control as the butterflies swarmed through me. My fingers itched to touch him, to feel the softness of his skin.

He started to pull back, and I could tell that he was going to apologize for it by the frown marring his forehead.

"I'm not sorry if you're not," I whispered, turning and sliding my hand behind his head before bringing my mouth to his again.

"I'm not at all," he muttered before my lips pressed against his.

I hadn't kissed a ton of guys in my life and had dated even fewer, but I didn't need a lot of experience to know that Dylan was a phenomenal kisser.

I leaned in closer, parting my lips as his tongue swiped across them. His hands wrapped around my waist as I climbed over and straddled him, not at all concerned that any of my nosey neighbors might be watching.

He deepened the kiss, his hands roaming down my waist to my ass.

I groaned into his mouth, my body slowly coming alive and wanting more from him.

My fingers scratched down his neck as my hips lifted, then lowered deeper over his groin.

"Calli," he panted, my name sounding beautiful on his lips.

"I want it too," I assured him, rocking back then forward to show him just how much.

"No, Calli. We have to stop."

His hands lifted from my ass, held out at his sides as if he was afraid to touch me.

"What happened? What's wrong?" I asked, not having the oxygen needed in my brain to process what had forced him to stop.

"We, um, have an audience."

He nodded behind me, so I turned my head and caught my mom's elderly neighbors watching us. The woman had a scowl on her face while her husband appeared to be amused.

"Hello, Sheriff Michaels. Evening, Sandra."

Dylan waved politely in their direction as I climbed off of his lap and adjusted my dress.

I heard a door slam shut and glanced over to find they had gone inside.

"Oh my God," I muttered, hiding my face behind my hands. "I can't believe that just happened. I'm so embarrassed. *That* was the *Sheriff*?"

"Yeah, but don't worry. He's pretty cool. I doubt we'll get arrested for it."

"Arrested!" My eyebrows shot up to my head. "What are you talking about?" I hissed, trying to keep my voice down so I didn't wake my mother.

"Well, this *is* a small town, and they don't take too well to people fornicating in public."

His eyes lit up as he said it.

"Stop it!" I laughed, smacking his arm playfully. "We weren't *fornicating*," I whispered the last word, too embarrassed to say it out loud.

"No, we weren't. But imagine if we had that invisibility power. That might have come in handy just now." He winked and held his hand out to help me off the swing.

"I should get going since it's getting late and the gossip is going to start any minute now."

"You're kidding, right?" I scrunched my face.

"No, it's really late. Look around you. The sun went down hours ago."

I shook my head and laughed, thankful that Dylan could easily lighten my mood.

"Well, thank you for coming over tonight. Maybe one day we can have a real date where it doesn't include my mom and where we don't become the town's gossip."

"Thank you for the invite. Tonight was wonderful, and I look forward to the next time we get to hang out."

He leaned in and kissed my cheek, giving me a hug before pulling away and heading to his truck. And just like that, I didn't want the night with him to end.

Seventeen

Dylan

"Did you kiss her again? Like *kiss her*, kiss her?" Ramona asked, sitting cross-legged on the floor in front of the coffee table.

We gathered around Maggie's living room, eating Chinese take-out since our weekly plans were foiled again last night. It was becoming more common that we missed our Saturday night dinners, and I wondered how long they would keep going before they stopped completely. Before, it was easy because we were all single. Now, not so much.

"Kiss her. Kiss her. Kiss her fucker face," Pablo said, squawking from his cage in the corner, his gray feathers ruffled as he shook them.

"That's enough out of you," Ramona scolded. "You need to use nice words."

"Nice words. Nice words. Pecker head is a nice word."

Ramona rolled her eyes, then stuffed the last bite of eggroll into her mouth before returning her attention to me.

"So," she said around her food. "Did you kiss her again? Did more happen?"

I felt my skin heat as embarrassment washed over me as I thought about Calli straddling me on her front porch and trying to take things further.

"Maybe." I lifted the chopsticks to my mouth and took a bite.

"Maybe?" Maggie questioned as she adjusted on the couch, balancing her take-out container on a pillow. "What does that mean?"

"It means he totally did. Look at how red his face is." Ramona pointed in my direction, completely calling me out.

"Red face. Red face. Someone sits on your face." Pablo bounced around in his cage.

Ramona had someone drop Pablo off at her pet shop, Cool Cats, a while back. She had taken the African Gray parrot in and tried to teach it some manners, but it was completely hopeless. He had lived in a *colorful* house, to say the least. Now he lived with Maggie and Owen, as well as an underwear-stealing turtle, who had snuck up on me and was trying to steal my napkin.

"Nope, not today, Leroy," I said, gently pulling it away and redirecting him to the plate of lettuce he had down by his cage.

"Do you think he thinks it's underwear?" Ramona asked, all of us watching him scamper off.

"I think he hopes that's what it is. He hasn't touched his real food in days, but the vet said not to worry just yet. It might be the summer heat getting to him." Maggie's face fell as she stared at him. "Or maybe he's just missing Owen while he's at his work conference. I don't blame him; I haven't wanted to eat either."

"I bet you he would start eating again in no time if you gave him some of *Victoria's finest.*" Ramona winked and then grabbed another eggroll from the bag.

"Victoria's finest?" I asked, completely confused as thoughts of Calli possibly wearing a thong the other night floated through my head.

"Yeah, from Victoria's Secret. He'll eat any panties he finds, but those are his favorite."

"I really didn't need to know that," I teased.

"So, how was it?" Maggie asked, tilting her head as she waited.

"How was what?" I took another bite and tried to get myself to stay focused on the conversation and not let my mind wander with thoughts of Calli.

"The kiss!" She threw her hands in the air, almost knocking over the container on her pillow.

I pretended that I had taken a big bite that I needed to chew to buy myself a few minutes.

"It was fine." I shrugged, feeling the heat of their gazes burning into me. It was weird being on the receiving end of this conversation and I wasn't willing to talk to them about the raging boner I constantly had for Calli.

"Fine? Just fine? Why does he always say that?" Ramona asked Maggie, completely ignoring me. "Whenever we ask him how things are going with Calli, he just says *fine* and acts like it's nothing." Finally, she turned to me and pointed a chopstick in my direction. "You're starting to piss me off."

Maggie's eyes widened though it wasn't really a surprise for either of us, given that we knew Ramona's love language was acts of violence.

"Okay, okay," I said, holding my hands in front of me to ward off the looks I was receiving. "It was more than fine. It was wonderful. Exceptional. The perfect kiss that I never want to end. And yes, it led to more, but we haven't acted on any of our urges yet."

"Awww," Maggie said softly, her eyes watering.

"There, that's better. Now we're getting somewhere," Ramona said, pleased with herself for getting an answer out of me that she liked. "When are you guys seeing each other again?"

I pushed my container to the side and leaned back against the recliner I was sitting in front of. I was too full to get up to throw my trash right away, and Leroy was on the other side of the room trying to eat the fake flowers painted on the side of one of Maggie's casserole dishes so I didn't have to worry about him.

"I don't know. We haven't made plans for another date yet."

"Why? Did something happen?"

"No," I said softly, picking at a loose thread on the bottom of my shirt. "We're just taking it slow. That's all."

The girls both made *aww* noises before Maggie shifted gears and asked how Cool Cats was doing with all of the new businesses popping up in that part of town. I let out a heavy sigh, thankful for Maggie saving me when she didn't even know how much I needed it.

Things were fine with Calli but I didn't want to talk about her and her mom with anyone without her being there. It felt too much like gossip, and that wasn't who I was when it came to people I really lov—shit. The realization that I was falling in love with Calli hit me hard and came from out of the blue.

Eighteen

Calli

"It has *what* in it?"

The older woman leaned in and tried to read the words on the menu board behind me, clearly not believing what I just said.

"It's a grilled cheese sandwich with a few slices of honey ham and mustard, then right before serving it, we add a layer of potato chips inside. It's served with a small side of chips and spicy maple bourbon pickle chips. It's that perfect combination of sweet and spicy with a satisfying crunch mixed in there."

"Okay," she sighed, slapping the counter as she smiled. "You sold me on it. I'll take one of the Poppin Grilled Cheese with water, please."

I grinned and rang her up before guiding her to the drink station to select her beverage, just in case she wanted something other than water.

It was busy for a Monday afternoon, but then again, it was busy all the time lately. We had a constant line out the door from the moment we opened until closing at 3:30. A handful of regulars had begged me to consider staying open through the evening since there wasn't a *decent* dinner place nearby.

I'd considered it, but until I could get the help I needed to keep Cravings afloat, it wasn't something I could do just yet. It would be amazing to reach that level of success so early on, but I would be lying if I said that I wasn't waiting for the other shoe to drop. It felt like things were going *too* well in my life right now, which was unnerving because I didn't know what was going to fall apart first. But history had shown that as soon as things felt like they were perfect, something always happened to mess that up.

I manned the register until Colby returned from his lunch and took over. I headed to the kitchen and checked on how everything was going, though there were no complaints up front, which should have proved everyone had a handle on things.

Paisley was at one of the back counters with my mom, laughing about something she had said. I smiled and walked over, grinning when I saw my mom making sandwiches. She had a loaf of bread out with a jar of peanut butter, a bottle of syrup, and a bag of chips she must have stolen from the guys when they weren't looking.

The grilled cheese was the most popular item today, and I knew we would have to stock up on more chips before we offered it again. But even though my mom had started out craving the grilled cheese sandwich this morning, her craving seemed to change by the time lunch came around.

"The key is to mix them together before spreading them on the bread," Mom said, guiding Paisley through the process for what was probably the millionth time in her life. But Paisley gave Mom her undivided attention and hung onto every word that came out of her mouth as if it were pure gold. Which, these days, we both did.

"Once you have the right consistency, you can start assembling your sandwich. Charlie always liked when I added an extra piece of bread so he could have a layer in between without it getting too soggy. Plus, I think he just liked having another spot to add more chips."

She nudged Paisley with her elbow, her eyes sparkling as she laughed.

Paisley caught my eye and held it, silently asking if I had noticed what my mom said.

It was the first time in—I couldn't remember how long, that my mom referred to my dad in the past. It was like she recalled that he had passed and was clearly present without the dementia taking over. These moments were so scarce that I didn't want to miss a single one.

"Hey guys, something smells good over here. What are you making?" I asked, pushing the emotion away so I could talk past the lump in my throat.

I stepped up to the counter and placed my hands on it to keep from nervously fidgeting.

"I'm making your favorite," my mom said, looking up at me with pride. "Peanut butter and syrup sandwiches with chips. Sit down and I'll make you one."

"Thanks, Mom." I pulled a metal stool over and sat down, glancing around the kitchen to make sure no one needed me. Lucas gave me a nod, letting me know he had everything under control so I could enjoy lunch with my mom.

Paisley grabbed the other two stools and set one to the side for my mom before taking a seat on hers. It felt like we were little girls again, eagerly awaiting lunch after spending hours playing outside in the sun and coming in famished.

Mom finished assembling the sandwiches and passed a plate to each of us before taking her seat and sitting down. She looked at the sandwich in front of her, a flurry of emotions swimming across her face, and worry began to fill me. Had the moment passed already? Had I already lost her to the fogginess of her disease again?

"What's wrong?" I asked softly, reaching my hand out and touching hers.

She looked up at me and shook her head.

"Nothing is wrong, dear. I just got lost in a memory. That's all."

She smiled, but it didn't reach her eyes. Without speaking another word, she lifted her sandwich and began eating. Paisley and I did the same, both too afraid to tarnish the moment.

****

By 3:15, my feet were aching, and I was ready for the day to be over. I was up front, sitting at one of the tables by the window when I heard the bell ding as the door opened. Dread rushed through me at the thought of another customer to serve when most of my staff had already gone home for the day. I tried to handle the end of day stuff by myself so I didn't stretch the team too thin when I really needed them during the peak busy hours.

I set the pen down and pushed away from the table, trying my best to put on a happy face even though I was too exhausted for it. Once I got to the register, I pulled my shoulders back and smiled.

"Welcome to Crav—." I shut my mouth and blinked a few times to ensure I wasn't hallucinating. "Dylan! What are you doing here?"

"Would you believe I'm here for a glass of water?" he asked, lifting his arm to wipe the sweat from his brow.

"I would, actually. It's hotter than a witch's tit out there."

"A what?" His cheeks showed off their deep dimples as he smiled, genuinely tickled by what I said.

"A witch's tit. It's something my grandma used to say." I waved my hand dismissively. "Let's just forget I said that. Did you want anything else besides the water?"

"Na, I'm good. Thank you. I didn't want to come bug you since it's so close to closing time, but I forgot my extra water bottle at home today, and the fountain outside is broken."

"You're never bugging me," I assured him. "Did you eat lunch?"

He shook his head.

"No time. We have to finish the rest of the strip mall by the end of September, and we're already a little behind."

"How many buildings do you have left?"

"Four if I can crank this last one out in the next few days."

"Dylan, it's like a hundred degrees out there. Spending that much time working in the sun without enough water and not eating can't be healthy. You're going to get sick."

"I'll be fine, I promise."

I glanced at my watch and then looked up at him.

"Can you give me five minutes?" I asked.

"Sure…." He eyed me suspiciously. "Does it take that long to get ice water?"

"No, smart ass. I'm going to make you lunch. Do you want something to drink besides water?"

"You don't have to do that, Calli."

"I know that I don't *have* to. I want to. Now sit down, take a break, and grab yourself some water. I'll make your lunch real quick."

"Thank you. I appreciate it."

Dylan grabbed the cup I handed him and went to the drink station, refilling his cup twice before I even had a chance to get started on his sandwich. I didn't want to cost him more time by cooking for him, but I also wanted him to take a break. It was sweltering outside, and I didn't want him to risk getting heat sick because he was so concerned with winning a bet.

I put together a grilled ham and cheese sandwich for him and looked through the fridge to see what fresh fruit I had left from breakfast this morning. I didn't want him to think he had to sit inside to eat it, so I packaged his sandwich with a side of chips, put the fruit in a separate to-go container, and bagged it all up. To make sure that he had everything he needed, I grabbed a few bottles of Gatorade out of the mini fridge I kept in my office and added them to his stuff.

When I went back up front, he was refilling his cup again, this time looking more refreshed with the redness in his face subsiding.

I held out the bag to him and smiled when he took it.

"It's nothing special. Grilled cheese and some fruit. Mainly watermelon and cantaloupe to help hydrate you."

"That was very considerate of you, thank you. How much is my total?" he asked, reaching for his wallet.

"It's my treat. Now get out there and finish that roof," I said playfully, loving the smile he was giving me.

He leaned in and pressed a light kiss to my lips. I walked him out and locked the door, officially closed for the day.

Nineteen

Dylan

My head hurt almost as bad as my body from working a double shift today. I wasn't sure if you could even technically call it that, but given that my day started at three this morning and didn't end until after seven, it felt like it should be.

I got home and fought the urge to pass out on the couch. I wanted nothing more than to sleep for seven days solid, but I was sweaty and sticky and needed a shower first. After cleaning up, I warmed a slice of leftover pizza and shoved it down my throat. More the process of eating because I had to than eating because I wanted to. I finally gave in around eight and crawled into bed, ready for sleep.

Just as my eyes fluttered shut, I heard my phone ding.

Normally, I would ignore it and let it go until tomorrow when I was hopefully well-rested and wanted to deal with whoever it was. But the thought that it could be Calli had me reaching for it within seconds.

A smile spread across my face as I saw her name.

Calli: Hey, just checking in to see how you're feeling. I'm sure you're used to working like this in the extreme heat, but I've been worried about you.

My fingers flew quickly across the screen, eager to talk to her.

Me: I'm fine, thank you for checking. I just cooled off in a quick shower and ate some leftover pizza.

Me: How are you? How was your day?

Calli: It was good. Busy. But I had a nice lunch with my mom. That was nice.

Me: How is she doing?

Calli: Today was a good day. She seemed more like herself and didn't struggle to remember things as much as she has been lately. It was weird, but I have never been more thankful to have my mom back.

Calli: I feel bad for saying that. I have my mom, but it just feels like she slips further and further away as this disease progresses.

Me: That's a valid feeling. You shouldn't feel bad about that. I can't imagine how hard this has been on both of you.

Calli: Sorry, I didn't mean to turn this into a sad text.

Me: You didn't. (Smiley emoji)

Calli: Yes, I did. It's okay; I can fix this. Let me think of something funny…

Me: Like the temperature of a witch's tit?

Calli: You're not going to let me live that one down, are you?

Me: I think the real question is how you know how hot a witch's tit is. Or better yet, how your grandma knew.

Calli: I'm trying so hard not to laugh right now. You're gonna make me wake my mom up.

Me: Hey, you started it.

Calli: It's better than the sad conversation.

Me: Any conversation with you is a good conversation. Good or bad—I'll take all of it.

Calli: Thank you. I enjoy talking to you too. Though it's getting late, and I have a feeling I'm keeping you up.

Me: It's worth it.

Calli: No, it's not. You need sleep.

Me: Says who?

Calli: Me.

Me: So bossy…

Calli: I have only the best intentions. The last thing I want is for you to fall off a roof because you were sleep deprived because of me.

Me: Again, it would be worth it.

Calli: I need to call it a night too. I've got an early morning tomorrow and slept like shit last night. Come see me in the morning, and I'll make you some coffee.

Me: What time will you be there?

Calli: Five.

Me: Cool. I'll see you in the morning.

Calli: Goodnight. Sleep well.

Me: You too. Sweet dreams.

I waited to see if another text message was going to come through, but she just hearted the message I sent and that was it. I put my phone back on the wireless charger and crashed out.

<u>Twenty</u>

Calli

It was funny how my body knew that Dylan was close by before I did. I felt goosebumps pebble across my skin as he pulled the door open, and the bell chimed above. I pulled my shoulders back, thankful I had taken the extra time this morning to get ready before he came in. I told him I would be here by five, but I hadn't been able to sleep last night and showed up at four-thirty instead.

"Good morning," he said, looking amazing even though I could tell he was still tired.

"Good morning," I replied, the stress in my body melting away as his fingers brushed mine when he took the to-go cup I offered him. "I made the same as last time, and there's a tray ready for you to take up to the guys."

"You're spoiling them, you know."

"Eh, it's just coffee. I wouldn't call that spoiling."

"Trust me—it's better than anything we make at home. It's definitely spoiling us but don't tell Maggie that I said that."

"Your secret is safe with me." I pretended to zip my lips. "Though I could totally go for a honey lavender latte from Spill The Beans this morning."

I grabbed one the other day while running errands during lunch and quickly became obsessed.

"Want me to bring you one later?" he offered, taking a sip.

I shook my head quickly.

"Oh no, that's okay. Thank you, I appreciate the offer, but you don't need to take time out of your day to bring me coffee."

I knew how busy he was this week with trying to finish the strip mall, so the last thing I wanted him to do was to fall behind because he did something nice and brought me a latte that I didn't need.

"The offer is always there." He winked and tapped his knuckles on the counter before grabbing the tray. "Thank you again for this."

I heard the bell chime as he left, leaving me alone with my thoughts of him and how I had never met anyone as nice and selfless as Dylan. I sucked in a slow, deep breath and tried to clear the fuzzy feelings he left inside me. When I looked down, I spotted a fifty-dollar bill where the tray had been and shook my head.

That little stinker.

I popped it into the cash register, then downed the rest of my coffee and got the day started before I had the chance to fall behind again.

By nine, I got a text message from Paisley that my mom wasn't feeling well. She had swung by to pick her up to bring her to Cravings with her since I came in so early. She asked if I wanted her to come to work or to stay with my mom. I immediately asked her to stay with Mom and to call me if anything happened.

Not having Paisley there meant we were busier than usual since we were shorthanded. I was running the kitchen as well as taking out orders, just to keep our heads above water. Since my mom wasn't there today, I didn't have her cravings to go off of, so I kept the menu simple. It was supposed to be another hot day with record-breaking temperatures, so I played on that and had a variety of spicy foods paired with some fun chilled salad options for those who didn't want anything hot.

I had spent the morning doing the prep work for the salads while Lucas worked on the sauce for the wings. We also had the spicy tuna wrap that everyone loved, which made it convenient that we didn't have to do a lot of explaining today about what each food was and what was in it.

Things were bustling in the kitchen when one of the kids that was helping out up front came back to get me.

"What's up?" I asked, barely looking up as I finished putting the cobb salad together.

"Someone is asking for you."

"Do you know who it is?" I lifted my head slightly, making eye contact with the overly angsty teenager who was way too emo and moody to work at Cravings. I was thankful for the help, but I could only imagine what people thought when they encountered him.

"Yeah."

I sliced the egg and added it to the top of the salad before pushing it to the side to finish the tuna wrap that went with the order.

"Okay," I said with an edge to my tone. "Who is it?"

The kid opened his mouth to say something but was interrupted.

"It's me," Dylan said, walking into the kitchen. "Sorry, I realized it was probably easier to come back here and tell you myself."

He gave me a sympathetic smile as the kid shrugged his shoulder, tossed his long bangs out of his eyes, and went back up front.

"Please tell me you have Kody clearing the tables and not helping customers?" he asked teasingly.

"That's what he's supposed to be doing. Colby should be at the register," I replied, standing on my tiptoes to confirm.

"Don't worry, he is. I was just teasing you. I know how *personable* Kody can be."

"You're telling me," I laughed as I placed the tuna wrap on the paper and rolled it up. "Kate, can you please run this order up for me?"

I wiped my hands on my apron and took a moment to catch my breath.

"You guys are super busy today," Dylan noted, handing me a to-go cup from Spill The Beans. "I thought you could use an afternoon pick me up."

My heart thumped wildly in my chest, touched by his thoughtfulness.

"Thank you, that was very sweet of you. I definitely need a pick-me-up. Paisley is out today, so we're short-staffed. My mom wasn't feeling well this morning, so she stayed with her to keep an eye on her."

Dylan's eyebrows pulled together.

"Oh no, I'm sorry to hear that. Do they need anything? I can make a quick run to the store and drop it off."

"They're good, but thank you. Paisley said that Mom has been sleeping most of the day. She seems run down and tired, nothing a little rest can't cure."

He nodded and shoved his hands into his pockets.

"I didn't get a chance to ask this morning, but were you able to get some rest last night?" I asked, taking a long sip of the latte. I closed my eyes and allowed myself to drift off to heaven for just a few seconds. Whatever Maggie put in here was pure magic.

"I did. I could've slept a few more hours, but I'm good."

I smiled and tried to ignore the calls flying through the kitchen as more orders came in. I wanted to talk to Dylan and spend time with him, but we were already sinking again with just the few minutes I had stopped to thank him for the coffee.

"I'll let you go," he said quickly, completely aware of how tense I was getting by the second. "I did want to ask if you have plans Friday night."

"Nope, none that I know of. Why?"

"Our guys got ahead of schedule, which means the new movie theater is opening. I thought maybe I could take you to a movie if you were up for it."

"I would love that."

"Cool. I'll text you later, and we can figure out the plans. Have a good day, Calli."

I could tell he wanted to lean in and kiss me as much as I wanted him to. But we had a kitchen full of people waiting for me to dive in and help get the madness under control, so I gave a small wave and got back to work.

Twenty-One

Dylan

"Can we get a large popcorn with extra butter, two large drinks, a box of peanut M&M's, and a box of Reese's Pieces?" I slid my card across the counter to the kid ringing up our treats for the movie tonight.

It was busy for opening night, just like I had assumed it would be. It was the first movie theater to open in Whiskey Mountain, so the locals were ecstatic about it. When I went online to grab tickets for Calli and me, almost everything was already sold out.

I lucked out and got two seats for some action-packed movie I had seen previews for. I wasn't sure whether Calli would enjoy it, but she assured me she liked anything and wasn't picky. I grabbed the big bucket of popcorn while Calli tucked the candy boxes into her purse and then grabbed the cups to fill them.

"What would you like?" she asked, standing in front of the soda dispenser.

"Root beer, please."

"You got it." She smiled and began filling the cup with ice before moving it over to fill hers. I watched her work, partly feeling bad that I couldn't easily help her with my hands full, but also thankful for the opportunity to take in her beauty.

She was breathtakingly gorgeous.

Once we had our drinks, we made our way to our seats. Unfortunately, when I got our tickets, the only seats that were left were in the very back, in the corner. I didn't want Calli to think that I had done that on purpose to try to take advantage of her in a dark theater, but it was either those seats or none at all.

"Sorry," I apologized as we sat down. "These were the only seats they had."

"They're perfect," she assured me, setting my drink in the cup holder.

I wasn't sure what to expect with the new theater, given that we were in a small town, but I was pleasantly surprised to find that each seat was plenty roomy and reclined. The amount of space we had between seats made me feel better that this wasn't an accidental step toward *creeper* status.

I wanted to say more and tell her how beautiful she looked tonight, but before I could, the lights dimmed, and the previews started playing on the big screen in front of us. I leaned back in my chair and handed her the bucket of popcorn, not trusting myself not to knock it over.

My phone buzzed in my pocket, so I quickly pulled it out and tried to hide it so I didn't disrupt anyone with the screen's brightness compared to the theater's darkness. There was a new text message from Maggie in the group thread with me, her, and Ramona.

Maggie: Have fun on your date tonight! Can't wait to hear all about it!

I grinned and texted back before shoving my phone back into my pocket. I felt it vibrate again but ignored it, knowing that either Maggie had hearted my *thank you* reply or Ramona had said something. I was there to spend time with Calli, so I wanted to make sure my attention was where it needed to be and not stuck on my phone.

"Everything okay?" Calli whispered, leaning in close enough that I could smell the light scent of her perfume.

Her hair was piled loosely on her head, with a few wispy curls tucked behind her ear.

"Everything is perfect." I lifted her hand and kissed it.

She grinned and turned back to the movie, not bothering to pull her hand away until the movie started and she needed it to fish out the candy from her purse. She handed me the box of Reese's Pieces and then opened her box of peanut M&M's, offering me one.

"Try them with the popcorn. It's the perfect combination," she gushed, her face lit up like a kid on Christmas morning.

I took a few and popped them into my mouth, then added a few pieces of popcorn. I chewed and closed my eyes, savoring the taste.

"That's delicious." I smiled at her and then offered her some of my candy. She took a few, popped them into her mouth, and added some popcorn. Her eyes widened in delight.

"I'm not sure which I like better," she admitted quietly.

"Help yourself to them whenever you want."

She smiled again and I felt it deep inside my heart.

I turned my attention to the movie so I wouldn't sit there and fixate on Calli, though it was hard not to when her arm would gently brush against mine. I took some deep breaths and tried to pay attention to the action happening on the screen instead of thinking about the action that could be happening between Calli and me every time her leg pushed a little closer to mine, making her sundress ride up higher.

Twenty-Two

Calli

"Thank you for the movie tonight," I said, pressing my hands together in front of me as we walked to his truck.

"Thank you for coming."

My eyes widened at the hidden innuendo he hadn't meant to put down, though I was quick to snatch it up. I couldn't stop thinking about Dylan lately, and the constant way my body buzzed every time he was around me had me taking everything he said the wrong way. Wishful thinking, such wishful thinking…

He cleared his throat and looked up at the night sky before looking back at me.

"I really enjoyed your company tonight, Calli."

I giggled, loving the moments when he would get so flustered around me. I liked to think that maybe it was because of me, but I didn't want to get my hopes up only to be let down if he wasn't exactly on the same page as me. It *felt* like he was, but I had been wrong before.

"I enjoyed yours too," I replied, taking his hand as he helped me into the truck.

I sat down and smoothed down the bottom of my dress as he climbed into the driver's seat and started the engine. I was disappointed that the movie was already over because I didn't want my time with Dylan to end. As if the universe could sense my unease, my phone vibrated in my purse.

I pulled it out and found a text message from Paisley, letting me know my mom had gone to bed and that she would stay there until I got back. She was starting a Harry Potter marathon which meant she would be staying the night and continuing any movies she didn't finish tonight tomorrow. Likely combined with mimosas and brunch that I would be lured into making.

"Everything alright?" Dylan asked, looking over at me before returning his focus to the road.

"Yeah, Paisley is staying at my house tonight, so she was just letting me know that my mom was already in bed, so I don't have to rush home."

I felt the heat rise through my veins as I thought about having a free night with Dylan without worrying about getting home. He hadn't asked me to stick around, yet he seemed to be driving slower than usual, delaying taking the street to my house.

"Oh. That's good. Is she feeling better?"

"She's been a little tired still, but overall doing good. Paisley has been great with helping out when I need her to. I didn't even have to ask her to stay over tonight; she just volunteered." I laughed nervously.

He shifted in his seat, seeming a tad bit uncomfortable.

"So, umm. Did you want to keep hanging out? I can take you home if you'd rathe—."

"I would love to," I interrupted, cutting him off before he could finish his sentence.

His cheeks split into the goofy grin I loved as his grip on the steering wheel relaxed a little.

"Was there anything you wanted to do?" he asked.

I shook my head, hoping he didn't catch the blush covering my face, giving away exactly what I wanted to do.

He chewed his lip while he looked around.

"I don't think much will be open this late. But we can go back to my place if you want to. I have more board games," he offered.

"Sounds perfect."

I leaned back in the seat and took a few steading breaths as I tried to remind myself that this wasn't my first time, nor was there even a guarantee that we were going to have sex tonight.

Once we got to his house, he parked and then came around to help me out. I loved the way his hands held onto me, gentle yet strong. It was nice having unexpected free time with him, and I didn't want to waste a single second of it, knowing that it might be hard to come by this opportunity again anytime soon.

He held my hand as I stepped down, his other hand sliding down to my lower back. I turned to face him, not realizing he had stepped closer, and smacked into his chest.

"Sorry," I murmured, not wanting to look up as my body pressed tightly against his.

"Don't be."

Without second-guessing anything or giving myself a chance to back out, I reached up, wrapped my hands around his neck, and brought my lips to his.

I thought the kiss would be soft and romantic, but his mouth swiped over mine hungrily, capturing the moan that floated through my lips. His hands slipped down my ass, lifting me to his hips as my legs locked around him.

We continued kissing, not bothering to care if anyone was watching, as he walked us to the door, unlocked it, and promptly kicked it shut with his foot. Nothing could stop us now as we made out, our hands grabbing whatever we could as we frantically tried to rip each other's clothes off.

"Are you sure?" he asked as my fingers desperately tried to work the button on his jeans.

"Yes," I breathed, finally getting it undone and pulling down the zipper. "I've wanted this for weeks, Dylan."

"Me too."

He gently pulled me off his body and set me on my feet while I tried to catch my breath. He grabbed the back of his shirt with one hand and pulled it over his ridiculously sculpted body. He was gorgeous. Absolutely perfect.

I licked my lips, ready to worship his body if he would just strip off the last of his clothes so I could.

"No. Me first," he said as if reading my mind.

I nodded, my brain struggling to process what was happening as all the blood rushed to my pelvis. He watched me with lust-filled eyes and kissed me gently while lifting my dress over my body and tossing it to the floor.

Thankfully I had planned ahead, *hoping* that this might happen, and had worn the new black lace lingerie I'd bought earlier this week. I knew things could happen between us at any time, given the constant combustible energy that flowed between us, and I was thankful that tonight was going to be the night.

He stepped back and looked me up and down, soaking up every detail as his eyes took their time going the length of my body. I didn't miss how his Adam's apple bulged as he tried to swallow when he landed on the thin patch of lace that was covering my sex. Wetness started to pool between my legs as I anxiously waited for his touch.

"You're so fucking beautiful," he whispered, dropping to his knees before me.

I was still standing there, wearing nothing but a bra and thong panties, as he leaned in and placed a kiss on my stomach while his hands leisurely roamed my body. His touch was feather-light, leaving goosebumps in their wake, but it kept me craving more.

He tilted his head, his tongue dancing across my skin as he pulled my panties down and slid them down to the floor. My pussy was lined up right in front of his face, and when he looked up at me with a wicked smile, I almost lost it.

"Dylan," I pleaded, closing my eyes while I tried to keep my composure.

"I've got you, baby. Don't worry."

Without saying another word, he leaned in and pressed his face between my legs. Normally I would have been mortified to have someone see me naked with the lights on, let alone plant their head in my private parts. But with Dylan, it was different. He made me feel calm and relaxed, but not only that. He also made me feel sexy with the way he was worshiping my body right now.

His tongue was warm and wet as he licked my lips, slipping it in between before pulling back and sucking my clit. I spread my legs wider, allowing him more room. I still had my heels on, which made me feel a little naughty, even if I was worried that I might break an ankle wearing them in this position if I came. As if reading my thoughts again, Dylan sucked harder, sending a jolt right through me that served as a silent promise that he was going to get me there.

I grabbed the back of his head and held on, pushing it harder against me as he drove me closer to the edge.

"Dylan," I panted, desperate to grind myself against him.

"I know, baby."

He pulled away, and the disappointment rushed over me in waves.

"Sit on my face," he instructed as he laid down on the living room carpet and extended his hand to help me.

"I—"

"Sit. On. My. Face."

"But—"

"Damn it, Calli. Get your sexy ass down here now and sit on my face so I can finish eating your pussy. I know you're not going to let yourself come standing up, so you're going to ride my face until you do."

I wanted to say more and continue to object, but the way he looked at me had me taking his hand and climbing down on top of him.

I did my best to get into a squatting position to hold my weight and not smother him, but he quickly squashed that idea by grabbing my ass and keeping me in place so I couldn't move.

Within seconds, his tongue had found my clit again and flicked it mercilessly as my back arched.

"Ride my face," he muttered from beneath me.

Knowing that I wasn't going to get out of it, I did as he asked. I took a deep breath and spread my legs before planting my hand on the side of his head. I rocked my hips back and forth, creating the friction I needed from him.

I felt the tingling in my spine and knew that I was close.

He sucked harder, continuing to grip me firmly against his face as I rode it to climax.

"Ahhh," I cried out, my eyes closed as my muscles clenched and spasmed. "Fuck!"

He continued his delicious torture until my body stilled around him and went limp. He placed his arms around my back and rolled me over, laying beside me so he could look into my eyes.

I tried not to freak out about the evidence of my arousal that was still streaked across his upper lip. While keeping his eyes locked on mine, he parted his lips and let his tongue slowly lick it off.

"If you were on the menu at Cravings, I would come in and eat you every day."

I arched an eyebrow while I tried not to laugh.

"Well, if I were on the menu, that would mean other people would too."

"Like fuck they would," he growled, pulling me closer to him. "I know we haven't talked about relationships and all that since we're taking this slow. But I can promise you one thing, Calli."

"What's that?"

"If I lick it, it's mine."

I covered my mouth and giggled.

"Oh really?"

"You bet your ass. Which I wouldn't mind licking either," he teased, his hand reaching down to grab it.

"Well, if the rule is that something is ours once we lick it, then your dick is about to be the property of Calli in just a few seconds."

His eyes darkened as I pushed him onto his back and began working his jeans off him. I stripped off his boxer briefs, not wasting any time getting what I wanted.

Once he was laid bare in front of me, I took a moment to take in the sight of him. How glorious his body was and how every single inch of him was ripped and defined by hours of hard work.

I grabbed his shaft and licked my lips, too eager to suck his cock to bother with starting slow. I brought him to my mouth and opened it, relaxing my jaw the best I could to accommodate his large size. He cursed under his breath as he reached the back of my throat and I felt his thighs tighten around me.

Dylan was beyond well-endowed, and I wanted nothing more than to have my fill of him—literally. I wanted to spend the entire night sucking his cock and then having him fuck me senseless because even though I had been with other guys before, none of them compared to Dylan.

I continued to work him in my mouth, pulling my head back before sucking him back down. My hands worked the rest of his shaft that didn't fit, teasing his balls as he got closer to coming. I wanted sex with Dylan to happen tonight, but I also wanted him to give in to his pleasure and come down my throat. How satisfying would it be to have a man lose control so quickly because of something I had done?

"I'm gonna come," he warned, trying to pull away from my mouth. Just like he'd done earlier, I gripped his hips and held him in place as I sucked faster and harder, taking him in and out of my mouth at the speed he liked until I felt the warm, salty ropes of cum shoot down the back of my throat.

I greedily sucked up every last drop, making sure I got it all before I slowly released his cock from my mouth. I chewed my lower lip as I laid down beside him and rested my head on his chest.

"You fucking own me, Calli. Whatever you want, it's yours." He closed his eyes as we lay there naked on the floor.

"Well, I kinda wanted your cock inside of me…" I teased playfully.

"Give me ten minutes to recover, and then I'll make that wish come true for you, baby."

I grinned and curled deeper into his side.

Twenty-Three

Dylan

"The pizza will be here in twenty minutes," I said, handing another bottle of water to Calli, who looked perfect sitting on my bed wearing nothing but one of my t-shirts.

"You didn't have to order food, but thank you."

"Like hell I didn't," I laughed. "I plan on fucking you senseless tonight and need the fuel to keep going."

"Two rounds weren't enough?" She giggled, and I loved the sound almost as much as I loved being with her. Being in her. Fuck, I just loved her.

"Not nearly. I hate to break it to you, baby, but I'm never going to get enough of you. Even while I'm fucking you, I'm going to be thinking about the next time I get to fuck you."

She shook her head and tried to hide her face behind a throw pillow.

I climbed on the bed and grabbed it from her, tossing it to the floor as I captured her lips with mine.

"Like right now, I already want you again," I said, pressing her hand to my crotch. After the second time being inside her, I stopped bothering to get dressed and just threw on a pair of sweatpants. They were easy enough to get off for moments like this when we knew we couldn't resist doing it again.

"This time, I want to be on top," she said quietly, chewing her lip again. They were already swollen from all the kissing we'd been doing, but the added nervous lip chewing kept them constantly puffy.

"Fuck yeah," I growled, grabbing another condom from the pile on top of the nightstand. Within seconds, I had my sweats off and sheathed myself before Calli climbed on and lowered herself onto my cock.

I hissed out a breath, so thankful that she seemed to be constantly wet around me. Even after cleaning her up each time, she was still so easily aroused by me that I felt a different connection with her. It was almost like it was a sign from the universe that we were meant to be together—we were a perfect fit, both figuratively and literally.

She didn't bother trying to keep her weight off of me—which I was happy about—as she ground her hips against me, rubbing her clit against my cock as she rode me. I could already tell she was getting close by the way she was tightening around me, and I wanted her to come again. I'd lost track of how many orgasms she'd had, but I knew it wasn't enough. It would never be enough.

"Use your fingers, baby. Rub your clit as you ride me. I want to see you touch yourself."

She nodded, locking eyes with me as she did as I asked. Her back was slightly arched, her nipples puckered through the thin fabric of the t-shirt.

"Wait," I said breathlessly. "Take your shirt off so I can see your perfect tits."

She grinned and pulled it over her head before tossing it to the floor.

I lifted my hips, meeting her thrust for thrust, wanting to be deeper inside her. She moaned as she used one hand to play with herself and the other to roll a tightened nipple between her fingers.

Right as she was on the cusp of coming, I heard the doorbell ring.

Fuck! On occasion, the pizza deliveries were quicker than they estimated, but tonight was the worst night for them to be ahead of schedule.

"Don't stop," I warned, grabbing my phone from the nightstand beside me. "Keep rubbing yourself until I tell you to stop."

She nodded and watched as I handled my phone.

"You can leave it there," I said, talking into the phone loud enough that the delivery person could hear it from the camera outside.

"Did you want any parmesan cheese or red pepper flakes?" the kid asked, looking up at the camera.

"No, thank you, we're good," I said, struggling to keep my composure as Calli rode me harder and faster. She had stopped rubbing herself with her finger, but I couldn't get mad when she was using my cock to get off.

"Okay." He turned to leave and then stopped and bent down to check the bag. "Sorry, I forgot the breadsticks in the car. Let me go grab them real quick."

I didn't bother to say anything as I closed my eyes and enjoyed Calli's soft moans. She dug her fingers into the sheets beside me, and her mouth parted.

The kid returned and set the other bag on top of the pizza box.

"Are you sure you don't want some cheese?" he asked, lifting his cap to scratch his head.

"Yes!" Calli screamed as she came hard and fast on my cock, her pussy clenching me so tightly that I struggled to hold off on mine while still watching the teenager on the camera app on my phone.

He nodded, grabbed a few from the outside pouch of the delivery bag, and set them on top of the breadsticks.

"Yes!" Calli screamed again.

He looked up and shrugged before adding another handful to the pile.

"Yes! Yes! Yes!" Her head tipped back as she finished spasming around me, but I couldn't take my eyes off my phone as I watched the kid dump the rest of the packets from his bag, shaking it vigorously to make sure they all came out.

"That's all I've got," he said, then turned and walked away.

I hadn't realized I had been holding the *talk* button the entire time. Thankfully I had already tipped him online, so I didn't have to face him after knowing that he heard Calli coming and thought her screams of ecstasy translated into a need for parmesan cheese packets.

"Oh my God," Calli sighed, rolling off of me slowly while I gripped the condom to make sure it didn't come off. "That was so intense."

I nodded, a cheeky grin consuming my face.

"It was fucking incredible."

"Did he hear me?" she asked cautiously, pulling the sheet over her.

"I'm pretty sure he did, given he brought a few pounds of parmesan cheese for us."

She covered her face and kicked her legs under the cover.

"Oh no! I'm going to get a reputation for being *that girl* in this town, aren't I?"

I grabbed the sheet and pulled it down despite her deathly cling to it.

"You're not *that girl*. You're *my* girl, and I don't care if people hear me fucking your brains out as long as I'm making you feel good. Now throw on a shirt so we can eat because I'm starving and if you dare try to eat pizza in front of me naked, I'm going to end up fucking you again *while* I eat it. Shit, I might even cover you in parmesan cheese, given that we have plenty."

I got up, pulled on my sweats, and winked at her before going out to collect our food.

Twenty-Four

Calli

"You seem distracted today," Paisley said as she wiped down the counter next to me. It was the first break we'd had at Cravings today and the first I had a chance to talk freely with her about what happened Friday night with Dylan. She'd stayed at my house that night, so she knew that *something* had happened when I didn't get home until six in the morning when she was already up and making coffee.

We'd spent Saturday on the couch continuing her Harry Potter marathon while my mom rested and tried to get into the movies. I knew Paisley had chosen them because they were Mom's favorite, but it was sad when she didn't know what they were and couldn't remember watching them before. Mom's knowledge of Harry Potter used to be so good that she could enter trivia contests and win.

Paisley and I had kept our conversations around safe topics that day, not venturing into anything that could upset Mom. Unfortunately, it left very little for us to talk about without excluding her, so we gave up and just spent the day watching other movies that Mom might enjoy once the marathon was over.

Yesterday I spent the day with Mom trying to do some light gardening, anything to get that light back in her eyes. I'd missed seeing it and it felt like it was diminishing more every day. By the time I made dinner, she was already tired and went to bed without eating. Her doctor assured me that she was okay and not to force her into doing things if she didn't need to.

I hadn't slept well last night after Dylan and I stayed up late sending dirty text messages about what we wanted to do to each other the next time we were together. After that, I was wound tight and overly sexually frustrated but unable to do anything about it. He had offered to call so we could have phone sex, but Mom had been just as restless as me, so I didn't want to risk her hearing anything.

"I'm just tired," I said dismissively with a shrug.

"Everything okay with you and Dylan?" she asked quietly, making sure no one else could hear our conversation. Most of the staff was in the kitchen, getting food prepped for the lunch rush, while a few were sitting at the tables in the front, wrapping silverware in napkins.

"Yeah, things are going good."

"But?" She turned and studied my face as if that would tell her the answer she was looking for.

"I don't know," I sighed, taking a seat on the stool behind me.

"Are you not feeling it with him anymore?" she pressed, hopping up onto the counter she had just cleaned.

"You're gonna have to wipe that down again," I said, pointing to where her butt was almost hanging out of her cutoff shorts on the counter.

She looked down and then wiggled some, making sure to spread her cheeks all over it.

"Everyone loves a little bit of ass," she teased with a wink.

Color filled my cheeks so quickly that I didn't have time to stop it.

Her eyebrows rose drastically high on her forehead.

"Did Dylan eat your ass?" she whispered loudly.

"Oh my God!" I screeched, swatting her leg. "PAISLEY!"

"What? I'm just saying that I wouldn't be complaining if someone ate my ass."

One of the guys from the back walked out right as she said it, then stopped, shook his head, and turned back to the kitchen. He was older and happily married to the love of his life, so I didn't expect him to linger around to hear whatever else came out of Paisley's mouth.

I arched an eyebrow in warning to her.

"Sorry." She shrugged. "Just saying that if Maverick busted through those doors asking if an ass sandwich was on the menu today, I would be the first to write it on the board so he could get what he wants."

I pressed a palm to my forehead and shook my head.

"What am I going to do with you?" I asked playfully.

"Tell me that you love me and thank me for packing up and moving down here with you—which you've already done."

"You know how grateful I am for everything you've done for me, Paisley. I couldn't do any of this without your help and support. And yes, I love you. You know that," I laughed.

"That I do. But I also know that something is going on with you and you're not telling me."

"There's nothing to tell."

"Bullshit."

I sighed heavily and folded my arms over my chest as I leaned back to rest my back against the wall. Thankfully the stool was old and didn't have wheels, so I didn't have to worry about shooting myself across the room.

"What's going on?" she pressed. "I know I tease and give you a lot of shit, but I also know you better than anyone, and I can tell that you're about to get in your head, which means you're going to get in your own way of happiness."

"You don't know that," I scoffed.

"Yes, I do. And if I had to bet money on it, I would say that something happened between you and Dylan—besides sex, duh. And whatever it is has you questioning whether or not you want to allow yourself to be in a relationship with him."

I opened my mouth to speak but snapped it shut when I realized she was right.

"It's complicated."

"Let's make it uncomplicated."

"It's not that easy," I muttered, desperate for the conversation to stop when I saw Dylan outside, heading in. "Can we please not talk about this right now?"

"Fine," she said, but then her tone changed from frustrated to flirty when she spotted Maverick walking in beside Dylan.

She hopped off the counter and tucked a strand of dark hair behind her ear before turning around and giving them her flirtiest smile.

"Hi, welcome to Cravings. What can we get you?"

I looked at her in disbelief, wondering if she was trying to sound like someone who worked at my restaurant or if she should pursue a career as a phone sex operator.

Maverick leaned against the wall, casually scanning the menu board behind us as Dylan headed straight for me.

"Hey," I said, standing up and leaning over the counter to hug him.

"Hey, beautiful."

I was thankful that even though we had spent hours together naked and licking every inch of each other's body that he didn't try to kiss me. We hadn't gotten around to talking about what this thing was between us, even though it felt like we'd both agreed that we were seeing each other. We also hadn't discussed whether this was exclusive, but the way he growled *mine* every time he got near my pussy told me that I probably didn't need to worry about that. We'd licked each other's privates, so obviously, we'd called dibs on them, and that was the rule. But I wasn't quite ready to show off my new relationship with him at work.

"How are you?" he asked, giving me space as Paisley flirted shamelessly with Maverick at the other end of the counter.

"I'm good. A little tired," I admitted, my cheeks flushed with color when I thought about our text messages from last night.

"I'm sorry. I wish I could have been there to take care of that for you." He kept his voice low so only I could hear.

"I wish you could have too."

"Maybe we can hang out again this weekend?" he offered, his voice still low as he glanced over at Paisley and Maverick. "It doesn't have to be all night like last weekend, but I also won't say no if you're available and want to stay over again."

I shook my head, hating the feeling that was bubbling up inside of me.

"I don't think I can. My mom hasn't been having the best days lately, and I think I need to be around more often for her."

He nodded but I could see the disappointment etched on his face.

"I'm sorry—"

"Don't you dare apologize to me, Calli," he said softly, reaching over and squeezing my hand. "I will *never* ask you to put me before your mother, and I know how important it is for you to be there for her. We have all the time in the world, so please don't feel like there's a rush to find time for me."

I pulled my lips in and tried to stop the quivering that wanted to take over. I tried to smile, but it fell short and never reached my lips.

"Hey, Calli, do you know where we would have some extra parmesan packets? I can't seem to find them anywhere," Paisley asked as she ducked beneath the counter to where the extra supplies were kept. "I swear, it's like everyone is out. Some kind of shortage or something."

I had just taken a sip of my iced coffee when she asked and sputtered it across the counter as I thought about what Dylan and I did with all of the cheese packets we had the other night. Paisley's head popped up and she gave me a weird look as I quickly grabbed some napkins and cleaned up my mess.

"They're in a box in the back," I answered.

Dylan smirked, licking his lips as he watched my flustered reaction. I took a deep breath and tried to remind myself that I was a businesswoman who needed to get her shit together and quit acting like a horny teenager.

Twenty-Five

Dylan

I missed Calli all week and the only thing that got me through not seeing her this weekend was the sexy picture she sent me a few hours ago. It wasn't a nude one—though I wouldn't have complained if it was. But Calli wasn't that kind of girl, and that's what I loved about her.

Instead, it was a selfie she'd taken in the kitchen while making dinner for her mom. Patti had been having a harder time this week, so Calli wanted to spend time with her one-on-one. They were having chicken pot pie with mashed potatoes for dinner, and Calli made the dough from scratch.

I tried to keep my attention focused on Maggie and Ramona while at dinner tonight but cut it short when they wanted to stay at La Salsa and have a few drinks. It was Saturday night, and I finally had a night to hang out with my friends where no one had to rush off to something else. But instead of hanging out, I faked having a headache, paid the bill, and got out of there so I wouldn't feel bad staring at my phone all night while waiting to hear from Calli.

As soon as I got home, I kicked off my shoes and headed to my room to change when I heard it ding with a new text message. I pulled it out of my pocket and grinned when I saw Calli's name.

Calli: How was dinner tonight?

Me: It was good. How was dinner with your mom?

Calli: It was fine. She wasn't up for much, so she ate and then retreated to her room an hour ago. I think she's asleep again. She sleeps so much these days.

I set my phone down for a minute while I pulled my shirt off and changed into a pair of basketball shorts. It was too hot to stay in the jeans and T-shirt I wore to meet the girls.

I picked it up and typed out a response quicker than I could think about it.

Me: What are you doing now?

Calli: Laying on my bed, texting you.

Thoughts of Calli spread out on my bed as I devoured her pussy rushed through my mind and sent an electrical jolt straight to my dick.

Me: You can't tell me you're laying on a bed…

Calli: Why not?

Me: Because I think naughty thoughts about it.

Calli: Like what?

I took a deep breath, hoping it would force some oxygen into my brain.

Me: I would spread your legs and eat your pussy.

Calli: Shit, I wish you were here.

I laid down on my bed, adjusting myself and the rock-hard erection that desperately wanted her touch.

Me: Me too, baby.

Calli: What else would you do if you were here?

Me: I would do whatever you wanted me to.

Calli: But what do YOU want to do? I want to hear what turns you on.

Me: You turn me on, Calli. Everything about you is an instant boner-maker.

Me: If I were there, I would eat your pussy until you came on my tongue. Then I would get some ice and rub it across your nipples, loving how hard they get. I'd suck them and tease them until you come again.

Calli: I'm already getting wet just reading this.

Me: I'm hard as a fucking rock.

Calli: I would ride that for you and help you out if I could.

I lowered my hand into my shorts and started stroking as I read her words. There was no way I was getting out of this conversation with her without coming.

Me: Touch yourself, baby.

Calli: Okay.

Me: Think about my cock sliding deep inside of you, baby. Almost as deep as you took it down your throat. You're so good at taking my cock, aren't you, baby?

Calli: So good. You fit so well.

Me: Tell me how wet you are.

Calli: Really wet.

I paused for a moment, not trusting that she was really touching herself. I knew that she had an iPhone like me, so without any hesitation, I opened the call window and pressed the button beside her name to FaceTime her.

It rang a few times, and I knew she was probably freaking out about me FaceTiming her.

"Hey," she finally answered, the phone pointed to the corner of the bedroom instead of at her. "I thought we were going to keep that going in the text message."

She laughed, but it was nervous laughter.

"We were, but I had a feeling that you were lying about touching yourself, and we can't have that. I know that I'm wound tighter than a fucking top right now, so if you're as sexually frustrated as me, then we're going to work this out between us. Which means I want to see you when you come so I know that you're not faking it. If I can't be there to take care of you, the least I can do is make sure you're taken care of over the phone."

"Oh, I'm fine. Really," she whispered as I heard her move around on the bed. Finally, a few seconds later, she turned the camera to face her.

"So, all that talk between us in those text messages didn't get you all hot and bothered?"

"It was hot…"

"But?"

"Nothing," she lied. She shook her head and looked away.

"Tell me how wet you are, Calli. Or better yet, show me."

"No!" she whisper-shrieked. "I can't do that!"

"Why not? You already told me in a text message that you were touching yourself. You weren't lying, were you?"

She squirmed as she looked everywhere but at me.

"There's nothing to be embarrassed about, baby. I wish I were there to watch you in person. I think it's fucking sexy that you play with yourself."

She chewed her lower lip and barely made eye contact with me.

"Do you want to see what you do to me?" I asked, hoping this would make her more comfortable showing herself to me. I reached into my shorts again and pulled my cock out, stroking it as I lowered the phone to show her.

I watched as her eyes widened, but she refused to look away from the screen. She licked her lips and stared as I pumped it for her.

"You make me so fucking hard, baby."

She let out a small gasp as I spat into my hand and used it to wipe away the drop of pre-cum glistening on the tip. I stroked harder and faster, lowering the phone so he was the star of the show. I could still see her on the small screen as she watched with fascination as I jerked off for her.

"I want to fuck you so bad, Calli," I gritted. "I wish this was your pussy instead of my hand. You remember how tight she clenches around him, don't you, baby? The way she grips him and milks him for everything he has."

"Yes," she whispered, chewing on her lower lip again.

I wanted to be there so I could free it before claiming her mouth with mine.

"Do you want me to come for you, Calli?"

I gripped the base of my cock and stilled my hand, waiting for her to answer.

"Yes. Come, Dylan."

That was all it took. Those words on her lips.

I held the phone as steady as I could as I jerked mercilessly, picturing Calli's tits on the receiving end as I shot ropes of cum up my stomach.

"Fuckkkk," I groaned, letting my head fall back onto the pillow as I closed my eyes and tried to catch my breath. "That was nothing compared to coming inside of you, but it will have to do."

"That was hot…"

I opened my eyes and lifted the phone back to my face.

"Now it's your turn."

Her eyes widened as she started to look away.

"You don't have to if you don't want to, Calli. I would never ask you to do anything that you were uncomfortable with. I just want you to know that you can trust me. I wouldn't ever tell anyone that we did this, I just want you to feel good, too."

Her shoulders lifted with the deep breath she took.

"I trust you," she said softly.

I smiled, relieved when she returned it.

She shifted on the bed, and I could see her hand dip below the waistband of her shorts. I could hear the blood rushing past my ears as excitement to watch her washed over me.

She closed her eyes and lowered the camera but then stopped. I couldn't see what was happening because the camera was now aimed at the wall.

"Everything okay?" I asked.

She brought the phone back up to her face, which now had a scowl on it.

"My mom is up." She sighed heavily. "Sorry, I need to go check on her."

"Don't be sorry."

"I'll talk to you later?"

"Of course. Call me whenever you're free."

"Goodnight, Dylan."

"Goodnight, Calli."

She ended the call and I hated the nagging feeling that said she wasn't going to call me back tonight.

Twenty-Six

Calli

"Son of a bitch!" I turned away from the stove and grabbed a rag to wipe off the bacon grease that had splattered onto my arm.

"Are you alright?" Lucas asked, stepping closer to look at the burn.

"I'm fine," I sighed heavily. "Can you please take over the bacon? We're never going to get these dishes out if I don't stop burning it."

"I'm on it." He smiled and then yelled throughout the kitchen, passing out new assignments as he took over the lunch rush.

Today's popular menu item was macaroni and cheese with maple bacon crumbles. Everyone else was doing their part to get the food prepared, but no matter how hard I tried, I couldn't stop burning everything I touched.

I had tried working up front, but my focus wasn't there, leading to me messing up orders and causing more chaos in the kitchen. Deciding that I was useless to everyone today, I went to my office and closed the door.

Mom hadn't come with me today, but instead of having Paisley stay with her at home, one of her neighbors had asked her to come over and play cards for a while. She promised to call me if there were any problems but assured me that she and my mother used to spend hours drinking sweet tea and playing cards. Her doctor had assured me again that I didn't need to hover around her and that it was good for both of us if she went about doing things she used to do.

I sat behind my desk, frowning when I went through my emails. There was nothing that had come through worth frowning about, other than a handful of spam ones, but my mood was sour, and no matter how hard I tried, I couldn't shake this mood.

"Hey, Lucas said you needed a break. Is everything okay?" Paisley asked, standing in the doorway. She was running the frontline and helping train a few new employees, so she hadn't been in the kitchen when I burned myself.

"Yeah, just having one of those days."

I didn't bother looking up at her because I didn't want my mood to rub off on her. I was better if I just stayed in my office and had as little interaction with people as possible.

"I'm sorry. Anything I can do to make it better?" she offered.

"No, but thank you. Just leave me to my misery."

"What about me? Is there anything I can do?"

My head whipped up as I spotted Dylan's head pop up beside Paisley's.

"I'll let you two talk," she said, ushering him inside my office before pulling the door closed behind her.

"Hey, what are you doing here?" I asked, standing up and coming around the desk to hug him.

He wrapped me in his arms and pulled me tight against his chest.

"I was waiting on the guys to get back with more supplies and thought I'd come down for lunch. I think they're so used to seeing me here all the time that they automatically just sent me back with Paisley."

I laughed but it felt hard and constricted.

"So, what's going on?"

"Nothing." I shook my head but refused to lift it from his chest. For once, I felt calm. "It's just been one of those days where everything that can go wrong does."

"I'm sorry. I hate those days."

"Me too."

I finally pulled away, brushing my arm where I burned myself against his side. I winced and hissed out a breath but didn't want to draw attention to it.

Dylan's eyes narrowed as he gently grabbed my wrist and turned my arm so he could see it.

"What happened?"

"I burned myself cooking bacon earlier. It's fine, just a little burn."

"It looks like it hurts. Did you put anything on it?"

I shook my head again. I'd had plenty of grease burns in my life to know that there wasn't much you could do for them other than wait it out and let them heal.

"You really should put something on it, Calli. Do you have any Vaseline?"

"Not with me. I already took some Tylenol. It'll be fine. Thank you, though."

"Do you have a first aid kit?" he asked.

"Yeah, it's in the kitchen."

He opened the door and walked out there like he owned the place.

"Hi, can someone point me to where the first aid kit is?"

I heard a few of the guys talking, and then a few minutes later, Dylan returned with the box of supplies and closed my office door again.

He opened it up, looked around, and smiled when he spotted what he was looking for.

"Aha! Bingo."

He pointed for me to sit and then pulled up a chair, resting my arm on the edge of my desk.

Without saying anything, he tore open the small packet of Vaseline and squirted some directly onto my burn without touching it. Then he grabbed another package and pulled out a thin piece of gauze that he set on top of it. A few minutes later, and some medical tape to hold it in place, and I was taken care of.

Or at least *my burn* was taken care of. The rest of me was aching for him to touch me more as his body brushed against mine. The way his leg was situated between mine so he could get closer made me want to reach across and trail my fingers over his body, sending goosebumps across his skin the way I did when I spent the night at his house.

That night was the best night of my life, and I hadn't forgotten a single detail about it. Not the way he looked when he came or the satisfied expression that lingered on his face after making me climax repeatedly.

My cheeks burned hot as the heat spread throughout me at the reminders of the things we did that night. My breathing had grown more rapid as well, my nipples hardening against the thin fabric of my bra while my panties got wetter by the second.

"Are you okay?" he asked lightly, a knowing smile on his face.

My eyes snapped back to his as I tried to regain my composure. I looked down to find that I had scooted as far off my chair as possible to get my crotch lined up with his knee, desperate for some friction where I needed it the most.

"Yeah. Of course," I said with a ragged breath. "Why wouldn't I be?"

"Oh, I don't know," he teased as he closed the first aid kit and looked at me. "Maybe because you were just about to hump my knee."

I gasped, my cheeks flaming with embarrassment again.

"I was not!"

He leaned back in his chair, his leg still painfully close to my throbbing pussy. Would it be such a terrible thing if I did hump his knee? Lord knew I had enough pent-up sexual frustration to make even the sanest person go crazy.

"I can help you with that before I go," he offered, subtly licking his lips.

"With what? I'm good. Totally good. Cool as a cucumber."

I fidgeted with the bottom of my tank top, hoping his eyes were focused on the delicate lace trim on the neckline and not my nipples that continued to give me away.

"Why do you push me away so much lately?" he asked, leaning close as he rested his elbows on his knees and lifted my chin with his finger. "You know that I can make you come, Calli. So why are you fighting it?"

My insides quivered as I thought about it.

"I don't know."

There—an honest answer.

"I don't want to push you into doing something you don't want to do, but I also don't mind having my lunch in here if you're okay with it."

There was a twinkle in his eye that I should have picked up on but didn't.

"Oh. Okay. Yeah. Sure. Do you know what you want? I can ask one of the guys to bring a plate back for you."

He pulled his lower lip between his teeth before letting his eyes roam down my body, fixating on the juncture between my thighs.

"There's no need for that," he said. "My food is already here."

"You can't be serious," I whispered, looking around the office even though there wasn't anyone else there but him and me.

"I sure am."

"But what if someone walks in?"

"Does your door lock?"

I nodded.

He winked and then got up and locked it.

"Problem solved."

"But what if they hear us?"

"Then I guess you'll have to be a good girl and stay quiet. Now get up on your desk so I can sit down and enjoy my lunch."

A chill spread through me as I saw the hungry look in his eyes. I took the hand he extended to me and stood up. I felt nervous about doing something like this when there were people on the other side who could hear us or, better yet—just know what we were doing behind closed doors.

But then Dylan pulled me against his body and wrapped his arms around my waist as his mouth lowered against mine. The kiss was soft and sweet, his way of reminding me that I knew him and trusted him. As he deepened the kiss, I started to feel the stress melt away, my arousal becoming more prominent.

He broke the kiss and nudged my head to the side with his before kissing along the side of my neck and nibbling my ear. Then I felt his hands slip down my waist and move to the front to work the button on my jean shorts. Within seconds, they were falling to the floor along with my panties.

He guided me to where he wanted me to sit on the desk and then spread my legs as he sat down and leaned forward.

"I could eat this pussy all day, every day."

Then he lowered his mouth to my lips and began his delicious torture.

I tried to stay quiet and found myself gripping his head as he used two fingers to fuck me while sucking my clit. I wanted to scream his name and make sure everyone knew that he was responsible for the orgasm that was pouring out of me.

My thighs trembled against his head as I felt the last spasm ripple through me.

He pulled away slowly, wiping his mouth with the back of his hand while looking up at me.

"You're too good at that," I joked, realizing that he had me coming in under five minutes.

"I know your body and what it likes."

"Well, it also likes your dick," I muttered, taking his hand as he helped me down. He was still sitting in my chair, a cocky grin spreading over his face.

"Is that so?"

"Very much so."

"We still have time." He wiggled his eyebrows.

I stood in front of him, wearing nothing but my tank top and bra, his hands leisurely roaming over my thighs.

This time, instead of being timid and afraid, I decided to go for what I wanted. I stepped closer and nodded to his crotch, where I could see the outline of his erection.

"Take him out."

His eyes stayed locked on mine while doing what I asked.

Once his cock sprung free, I found myself climbing on top of him in record time.

"Shit," he muttered, tipping his head back. "I don't have a condom."

I frowned, not wanting to stop.

"I'm clean and on the pill," I offered, chewing my nail nervously.

"I'm clean and not on any pills. Other than Ibuprofen," he joked.

I shook my head and lowered myself onto his lap, going slowly as he lined himself up at my entrance. I slid down, closing my eyes as I felt him going deeper inside me.

"Fuck," he breathed, pinching his eyes closed.

"What's wrong?"

"Nothing." He shook his head. "This feels so fucking good that I'm trying not to blow my load right away."

I giggled and began riding him slowly until I knew he was okay.

He tugged my shirt down enough to expose one breast and then the other. My bra was a thin black see-through material that seemed to drive him wild as he licked at it before attempting to suck a nipple into his mouth.

Finally, I reached up and pulled the cups down, freeing my breasts which were immediately cradled in his hands. He sucked hard, taking his time going back and forth between nipples.

I arched my back and ground my hips harder, building the friction we both needed.

"You feel so fucking good," he breathed, releasing my nipple for a split second.

"You too. I feel like I'm going to come again already."

"Touch yourself, Calli. Rub your clit while you come on my cock."

I nodded, this time not too shy to do what he asked. Maybe it was different because we weren't on the phone, and his dick was literally inside me. But I did as he asked and rubbed my clit the way I needed it, feeling the tingle creep up my spine.

"I'm going to come," I warned, panting as my breaths grew heavier.

I rode him harder, thrusting my hips forward while pushing myself over the edge.

My body trembled at the same time his fingers dug into my ass, and he clenched beneath me, shooting his load inside me.

 Once we were done, we sat there resting our foreheads on each other's as we tried to catch our breath.

"I love you," he whispered.

My body froze, and I knew he could feel it because he started to pull away. He didn't look at me or question why I didn't say it back.

I knew Paisley would be coming back to check on us soon, so I got up and got dressed, Dylan following suit behind me. I felt like an ass for not talking about what just happened, but I also knew that I wasn't going to be able to say the words I knew he was hoping I would say.

I made sure we both looked decent and that all of our clothes were put on the right way before opening the door and finding Paisley heading our way.

"Thank you for lunch," Dylan said, giving me a quick peck on the cheek before making his way through the kitchen and out the door. He was rushing to get out of there, and I couldn't blame him.

"What did he eat?" Colby asked another kid with a confused look on his face. "I didn't see him take any food back there."

"Get back to work," Lucas scolded, not daring to look me in the eye.

Paisley shook her head as her grin spread wider across her face.

"Oh, he ate alright."

"Shut up," I hissed, heading back to my office and closing the door. Thankfully she didn't follow me in because there was no way I could deny what had just happened in there.

Twenty-Seven

Dylan

"I didn't think you were going to be able to do it," Curtis said, shaking his head as he looked around at the work we had done. "And a few weeks early at that."

"I told you." I winked when he rolled his eyes at me.

"And it's not bad either," he added, walking around as he inspected the last roof.

"Of course it's not. I was in charge, and I only deliver the best."

"Except for in the bedroom, then that's where I reign supreme," Maverick said as he joined us. His team was getting ready to start the HVAC work now that we were done. All of the vent pipes had already been installed in the roof, so he was up there to ensure their work was done properly before giving them the green light to proceed with the rest.

"You wish," I muttered, my shoulders tightening when I thought about what he said. Calli seemed more than satisfied with me, but that still didn't stop the intrusive thoughts that were forcing their way in, wondering if Maverick would be the better lover if given a chance.

It wasn't that I doubted my abilities as a man to please a woman in the bedroom, but Maverick had far more experience with it than me. Hell, he could probably make someone come just from looking at her the right way. He didn't boast about his sexual abilities, other than when taking jabs at someone, but we all knew that he was never lacking when it came to sex.

Maverick wasn't a *settle-down* kind of guy. Everyone in town—and the neighboring towns—knew that. He built his reputation on being a handyman, and when they said *handy,* they meant it. He had broken more hearts than anyone could count, but the one thing that was consistent with him was that he never led anyone on to think there could be more. He was clear with his intentions, which set him apart from everyone else.

Curtis went on about the next project we would be starting next week, but my mind was scattered, unable to focus.

"She's gotten that far under your skin, hasn't she?" Maverick asked, nudging me with his elbow as we walked behind Curtis.

"Who?" I asked dumbly, thankful we were heading into cooler temperatures and that it wasn't blistering hot up on the roof. We were still having a hotter September than usual, but I was hopeful that it would change soon.

"You know who."

I shrugged, not wanting to admit anything.

"You don't have to say anything, but it's written on your face."

"What about you?" I asked, deferring the conversation to him. "Have you talked to Paisley lately?"

He shrugged and looked around, making a note in his phone before putting it back into his pocket.

"We've talked a few times when I've gone in for lunch."

"Are you going to ask her out?"

"I don't know," he sighed. "Probably not."

I frowned and stopped walking. While Maverick wasn't the settle-down, relationship type of guy, he wasn't usually an asshole to women, either.

"Why not?"

He looked at me and then looked away.

"Because," he said slowly. "I kind of like her. She's different than the other girls I talk to."

I tipped my head back and laughed.

"And that's a problem why?"

"I don't know. It just is." His brown eyes pinned me with a look that said he didn't want to get into it. "I don't do the whole relationship thing."

"Has she said that's what she wants?"

"No. But have you ever met a woman who *doesn't* want that?"

"No," I agreed. "But I've also never met anyone like Paisley. She knows what she wants and isn't afraid to go after it. If she hasn't hinted at wanting a relationship, then maybe don't assume she's looking to trap you."

"You make it sound so easy," he laughed.

"It is. You talk to people, figure out what everyone wants, and then you work together to make it happen. Easy peasy."

"And that's what's happening between you and Calli? You're *both* opening up and telling the other what you want so you can *both* make it happen?"

My jaw tightened as I kept my head looking forward. I knew that if I looked at Maverick, I would see the same truth in his eyes that I heard in his words. I hadn't told anyone about how I had told Calli I loved her, only to have her not respond. I was too embarrassed by it but even worse, I didn't want to think about what it meant for us and our relationship—if we even had one at this point.

"Shut up," I said, elbowing him in the side like he did to me earlier. "Our situation is different."

"Why's that?"

I could hear the change in his tone and knew that he was asking with sincerity, not to mock me.

"I have no fucking clue," I muttered, picking up the pace to keep up with Curtis before I completely missed everything he said.

Twenty- Eight

Calli

"Why don't you ask Dylan out tonight?" Paisley asked, sitting on the island as I worked on basting the short ribs before taking them out to the smoker.

"Because I need to be here with Mom." I looked into the living room to find her sitting in the recliner that Dad used to love, wrapped with a blanket even though it was hot today. I was used to the constant heat in Florida, but the locals were constantly griping about how we were having a hotter than usual September and how they couldn't wait for it to cool off. Thankfully it was already cooler than the past few months, so I wasn't going to complain.

"I can stay with her. It's not like I have any plans." Paisley pouted, swinging her legs in front of her.

"Call Maverick, ask him out."

"Nope. Can't do that."

"Why not?"

"Because I'm waiting for him to ask *me* out."

"It's not the 1920s, Pais. You can ask a guy out. It's the cool new thing to do, and spoiler alert—they love it." I brushed the ribs with another coating of the sweet chili glaze and then pulled the foil up around them.

"I know that I *can*. I just don't want to. *If* Maverick wants to ask me out, then he can do so. It doesn't matter any to me."

"Is that why you're sitting there pouting? Because it doesn't matter?"

"I'm not pouting," she said with a sigh. "I'm just saying it would be great *if* I had plans, but I'm quickly learning that there's not much to do in a small town on the weekend."

I pulled my lips together into a line and tried to fight back the tears. This week had been more challenging than usual for me, and I found myself regretting so much about my past. Now hearing that Paisley wasn't happy here was the last straw.

I took a slow, steadying deep breath, grabbed the tray, and headed outside to the smoker. She hopped off the counter and followed me, quietly closing the door behind her.

"What's going on?" she asked, staying out of the way as I set the foil packets inside.

"Nothing," I lied, closing the lid and wishing I had something else to keep me busy and distracted.

"You're such a terrible liar." She folded her arms over her chest and stared at me.

"I don't know what I'm doing!" I flung my arms at my side helplessly. "I'm screwing everything up, and now you hate it here."

"I don't hate it here," she assured me, her eyes softening. "And you're not screwing anything up."

"Yes I am." I sniffed, trying to will my tears not to come down my face.

"Oh yeah? Like what?"

"Everything, Pais. Things with my mother aren't going how I thought they would. The restaurant is busier than I can handle, but I don't have time to focus on that because I'm worried about my mom. Things with Dylan—it's just all too much."

I let my head fall back as I closed my eyes so I didn't have to see the pity in her eyes as she looked at me.

"Hey," she said, shaking my arm to get me to look at her.

"You're not screwing things up. Your mom is fine. This is all normal and what the doctor said to expect. You're doing your best, and no one thinks otherwise. The restaurant is doing well, and the newbies should be trained soon. You're doing great with running your own business, Calli. Be proud of that."

I let out a shaky breath and opened my eyes, now filled with tears.

"This is all so much harder than I thought it would be," I sniffled.

"I know it is. But you have me here to help you. It's going to be okay." She squeezed my hands gently. "Now, what's going on with Dylan?"

"Nothing, but I'm sure that will change soon when he realizes that he fell for a girl who can't love him how he deserves to be loved."

"Why not?"

"Because it's too much, Paisley."

"Loving him is too much?" She furrowed her brow. "How so?"

"Because he deserves so much more than I can give him." I threw my hands up in the air. "I can't even find the time to go on a date with him because I need to be here for Mom. He's been patient with me so far, but you and I both know that will only last for a little while. Then he'll decide that he's had enough and leave."

She shook her head sympathetically. This was exactly what I *didn't* want to see from her.

"You're wrong," she said softly.

"No, I'm not. There's not enough of me to go around for everyone, Paisley. If I let myself fall for Dylan, I'm going to fall hard because I think I might already be in love with him. Never mind the fact that he already said it to me, and I couldn't bring myself to say it back. But that's neither here nor there, and it doesn't matter because I can't be in love right now. Being in love means spending all your time with that person and building a life together, but my life is my mom right now. I came here to help take care of her and be there for her. It's the least I can do after moving to Florida and not getting to see my dad before he passed. I don't want to lose my mom and regret not being there for her too." My voice cut out as the raw emotion consumed me, my body shaking as I cried.

Paisley wrapped her arms around me and hugged me as I fell apart.

Twenty-Nine

Dylan

After not seeing Calli in over two weeks, I started to worry that she had ghosted me. Since I was done working at the new strip mall and had been moved to a new job on the other side of town, I couldn't sneak in and see her on my lunch like I used to. We texted here and there, but the messages were short and seemed to lack effort on her end. It was almost like she was trying to give the bare minimum so I would walk away and leave her alone.

It was after ten on a Friday night, and I was throwing back tequila like it was water and I was stranded in the desert. Not a wise idea, but I'd done worse. I had my phone out, scrolling through social media, when I came across a blog post from Spill The Beans, Maggie's romance advice column. She'd recently branched out and decided to have a presence online, which was bad news for me tonight.

Before I could talk myself out of it, I clicked the link to the blog page and started a new message.

Dear Ask Mags,

Hi. It's me again. The one man who can't seem to stop falling in love with women who don't want to love him back. Don't worry, this time I'm not coming to you because I'm in love with my best friend again. This time it's worse than that.

I found a woman who stole my breath—not in a literal way. It's not like she was a terrible kisser and I couldn't breathe while we made out. She's a fantastic kisser, by the way. Really knows what she's doing and even has this little trick that she does that drives me crazy.

Not crazy in a bad way—though I think I'm heading there too. But crazy in a good way. In such an amazing way that I fell in love with her without even trying. She's the sun to my moon or to my stars or maybe to a planet? I don't really know. But I think I want to orbit around her and save her from any sort of meteor attacks.

I mean, I know that's hard because you can't stop a meteor, but I would die trying for her. Not that I'm coming to you with a death wish or anything—it's not like that. I'm just saying I would do whatever I could for her. Does that make sense? Probably not.

Where was I?

Oh yeah. I love her, but she doesn't love me back. She's ghosting me, and I don't know why. Am I so unlovable that no one wants to be with me? I mean, LL Cool J wasn't lying when he said he needed love, and guess what? So do I.

But why can't I find it? And more importantly—why are pizzas round, but the box they come in is square? I know that's not related to what we're talking about, but it's been weighing on my mind for a while now, and I'd really like the answer.

If you know, please reply back and tell me. Why doesn't she love me, and why is the pizza not the same shape as the box?

Sincerely,

Unlovable Pizza Lover

I tossed my phone onto the couch and let myself sink lower, thankful I didn't press send.

****

I had no clue what time it was, but the light burned my eyes as I looked around to find my phone as it rang from somewhere close by.

My head throbbed as I tried to wake up, surprised to find myself still on the couch and not in bed. The ringing finally stopped, and I was going to give up locating my phone until it started again.

I tried really hard to focus on where it was coming from as I slid my hand across the couch cushions. Finally, I found it in between the cushions and retrieved it. The call ended by the time I got it out, but the caller ID showed the missed calls were from Maggie, which meant she would be calling again in a matter of seconds. *Just great.*

"Ugh," I grunted as I answered it and held the phone to my ear.

"You sound like you're feeling mighty fine this morning," she teased, though I had no idea how she knew I would be this hungover.

"It was a long night," I muttered, forcing myself to sit up right.

"I can imagine."

"Why do you say that?"

"Oh, no reason, *unlovable pizza lover*."

I frowned as fuzzy memories tried to shove their way back into my head. I shook it, trying to clear the fog, when I remembered going to her blog page last night.

"Fuck. Please tell me I didn't send that to you."

"You sure did. And I believe the saying you were looking for is that she's your sun, your moon, and all of your stars. However, given the turn the email took, it could also be taken as a medieval political theory in which she is the only source of her own light, and you're the moon which merely reflects lights and has no value without the sun. Either way, there seems to be astrological love involved."

"I don't think so. The only love out there is my one-sided love for her," I muttered, shifting as I pulled a remote control out from under my ass.

"Oh, Dylan, what happened?"

"I don't know. I fell in love and thought she felt the same way, but I've hardly talked to her in two weeks. Pretty much ever since I told her that I loved her," I lowered my voice as the embarrassment crept over me.

I could hear sniffling on the other end of the line and pressed the phone closer to my ear.

"Are you crying?" I asked, knowing that Maggie had the biggest heart of anyone I'd ever met and she was "love's" biggest fan.

"No," she lied, blowing her nose.

"You're as bad of a liar as Calli."

"It's not fair," she said angrily into the phone.

"That I called you a liar?"

"No, that you love her, and she won't say it back, you big ol' dummy. Why didn't you tell us about this sooner? Two weeks is a long time to keep something like this from your best friends, you jerk."

"Wow. You really know how to cheer people up, Mags. You should start an inspirational and uplifting blog where you help people with your kind words of encouragement," I teased, happy to deflect.

"Shut up," she laughed. "You know that I love you."

"At least someone does."

"Oh, stop it. I know it sucks right now, but you cannot tell me that you honestly believe you're unlovable."

"Aren't I though? I mean, tell me I'm wrong, but I seem to fall for the ones who can't love me back. First, there was Ramona. Now Calli. What's next? Is the universe going to tempt me into falling for you, another best friend who's already taken?"

"Ramona doesn't count, and neither do I. We love you the same way you love us, and that will never change. The love you have for Calli is different. It's something I've never seen with you before, Dylan. So, stop disregarding it as if it isn't there."

"Why not? It would be so much easier to pretend that I didn't love her when she doesn't love me back."

"Because love is full of challenges! If it were easy, it wouldn't be worth it."

I chewed the inside of my cheek for a moment while I thought about that.

"But should it really be this hard?" I asked.

"That all depends on you."

"What does that mean?"

"It means that it's up to you and how much work you're willing to put into making this work. Are you going to sit on your couch and drink tequila until you pass out and send hilarious messages to my blog, or are you going to man up and go get the girl you love? You're the only one who can decide this, Dylan. One way or another, you're the only one responsible for your future and whether Calli is in it."

"I think you're giving me too much credit if you think that I'm going to be able to make Calli fall in love with me. If I haven't already, then there's really no hope for the future."

"Do you really think she doesn't love you?" Maggie questioned.

"She didn't say it back when I said it, and then she ghosted me shortly after."

"And you think that means she doesn't love you?"

"What else could it mean?"

"Gah, boys are so stupid sometimes," she muttered in frustration.

"Really, Mags, you need to get that inspirational site up and running ASAP. I can't be the only one who benefits from these uplifting messages."

"Oh, stop it. I mean you're being stupid because you're so stuck in your head right now that you're fixating on the fact that she didn't say she loves you back when you should be considering that she *does* love you and that it scares her to admit it."

Fuck.

I laid my head back against the couch cushion and rubbed at my temple with my free hand. Why hadn't I considered that?

"You don't have to say it," she replied cheerfully. "I know that I'm right."

"And a huge pain in my ass," I muttered sarcastically.

"The best pain in your ass you could ever ask for. Now pull yourself together and figure out a way to get your girl. If you need some help, I can whip up some banana nut—"

"No," I interrupted. "I don't need help with my stamina, Maggie. Trust me; we're fine in that department."

"Well, if you change your mind, you know where to find me."

"Thanks."

"Anytime. Keep me posted on what happens?"

"Will do. Thanks for calling, and sorry for sending that to your blog last night. Please delete it, and let's never speak of it again."

"Nope, no can do. I'm printing it as we speak. I'm taking it to our next weekly dinner so I can show Ramona."

"You're so mean," I grumbled, knowing how much Ramona would enjoy reading it.

"Yeah, but you love me. Talk to you later."

I hung up the phone and allowed myself a few minutes to rest before getting up to wash last night's tequila off of me.

<u>Thirty</u>

Calli

I woke up sore from sleeping in the hospital chair beside my mom's bed last night. She had fallen while I was out running errands this morning and Paisley called to let me know they were taking her by ambulance.

The doctors wanted to watch her overnight to make sure she was okay before releasing her. I had sat on pins and needles while waiting for the results of her tests to come back, praying that there were no serious injuries. Paisley stayed with me until around eleven, when I was finally able to send her home. She'd asked if I wanted her to call Dylan for me, but I declined.

It wasn't that I *didn't* want to talk to Dylan; it was that it was too hard. Things were too complicated in my life to allow myself to fall even harder for him. There was no way I could run a restaurant, care for my mom, and make a relationship work. He deserved better than that, even if it hurt to admit.

"How's she doing?" the doctor asked quietly as he stood at the end of her bed.

"She seems good. Sleeping a lot."

He nodded and gave her a sympathetic smile.

"Well, the good news is that her tests returned normal, so we don't need to keep her for additional monitoring. She's a bit dehydrated, which might be why she fell. Her urine sample confirmed that when she was first brought in, but having her on an IV has helped."

I bent forward and pressed my face into my hands.

"I'm sorry. I make sure that she has water and try to confirm that she's drinking it throughout the day, but it's hard to tell whether it's the same bottle I've given her from the start or if she's refilled it."

"You have nothing to be sorry for."

He grabbed the chair from the corner and pulled it close to where I was sitting.

"Calli, can I talk to you for a minute about your mom's condition?"

"Of course," I said, lifting my head and pulling my shoulders back. He was going to tell me just how much I was failing with taking care of her; I just knew it.

"I understand that you're her caretaker and you're doing a great job."

"But…" I sighed heavily, just waiting for it.

"But the level of care that your mother needs far exceeds what you're able to do while running your own business."

I lowered my head and nodded.

"I don't know what to do," I admitted, the overwhelming feeling of defeat washing over me.

"I'm not saying that you're not doing the best you can, Calli. I'm saying that her dementia is progressing quickly and that you need help. Both of you do."

"Okay," I pulled in a deep breath. I needed to keep myself together for Mom. "What do you propose we should do?"

"My recommendation would be either to bring in help through in-home care services or to transition her to a nursing home where they can provide care for her 24 hours a day. There's one in Whiskey Mountain that I strongly recommend, as well as a new one that just opened in Fallen Oaks."

I looked at my mom and felt the burning sting of tears in my eyes.

"I can't move her out of her house. That's her home. That's where she and my dad spent their lives together until he passed. I can't ask her to walk away and leave all of that behind."

"I understand. It's hard to make these decisions, and I won't push you one way or another, but I do want to remind you that as this disease progresses, she may lose those memories that you hold dear. To you, that will always be the house that your parents shared special moments together in, but to her, it may become a house that she may not remember at all."

"So, you think it would be better to move her into a nursing home?" I asked, hating the way the words sounded coming out of my mouth. I promised my dad at his funeral that I would move here and take care of Mom, but was I really doing that if I was so quick to give up and put her in a nursing home?

"I think she needs a level of care that you can't provide without quitting your job and taking care of her 24/7."

I swallowed hard, the rising bile burning my throat.

I looked from him back to her and let the first tear fall without wiping it away.

"Give it some thought but don't feel like you have to rush to make a decision," he said as he stood up. "We're here to support you and your mom, so please let us know how we can help."

"Thank you."

I tried smiling, but it fell flat, so I gave up and returned my focus to my mom as the doctor walked out and closed the door behind him.

I lowered my head to her side of the bed and cried into the blanket. This was harder than I could have ever imagined, and I was stuck having to make a decision I didn't want to make. The emotions rolled over me in waves, and no matter how hard I tried, I couldn't force them to go away.

The door opened again, and I quickly wiped my face with the palms of my hand, desperate to get rid of the proof of my undoing. I turned my head, assuming the doctor had returned or a nurse was coming in to collect Mom's vitals. But standing there instead was Dylan.

"What are you doing here?" I asked, noticing the concern on his face as he approached me holding a to-go bag from Spill The Beans along with a tray filled with drinks.

"Paisley called me."

"Of course she did," I sighed with a laugh.

"Is it okay that I'm here?"

He seemed so timid and afraid, making me deeply regret how I'd been keeping him at a distance lately.

I nodded, too overwhelmed with emotion again to speak. I lowered my head, feeling the tears slide down my face.

He set the items on the table beside me, and then I felt his hand on my elbow, lifting me up. I couldn't bring myself to look at him, to know he was seeing me at my absolute worst.

But Dylan didn't seem to care. He just wrapped his arms around me and provided the comfort and safe place I needed to fall apart against his chest. I gripped his shirt tightly as everything I had been holding in for weeks finally came spilling out.

"Shhh, it's okay," he whispered, rubbing his hands up and down my back.

A few minutes later, I was a snotty mess and accepted the tissues he handed me so I could clean my face before looking at him. I was surprised that my mom had slept through all of this, but her soft snores were comforting, knowing she wasn't witnessing me falling apart.

"I'm sorry," I apologized, grabbing a few more tissues to wipe his shirt.

He lifted my chin with his finger, forcing me to look at him.

"You don't get to apologize to me, Calli."

"I feel like it's necessary," I laughed. "I made a mess out of your shirt."

"I don't care about the shirt. All that I care about is you."

My heart swelled at his words as the words I needed to say tickled my lips.

"I love you, Dylan."

He looked shocked by it for half a second before his grin spread across his face.

"I should have told you a while ago when you first said it to me, and I'm sorry for that. I just couldn't bring myself to say it because I thought you deserved better than me, and hell, you probably still do. I'm a hot mess, and I don't know how to do the whole dating thing while caring for my mom and trying to run a business. So yeah, maybe you deserve someone who can make the time for you, but she won't love you like I do becau—"

"No more talking," he interrupted before closing his mouth over mine.

My body immediately betrayed me, and all of the fight I had left to prove that we shouldn't be together vanished.

"But," I objected, pulling away for a quick second before his hand rested against the back of my head and held me in place.

"No," he murmured against my lips.

I felt the giggles bubble up inside me as I kissed him back.

Finally confident that I wouldn't talk any more nonsense, he let go of my head and stepped back so we could both catch our breath.

"I brought you a honey lavender latte and an apple crumble muffin. Maggie said you've ordered those several times, so I figured it was a safe bet."

"You brought me coffee," I said dumbly, accepting the cup he offered.

"And breakfast," he added, nodding for me to sit down before he handed me the muffin.

"Are you eating too?"

"Yeah, Maggie packed a banana nut muffin for me. I grabbed a few extra in case your mom was up and wanted something besides hospital food."

"Thank you, Dylan. That was very sweet of you. All of this is just so…."

"Sweet?" he offered with a wink.

"Yes, very sweet. But I didn't do anything to deserve this. If anything, I wouldn't blame you for not speaking to me again after I practically ghosted you."

"I won't lie; that sucked. But a very wise person told me that if I love something, I need to fight for it. And Calli, you're very much worth it. I will fight for you for as long as I live if you just give me a chance to show you that I can be there for you. For both of you." He looked at my mom and smiled.

"I know you don't want me to apologize, but I still feel like I need to. I just got overwhelmed and couldn't figure out how to do all this. It felt like I was failing and I didn't want that for us. For you."

"I know. I get it, Calli. I can't imagine how much pressure has been on you to do everything, but I promise you that I'm here to help. Whatever you need, you just tell me."

I worried my lower lip between my teeth.

"The doctor thinks my mom needs more care than I can provide. He recommended either having someone come in for in-house health care or that I put her in a nursing home where she has access to care 24/7."

"How do you feel about that?" he asked gently.

"I feel like no matter what decision I make, I'm failing her." Another tear slid down my face.

"Well, let's just take it one day at a time. You don't have to make a decision right now. Let's focus on getting her home, then we can return to this conversation later."

I nodded, the tears burning the back of my throat too much to want to talk. We sat there quietly, eating our muffins and sipping our lattes.

"Did they say when she'll be discharged and able to go home?" he asked a few minutes later, breaking the silence as we finished our food.

"Her tests came back normal, so I'm guessing they'll be working on her discharge paperwork soon. He said there was no reason to keep her for monitoring."

"Okay, cool." He nodded, clearly thinking through something without saying what it was.

"You don't have to wait around here, though. You can go if you want to. I'll be fine getting her home."

He glanced at his watch and then back to me.

"I have a few errands that I need to run, but I'll call you in a little bit to check in. Is that okay?"

I nodded and smiled, finally not feeling the strain of faking it.

He pecked me on the lips and then headed out. I sat back in my chair, staring at my mom while praying that the right answer about what to do for her would come to me.

Thirty-One

Dylan

I stood in Calli's kitchen, nervous as hell as I worried that this was a terrible plan.

"It's fine. Stop worrying," Paisley scolded, leaning against the counter as she finished highlighting the calendar she was working on.

"What if she hates it?"

"She won't."

"But I didn't ask first."

"You led with your heart. That's all that matters," Maggie said as she walked in, carrying another armful of casserole dishes that she loaded into the freezer.

"Don't be so scared," Ramona teased, bumping her hip into mine before stocking the K-cups into the organizer we had bought. "Everything is going to be just fine."

I inhaled deeply and let it out slowly.

But then I heard keys in the front door and started to panic again.

"Stop it!" all three women scolded before Maggie opened the door.

Patti was the first to come in and looked as shocked as I imagined she would be when she saw the four of us in her kitchen.

"Oh my goodness," she said, holding her hand to her heart. "You brought me daisies again!"

I grinned stupidly at the giant bouquet I'd assembled for her with Paisley's help.

"What's going o—" Calli said but stopped when she spotted us. "Oh, hi!" She waved nervously, looking around as she tried to figure out what was happening.

I grabbed the flowers from the island and took them to Patti, unsure if she remembered me. But the way she smiled before pulling me in for a hug was reassuring.

"Thank you for the beautiful flowers. What a treat to come home to."

"You're very welcome. I'm so happy you're feeling better."

Patti brushed her finger over my cheek before heading into the kitchen. She said hi to Paisley and then waited for her to introduce her to Maggie and Ramona.

"Hey, what's all this?" Calli asked softly as she stepped beside me and wrapped her arms around my waist. I cuddled her against me and loved the feeling of having her there.

"We all wanted to do something to help. I hope you don't mind, but I talked to Paisley and Maggie about what was happening, and things kinda just went from there."

Paisley gave me a wink before leading Patti to the back patio, where a few of her friends were waiting for her.

"Dylan asked for help with recipe ideas and then told me what was going on," Maggie explained. "I know you're not used to small-town life, but one thing about it is that we take care of each other. We're one giant family, so when we say you're not going through this alone, we mean it."

I kissed Calli's head when I noticed the tears in her eyes again.

"My friend's mom runs the town's food chain, meaning that when someone is in need, we rally together, and everyone prepares a dish. I spent the afternoon collecting them, and they're all packed up in your freezer with dates, heating instructions, and a little pick-me-up note from the person who made it. We didn't leave anything out for tonight since Dylan said he's got that covered."

Maggie winked at me, but I shook my head, not wanting to get into the debate again over whether I could grill for dinner tonight without burning the food. It had happened *one time*.

"I also baked some muffins and assorted breakfast breads, so you guys will have ready-to-eat options. I'll come by next week and bring some fresh goodies, but let me know if there's anything you want in particular. Since we're heading into fall, I'll be adding some pumpkin and apple items to the menu at Spill The Beans, but I'm happy to bring some here too."

"Thank you so much. That's too kind of you," Calli said, accepting the tissue Ramona handed her. "This is all too much!"

"It's not at all," Ramona said. "Now, I might not make delicious muffins, but I know good coffee, so I wanted to make sure you had some here too. Dylan told me your Keurig recently broke, so we all pitched in and got you the Keurig K-Café Single Serve Coffee, Latte & Cappuccino Maker. It may not make the over-the-top delicious drinks that Maggie makes, but it is definitely better than the crappy coffee Dylan makes at home."

"Hey now," I objected. "I'm a busy man; gotta have something quick and easy."

"Don't worry. I'll share some of my fancy coffee with you."

"We stocked you up on a variety of options," Ramona said, opening and closing the drawers of the organizer to show Calli the K-cups. "And we chose one that was safe for your mom, so you didn't have to worry about her burning herself on a hot pot of coffee."

"Thank you, I appreciate that."

Paisley came back inside, closing the patio door behind her.

"Where's Mom?" Calli asked, pulling away with a concerned look splashed across her face.

"She's outside with the girls." Paisley smiled, pulling Calli in for a hug.

"Girls? What girls?"

"Her friends," Paisley said softly. "Rita from across the street rallied the girls together. It turns out that they used to get together a few times a week to play cards, but it stopped shortly after your dad passed. When I told them what was happening, they all stepped in and wanted to help."

"Okay," Calli sighed, shaking her head. "What does that mean?"

Paisley grabbed Calli's hand and led her to the calendar on the fridge.

"It means that family takes care of each other, and we're all family, Calli. We know how important Cravings is to you, but we also know that your mom needs care 24/7 and that you can't do both."

"I know, bu—"

"BUT," Paisley interrupted. "You don't have to do all of this on your own, Calli. That's what we're saying. Everyone is rallying around you guys right now because we see that you need help, and that's nothing to be ashamed of. You're doing an amazing job with Mom, don't ever second guess yourself. But when you moved out here to take care of her, there was no way you knew what to expect. Neither of us did."

Calli covered her mouth as a sob escaped her throat.

"We've got this," Paisley assured her, squeezing an arm around her shoulders. "Aside from the meals that have been brought over, we also have a schedule going. I'll keep track of this and help you update it every month. But for now, we're all set. You'll see everyone's name on the right side, highlighted in their color. Then on the calendar, it shows who will be staying with Mom on those days. The ladies have taken the days during the week while you're at work and will take turns coming every day. You'll be home most evenings; however, you'll see the spots where I've added myself to stay the night."

I felt my stomach tighten as I worried about how Calli was going to handle all of these decisions being made for her.

"Why are you staying over those nights?" Calli asked quietly, her body stiffening.

"Because those are the nights you're going to take a break and stay with Dylan. I know you're afraid this can't work because it's all too much, but we've got this."

"And I'll be staying over here a few nights a week, too," I added, coming to stand on the other side of her. "I'm not coming to take advantage of being in your room. I'm coming so I can be on night duty those nights so you can get some sleep. I'll camp out on the couch, and you won't even notice I'm here."

Calli turned toward me, eyes filled with tears again.

"I can't believe you put all this together, Dylan."

"Are you mad?" I asked quietly, pulling my mouth to the side.

"No," she laughed, wrapping her arms behind my head. "Not at all. The only thing I'm mad about is that it took me so long to tell you I love you."

"Well, there's no need to worry about the past, my love," I assured her, resting my forehead against hers. "We have the rest of our lives to make sure we tell each other how much we love them."

Epilogue

Calli

Three Months Later

"The snow is really coming down. You better go if you want to make it home before the roads freeze," I said, looking out the living room window.

My mom had already gone to bed after dinner, which had quickly become the new norm for her. Dylan spent most nights with us, except for the prescheduled ones where Paisley kicked me out of my own house once a week to give me a break.

I was pleasantly surprised by how well things were going and even more so with how much pressure had been lifted from my shoulders with everyone helping out. The ladies loved spending their time with Mom during the week, and instead of only one of them coming per day, all four of them would show up, and the Feisty Five, as I called them, would spend the day laughing and having fun.

Mom still had her ups and downs, but now that I had so much support, we were able to set up a routine that worked for everyone.

"I don't want to leave you and your mom by yourselves in the storm," Dylan said quietly, wrapping his arms around my waist and pressing his hands firmly against my stomach.

"We'll be fine. It's just snow."

Not that I had much experience with snow until now. Living in Florida was nice because we didn't get this bitter-cold weather, but I wasn't sure which I disliked more—having to worry about alligators sneaking up on me or shoveling snow and ice.

"You don't know how bad these storms can get. We might lose power." He leaned down and kissed behind my ear.

"I have candles," I giggled, leaning into his touch.

"Yeah, but what about food? How are you going to feed my little peanut? You know she gets hangry."

"We don't know that it's a girl," I laughed as he tickled my sides.

He moved around and kneeled in front of me, lifting the bottom of my hoodie before lowering the waistband of my sweats. He closed his eyes and kissed my stomach, already so in love with our baby.

"What if I'm not worried about the storm, and I don't doubt you can feed yourself if the power goes out," he said softly. "What if I just don't want to leave?"

"Then don't," I said a little too eagerly.

He stood up, lifted me to his hips, and grabbed my ass.

"Move in with us," I whispered in his ear.

It wasn't the first time I'd asked, but he wanted to take things slowly so we didn't disrupt the routine we had going for Mom.

"Do you think it's too soon for her?"

I shook my head and cupped his face in my hands.

"She's already used to having you here as it is. It wouldn't be that much different if you moved in."

"That means we can't sneak off to my house to have loud, crazy sex anymore," he whispered.

"True. But I've learned to be quiet… for the most part." I giggled when he nipped my ear.

"So, what do you say?" I pressed, sighing heavily as I waited for his answer. "Will you move in with us?"

He nodded and squeezed my ass harder before carrying me down the hallway to *our* bedroom.

Something To Live For

Whiskey Mountain Book 4

Samantha Baca

548

Copyright © 2024 by Samantha Baca

Cover Design: Oh So Novel

One

Paisley

"Can I help you?" I asked grumpily, my foot tapping impatiently on the floor as Maverick lowered his head and approached the counter. I had done well with ignoring him this week, but we were shorthanded today, so I agreed to handle the register for a while until Calli caught up on orders in the kitchen. Of course, he just had to pick today to stop in for food. *Fucker.*

"Yeah, can I get the chicken and waffles?" He grinned a dimpled smile, his stupid voice deep and sultry.

"No." I glared at him and then leaned to see past him. "I can help who's next."

"Really?" He cocked his head to the side as a smirk graced his full lips that had once devoured mine.

"Paisley," Calli hissed, bumping my hip with hers as she walked past me. "Stop it."

"I'm not helping him." I folded my arms over my chest and raised an eyebrow at her.

"You're on the clock, which means it's your job to help *everyone* who comes in," she replied with gritted teeth. Thankfully, she was my best friend and needed me more than I needed this job, but I knew my attitude wasn't making things any easier for her.

"Fine." I turned my head, my eyes narrowing as they found his. "Chicken and waffles with extra spit. Can I get you anything else to eat?" I forced a smile on my face, pretending to give the best customer service I could muster.

Calli sighed heavily as she walked over to the other register and called the next person up. It was a good sign that we were finally catching up and the rush was coming to an end, but that meant Maverick had no real pressure to move through the line now.

"What are my options?" he asked softly as he licked his lips.

"There was a dead cat out back in the alley. I can see if Frank can get it on the grill for you."

"That's not the kind of *cat* I usually enjoy eating."

I felt the heat flush through my skin as I looked down and jabbed the order into the computer.

"$17.37," I said, keeping my tone clipped.

"I thought it was the lunch special for $12.99?"

"I added a brownie."

"Oh. Okay. I wasn't really in the mood for a sweet treat, but why not."

"It's for me."

The corners of his lips turned up into a devilish smile as he passed his credit card.

"Well, in that case, why don't I take you to dinner tonight? I'll gladly buy you more than a brownie. Something more *filling* and *satisfying*."

"No thanks. I'd rather take my chances on the brownie and my vibrator leaving me fulfilled and satisfied, if you know what I mean. At least I know they won't flake out on me." I winked and held my hand up as I pretended to whisper but said it loud enough for Calli to hear. She had already cleared the line, so at least I didn't embarrass her in front of any customers.

Maverick let out a long, heavy breath and locked eyes with me.

"I'm sorry that I had to cancel our date."

"Which one?" I replied curtly.

"Fair point. I'm sorry that work has been so busy and that I've had to go out of town so much on such short notice. I didn't mean to upset you by canceling so much. Trust me, I was looking forward to it as much as you were."

"I seriously doubt that."

"Then give me a chance to prove it to you. Have dinner with me tonight."

"No."

He rubbed his lips together, unsure of what to say as I passed his credit card back to him.

"Your order will be ready in a few minutes. You can wait over there for it."

He nodded and lowered his head as he walked off. My insides felt like they were on fire as I fought off the flurry of emotions that were storming inside me.

"What the hell was that?" Calli asked as Maverick left with his food.

"Nothing."

I grabbed the towel and began wiping the counter down, even though it was clean from when I did it five minutes ago.

"Bullshit."

"We were supposed to have a date last weekend, and at the last minute, he had to cancel. It wouldn't have bothered me so much, but it was the third time in two weeks. I'm just over it."

"What happened to you being so obsessed with him?"

"I guess constantly being pushed to the side will do that."

"But you liked him," she pressed.

"Yeah, and sometimes things change. It's not a big deal, Calli. Let's just let it go and get through the rest of the day."

I walked off and hated the nagging feeling that told me she was right. I had liked him, but none of that mattered if he didn't like me enough to make an effort to really get to know me.

<u>Two</u>

Maverick

"How long do you think we'll have?" I asked, pressing the phone to my ear as I took a bite of my food. I didn't technically have time to stop for lunch, but Paisley had gotten so deep under my skin by not answering my texts that I made it a point to stop in and see her today.

"Two, three weeks tops. That storm is coming sooner than we expected."

"Alright. I'll shuffle some stuff around and get a crew out to finish the job in Claremont. After that, we have one more to do in Fallen Oaks, and then I plan to slow down some for the winter. Send me over the details, and I'll approve everything tonight."

"Will do, Boss."

I hung up the phone and took a drink of water, washing down my food.

Business had been busier than usual lately, with all of the new shops opening in Whiskey Mountain. On top of that, I had taken on a lot of jobs outside of town to help my cousin while he recovered from injuring his back. It had been more than I could chew, but I did my best to keep my head above water until things slowed down. The nice thing was that even though we were headed into winter, HVAC work never stopped, so I didn't have to worry about pulling in more business during the slow months.

What I did worry about was getting Paisley to talk to me and better yet, to give me a second chance to take her on a date. I'd finally gotten up the nerve to ask her out, only to have a slew of unexpected things thrown at me to the point I had to cancel after trying to reschedule several times.

Paisley wasn't like other girls, and I knew that. That was what attracted me to her the most. Any other girl would be jumping at the opportunity to have me take them out, but Paisley was far from giving in any time soon. *If* I was going to get the chance to take her on a date, I was going to have to work hard for it—which I kinda looked forward to. I was accustomed to hard work and going after the things I wanted, which meant getting Paisley's attention was no different.

I threw my trash away and got back to work, ready to wrap up a few jobs so I could finally stop and breathe.

By the time I got home, it was already past nine and I'd gone all day with only stopping to eat lunch. I grabbed a slice of leftover pizza out of the fridge and scarfed it down, not bothering to warm it first. I wanted to take a shower and relax but found myself reaching for my phone instead.

Me: I know you're still mad at me, but I just wanted to say you looked beautiful today.

I didn't expect Paisley to respond, so I set my phone on the charger and hopped in the shower. When I came back, there was a new text message waiting for me.

Paisley: Unsubscribe.

My cheeks split with a grin as I shook my head and climbed into bed. Paisley might just be the death of me, but what a way to go.

The next day, I got up early to get a head start since I was starting a new job on the outskirts of town, and there was a snowstorm moving in. I wasn't sure how bad it would get, but I didn't want to get caught in it and not be able to get home before it hit.

When I pulled up outside of the general store, I took a look at the old, worn-out building and sighed. The owner had informed me that they would be closed for a few weeks while they worked on renovations inside, though the outside needed a facelift as well. It surprised me that they were even willing to put so much money into fixing up the place, given that there were at least three other general stores in town that were easier for people to get to. It didn't make sense to me to fix something up that wouldn't get a lot of traffic, but that wasn't what I was hired for.

I climbed out of my truck and headed inside, shivering at the chill already in the air. A few guys were finishing up painting the walls while Mr. Crawford sat in front of the register, watching. I'd met him a handful of times, and while he looked rough and rugged on the outside, he was one of the kindest people I'd ever met.

"How's it going?" I asked, nodding to the workers as I stood beside him.

"It's looking good. The store needed an update, and Clara said that yellow and gray were the new popping colors. I don't know about it, though."

I scrunched my face and looked at the paint sample cards in his hands.

"Which wall are they painting yellow?" I asked, looking around the store at the gray and white walls that hadn't been painted yet.

"The one right behind me." He jabbed his thumb over his shoulder and shook his head. "She said it wouldn't hurt to have a little bit of sunshine behind me when people come to talk to me."

I chuckled and took the cards from him.

"Is this the yellow you're going with?"

"Yup. Sunny Side Up."

I held it against the wall and then leaned back to see it behind him.

"I think it'll look good."

"Yeah, like sunshine coming out of my ass. Maybe we can put a rainbow up and I can tell the kids I farted that out."

I shook my head and laughed, enjoying the way the corners of his eyes wrinkled as he grinned. He was ornery, but that was what I enjoyed the most about him.

"Did you decide on whether you wanted to go with another swamp cooler or if you wanted to try refrigerated air?"

"Clara wants the refrigerated air, but I told her that we could save that money and go to Italy someday before we die."

"What did she say?"

"She would rather be cool on a hot summer day than sit around and wait for my old ass to take her to Italy."

"So, then we're doing the refrigerated air?" I asked, my lips turning up in a smile.

"Nope. She can be hot and moody, as usual. I promised her when I proposed that someday we would go on a romantic getaway to Italy, and I've never lied to her yet. We'll go with a new swamp cooler, and she'll just have to get one of those little neck fans I see people wear at the baseball games."

"You're a good man." I clapped him gently on the shoulder. "Do you mind if I get started and take a look at what we're working with?"

"Not at all. But that storm is moving in quickly, so I don't know how much time you'll have. I'll need to close up early so I can get home before I get stuck here, and I imagine you'll want to do the same."

"Not a problem. I would like to take a look at the heater so I can get that working for you again. I don't want you to be stuck without heat while they're finishing the rest of the renovations."

"Thankfully, most of it is already done. Plus, once that storm hits, I won't be able to get in here for a while. The roads get covered in ice, the snow piles up in the blink of an eye, and it takes forever to get the roads cleared out here. I was planning on being closed the rest of the week due to the storm anyway. I know most of the guys won't be back until after the roads clear, so don't stress yourself about trying to work a miracle with that heater."

I nodded and looked around the store. A lot had been done already, but I didn't want to drag this job out for a few weeks since I had others lined up. If I could get the heater up and running, then at least I wouldn't have to worry about him being here in the cold. I could always come back later to get the swamp cooler set up since it would be a while before he would need it.

I was so focused on figuring out what was wrong with the heater that I hadn't noticed everyone else had left for the day until I went into the store to see if Mr. Crawford had a flashlight I could borrow. He was standing by the register, stuffing the newspaper into his bag when he lifted his head and smiled at me.

"All done?" he asked.

"Not yet, but I think I figured out what's wrong with it. My flashlight died so I was coming to see if you had one I could borrow."

He reached beneath the counter and pulled one out.

"I need to head home before the snow gets much worse. I worry about Clara being by herself and trying to start a fire. I know she can do it, but I like to take care of my lady."

"Okay," I said, nodding though my mind was still going a mile a minute about fixing the heater.

"I don't want to leave you by yourself to lock up, but I can see that you're not ready to go yet. I can leave the keys with you if you want to stay a little while longer to work on that damn heater, but I wouldn't stay too long, or you'll risk getting stuck here."

"Are you sure you don't mind?" I didn't want to make him uncomfortable with leaving me alone in his store, but if I could have at least twenty more minutes to work on it, I could possibly get it up and running for him.

"I don't mind one bit." He handed me the key after taking it off of his keyring. "But you get yourself out of here before you get stuck. These roads back here aren't anything to play around with."

"Yes, sir."

"I'll get in touch with you next week, and we can see where everything is. Be safe heading home."

"You too. My goal is to get it up and running here in the next thirty minutes if I'm lucky."

He nodded and then pulled on his wool cap before heading out into the storm. I knew that I should probably be smart and leave with him, but I also couldn't stand the thought of him coming back before I could and being stuck in the freezing cold with no heat in the place.

Three

Paisley

"You want me to get what?" I asked, gripping the steering wheel tighter as the snow fell in a heavy blanket around me. My phone was in one of the cupholders on speakerphone so I could hear Calli.

"They're these cute little Thanksgiving gnomes. Clara said I could have them to decorate Cravings before the holiday, but I needed to go by and grab them. I don't think I'll get over there before this storm hits, and since you're already headed that way, I thought maybe you could pop in and grab them. She's not at the store, but Mr. Crawford should be."

"Gnomes?" I questioned, a shiver running through me. "You know how much I hate gnomes, Calli."

"I know, but these ones are cute. They're holding pumpkins and have rosy cheeks. They're so adorable."

"You're lucky I love you."

"Does that mean you'll go get them for me?"

"Yeah, but only because I'm already headed that way. But you owe me. It's freezing out here, and I just want to get home so I can curl up in front of the fire with my fuzzy socks and read a dirty book."

"I'll buy you new fuzzy socks and more smut books for doing this for me. Just send me the links to the ones you don't have yet."

"Deal."

"Be careful and let me know as soon as you get home. Okay?"

"Will do. You be careful, too. This storm is insane, and the weather report on the radio a few minutes ago said it's only going to get worse."

"Yeah, I'm closing early and heading home to check on Mom. I'll let you know when I get there."

"Sounds good. Talk to you soon."

I didn't bother to press the button to disconnect the call since I was too focused on the road I could no longer see in front of me. Calli hung up, and a few minutes later, the store came into view. I put my SUV in park and rushed inside, hoping the gnomes were already waiting for me.

I knew the place was being renovated, but I didn't expect it to be so eerily dark and quiet.

"Hello?" I called, walking through the front of the store and peeking down the aisles. "Mr. Crawford?"

I couldn't imagine that he was just hanging out in the store with the lights off, but I hadn't been in here before, so I had no idea where his office might be—assuming he had one. I kept walking, going up and down the aisles as I struggled to listen for any sounds of movement.

Just as I was getting to the last aisle, I rounded the corner and smacked right into someone coming out of a narrow hallway.

"Holy shit!" I gasped, clutching my hand to my chest as the blood rushed through my ears.

"Hey, are you okay?"

Strong hands wrapped around my waist, the intoxicating scent of soap and cologne filling the air around me.

"What are you doing here?" I demanded as I looked up and found Maverick looking me over.

"Working. What are you doing here?"

"I came to pick something up for Calli." I pulled out of his grasp and stepped back. "Where's Mr. Crawford?"

"He already left for the day."

I rolled my head on my neck, the frustration mounting quickly.

"Okay. Did he by chance say anything about some gnomes he was leaving for me to pick up?"

"He did not."

"Great. Looks like I came all this way for nothing."

I turned on my heel and headed for the door with Maverick right behind me.

"Maybe you came to see me."

"Nope."

"Well then, maybe it was destiny bringing you here knowing I would be here."

"Again, nope. It was gnomes. Stupid Thanksgiving gnomes that Calli asked me to pick up that aren't even here. A wasted trip out here for nothing when I could already be home by the fire, warm and toasty."

"Do you want me to follow you home to make sure you get there safely?" he offered, though I didn't hear any flirting in his tone. He looked past me to the storm raging outside, concern heavy in his eyes. The snow was still coming down in sheets, but the wind was intense as it howled around us.

"No, I'm fine, but thank you. There's nothing my four-wheel drive can't handle—"

Before I could finish my sentence, there was a loud cracking sound as snow flew in the air. We rushed to the window to find a large tree had been knocked down, likely due to the weight of the snow on it combined with the forceful wind pushing it over.

"I'm gonna venture to say that it can't handle that," Maverick said with a heavy sigh.

I stared at the parking lot and our vehicles that were now trapped beneath the tree.

"This seriously cannot get any worse," I muttered, pinching the bridge of my nose and closing my eyes.

"I mean, it could, but the good news is that at least we're stuck here together," he offered.

"You think that's *good* news?" I arched an eyebrow and glared at him.

"I think it's destiny forcing you to give me another chance."

"You've had your chances, and you chose not to do anything with them." I folded my arms over my chest and stared out the window, wondering if there was any way I could get the stupid tree off of my car and safely drive it home. There was a massive dent in the roof and I wasn't a tree expert or anything, but my guess was that this one weighed at least a couple hundred pounds. It looked like his truck had taken the brunt of it, but there was still damage to my car.

"Well, it looks like fate has decided to give me another one now that we're stuck here together."

He rocked back on his heels, smiling smugly as if this wasn't the worst thing in the world that could happen to us.

<u>Four</u>

Maverick

I wouldn't necessarily call being stuck in a snowstorm with Paisley hell, but apparently, that's what it was when she called Calli and told her that hell would have to freeze over before she would consider being nice to me. I knew most women thought I was hot but devilishly hot was a whole new level, and I was ready to show Paisley just how devilish I could be.

"Well, you're not getting your gnomes, and who knows how long it will be before I get out of here," she said into the phone, pacing the small space in the aisle.

I had already told her that there was no point in calling for help because everyone in town had already turned in for the day. Even Mr. Crawford hadn't answered my call when I tried letting him know we were stuck here. Unless it was an absolute emergency, no one was going to risk coming out here to save us. And being stuck in a fully stocked general store wasn't such a bad thing. We had access to food and running water, and once I had a chance, I planned to get the heater up and running. Sure, we didn't have a comfy bed to sleep in, and there was no way to start a fire if we got cold, but things could be a hell of a lot worse.

"Yeah, I tried calling, but they said no one would come out to take care of the tree until the roads were cleared. I'm hoping that means a day or two tops." She looked up at me and glared before turning and walking down another aisle.

I knew Paisley didn't want to be stuck here with me, but I was feeling quite thankful that I finally had a chance to talk to her without her running away. Sure, I would have to hide anything she could use as a weapon against me, but if I could just get through that icy wall she'd built, I knew I could find the Paisley I had gotten to know and was quickly falling for.

I browsed the back of the store where the camping supplies were kept while Paisley finished her phone call. So far, I had grabbed a few flashlights for when the power went out—which I expected would be any moment, given how much the wind had picked up, and a double sleeping bag for us to share. I knew that she wouldn't be ecstatic about sleeping next to me in the same sleeping bag, but it was the best way to share body heat to keep us as warm as possible. I also grabbed some hand warmers and extra blankets since we wouldn't have any heat tonight.

"So, what is the plan?" Paisley asked, hand on her hip as she stood above me.

"I'm getting the stuff we'll need for tonight and thought we could set up in the breakroom. It's the smallest space in here, so it'll be the easiest to keep warm."

"Are you supposed to be helping yourself to everything?"

"Yes. We're stuck here whether we want to be or not. My only focus right now is keeping both of us from losing a limb to frostbite. We have no way to get out of here to get the resources we need. Therefore, I'm utilizing what's available to us."

"That's stealing," she scoffed, shaking her head.

I stopped what I was doing and stood up, my body painfully close to hers. She sucked in a breath, her eyes widening when I invaded her space, easily towering over her petite frame.

"It's not stealing if I intend to pay for everything. I've known Mr. Crawford for years and know that he would want us to use what we need. I've already started a list of what I'm taking, and then I'll settle with him once we're able to get out of here."

"I guess it's not bad if it's just a day or two worth of stuff."

"Try weeks."

Her eyebrows shot up on her forehead as she stared at me in disbelief.

"This is day one of the storm, Paisley. We haven't even had the worst of it yet. No one is going to risk their lives to deal with that tree until it's safe to do so. We have food, water, and a dry, safe place to sleep. We'll be just fine."

"You think that we'll be *just fine* spending weeks cooped up together in here? I don't think so."

"We don't really have much of a choice, now do we? Instead of standing here, throwing a fit, why don't you find something for us for dinner? Nothing that has to be cooked because we're limited to a microwave, and the power is probably going to go ou—"

Paisley gasped loudly as the lights went out, leaving us in darkness. I grabbed one of the flashlights, turned it on, and handed it to her.

"Go figure something out for us for dinner," I instructed, knowing that she needed me to be firm with her right now. She was frightened, and I understood it. But I needed her to get on board with things or it was going to be a long, dreadful time stuck together.

Five

Paisley

"You've got to be kidding me," I grumbled as I struggled to get the flashlight to sit right on the small counter space in the breakroom so I could see what I was doing.

"Need help?" Maverick offered, startling me.

"No."

I knew I would eventually have to give in and stop being so mean to him, but right now wasn't the time. I just wanted to go home, get comfy in my warmest pajamas, and sleep in my own bed. Instead, I was stuck with him for who knew how long in a general store without power or heat.

"Eventually, you're going to have to get over hating me so we can work together as a team," he said softly, his hand brushing against my lower back as he grabbed the flashlight and held it for me.

"Not today, Satan."

His chuckle vibrated through the air as I worked on cutting the blocks of cheese into bite-sized pieces. There wasn't any fresh produce, which left us with few options for dinner. I had decided to do a mini version of a charcuterie board and grabbed a few packs of different cheeses, lunch meat, and some assorted crackers. I knew it wasn't much, but it was the best I could do for now.

I tried to ignore the way my body automatically wanted to lean into his or how I could feel the heat radiating from him. I had been cold the moment I got into my car earlier and still hadn't warmed up. I didn't have high hopes for tonight, given we had no power for the heater to run, nor could we safely start a fire.

"Do you want something to drink?" he offered as I finished cutting the last few pieces of cheddar cheese and laid them on the paper plate.

"What are the options?"

"Bottled water, milk, soda, beer, or wine. There might be juice in the other cooler. I didn't go that far to check yet."

"Wine," I answered quickly, hoping it would warm me up.

He arched an eyebrow at me and then nodded, handing me the flashlight before heading back into the store.

"Aren't you going to ask what kind I want?" I called after him.

He stopped and popped his head back in through the doorway.

"You only drink sweet wine unless you're drinking a glass with dinner, and then you'll drink red, but only if you're having steak. You don't like dry wines and can't stand anything that fizzes," he said matter-of-factly. "I hate to break it to you, Pais, but this is a general store—not a winery. Your options are going to be limited and the selection an assortment of cheap wine. I'll do my best to pick something that *might* meet your *constantly changing* expectations."

My jaw hung open, my mind processing his words as he disappeared as quickly as he appeared.

Did he just get snarky with me? Was he insinuating that I was hard to please?

I moved the charcuterie plate to the rickety table in the corner of the room and sat down. It wasn't fancy, but it would have to do.

The room was bigger than I expected, though I knew that would change as soon as we put down the sleeping bags and had to share the space—which I still wasn't looking forward to. A few weeks ago, I would have been balls to the walls excited about being snowed in somewhere with Maverick. But a lot had changed since then. Okay, so *feelings* had been hurt since then.

My heart was angry with him, but my vagina was flashing a "now open" sign because she was stupid like that. I blamed it on the soft, lingering scent of his cologne floating through the air, making my head even more confused and foggy. He did smell good, though.

"This is the best I could find," Maverick said, setting the bottle on the table and taking a seat.

"Thank you." I reached for the bottle, but before I could grab it, he pulled it away.

"Na uh." He shook a finger at me, the bottle firmly in his grasp.

"Are you holding my wine hostage?" I cocked my head to look at him. I narrowed my eyes and leaned into the dim light of the flashlight, making sure he could see the glare I was giving him.

"Yes. Until you stop being so mean to me. I said I was sorry, and I meant it."

"Doesn't mean I forgive you."

"Then let me work for it."

"For what?"

"Your forgiveness."

"And how do you plan to do that?" I rested my arms across my chest, more so to keep warm than to look annoyed—but it helped.

"However you want me to." He pulled his chair in closer to the table and slowly unscrewed the lid. It was definitely a less expensive bottle, but I loved that we didn't have to worry about finding a corkscrew to open it. The convenience outweighed the cost or quality of the wine right now.

"I know that I let you down by having to cancel our dates repeatedly, and I feel terrible about it. But I was trying to help my cousin while he was in a bind. It wasn't like I purposely chose him over you, Paisley. I was trying to do the right thing, but in hindsight, I can see that it also meant that I was hurting you, and that was never my intention. This may come as a surprise, but I don't chase after women. Never had to. But, as you can see, that's all changing with you."

I sank back against the chair and exhaled heavily. Calli had mentioned that his cousin needed help, but I didn't ask for any details. It didn't really matter because I couldn't fault him for helping his family, no matter how much I wanted to. Plus, he just admitted to being willing to chase after me, which was insanely flattering.

"So, you tell me what I can do to earn your forgiveness, and I will."

He spoke softly, the dim light casting a warm glow over his features as he grabbed a disposable cup from the coffee bar and opened the bottle.

"You don't have to earn my forgiveness," I replied with a sigh, earning another arched eyebrow from him as he poured.

"I feel like this is a trap," he teased, handing me the cup.

"It's not. I mean, I'm still mad at you, but it's nothing you have to be forgiven for. That's a bit drastic, especially considering that we're not even dating or anything."

"So, you're just going to stay mad at me until you decide you're not mad at me anymore? And there's nothing I can do to fix it in the meantime?"

 I shrugged and took a drink, enjoying the sweetness on my tongue. I felt more comfortable staying mad at him, even if it was over something that now seemed so silly. But I wasn't willing to put myself out there again and risk being the one to get hurt if things didn't work out the way I wanted them to between us.

"I'm just saying we might be stuck together for a while. It *might not hurt* to clear the air between us so we can try to make the best of it." He offered me a sympathetic smile.

"Can I ask you something?"

"Of course."

"Why do you keep saying we might be stuck here for a while? Why not a few days?"

"Have you ever spent a winter in Whiskey Mountain?" he asked, cocking his head to the side.

"No, but it can't be that bad."

His face softened as he waited for it to sink in.

I closed my eyes and let my head fall forward.

"It's going to be *that bad*." I groaned, finally acknowledging the reality of our situation.

"Now you see why I want to make the best of it. A few weeks stranded with someone can really change your perspective about them." He grabbed a small piece of cheese from the plate and popped it into his mouth while I felt any remaining hope I had left drain out of me.

<u>Six</u>

Maverick

"I have good news and bad news. Which one do you want first?"

Paisley was still sitting at the rickety table with her legs pulled up against her chest as she finished her second glass of wine.

"I'm honestly surprised to hear that there could be any good news at this rate. Let's start with the bad, I guess."

"Okay, the bad news is that I could only find one sleeping bag." I held up the bag to show her, trying to keep my face from giving away that I was lying to her.

"What's the good news?" Her brows pinched together as her body stiffened.

"The good news is that it's a double, so it's big enough for us to share."

Her face went through a flurry of emotions before deciding on anger, her green eyes blazing.

"I'm not sleeping with you."

I pulled my shoulders back, took a deep breath, and slowly let it out. Now wasn't the time to fight with her, especially since it was getting late and I was already exhausted from the past few days.

"Relax, Paisley. It's not like I'm going to fuck you senseless and give you multiple orgasms in it. Regardless of whether you like it or not, this is where we're sleeping tonight. Once I get the air mattress blown up, I'll set this up, and we can go to bed."

"You can sleep in there all by yourself," she said bitterly, standing up and heading toward the door.

I stepped to the side, blocking her path as my hand shot out and wrapped around her waist to stop her.

"Trust me when I say you don't have a choice in the matter," I warned, my voice low and gravely. "The power is still out, which means we don't have any heat options other than this sleeping bag and relying on each other's body heat. So come hell or high water, I will drag your stubborn ass back to this sleeping bag if you attempt to leave. I would appreciate it if you would just stop being difficult because it's been a long fucking day, and all I want to do is get some sleep so I can figure out the next steps tomorrow."

Her body froze against my touch, her breaths soft and shallow, though I could see the vulnerability in her eyes.

"Fine, but if you so much as touch my ass in your sleep or if I wake up with a cock pressed against it, I'm cutting your balls off."

"Trust me, if you wake up with anything against your ass, it'll be my tongue."

Her face darkened in the dim light as she blushed and looked away.

I grinned a smug smile she couldn't see as I headed back into the store to grab the air mattress. When I came back, Paisley was finishing sweeping the floor and had pushed the chairs against the wall to give us more space. It was such a small room that it almost made me feel claustrophobic, but I took comfort in knowing we would stay the warmest in here, given how much colder the rest of the store had been when I went in to grab stuff a few minutes ago.

Once everything was set up, I pulled the top cover back and motioned for Paisley to get inside. She rolled her eyes and shivered as she climbed in.

I might have lied when I told her this was the only sleeping bag there was. There were a few other ones on the shelf, but this one was the thickest and looked most promising. Plus, there was something comforting about knowing that Paisley would be next to me so I could keep an eye on her and make sure she was okay. If we did individual sleeping bags, I wouldn't be able to do that as easily and would probably lose an eye if I looked over to check on her.

I climbed in beside her and pulled the top over us. I had been able to find a few pillows, so I added those, hoping it wouldn't be terribly uncomfortable for either of us.

"Are you comfortable?" I asked.

"Mmm hmm," she mumbled through chattering teeth.

Without considering the consequences first, I reached over and grabbed her, pulling her back flush against my chest.

"It hasn't even been two minutes," she grumbled, pulling her hips away.

"Relax, Paisley. This isn't an attempt to try to have my way with you. I can hear you shivering from here, and I'm not about to willingly let you lie beside me and freeze. I run hot, so I have plenty of heat to share."

"Are you seriously making this about how hot you are?"

"Yes, because it comes in handy. And if for some reason we don't make it through this, you can say you went out cuddled by one of the *hottest* men in Whiskey Mountain."

I totally meant it as a joke, but her head whipped around as panic filled her eyes.

"You think there's a chance we won't make it?"

I reached up and pinched her chin between my fingers to keep her gaze on me. I needed her to look me in the eyes as I said it and know that my words were true.

"I promise you we will, Paisley. I just need you to trust me and allow me to take care of you the way I need to."

She nodded her head slightly, not bothering to break the physical contact between us. Maybe this was the fresh start we needed.

<u>Seven</u>

Paisley

I woke up with a rock-hard cock pressed against my ass.

While I wanted to be mad at Maverick for it, I knew it was out of his control as he snored loudly, completely unaware of his *little friend,* locked and loaded, fully prepared to storm my gates. Only he wasn't little—not by any means.

I shifted my weight slightly, trying not to wake him up, and unintentionally grazed his cock harder. I froze for a second, ignoring the heat that rushed between my legs at the promise of a good time behind me. If he was already this hard without trying, I could only imagine how hard he could get when awake.

I wanted to press my luck and see if I could get him there, but the last thing I wanted was for Maverick to wake up and catch me. I still wasn't ready to let go of the anger façade I was carrying, even if he had the kind of cock that wet dreams were made of.

My back arched as I attempted to stretch, pressing my ass further down on his erection. Almost immediately, strong hands reached out and grabbed my hips, stopping me from moving any further.

"What are you doing, Paisley?" he asked, voice still thick with sleep.

"Stretching," I said, half lying, half telling the truth. "Why? Am I bothering you?"

"You know damn well what you're doing, and you're doing it on purpose."

"So, what if I am?"

I suddenly felt bold, the pressure building between my thighs too much for me to think straight.

"Is that your way of torturing me? To prove your point?"

"No," I breathed out, wrapping my hand over his until he relaxed his grip on me enough to allow me to press my ass over his cock again. "But it turns out there is a path to forgiveness, and it's a little bit south of where you're currently at."

"Fuck," he hissed under his breath as I lowered his hand to where I desperately wanted it.

"Are you sure about that, Paisley?"

I nodded my head against his chest, eyes closed as I waited to feel his touch.

He pulled my hair to the side and kissed along my neck, sending shivers up my spine. Maybe *this* is what we should have done last night to stay warm because my body was on fire.

His palm flattened against my stomach as his fingers inched their way down under the waistband of my leggings and skimmed the top of my panties.

I held my breath as he continued kissing my shoulder, his touch electrifying. The heat from his skin radiated through the thin fabric covering my pussy, making me ache with need.

"Your pants are really soft," he said, catching me off guard as he shifted from slipping his fingers inside my panties to rubbing them against the inside lining of my pants.

"Thanks, they're fleece lined. I get cold easily."

"Those will come in handy out here. The winters get bad. Definitely softer than wearing thermals, but those really help keep you warm as well."

"Umm, Maverick?"

"Yeah?"

"While this is all very informative, my pussy is going to explode if you don't touch her in the next twenty seconds."

"Well, we can't have that happen, now can we?"

His breath was hot on my skin as he chuckled and nibbled my earlobe before pushing my panties to the side and running a finger through my slit. A hiss rushed through my lips before I could stop it.

I didn't bother answering him as I closed my eyes and leaned into his touch. His fingers glided effortlessly through my wetness as he brought me closer to climax. I wanted him to roll over, crawl on top of me, and own my body, but he didn't. He stayed behind me, teasing me with his cock that I wanted—no, *needed* inside of me.

"Mav—" I started to object right as his fingers found my clit and began rubbing just the way I needed. Before I could get my words out, he was sending me over the edge as my pussy spasmed with the best orgasm of my life.

Eight

Maverick

"Where are you going?" Paisley asked as I stood up and stepped around the air mattress without tripping in the small space.

"I want to get a head start on the heater since the power is back on. It'll take time to warm things up, so it's better to get going."

"How about finishing with the thing you already got all hot and bothered?"

She rolled onto her side and stared at me, that same vulnerability in her eyes that I saw yesterday.

"As much as I would love that, Pais, it's not going to happen."

"Why not?" Her head pulled back in surprise as anger flickered in her eyes.

"Because as much as I would love to fuck you senseless, I'm not touching you again while you're still mad at me."

"Fine—I'm not mad anymore. There. Settled. Let's go."

A smirk tickled the corners of my mouth as I tried to hide it.

"I'm afraid it doesn't work that way."

She took in a harsh, deep breath and blew it out, clearly indicating her frustration with me.

"It could—if you weren't being so *difficult*."

"I'm not the difficult one, Paisley. You're the one who's been mad at me, remember?"

"Yeah, and I just said I was over it. So what's the big deal? You're just doing this to punish me."

"No, I'm not. I'm doing this because I'm not going to take advantage of you being horny now, and then you regretting it later when you remember that you're mad at me. When you're ready to talk things out, I'll listen. Until then, sex is off limits."

"You'll finger me until I come, but sex is off limits?" she countered snarkily.

"Exactly."

I winked as she opened her mouth to spout off a sarcastic response before closing it. I could stand here and fight with her all day, or I could get my ass in gear and get the heater working. I turned and grabbed my tool bag from the floor before heading out to get to work.

A few hours and several curse words later, I had the heater up and running again. I made a note of the things that I would need to come back and fix later, but for now we had heat. I put my stuff away and then went in search of Paisley.

It wasn't like there were many places for her to hide, yet it felt impossible to find her. I went down every aisle of the store, calling her name but not getting a response. Finally, I went back to the break room, hoping she was just hanging out in there, only to find it empty.

Just as I was getting ready to call Dylan to see if Calli had heard from Paisley, I heard water running in the bathroom. I let out a long sigh and leaned against the wall, wondering what in the world she was doing in there.

I raised my hand to knock but waited as I heard singing on the other side. I didn't want to interrupt her and have her stop, so I stood there listening like some creeper as she belted out a popular love song. She had a beautiful voice, which wasn't surprising given everything about her was beautiful. Even her attitude when she was mad at me—though I would never openly admit that.

I leaned against the wall, enjoying the next song until she stopped abruptly, and the door swung open.

Paisley walked out, wearing nothing but a smug smile as if she knew I had been standing there the entire time.

"You've got to be kidding me," I groaned under my breath, closing my eyes and resting my head against the wall.

"You're the one who said sex was off-limits," she replied nonchalantly.

I heard her footsteps as she walked past, making sure to keep my eyes closed so I wouldn't be tempted to change my stance on the no-sex rule.

<u>Nine</u>

Paisley

It was much colder than I expected, especially since I was prancing around naked without a care in the world.

I wanted to show Maverick what he was missing after his whole *no sex until we talk* speech this morning, but I hadn't stopped to think whether there were cameras in the store and if my little antics were being put out there for all the world to see.

It wasn't like I had clean clothes to change into, so I grabbed my hoodie and slipped it on before heading into the store in search of something to wear. Freshly laundered clothes were out of the question at this point, but I had noticed a small section of clothing when I was wandering around earlier—before I got the wild hair to attempt to *shower* in the bathroom and strut my stuff. However, I didn't know if you could technically call it a shower when you were forced to use the cold water from the sink and ended up splashing around like a wild bird. Thankfully, I had found a razor so I could at least shave, even though my skin immediately prickled from the cold, so it was rather pointless on my legs.

As I walked down and browsed the aisles, I found there was an odd selection of stuff, and I couldn't quite figure out what kind of store it was supposed to be. There were plenty of groceries and household essentials, but there was also an entire section that felt geared toward wilderness survival, which could come in handy. I recognized the air mattress and sleeping bag that Maverick had put together for us last night, then frowned when I saw the assortment of single-person sleeping bags on the same shelf.

"I was hoping you wouldn't see that," he said, nodding to the shelf where I was looking as he rocked back on his heels next to me.

"Why? So I wouldn't know what a big liar you are or because you didn't want to get caught making up stories to get me to share a bed with you?"

"I did lie about there not being any other sleeping bags," he admitted with a shrug. "But I knew that if you had the choice of sleeping next to me or on your own, you would have chosen to sleep on your own."

"Surprise, surprise. I wonder why, *Pinocchio*." It wasn't his nose I was worried about growing right now; it was the cock he was purposely withholding from me, leading to my increased frustration.

"I did what was best for everyone last night, Paisley. You don't have to believe that, but it's true."

"And how was lying to me about there not being any other sleeping options the best for everyone?"

"Easy. By us sleeping in the same sleeping bag, it kept us warmer than we would have been sleeping on our own. Our shared body heat was essential given how cold it got last night."

"Yeah, and you having your cock pressed against my ass this morning was just a bonus for you?"

"No, but shoving it in your tight little pussy would have been."

My cheeks flushed with heat as I looked away, not wanting him to see the effect his words had on me.

"What were you looking for?" he asked, changing the conversation.

"Something to wear," I answered with a heavy sigh. "I don't want to wear the same stuff every day, but it's not like there's a laundromat close by. Not that I want to wear clothes from the rack that haven't been washed either, but beggars can't be choosers."

"The sink in the bathroom should be big enough to wash stuff in small batches. They have laundry detergent over there, and I think I saw some rope we could use to make a line to hang everything while it dries."

"That could work," I said, thinking it over. "I think I saw some T-shirts over on the other side of the store. I can grab a few, that way I have something to wear while I'm washing the rest."

"Let's go check it out." He smiled and walked off, leading the way down the aisles.

It felt weird shopping when there was no one else in the store, but it felt even stranger to be living in the store for the time being.

Maverick and I shopped the limited clothing options, and I cringed when the only underwear they had were full on granny panties. I set my pride aside and grabbed a pack, knowing no one was going to see them anyway. Maverick grabbed a pack of plain t-shirts and a few pairs of sweatpants, calling it good. I didn't question why he didn't need underwear because I couldn't stand the thought that his junk was just hanging around freely. That would be a slippery slope that I had no right to be on.

Once we had what we needed, we went to the small bathroom and crammed ourselves inside as he worked on plugging the sink before adding some detergent to the water. It wasn't big enough to do a lot at once, but being stranded in the store meant we had all the time in the world to get our laundry done.

I grabbed the clothes I had been wearing yesterday and added them to the water before discreetly pulling my panties off and tossing them in. The lone thong swam alongside my new grannie panties, probably wondering what in the world those hideous white things were.

Without batting an eye, Maverick grabbed them and swished them around in the water as if he wasn't standing there washing my panties.

"You don't have to do that," I whispered, looking down into the water to avoid meeting his eye.

"It's not a big deal, Paisley. They're just panties. Besides, my fingers have already been inside your pussy, coated with your arousal, and felt as you spasmed against them as you came. Washing them is the least offensive thing I plan on doing. You know, once you're not mad at me anymore."

Heat spread throughout my body as I watched him grip them tightly in his hand as he squeezed the water out of them before plunging them back into the water. As much as I tried not to, I couldn't help but imagine his hands grabbing my ass the same way he was currently manhandling my panties.

<u>Ten</u>

Maverick

"What do you feel like for dinner?" I asked, sitting down in the cramped space at the table in our temporary room.

"That's not a fair question because everything I could possibly want isn't an option," Paisley said with a sad-sounding sigh.

"What is it that you want?"

"I would kill for a steak and baked potato."

"I can make that happen."

"Oh yeah? How exactly are you going to do that? There's not even a stove, and while I hate to burst your bubble, I don't think microwaved steak is going to be very appetizing. Plus, I've looked inside that thing, and I don't think I would trust cooking anything in it." She shuddered and wrapped her arms around her legs, pulling them to her chest as she sat on the air mattress.

"No, you're right. The microwave is out of the question. I did, however, see an air fryer that we can use."

"Where?" Paisley looked around the small room, and I grinned, loving how cute she looked.

"They don't have one in here, but I saw some on the shelf. I can add it to my tab, which I technically needed a new one anyway."

"You don't have to do that. Not for me. I don't want to be the reason you rack up a lot of debt here that you wouldn't have if I weren't with you."

"Relax, it's not that big of a deal. Plus, it's not racking up a lot of debt. We're buying stuff we need, and I refuse to live off cheese and crackers for a few weeks until someone can clear the roads out here."

"Excuse me, *Mr. Fancy Pants*. Those cheese and crackers were delicious."

"Yes, they were. You make a very tasty charcuterie board. But you even said it yourself that you were craving something else."

"Okay. Fair point. But don't talk shit about my cooking."

"I won't. But that means you actually have to cook," I teased. "Cutting up cheese and putting it on a tray with crackers isn't cooking."

"You better watch yourself before I cut *you*," she warned, green eyes dancing with humor.

"Promises, promises." I shook my head and stood up. "Come on, let's go pick stuff for dinner."

I held my hand out to help her up and then looked away when I remembered she was still wearing just a hoodie while waiting for the other clothes to dry. She had been covered up with a blanket, but now that she stood there with long legs leading up to heaven, I couldn't remember what I was supposed to be focused on.

"Was there something else you wanted to eat?" she asked coyly, batting her eyes playfully as mine finally made their way back up her body and landed on her face. She chewed her lower lip, which was already moist from her licking it a few seconds before.

"Yeah, there is, actually," I answered, wrapping my arm around her waist and pulling her against me. A gasp escaped her plump lips as her eyes widened. Her chest rose and fell heavily as her body reacted to my touch.

I allowed my hand to fall from her waist and gently brush against her ass before I moved it in between us, painfully close to her bare pussy. She arched her back slightly, taking a small step as her feet spread apart, allowing me to feel the warmth radiating from her body.

All I had to do was lift my fingers a fraction of an inch and I could feel the wetness that was pooling between her legs. I could slide my finger inside and fuck her with it until she came again like she did this morning. But I wasn't ready to keep fucking around with Paisley, not until we cleared the air between us.

"Yeah, I think I'll cook some chicken too." I nodded my head as if I had just made the biggest decision in the world and turned to head into the store. I didn't stop or look back at Paisley as she cursed me loudly because I knew if I did, that would be the end of me. I would be balls deep inside of her within seconds, and there was no coming back from that.

<u>Eleven</u>
Paisley

That fucker.

Twelve

Maverick

Paisley had been mad at me for at least an hour, hissing at me every chance she could get. Which, in all fairness, I didn't mind. I kinda liked the feisty little demon she was acting like because it would be that much better when I fucked it out of her.

The clothes were still wet, so she was running around in the hoodie that seemed to be getting smaller by the minute. Either she was purposely pulling it up to drive me crazy with glimpses of her ass, or it was so cold that it was literally shrinking like my balls would when I attempted to shower later.

I had picked out food for both of us after she refused to help me earlier. I knew she was mad at me for teasing her, but then again, she didn't *have* to wash all of her clothes at the same time. She could have found a pair of sweatpants to put on but had decided to tease me by showing me what I was missing out on. The problem was that I was a man and Paisley was a woman I had wanted for a long time, which meant my resolve was quickly fading.

Cooking the steaks in the air fryer was a new experience for me, but thankfully, I had found some seasonings and was able to figure everything out. While I might have lied about needing a new air fryer—especially since I had no idea what to do with it—I was pleasantly surprised that this one had two large racks so I could cook the potatoes at the same time, as well as a handy booklet with tips on how to cook everything.

I wasn't sure how she wanted her meat cooked, so I went with medium, knowing I could throw it back in if she preferred it well done. Right now, if I had to go based on her temperament, I would have just thrown it in for a few seconds and then called it good so I could offer her the blood of an innocent animal as some sort of sacrificial offering.

"What would you like on your baked potato?" I asked, hoping she would at least make this part easy since it was her food at stake.

"Just butter and cheese if we have any."

I felt my lips curl into a smile, thinking about how we still had plenty of cheese, thanks to the blocks she had cut up for dinner last night. I had grabbed a small container of butter earlier to cook the steaks with and then decided to clean out the fridge so we could use it now that the power was up. It was more or less clean, aside from some take-out containers that needed to be thrown away—nothing like the microwave that was sure to give me nightmares.

"Dinner will be ready in a few minutes," I replied, cutting the potato open and moving my fingers away to keep from getting burned by the steam. "The steaks are medium, but I can cook yours longer if you'd like."

"Medium is perfect. Thank you."

I nodded my head, unsure if she could see me, as I worked on finishing the potatoes. This wasn't how I would have envisioned myself making dinner for Paisley, but then again, I hadn't imagined getting stranded with her, either. Had Calli not sent her for the gnomes, I would have been stuck here by myself with far less to keep me entertained.

I plated our food on the paper plates I'd grabbed from the store and set them down on the table. Paisley had already set some bottles of water on the table for us—or at least I assumed one might be for me—who knew with how she was glaring at me right now—and a bottle of wine. I didn't bother to ask if she needed a glass for it, given that I didn't want to lose an eye as she picked up the steak knife I had given her and stabbed the meat with it.

At this rate, I was going to be leaving here with a fully stocked kitchen and new appliances with how much stuff I was casually borrowing and adding to my tab. But if there was a way to make things a little easier while we were here, I was going to do everything I could.

I cut into my steak, giving her a few minutes to get some bites into her before I attempted to start a conversation. I was learning so much about Paisley in such a short time, but I had yet to find a part of her personality that I didn't like. Even when she was angry—that turned me on the most, yet I wasn't willing to dive down that rabbit hole to question why.

She lifted her fork to her mouth and bit the piece of steak off, closing her eyes and moaning softly as she chewed. I tried to look away, but her features pulled me in, keeping me locked in another trance as I watched her eat.

"Oh my God, this is so good."

Her eyes fluttered open and landed on mine. I took a bite and held her gaze, not bothering to let her see how affected I was by her compliment or the tender meat swishing around in my mouth. *Also—holy hell, why hadn't I ever used an air fryer before? That thing was pure fucking perfection and 90% less work than grilling.*

"So, why are you mad at me?" I asked, getting straight to the topic we needed to discuss as I shifted in my seat and took another bite.

She raised an eyebrow and glared at me under her thick lashes as she looked down to cut another piece of steak.

"You really want to do this *now*?"

"It's not a matter of what I *want*, Paisley. It's a matter of this conversation is happening—right here and right now."

She set her fork and knife down on her plate and folded her hands in front of her on the table while giving me the coldest expression I had ever seen. Normally, this kind of behavior would have me zooming out the door and not looking back. But with Paisley, it made my dick twitch.

"So, what, you think I'm just going to tell you because you've *demanded* it of me?"

I lowered my fork and knife to my plate and steepled my fingers in front of me as my gaze locked onto hers and held it. The way she shifted in her seat and how her breathing changed didn't go unnoticed by me.

"No, we're going to deal with this because we're two powder kegs one spark away from exploding. I refuse to fuck you until we've cleared the air between us, Paisley, but that's getting harder to do. So, for the love of God, we're going to deal with whatever this is between us so I can bury my cock inside of that tight little pussy of yours and fuck it like it's begging to be fucked."

Her jaw dropped open for a split-second before she composed herself and pulled her shoulders back.

"I feel like I put myself out there by letting you know I was interested in you. Then you canceled our dates repeatedly, and that made me feel like I wasn't worthy of your time since you kept choosing to do something else instead of what we had planned. I know you've said it was work-related, however, I don't know whether to believe that or if I should trust my gut when it says I'm being blown off. I also have to take into consideration that if this is truly your work that is pulling you away, then I would have to be comfortable going into something knowing that this would continue to happen. I'm not saying that everything has to be about me all the time and that your attention has to always be on me, but I also need to make sure that I continue to value myself and make sure that you do, too. I'm not interested in starting something with someone who sees me as a disposable toy to play with when he wants and then be done with me."

"Wow. Okay. I didn't expect that to be so easy." I shook my head, giving myself a few seconds to process her words before responding.

"I'm sincerely sorry that I had to cancel on you so many times, Paisley. I assure you that it wasn't because I was blowing you off. My cousin injured his back on the job and had to have surgery. I knew that he couldn't afford to take time off for it because he had a wife, three kids, and one on the way to take care of. I stepped in and took the jobs he had lined up so he could work to get back on his feet. I took extra jobs as well to help line their savings so they wouldn't have to worry about things for a few weeks while he recovered. It was never about picking something or someone else over you. But he's my family and needed help, and I was fortunate enough to be in a position to do that for him. I'm sorry that I hurt you in the process, though."

"Thank you. I'm sorry to hear about your cousin."

"He's doing better and recovering well. My other cousin was able to go down there for a few months to help out, which means I won't have to keep going up there for a while. We're a big family, but everyone pitches in when and how they can."

She nodded her head in understanding and cut into her potato. It already felt like the air between us had started to shift with less tension filling the space.

"Thank you for talking to me," I added, cutting a piece of steak and sliding it into my mouth.

"Well, your cock was on the line, and I wasn't about to keep missing out on that."

She chewed with a smug smile on her pretty face while I nearly choked on the bite I had just taken.

Thirteen

Paisley

"Do you want anything for dessert?" I asked, looking over my shoulder at Maverick as I washed the forks and steak knives we had used for dinner. "I think I saw some of those individual serving-sized ice cream containers in the frozen food area."

"I absolutely want dessert," he answered, coming up behind me and wrapping his arms around my waist as he kissed the back of my neck. "But it's not ice cream."

"Maverick…." I laughed, squirming as he tickled my sides while possibly leaving a hickey on my shoulder as he kissed and sucked in a way that had me instantly wet. "This is all good and fun, but I really, really want ice cream. You can't deny the heart what it wants."

"I think it's that you can't deny the *cock* what it wants. And this cock wants this warm pussy."

His fingers slipped down over my hips and lifted the hem of the hoodie I was wearing, feathering over my pussy as my ass pushed into his groin.

"What kind of ice cream do you want?" he asked, mercilessly nibbling my ear as his finger slid inside me.

My eyes rolled back in my head as it tilted back to rest on his shoulder.

"Cookies and cock," I answered, not fully paying attention as he rubbed my clit with his thumb. "Better yet, just the cock."

"I'll go get you ice cream, Paisley. Just tell me what you want."

He acted like he wasn't driving me crazy with his expertly skilled fingers.

I spun around, forcing his fingers out of me as I jumped up, my arms locking behind his neck as my legs wrapped tightly around his waist. My mouth instantly found his, our tongues doing a frenzied dance as the electricity pulsed through us.

My hips began thrusting on their own free will, eliciting a deep groan from the back of his throat. It was harder for me to control myself when I had no panties on and all of the friction was stimulating my clit in the best possible way.

"I don't want to wait anymore," I said breathlessly. "I've waited far too long for you to fuck me, Maverick, so you're going to give me that cock, and you're going to give it to me now."

"Yes, ma'am." He grabbed handfuls of my ass as he lifted me higher and set me on the small countertop.

His mouth found mine as he lifted my hoodie and threw it across the room. Even with the heater working, there was still a chill in the room, instantly hardening my nipples. His hands eagerly reached up and began caressing my breasts, setting my body further ablaze.

My legs spread, inviting him in, though I desperately wanted his cock out.

"You're wearing too many clothes," I muttered between kisses, my hands reaching down to lift his shirt.

"We can fix that." He grabbed the back of his shirt and pulled it off in record time before taking off his sweats. Just like I'd expected, he had been going commando this whole time.

"I don't like to be restricted," he commented, somehow reading my mind.

I reached down and grabbed him, loving how heavy he felt in my hand. I wanted to stroke him and watch ropes of cum squirt across my chest as much as I wanted to take him deep in my throat and feel him release his load. But everything would have to wait until after we fucked this energy out of each other. There was a carnal need, and we were both obsessed with fulfilling it.

He leaned down and pulled a pebbled nipple into his mouth, sucking it to the point I moaned from the pleasure, but borderline painful. I continued to stroke him as I spread my legs wider and lined him up at my entrance. He paused for a second and looked up at me, a million questions flashing across his face.

"I don't have a condom. I get tested every year and am clean. I haven't been with a guy since before I moved to Whiskey Mountain. And I'm on birth control," I said in one long-winded breath. "I just want to feel you without any barriers. Please."

He nodded, his jaw tight as he worked it slowly back and forth as if he was struggling to keep his composure.

"I get tested with my annual physical and got the results back a few weeks ago that I'm clean as well," he confirmed.

I leaned back as much as I could and kept my eyes locked on his as I guided him inside. He was larger than I had expected and I had to pause for a second to allow my body to adjust to his size as he stretched me.

"Shiiitttt," he growled, closing his eyes and gripping my hips tightly to hold me still. "Fuck, Paisley."

"I know," I panted, wrapping my legs tighter around his waist as I pulled him in further. I held my breath as I felt the sharp sting as he slid in deeper, still not fully seated inside me.

"Breathe, baby," he coaxed, gently rubbing his thumb across my cheek. "I know it hurts with how much I'm stretching you, but you can take this cock. I promise. Show me how well you can take it, Paisley."

I nodded my head and closed my eyes, trying to focus on the pleasure part of it as I tried to get my body to relax enough to let him in. He leaned in and nudged my head to the side as he began kissing the side of my neck, my one true weak spot.

My fingers scratched along his back, loving the way he groaned every time I increased the pressure. He lowered his mouth, licking his way down my chest and back to my nipples before pulling one in and sucking hard. This time it was more intense, almost immediately sending me to a mind-blowing orgasm as his fingers found my clit and began rubbing.

"Lean back and rest your head on the cabinet," he instructed, pulling my attention back to him the best I could before he assaulted my other nipple. I did as he asked and felt him grip my waist and pull me closer to the edge of the counter.

His dick was hard inside of me as he rubbed my clit, my legs trembling in response. He wasn't fucking me yet, but he was already bringing me more pleasure than anyone ever had. Within seconds, I felt the tingle up my spine, and then my orgasm washed over me, my pussy violently pulsating against his fingers.

"That's my girl," he said proudly. "Giving me those orgasms when I ask for it. Now you're gonna take this cock and come for me again."

I shook my head, my eyes too heavy to open as he removed his fingers from my clit and held onto my hips again. He began slowly thrusting in and out, each movement deliciously perfect as my pussy adjusted to his size. I was beyond full, loving how deep he was inside of me.

"Are you ready to take this cock, Paisley?"

His thrusts increased as he pulled out and then slammed inside me again before I could even process what was happening.

"Oh my God," I cried, immediately loving the sensation of him thoroughly fucking me.

"I told you that you could take this cock, baby. You're doing such a beautiful job, but I'm not done with you yet. I'm going to fuck you so good you won't be able to walk for days. Which is fine because I plan on eating your pussy while you rest and get your energy back so you can suck my cock like you want to."

His dirty words turned me on so much, and before I knew it, I was on the verge of coming again.

"There it is," he said proudly. "My good girl, already ready to come for me again, aren't you?"

"Yes," I whined, part panting. I shifted myself so I could feel him rub his cock along my clit, the friction and pace precisely what I needed.

"Oh, fuck!" I tried breathing through it, but it was impossible. I grabbed onto him the best I could and closed my eyes as he fucked me hard and rough—exactly how I liked it. The small room echoed the sounds of our bodies slapping against each other, but it was nothing compared to the sweet guttural noise he made as he came inside of me, bringing me to another orgasm.

Fourteen

Maverick

"Do you want to try the strawberry one?" I offered, extending my spoon to Paisley as we cuddled on the air mattress.

"Sure. Try some of my cookies and cream. It's delicious."

We leaned in and took the bite of ice cream off each other's spoons.

"I like that one, but the strawberry might be my favorite," I said, swallowing my bite before the cold burned my mouth.

"It is quite refreshing. Reminds me of something I would crave on a hot, sunny day."

I nodded, enjoying how relaxed we both were now that we'd fucked all the tension out of our bodies.

"Do you like what you do?" she asked randomly, turning her head to look at me.

My brows pulled together in confusion since there was no context as to what she was asking.

"Like in life? Or as in how I fucked you? Cause if that's what you're asking, yes, I love what I do and can't wait to do it again. I can go now if you're ready." I turned to set my ice cream down as she giggled and grabbed my arm to stop me.

"While I enjoy your honesty, that's not what I was asking."

"Oh."

"I meant, do you enjoy your job? Is heating and cooling what you've always wanted to do?" she clarified.

I shrugged, not really having given it much thought before now.

"I guess so. I don't think I've ever stopped and thought about it. My dad and uncles did it their whole lives, so I was exposed to it at an early age. I enjoyed helping my dad when I was growing up, but I really loved trying to problem-solve why something wasn't working. He always loved watching me struggle to figure it out when he knew what it was within minutes of looking at it. I always hoped I would be as smart as him some day, so it wasn't really a surprise when I went into the same line of work. For others, it can be hard and challenging, but for me, that's what I like the most about it."

"That's awesome. You don't find many people these days who actually love what they do. I always thought Calli was the weird one, but I guess both of you are," she teased, nudging me with her elbow.

"Gee, thanks," I replied sarcastically, nudging her right back. "What about you?"

"Well, I originally moved down here with Calli to help with her mom after her dad died, but there wasn't much more I had planned to do. But now Calli is doing well with the business, and her mom has more support than I could ever give her, so…"

"So…" I prompted, asking her to continue.

"So now I don't know what to do with my life. Everyone else has a purpose, something they love. But not me. I go to work and help Calli, but it's not like she really *needs* me anymore. Do you know what I mean? When we first got Cravings opened, and she was just getting started, yeah, she needed me. Not just for support and to be there as a friend but for help with marketing and drawing in business. Now she has all of that, and the most I do is help at the register or wipe down the tables. I'm easily replaceable now, but not only that, I'm not even doing something that I enjoy. I love going in to work and spending time with Calli, but honestly, she's so busy when we're there that I don't even get to see her as much as I want to."

"If you could do anything in the world, what would you do?" I asked, taking another bite of ice cream.

"Anything—as in there's no monetary restrictions, and I don't have to jump through a million hoops?"

"Yup. Anything. The sky is the limit."

I set my empty ice cream carton down and leaned back against the cabinet the air mattress was pushed up against while I waited for her answer.

"If I could do *anything*, I think I would want to do marketing for a large corporation. I like the idea of being constantly challenged to think of new ideas and see what works."

"Have you looked into any jobs like that here in Whiskey Mountain?"

"No," she said, shaking her head. "I feel bad for even considering doing something different. I agreed to come here to help Calli, so the last thing I want to do is make her feel like I'm abandoning her."

"Yeah, but you said yourself that Calli is doing well, and so is her mom. She is doing what she wants with her life. Isn't it fair that you should be able to as well?"

"I think we all know that life isn't fair, Maverick. I made a commitment to my best friend, and I plan to honor that. But that doesn't mean that I don't sometimes think about what *could* happen if I did something different with my life."

I smiled, but it wasn't one of happiness. I felt sad that she felt like she didn't deserve to live the life she wanted because she was trying to do what she thought was right for her friend. I could get where she was coming from, as someone who always strived to do the right thing and stay loyal to those I loved. But no one had ever asked—or even insinuated—that I put their happiness above my own. It wasn't that Calli was asking her to either, but she also wasn't asking Paisley what she wanted out of life, and that got under my skin deeper than I would have imagined.

"Please don't say anything," Paisley said, turning to face me. "I don't want you to tell Dylan, and then it gets back to Calli. I shouldn't have said anything."

"I won't," I promised, leaning in to kiss her cheek.

But just because I wasn't going to say anything didn't mean I was going to let this drop and not try to find a way to give Paisley the life she wanted.

Fifteen

Paisley

I was more tired than expected, probably from having my brains fucked out a few times today—not that I was complaining.

Maverick had been just as good in bed as I had imagined—technically better—but I wasn't going to tell him that and inflate his ego bigger than it already was. Hell, I had already lost track of how many orgasms I'd had today, but I knew if I asked him, he would be able to give me an exact number with a smug smile on his perfectly beautiful face.

We brushed our teeth and climbed into bed, though I wasn't sure you could technically call it that. Sure, it was comfortable for an air mattress, but it was nothing compared to the plush pillowtop one I had waiting for me at home. It hadn't even been a full 48 hours and I was already missing the luxurious conveniences of my house, like having a hot shower and being able to do laundry.

I rolled on my side, facing the wall instead of Maverick, when I felt strong arms grab me and pull me to his chest.

"What are you doing?" I asked with a giggle.

"I thought it was clear when I fucked you earlier that you're mine, but just in case it wasn't, this is me claiming ownership again."

His body pressed against mine, bending and wrapping perfectly against each other.

"I mean it, Paisley," he said when I hadn't responded to him. "Like it or not, you're mine. I licked you. That's the rules of the game: you lick something, and it belongs to you."

"Well, then remind me in the morning to lick your cock, because I'm going to want to take ownership of that if that's what we're doing." I covered my mouth to stifle a yawn as my eyes fluttered closed.

"That's absolutely what we're doing. Goodnight, Paisley. Get some rest."

I tried to say goodnight back to him, but my body was blissfully relaxed, and I was drifting off to sleep within seconds.

When I woke up, I had no idea what time it was—only that my phone wouldn't stop ringing.

I rubbed the sleep from my eyes and tried to open them as I looked around to find it. Maverick's hand extended across my chest, handing it to me as he lay on his back with his eyes closed.

"Thanks," I said, still trying to wake up as I slid my finger across the screen to unlock it. There were two missed calls from Calli, both back-to-back, and I immediately panicked, worried that something had happened to her mom.

"Hey," I said as soon as she answered. "What's wrong?"

"I just saw on the news that there's another storm headed your way. I was waiting for the doctor to come in, and one of those emergency alert things happened. They interrupted the show I was watching to warn everyone about this one."

"Wait—why are you waiting for a doctor? Where are you? Is Mom okay?"

"She's alright. We're at the hospital because she wasn't feeling well. They think it's a cold, but they're going to do a chest x-ray to rule out pneumonia."

"Oh my gosh, poor thing. Let me know what they say."

"I will. But the more important question is, how are you? I know it's only been a few days, but you're literally living in a general store."

"It's surprisingly going alright," I said, glancing over to see if Maverick was awake. "They have everything we need, so we don't have to worry about running out of food or water for a while. Maverick got the heater running, so we're good there. And we're camping out on an air mattress, so at least we have the basics."

"Something is off," she said cautiously.

"No, nothing is off. What are you talking about."

"Yes, there is. You're not all angry and spitting venom when you talk about Maver—"

I closed my eyes and waited for her to say it.

"Paisley!" she shrieked loud enough for me to pull the phone away and lower the volume before pressing it to my ear again.

"Shhh," I hissed, turning my body so I could at least shield myself from having Maverick see the embarrassment flushing across my cheeks.

"You *slept* with him!"

"We're sharing a sleeping bag so we can stay warmer," I countered, trying to get up as gently as I could without falling on him. I couldn't talk to Calli about this sitting right next to him, and I knew she wasn't going to hang up and *not* demand that we discuss what happened.

I walked down the hall, thankful that we had left the lights on, and then wandered out into the store. It was colder in here, likely due to the large glass windows that seemed to take up the entire wall. Maverick mentioned that he was upgrading the heating and cooling system once the storm passed, which made a lot of sense with how cold it was with the heater running full blast.

"Okay, so by sharing a sleeping bag to stay warmer—did that mean you offered him your vagina so he had a warm place for his dick—because if so, that makes total sense," Calli said. I could just picture the smug smile on her face when she said it.

"Does your mom know you talk like that?" I asked, finding a spot on the counter by the register and hopping up to sit on it.

"We both know that I don't talk to anyone like that except for you. And Dylan," she replied with a giggle.

"Speaking of, how's he doing?"

"He's fine. Stop changing the subject."

I rolled my eyes, hating that she was acting like a total best friend.

"Did you guys sleep together?" she asked.

"Yes."

"Like as in had sex, not just shared a sleeping bag?"

"Yes."

"And was it everything you thought it would be?"

"Yes."

"Okay, so what's the problem? Why aren't you more excited about this?"

"Because it's God knows what time in the morning, and you called and woke me up. I haven't even had coffee yet," I muttered, looking around to see if they had any fun coffee drinks in the cooler. "You know I'm not a functional human being until I've had some coffee in me."

"I don't know; maybe you should try some Maverick in you and see how *that* starts your day."

"You're so bad." The corners of my lips curled up into a smile as I wondered how that would be. It definitely wouldn't be a bad start to the day…

"The doctor just came in, so I gotta let you go. I just wanted to warn you about that storm. I don't know if anyone can get out to you guys before it hits, but if not, just be prepared that you might be stuck there longer. This one is supposed to be worse than the last."

"Okay, thanks for the heads up. Keep me updated on Mom."

"Will do. Love you."

"Love you too."

I hung up my phone and set it next to me on the counter, wondering if I was truly disappointed that I would be stuck here even longer with Maverick and his wondrous cock.

Sixteen

Maverick

"Wow, that snow is really coming down," I commented, looking out the window as it fell in thick blankets around us.

I knew this meant it would be even longer before anyone got to us, but I didn't feel a single ounce of anxiety about being stuck here. It was probably because I had fucked Paisley, so nothing else in the world mattered right now except being in between her legs.

"I don't think I've ever seen snow like this before." She looked past me, her eyes wide as she took in the storm that had officially rolled in. "How long do you think we're going to be here before someone gets to us?"

"Honestly, I don't know. I've never seen it snow this much in such a short time. I don't know if Whiskey Mountian is even equipped to deal with this storm. They have a lot of resources, but at the same time, it's a small city, which means they're still going to be shorthanded, even if they have all hands on deck and get everyone working to clear the roads."

"So, I guess it's safe to say we're stuck here for at least a few weeks after all." She rubbed her hands nervously up and down her arms as her voice rose an octave.

"Hey, it's going to be okay. I promise." I pulled her into my arms and held her, meaning every word I said. "We have everything we need here. Running water. Food. Power. It might not be anything luxurious, but we have what we need to survive being stranded here."

"Okay." She nodded her head, but I could tell she was still freaked out. "I really wish I could just crawl into a hot bath and soak the stress away."

"I think I saw some inflatable kids' pools in the stock room," I offered, a smile teasing my lips as I hoped to lighten the mood.

"I would say that I'll pass on it given that a cold bath sounds terrible—but I also hate the thought of trying to take another shower in the bathroom sink. This place is huge. You would think they would have used some of it for a full-sized bathroom."

I knew by the smile on her face that she was kidding, but something she said sparked something inside that had the wheels in my mind instantly turning.

"Follow me," I said, grabbing her hand and leading her down the aisles as we rushed to the back hallway.

I had been back here a handful of times as I climbed up into the attic to work on stuff, but I'd never opened any of the doors to see what was inside. Before, it was out of respect for Mr. Crawford because I was only here to work on the heating and cooling. But now, who knew how long we would be stuck here, forced to find ways to survive the storm. If I could figure out a way to make that slightly easier, I was going to. I would just have to make it up to Mr. Crawford later.

Paisley followed behind me, not asking a single question as I opened doors and shut them without any explanation of what I was doing. Finally, we reached the end of the hall and I paused, praying that I wasn't wrong about this.

I opened the door slowly and felt the grin spread across my face.

"Bingo."

Seventeen

Paisley

I had no idea what Maverick was up to, but when he led me inside the room, I gasped and covered my mouth.

The room was huge, with a massive king-sized bed that looked so much more comfortable than the air mattress we had been sleeping on. Maverick turned on the lights as I walked around, staring in disbelief. There was a nightstand on each side of the bed, bringing an earthy vibe to the room with the dark wood. It was a nice contrast to the light gray and white comforter that covered the bed.

Off to the side was a large walk-in closet that was surprisingly empty. It was big enough that it could probably fit the air mattress we had been sleeping on if we tried. I continued my self-guided tour and turned the corner, walking into the en-suite bathroom and the large soaking tub sitting in the corner.

I continued to stare in disbelief, not quite able to believe all of this was real.

"It looks like that bath is going to happen after all," Maverick said, standing behind me with one hand on my hip.

"I can't believe this. Look at the size of that walk-in shower. We don't have to act like birds and struggle to use that tiny sink in the other bathroom." I turned and faced him, feeling a strange tug on my heart when I did. "How did you know this was back here?"

"Technically, I didn't," he admitted. "When you mentioned it being big enough to have a bathroom, that tickled a memory buried deep in my brain about Mr. Crawford and his wife living here for a bit while their new house was being built. I wasn't sure what, if anything, we would find, but I'm glad we came and checked it out."

"Do you think they'll mind if we use their stuff?"

"I doubt it. The closet and all of the dressers have been emptied," Maverick replied, letting go of me to check the bathroom stuff. "Same in here. Looks like they cleared everything out when they moved into the new house. I can't imagine he would have a problem with us using this space while we're stranded here."

"This feels so unreal," I said, still staring at the giant bathroom in disbelief.

"Want to go get our stuff and bring it in here?" Maverick offered.

"Yes, please. That sounds amazing. I know it's still morning, but I swear, I could climb into that bed and sleep for days. My body already hurts from sleeping on that air mattress."

"Well, how about we go grab our stuff, move it in here, and then you can soak in a long bath. I saw some bath stuff in the store, so there should be a few things to choose from. I also found a washer and dryer in the other closet so we could wash our clothes and pick out some towels. We can even get new bedding if you'd like."

"Why does it feel like we're moving in together?" I joked, meaning for it to sound light and like a joke. But the way Maverick looked at me said he saw nothing funny in it.

****

"Oh. My. God." I sank lower into the hot bubbles, closing my eyes and breathing in the calming lavender scent as it floated in the air around me.

"You sound like Janice," Maverick said, standing over me.

Typically, I would be jealous and demand to know who she was, but my body was so relaxed that I didn't have the energy for it.

"Who?"

"From Friends. You know, Chandler's girlfriend?"

"Never seen it."

The water shifted around me as he climbed in behind me. I leaned forward, making sure he had room even though the tub was more than big enough for both of us.

"That's a crime, you know."

"No, a crime is getting out of this tub. It's pure heaven."

"Well, I would agree with that, but I also have fresh, clean towels for you when you're done, and I found new bedding for us and washed it. It's drying as we speak, but a nice, comfy bed will be awaiting you when you're ready."

"Too bad we didn't find a full-sized kitchen," I joked. "I'm not kidding about moving in here just for this tub. This tub is the tub that makes all other tubs jealous."

"I don't think I've ever heard anyone say the word 'tub' that many times in five seconds."

I reached down and pinched his leg, giggling when he tried to pull away.

"Don't talk shit about my tub, or I'll kick you out of it," I warned.

"I think it's technically Mr. Crawford's tub. Or possibly his wife's. I don't know that you can come in and demand that he give it to you."

"I'm going to ask him to rent that bedroom to me. I'll gladly pay him to live there. Plus, it comes with this bathroom and, therefore, the tub. And I wouldn't have to go far to do my grocery shopping. It's like a win/win and dream come true."

"So that's what your dreams are made of?"

"Yup. I've decided what I want to do with my life, and this is it. I can still work at Cravings and live here, enjoying my tub."

While I was technically kidding, I couldn't help but notice how my heart fluttered at the thought of doing something different with my life.

Eighteen

Maverick

I got out of the bath a little before Paisley was ready to be done so she could have some space, and so I could get the clean bedding out of the dryer. I was not only relieved to find this room but also ecstatic to find new bedding and a washer and dryer so we didn't have to keep washing our stuff in the tiny sink and hanging it to dry.

The bedroom was more than nice, and the bathroom was an added bonus. I didn't blame Paisley for wanting to live here. I did, too. But that didn't stop my heart from skipping a beat when she jokingly said we were moving in together. If I had my way, I would move in with her in a heartbeat. If she *had* to have this place, I would buy the whole damn place from Mr. Crawford and send him into early retirement while I became the proud new owner of a general store in Whiskey Mountain.

I heard the shower running and knew that she was washing her hair since she didn't want to do it in the bath. The amount of relief that washed over me when we found this space created a sense of peace that I hadn't felt in a long time. It wasn't just about me anymore, but the fact that I was able to keep Paisley as comfortable as possible while being stuck here. While we would have a funny story to later tell our grandkids about us falling in love while stranded in a general store, I couldn't get past the smile on her face, knowing that we had an actual bed to sleep on tonight and that we could do basic things—like taking an actual shower.

A few minutes later, the shower turned off, and Paisley came in with a towel wrapped around her body and one on her head.

"I honestly think I could live here," she teased, pulling the fluffy fabric tighter against her body. "These towels are better than the ones I have at home, which just goes to show that I need to start shopping here instead of the market in town."

"Are you hungry?" I asked, ignoring the lump in my throat as I thought about us living together.

She'd been soaking for a few hours, refilling the tub with hot water when it would go cold. We'd somehow skipped breakfast, which my stomach was currently reminding me of with a loud growl.

"I'm starving. Let me get dressed real quick, and I'll help you fix something if you want."

"Sounds good. Your clothes are in the closet, and your panties are in that drawer," I said, pointing to the large dresser across from the bed with a TV mounted above it. And to think, we spent the first 48 hours stuck in a break room with nothing to entertain ourselves aside from our constant banter.

I left to give her some privacy while she got dressed and went in search of food for lunch. Now that we had the air fryer and power, we had a lot more options. There wasn't much in the way of fresh produce or meat, for that matter. But there was a lot of frozen food that could be easily heated up.

I was scanning the frozen pizza options when Paisley joined me, looking around my arm before grabbing the sausage one.

"Sausage is always the answer," she said, holding it to her chest like some sort of prized possession.

"I'm curious to know what the question is," I teased, picking up a supreme pizza before putting it back and grabbing the pineapple and ham one.

"That's a sin." She pointed to the box in my hand and shook her head.

"You're kidding, right?"

"Nope. Pineapple doesn't belong on pizza."

"I beg to differ."

"You could do the right thing and be Team Sausage. Everyone loves a good sausage."

I grabbed her by the waist and pulled her into me.

"If I were Team Sausage, I wouldn't be giving you mine," I teased, leaning in to nip her earlobe.

"Well, when you put it like that…"

Just before I could nip her again, she pulled away and took off running through the store as I chased behind her. There might have been a storm raging outside, dropping more snow than we could dig our way out of, but there was nowhere in the world I would rather be than here with Paisley.

Nineteen

Paisley

"Okay, I'm officially moving in here. I don't care if Mr. Crawford wants to rent this room to me or not. He's either going to take my money and accept it, or he's going to have to find a way to get rid of me because I'm not going easy."

I climbed onto the bed and pulled the comforter and sheet over me, closing my eyes as I inhaled the soft scent of fabric softener. This was so much better than sleeping on the air mattress and being confined to the sleeping bag. The bed was super firm but soft, and the pillow-top mattress added the perfect amount of softness. Not only that, but I had the hottest man in the world in bed beside me, ready to tuck me in or fuck me—either was fine with me.

"I'm glad you like it. Anything would have been better than the air mattress, but this is definitely leveling up a bit." He fluffed the pillow under his head and then laid on his side, facing me.

"I really want you to fuck me senseless on this nice bed we have the privilege of using, but I'm afraid I might fall asleep in the middle of it," I said sleepily, followed by a yawn. "That bath really did me in, and I can barely keep my eyes open."

"No, I would rather you get some rest, Paisley. It's been a rough few days, and we've slept like shit trying to sleep in the other room. Let's get some good sleep and then see what tomorrow brings. It already feels one hundred times better being stuck here now that we found this room. Let's enjoy it, and then we can fuck all day tomorrow."

"Like a full day fuck-a-thon?" I asked, lifting up on my elbow to see him better.

"If that's what you want to call it." He laughed.

"That's the official name. Now get some sleep and be ready for it."

He leaned in and lightly kissed my lips.

"Goodnight, Paisley. Sweet dreams."

"Goodnight. Sweet dreams. Love you."

My eyes felt heavy as I drifted off to sleep.

****

The next morning, I woke up feeling relaxed, refreshed, and suddenly mortified.

I shot up in bed and stared at the spot where Maverick was supposed to be sleeping. The curtains were still closed so it was hard to tell what time it was, but my guess was that it was too early for him to be up and getting the day started.

I reached over and grabbed my phone, groaning when it showed it was already after eight. I had slept longer and harder than I expected. Last night had felt like such a dream, but I knew for certain that I had said *those words*. I had fallen asleep right away so I had no idea how he'd responded to them, but I was willing to bet money that it wasn't with *I love you too, Paisley*.

Gah, I was such an idiot. Who confesses they love someone while they're delirious and sleep-deprived? Not only was it the least romantic way to say it for the first time, it was too freaking early.

We weren't even dating, and it hadn't been twenty-four hours since we'd had sex. I knew Maverick wasn't a commitment or relationship type of guy, so I could only imagine how much this scared him off when I confessed it right after he got in my pants. However, I do blame the lack of pants for what happened between us—not that we needed any excuses.

I climbed out of bed and headed to the bathroom to relieve myself before I burst. A quick glance in the mirror confirmed I looked like the hot mess I was. My hair was tangled and stuck to the side of my face, likely from getting too hot and sweating in my sleep, but also because I went to bed with wet hair. I finished up and washed my hands, quickly brushing my teeth before I had to see Maverick and talk to him about what happened.

It wasn't like I could just ignore it or pretend it didn't happen. There was no way he hadn't heard it, and if I could remember saying it, he definitely remembered as well. The best course of action was to address it head-on and admit that it was a silly slip of the tongue. I was tired, and I'm used to saying goodnight to Calli and her mom, so that's all it was—just a habit of wishing them sweet dreams and telling them I loved them.

But then *why* did it feel so different? If it was really just a tired mistake, why was I so nervous for him to have heard me? I didn't tend to care what people thought about me, but Maverick was different and knowing that what I said must have freaked him out enough to make him get out of bed early was eating away at me in the worst way possible.

By the time I found him, he was pacing in the corner of the store with his phone held against his ear. He was already dressed and wearing new clothes, while his hair looked wet. How had I not heard him in the shower? How long had he been up?

I browsed the refrigerated coffee drinks, pretending to look for a new one to try while he wrapped up his call so I didn't look like the creepy stalker I was. There were three options to choose from, so I grabbed the caramel one and immediately turned it around to read the label on the back as he approached me.

"Good morning," he said, his voice normal and even, revealing nothing about how he felt about what happened last night.

"Oh my gosh!" I said, wayyy too dramatically as I clutched the bottled drink to my chest. "I didn't see you there."

At least the bottle was cold enough to help defuse some of the heat coming off my skin from the embarrassment I was feeling from the lie I'd just told.

"You mean you didn't see me over there taking a phone call when you came out here and watched me for a few minutes before pretending to check out the coffee drinks you've been drinking the past few days?"

"Shit," I muttered under my breath, looking down so he couldn't see my face.

"Look at me, Paisley," he directed, lifting my chin with his finger.

My head lifted, but I looked off to the side to avoid looking at him.

"Nope. Look at *me*."

My heart beat wildly in my chest as I tried to calm myself by counting the types of cheese. I got through Colby Jack, Mozzarella, and Cheddar before he snapped his fingers in front of my face to get my attention again and pulled me out of it.

"What's going on?" he asked, his eyes searching my face for something.

"I don't know what you're talking about."

"Yes, you do. You're being weird and fidgety. Why?"

I blew out a frustrated breath and tried to look away, but he wouldn't let me.

"I don't want to talk about it."

"Well, that's too bad."

"You're quite bossy, don't you think?" I countered with a raised eyebrow.

"No. But I have a *no sex while we're fighting* rule, and I'd like to be balls deep inside you this morning. So the sooner you tell me what's wrong, the sooner I can finally eat your pussy and fuck you again."

My palms started sweating as heat washed over me from his words.

"I said I love you last night when I was falling asleep."

"I know."

"And then it freaked you out, and you weren't in bed when I got up."

"It didn't freak me out. I got up because I had to pee, then I took a shower and when I got out, I had a missed call from Mr. Crawford."

"Mr. Crawford? What did he want?"

"He was calling because he didn't know we were stranded here until he went in for breakfast and Calli told him. I guess he didn't get the voicemail I left him the other day. He wanted to make sure we knew about the bedroom and to tell us to use whatever we needed in the store."

"That was nice of him," I said softly, feeling my heart rate start to come back down a little.

"It was." He held my gaze, not looking away as I started to fidget again.

"You know that I said I love you, and you're acting like it's not a big deal," I blurted out. "Of course I'm going to freak out right now, Maverick. Who wouldn't be?"

"Me."

"Yeah, right," I scoffed.

"I wouldn't be freaked out, Paisley, because I would mean it. I haven't said that I loved you back because I wasn't sure if you meant it or if you said it out of habit. Maybe you say it a lot to Calli or your parents. It's a common thing to say when you're saying goodbye or goodnight."

"Are you saying you love me?" I asked nervously, ignoring everything else he said.

"Yes. I'm saying that I love you, Paisley. I'm head over heels, without a doubt, in love with you. I have been for a while now, but being stuck here together only solidified what I already knew."

"Oh," I whispered, feeling my body flush again, this time with excitement.

"So, what about you? Did you mean it, or were you saying it out of habit?"

I rubbed my lips together, trying to figure out how I really felt. My instinct was to tell him that I loved him too and that I meant it last night when I said it. But I couldn't stop overthinking it and trying to convince myself that I might *not* have said it had I not been so tired.

"Come on, Paisley. Tell me what you're thinking. I've already said it, so you know where I stand. Put me out of my misery one way or another. It's okay if you're not there yet—"

"I love you too, Maverick. I meant what I said last night, and I mean it now. I'm also madly in love with you."

Before I could say anything else, he pulled me flush against his body and kissed me with more passion than I'd ever felt before in my life.

Twenty

Maverick

It turned out that having a full-day fuck-a-thon was precisely what we needed. My tab with Mr. Crawford was growing by the minute, but we totally needed the extra carbs and hydration to keep up with each other as we kept going at it.

Paisley wasn't just sassy—she was a full-on brat, and I loved every second of it. It wasn't just the way she taunted and teased me; it was the way she trusted me with her body to deliver the pleasure she deserved.

By the time dinner rolled around, I sent her to take a bath while I worked on figuring out what to make. There weren't a ton of options, but I wanted to make something nice for her. I'd taken the time to look up some air fryer recipes and prayed that I could pull them off with a somewhat limited selection of ingredients in the store.

It was nice being stuck here with Paisley, but I hated the idea of what would happen to us once the storm cleared and we were able to get back to our regular lives. We'd said we loved each other, but we hadn't talked about what that meant or what it would look like after we left here. While I would love to move her in with me and spend all of my free time making love to her, I needed to focus on what Paisley wanted.

I knew she wanted to someday work for a large corporation doing marketing, but I didn't know what that meant for us. There were plenty of people in town who worked for large companies remotely, but I didn't want to assume that would be what she would want to do. She was a free spirit, and I could imagine her wanting to travel the world and branch out of this small-town life.

"Something smells good in here," she said, startling me as she came into the breakroom where I was finishing up dinner.

"Thank you. I attempted to make some seasoned chicken breasts with crispy potatoes, but I'm still trying to master this whole air fryer thing." I laughed as I pulled the drawer open and checked on the food.

"Well, I think you're there. It smells better than anything I ever make."

I smiled at her over my shoulder as she took a seat at the table. I had packed up the air mattress and sleeping bag so we could walk easily in here. It was nice having the large closet space in the bedroom to store stuff since I now had a lot to take home.

"Do you want something to drink?" I asked, knowing that the food had at least ten more minutes to cook.

"I'm craving a Diet Dr. Pepper but didn't see any in the drink fridge up front so that probably means I need to stick with water." She laughed lightly, and I loved how much the energy between us had shifted already.

"I'll go see what I can find."

She opened her mouth to object, but I was out the door before I could hear what she said. I scanned the aisles quickly, looking for the section that had the soda. Once I found it, I grabbed a 2 liter and tucked it under my arm while I went in search of a few other things I needed for dinner.

Once I made it back to the breakroom, the food was ready. I served Paisley first, setting her glass of Diet Dr. Pepper down on the table beside her plate. The way she looked at me with genuine appreciation sent butterflies fluttering through my stomach. I had never felt this way with anyone before, and I couldn't imagine not feeling this way again. Now that I had Paisley, it was my goal to make sure I never let her go.

After we ate, I cleaned up and sent Paisley to the room to pick something to watch on TV. Thankfully, the majority of the storm seemed to have passed, and we hadn't lost power again. I wasn't sure how much signal we would get here, but I had noticed a

DVD player set up, and a large selection of movies was stored on the bookshelf beside the dresser. Either way, we would have something to entertain us for a bit tonight.

When I walked into the room, she was cuddled up on the bed, her hair tossed in a loose bun on her head, and she looked incredible. She patted the side of the bed beside her and smiled as she waited for me to join her, but I couldn't stop thinking about how much I wanted this to be our new life.

"What did you pick?" I asked, crawling beside her and inhaling the soft scent of her shampoo from her freshly washed hair.

"There weren't a ton of options to choose from, and most of the DVDs are kinda old," she replied, her nose scrunched. "But I thought this one might be fun. I haven't seen it before."

She held up the case for *What Women Want* and I grinned. It had been a while since I'd seen it, but it was light and funny, while Helen Hunt kinda reminded me of Paisley—a take-charge woman who goes after what she wants.

I shifted and got comfortable while Paisley pressed play to start the movie. It felt like we were on another date, but there weren't any of those first-date jitters to go along with it. We had only been stranded together for a few days, but somehow, it felt like we'd been doing this for years. It felt comfortable, like we were just meant to be together.

Twenty-One

Paisley

"That's what I want to do when I grow up," I said wistfully, my attention still fixated on the TV as the movie came to an end and the credits rolled. "I want to be Darcy Maguire, a woman on a mission who goes after what she wants in life. Not letting any chauvinistic weasels like Nick Marshall get in my way or sabotage me."

"Yeah, but he ended up redeeming himself and supporting her in the end," Maverick replied, softly brushing a strand of hair out of my face. "But don't worry, that won't be you."

I pulled my head back in surprise, not sure how to take his words.

"Sorry, I didn't mean that how it came out. You'll definitely be successful in anything you do, Paisley. You're determined, focused, driven. I just meant you won't have to worry about some chauvinistic weasel trying to sabotage you because I'll beat their ass before they have a chance."

The corners of my lips pulled up as my heart swelled at his words.

"Well, lucky for us, we don't have to worry about that anyway— since I won't ever have a highly competitive corporate job. I don't think anyone in Whiskey Mountain is out to sabotage me." I winked to let him know that I was playing, but it seemed to fall short.

"Not yet you don't."

"I hate to break it to you, but I don't think there's ever going to be *that* kind of job here. It's such a small town, I can't imagine they would want to allow a big corporation in like that. Nor could I imagine that a big corporation would want to set up shop in a small town."

"I actually have a friend from college who runs a very successful advertising company in Sugarplum Falls, Idaho. Though he originally started it in New York, he moved to Idaho when his sister passed away and he became the guardian of his niece. While he started in a big city, his branch in a small town is thriving and is actually more profitable than the NY office."

"Wow. I guess I didn't think about it that way. But I think there's a huge difference in success when you already own the company. I don't see anyone doing something like that here."

"No, but that doesn't mean you can't branch out and go somewhere else," he said softly as he felt my body tighten against him.

"You know that's not an option. I can't just up and leave everything here to chase some crazy dream. People might do that in movies, but they don't do it in real life."

"Calli did."

I pulled a deep breath slowly between my lips before letting it out.

"That's different. She came here for her mom. Opening her restaurant was an added bonus."

"Or, maybe it was fate. Maybe she was meant to be here so she could help her mom *and* bring her dream to life."

"You make it sound like it's so easy." I laughed, though I felt nothing was funny about this conversation. He was getting too close to digging up the truth I had been trying to keep from everyone.

"I never said it would be easy. It won't. Change is hard, but so is life. Why go through all of this if you don't have something to live for? Something that brings you so much happiness that you can't wait to wake up the next day to bask in that joy?"

"And what about you? Do you have that?"

"Sometimes." He shrugged. "Maybe not as much with my job anymore, but with you, yeah. If I could wake up every morning to you in my bed, that would be my joy. Having you in my life would be worth waking up every day, getting to love the person who makes my heart whole."

"Then what happens when I find my dream job, and it's not in Whiskey Mountain?" I challenged, holding his gaze as I desperately tried to read the reaction he was hiding from me.

"We would find a way to make things work, Paisley. If you thought I was a pain in the ass trying to get you to talk to me before, then you'll think I'm crazy when you see the lengths I would go to just to keep you in my life."

Butterflies fluttered through my stomach as I tried not to get my hopes up too high. Things right now felt wonderful and perfect, but everything would change once we were forced back into the real world.

Twenty-Two

Maverick

I knew Paisley would be mad, but that didn't stop me from reaching out to my friend Jackson this morning to pick his brain about advertising. He had taken Mason, Inc. and built something from the ground up to a multimillion-dollar advertising company all on his own. If anyone could help get me the info on how to get Paisley started, it would be him.

He hadn't answered when I called, which wasn't a surprise, given I knew how busy he would be right now. I left a voice mail, but then not trusting it to go through, shot him a text message letting him know it wasn't urgent but that I wanted to touch base soon if he could.

Paisley was still in the shower while I figured out what to make for breakfast. Even though we had more accommodations than I expected, I was starting to feel frustrated that I didn't have the things I needed. Like a stove. Or more than two dishes. I knew things would change for us as soon as the roads were cleared and we were sent on our merry way, but I was terrified of how much would change for us once we had to figure out what our relationship looked like outside of being stuck together.

I knew she was already feeling frustrated about our conversation last night. She didn't seem to have much interest in looking into a new career path because it felt hard, but I also couldn't just move forward and not want the best for her. Which meant it would be up to me to guide her down that path, whatever it might be.

By the time she finished, I was in the breakroom, plating our food. It wasn't anything fancy, just some potatoes and bacon that I had cooked in the air fryer. Thankfully, it was the pre-cooked kind, so it didn't produce as much grease since I was already worried about it setting the air fryer on fire.

"You didn't have to make me breakfast," she said softly as I set her plate down on the table in front of her. "But thank you."

"It's not what I would have normally made for you, but it's the best I could do with limited resources."

I knew she could hear the agitation in my voice when she reached over and placed her hand on top of mine.

"It's wonderful. Really."

"Sorry," I said with a heavy sigh. "I'm just feeling out of sorts this morning, and I think it's starting to wear on me being stuck here and not having the comfort of being at home. I could have made you a killer breakfast in bed there."

"Yeah? Like what?" She smiled playfully as she picked up a piece of bacon and bit into it.

"I would have made you the most amazing omelet with fresh veggies and the creamiest eggs you've ever tasted. Then I would have made real fried potatoes, the kind my grandma used to make with onions and peppers. I would have cooked bacon and sausage so you could choose what kind of meat you wanted in your mouth—" I stopped and wiggled my eyebrows. "And then I would have topped it all off with a homemade Belgian waffle with fresh whipped cream and berries."

"Sounds like I would have been in a food coma from all of that, but I can't lie—that sounds amazing, and I am super bummed that we're stuck here."

"Me too." I tried to make it sound like I was joking, but I wasn't.

I was used to constantly being on the go, never being in one place for too long. While I enjoyed her company and didn't want that to end, I couldn't help but find myself wishing we had somehow gotten stuck together at my house instead. Not that there was any chance of that actually happening, but it would have been far more comfortable.

"So, what do you want to do today?" I asked, hoping to change my mood.

"Are there options?" Her eyebrows raised in question.

"Not really. Yesterday was a fuck-a-thon, and as much as I would love to do that again, your body needs a break."

She smiled and lowered her eyes bashfully.

"I think I saw a small stack of games. We could always make it a game day," I offered, but I wasn't enthusiastic about it.

"Honestly, I am going stir crazy being cooped up in here and not being able to get fresh air. I know it's only been a few days, but I don't know how people do this. I know it's frigid outside, but I *desperately* want to go out there. Even if for just a few minutes."

"Let's make it happen," I said with a burst of excitement. "It's not like we can't get the front door open. We might not be able to leave and go anywhere, but at least we can get some fresh air."

Paisley smiled as she quickly finished her breakfast. Thankfully, there wasn't much to clean up, so that was a breeze. We changed into warmer clothes, layering with thermal and fleece to keep the cold at bay. I wasn't sure how long we would get to be outside, but even a few minutes would feel like a win right now.

I helped her get snow boots on and then pulled the insulated face mask over her face. She looked adorable, like a cute little snowman that could wobble over at any moment. I pulled mine down and then tightened my gloves, making sure I was ready before attempting to open the door. The wind had died down, but I knew it was going to be blistering cold outside and wasn't sure if it was the best idea to do this after all.

There were a few feet of snow piled against the glass door that led into the store and I wasn't sure I was going to have the strength to push it open. There was a good chance it had froze to the door, and I didn't want to risk breaking the door and then having to deal with finding a way to secure it to keep the heat inside.

I pushed gently, relieved when the snow started to move. It was heavy but thankfully not frozen. I put my full weight against the door, trying not to let Paisley see me struggle as I tried to force it open. Before I could stop her, she was standing beside me, pushing with everything she had.

Finally, we got traction, and a few minutes later, the door opened.

"Holy fuck!" she shrieked, lifting her hands to cover her face as a small gust of wind whipped past us and blew frigid air at us. "It is freezing out here!"

"Maybe this wasn't such a good idea," I muttered loud enough for her to hear.

"It's fine. I'll adjust in a minute. I just didn't expect that."

I guided her as she stepped around the big pile we had created from the door. There was an old wooden bench close by, so I helped her to it and brushed off as much snow as I could so she could sit down. Her teeth were chattering, but I knew she wasn't going to go back inside, even if I asked nicely.

I grabbed the snow shovel from inside and began clearing the mess in front of the door. It felt nice to be moving my body again, even if I was freezing doing it.

Soon, I no longer felt the cold and Paisley seemed to have adjusted to it as well as she sat happily on the bench in her snowsuit. There were more things added to my tab with Mr. Crawford, but I felt better knowing she was as warm and comfortable as she could get, given the circumstances.

I continued clearing the snow, making a pathway from the store to the parking lot. It wasn't like anyone was coming any time soon and would need to use the sidewalk, but it felt good to clear it anyway. I finally reached the parking lot and set the shovel against the wall of the store before heading over to check out the damage to our vehicles from the tree that had fallen.

"How bad is it?" Paisley asked, coming over to join me.

I looked back at her, making sure she was okay before I answered.

"It doesn't look as bad as I thought. Both vehicles are definitely pinned beneath it, but it looks like my truck is taking the brunt of it. If I had a saw, I might be able to cut off enough to free your car."

"You mean like *free* my car, as in we would be able to get in it and leave here?" she asked, desperation in her voice.

"Possibly." I worked my jaw back and forth as my mind ran a mile a minute, trying to figure out how to do this.

"Do you think there are tools inside we can use?"

"I can go check. I don't want to leave you out here by yourself, though."

"Maverick, it's not like I'm going anywhere. Look around; there's nothing for miles. I'll be fine."

I knew she was right, but I still hated the nagging feeling in my gut I had about leaving her.

"Okay, I'll be quick. Stay right there."

"10-4."

Her lips curled into a playful smile, but I missed it as I turned and headed back into the store to see what I could find.

<u>Twenty-Three</u>

Paisley

"Oh my God!! I can't believe it!" I squealed, clapping my hands excitedly as I watched Maverick slowly move my car out from beneath the fallen tree. He had been able to cut most of it away, but there was still a tiny bit left that he couldn't get to so he wouldn't allow me to get anywhere near the car while he attempted to move it.

I hated that his truck had been totaled and he would be stuck dealing with the insurance company to get it taken care of, but I was too excited about the idea of going home that I didn't focus on it.

He moved the car to an open section of the lot and parked it before getting out and rushing over to me with a huge grin on his face.

"You did it!" I jumped into his arms, hating how the thick layers of clothes kept us from being as close as I wanted.

"I'm honestly surprised I was able to get it out," he admitted with a grin. "I was even more surprised when it started. Looks like luck is on our side today."

"I can't believe we can actually leave and go home. I can drop you off at your place before I head—"

I stopped speaking when I saw the look on his face.

"Sorry, I just assumed…"

"This is what I was worried about," he admitted, taking a step away from me. "I knew the moment we were able to get out of here, you would take off."

"I'm not taking off," I assured him, reaching for his face when he pulled away. "Maverick, look at me."

His brown eyes refused to meet mine, and that broke my heart.

I lifted my fingers and gently stroked his cheek, hoping he would feel the love I had for him in my touch.

"I'm not taking off," I repeated, stepping to the side so he was forced to look at me. "I'm sorry, I didn't mean to upset you. We haven't talked about what any of this looks like for us once we leave here, and I just figured you would want your space. We've been cooped up together for days, and I wouldn't blame you if you wanted time for yourself."

"No, Paisley. I want time with you. That's all I want."

"Oh. Okay." My heart was racing, and despite how cold it was outside, my palms started sweating.

"But if *you* need time to yourself, that's fine. I'm sorry for acting the way I did. I've just been worried about what would change for us once we weren't stuck here anymore, and I felt like my worst fear was coming true."

"That I would go back to my place?"

He nodded and looked away.

"Don't you think it would be kind of silly of me just to assume that I would go straight to your house? I mean, we've only been dating a few days. It's all kinda moving a little quickly, don't you think?"

I wanted to offer him a way out because there was no way this was what he wanted. How could he? Maverick was adamant about not wanting to be tied down and committed to anyone. He bragged about his lifestyle and how he had the freedom to do what he wanted when he wanted. If I just jumped into this head first, all of that would change.

"I said I love you, Paisley, and I meant it. If I could convince you to move in with me today, I would. And the moment I get a new truck, I'll be at your place, packing your things so you don't have to worry about any of that. So, no, I don't need space. I need you."

I rubbed my lips together, buying myself a few minutes while I considered what he was saying. I didn't have to *move in* with him right now. I could grab a few things and stay with him for a little while to see how that felt. There was no need to rush anything when we were just starting to figure things out.

"Okay, I have a deal," I offered with far too much uncertainty in my voice.

"Let's hear it."

"I'll go to your place and stay for a while, but I don't want to rush moving my stuff over just yet. If we can make it through New Year's without trying to kill each other, I'll officially move in then. That gives us a few months to try this and see where it goes."

"Deal."

He extended his hand for me to shake, but once I took it, he pulled me against his body as his lips crashed down over mine.

"I already told you you're mine, Paisley," he said once we caught our breath. "But if you need a few months to convince yourself that this thing between us is real, so be it."

652

Twenty-Four

Maverick

"This is the master bedroom, and through that door is the ensuite bathroom. I don't know that the tub compares to Mr. Crawford's, but I like to think that it's impressive." I leaned against the doorframe while Paisley looked around, ignoring the feeling inside that told me she was meant to be there.

It took us longer to get home than I had wanted, but between cleaning up our mess at the store and getting Paisley's car loaded with everything we were taking, it was a busy day. I left a note for Mr. Crawford by the register, letting him know that we had left and that I would be back in soon to settle what I owed for the stuff we had used. I left a detailed list of everything, making sure he would find it with the note. I had left him a voicemail as well, just to make sure he was aware that we weren't staying there anymore. It would be a while before I could get back to deal with my truck, but at least we were able to leave and get home.

I expected the drive back to be extended because of the weather, but the trickiest part was making sure it was actually safe enough to drive Paisley's car. There was noticeable damage that she would need to have repaired, but we were both determined enough to get out of there that we figured out a way to make it work. Thankfully, the roads were clear through Whiskey Mountain all the way to Fallen Oaks, where I lived. It wasn't typically a long drive, but we went slower than needed just to be sure the car could handle it.

"This is better than the tub I have at my place, so you won't get any complaints from me." She smiled as she walked in front of it, running her fingers along the sleek edge.

"Well, you're welcome to soak while I figure out something for dinner. The good news is that most of the roads are clear here, so the sky is the limit. I can order food too if you'd rather.

Tomorrow, I'll go grocery shopping and can grab whatever you need here."

"You know what I'm craving?" she asked, standing in front of me and batting her eyelashes.

"Chinese food?"

She shook her head, her fingers feathering across my skin as they inched under my shirt and dipped down to my joggers.

"A nice, thick, juicy steak?"

"Nope, but it is thick and juicy."

Before I could stop her, she dropped to her knees, taking my pants down with her.

My eyes rolled to the back of my head as her lips wrapped around my shaft, taking me to the back of her throat.

I had plans of feeding her since we had worked through lunch—but my cock wasn't what I thought would be on the menu. Not that I was complaining.

She hollowed out her cheeks and gripped my ass tightly as she bobbed up and down, her eyes looking up at me from under her dark lashes. I tried to steady my breathing so I didn't come right away, but Paisley was way too good at what she was doing.

"Fuck. I'm going to come, baby," I warned, my hands grabbing the back of her head and holding her steady.

She maintained her rhythm, not bothering to pull away as I exploded in her mouth, a sharp breath leaving my parted lips.

Once I was done, Paisley slowly released me and stood up, gently wiping the corners of her mouth as she gave me a devilish grin.

"That wasn't what I was thinking when I mentioned dinner, but if that's what you're in the mood for, I'm more than happy to have my turn eating my favorite thing," I said with wiggled eyebrows.

"While I would love that, my stomach is loudly protesting and wants real food."

"I might have some frozen pizzas in the deep freezer," I offered, not wanting to disappoint her if she wanted something else.

"That sounds perfect. Do you need any help?"

"Nope. I've got it, but thank you. Feel free to look around and make yourself at home. There's plenty of room in the closet for your clothes, and I can go through the dresser soon and clear out some drawers for you. Just let me know what you need, and I'll make it happen."

"I don't want to go all crazy and just take over your house, Maverick." She let out a soft laugh. "I know we agreed to do this for a couple of months to see how it works, but I promise, I'm not coming in to invade your space."

I pulled her against my body and lifted her chin with my finger to force her to look at me.

"I want you to invade my space, Paisley. And I'll keep reminding you of that every single day through New Year's. Then I'll remind you every minute after as I'm packing up your stuff and moving you in with me—permanently. *You* might need the time to adjust to everything and figure out if this is what you want, but I've already made up my mind, and there's nothing in this world that could change it."

Twenty-Five

Paisley

"So you're living with him now?" Calli asked as she arranged the creepy little gnomes on the counter by the registers.

"I mean, I guess *yes*, but I haven't *officially* moved any of my stuff in yet. We agreed that we would look at things after the new year and see if everything was still working for us. If he had his way, I would be completely moved in *today*."

"Wow. I honestly didn't expect such a sudden change." She shook her head and kept decorating, but I couldn't help the bitter feeling rising up deep inside at her words.

"What does that mean?"

She looked up at me, then softened her features.

"I didn't mean it in a bad way," she said softly. "It's just that you were adamant about *hating* him a few days ago, and now you guys are suddenly in love and living together. It's a big change in a little time, that's all."

"Trust me, I know." I sat down on the edge of the counter opposite her and sighed heavily. "I've liked Maverick for a while now, and it's not like we haven't gotten to know him here and there. But saying I loved him felt right—which I know sounds crazy."

"It does, but sometimes love happens quickly and you can't stop it. It seems silly to try to fight it if you both already admitted that you're feeling it."

"What if I'm wrong though?"

"What do you mean?" She pulled her brows together as she moved the gnomes again. I hated that I was going to have to see them every day when I came in to work. They gave me the creeps, and I couldn't help but think about the scary movie I watched with Calli a few years ago, where they came to life at night and haunted people.

"What if it's not *love* but maybe just *lust*?"

"As in?"

"As in, I like his cock more than anything else about him. What if I'm so dick-sided by it that I can't see straight, and I think I'm in love, but I'm really just horny or something?"

"Dick-sided?" she questioned with a giggle.

"Yeah, it's like being blindsided, but by a dick."

"I don't think that's a thing…"

"Trust me. It is. If you saw what he was packing, you'd know."

"I'll take your word for it."

She stopped messing with the gnomes and turned to face me. Cravings was already closed for the day and the staff had gone home an hour ago, so thankfully, it was just us.

"I don't think that you're being *dick-sided*. I think you have liked Maverick for a while, but you let your anger and pettiness stand in the way of allowing yourself to get to know him better. Then you got stuck together and were forced to spend all of your time with him for several days, and that helped you guys clear the air. I'm sure that the apparently satisfactory sex helps, but I can tell that there's more to whatever this thing is between you two."

"How?" I threw my hands up, exasperated. "How can you possibly tell that there's more than good sex between us? Because I seriously haven't been able to figure that shit out for the life of me."

"Because you wouldn't be sitting here, freaking out if you didn't genuinely care about him. If it were just sex, you would be forcing me to hear all of the dirty details of the ways he fucked you—even after I beg you to stop. But you're not. In fact, you haven't given me a single detail."

She arched an eyebrow and pinned me with a look that had a rush of heat flushing my cheeks.

"What I'm saying is that you love and respect him enough to treat him as something more than just a good fuck, Paisley. And you're freaking yourself out because you've never been here before."

Why did she have to know me so well?

"So what am I supposed to do now?" I asked, staring at the floor so she couldn't see the look on my face, knowing she was right.

"Enjoy being in a relationship. Put in the effort to make it work. And when you're ready, move your stuff into his house and sell your place. Then get knocked up so I can have a cute little baby to spoil."

My eyes bulged at that last sentence. There was no way I was ready to think about settling down on that level. Living with Maverick—maybe. I could work toward being more comfortable with that. But diving in headfirst and thinking about starting a family right now—no way in hell was that going to happen.

Twenty-Six

Maverick

"You're what?" I asked, staring at my dad in disbelief as my jaw hung open.

"I'm retiring. I've reached the age where my body doesn't move like it used to, and I'm too old to be climbing into attics. My knees are getting bad, and my hips constantly hurt. Your old man has worked his ass off for years. It's time I give myself a break and enjoy the life I've created with your mom."

"Wow. Congratulations." My head was still spinning as I tried to process the news. I knew my dad would eventually slow down and consider retiring, but I hadn't expected it to be so soon. He was in good health, but he was getting older, and I would be lying if I said I hadn't noticed he had been slowing down recently when we did a few jobs together.

"Thank you. But the reason I asked you to stop by today is because I wanted to talk to you about the business. I know you've worked hard to get to where you are with your company, but I thought I would see if you were interested in taking over Thompson Mechanical."

My eyes widened as I sat in the chair across from him at the kitchen table, taking it all in.

"But Dad, that's the family company…."

"I know. And you're next in line—if you want it. The business is well established, you know that. I imagine you could easily merge your business with it. The only thing I ask is that you keep the Thompson Mechanical name. People in Whiskey Mountain have known that name for over sixty years. They trust it."

"I don't know what to say." I scrubbed a hand down the scruff of my jaw, shaking my head in disbelief.

While I had assumed this might happen someday, it never occurred to me that it would happen now.

If I took over the family business, that would keep me busier than I was already. I would step into my dad's place and continue running things the way he had and the way my grandfather had before him. My uncles had worked there, too, before they moved away to start their own families. I wanted to make my dad—hell, my whole family—proud.

"The current team would stay in place, so you don't have to worry about any of that. They're good guys and have been with me for years. They know what to do and how to do it. It might be a slight adjustment for some of the older guys since they're so used to me, but they'll be fine."

I nodded, quickly picturing it in my head. I'd dreamed of this since I was a little boy, and now that dream was being offered to me.

 "I'll do it," I said, extending my hand to my dad and shaking his firmly. "I promise I won't let you down."

"I would never offer it to you if I ever thought it was a possibility, son."

He stood up and pulled me with him, wrapping me in a warm embrace as we accepted the new change in the dynamic between us.

****

By the time I finished with work, ran errands, and got home, I found Paisley in the kitchen making dinner. I set my stuff down on the island and immediately wrapped my arms around her waist from behind as her body swayed to the music coming out of her phone.

"Hello," she said with a giggle as I kissed the side of her neck. "Welcome home."

"Thank you. I'm very happy to be here. Seeing you in my kitchen is the best thing I've seen in a while."

"Is that so?" she asked, turning around slowly as my hands grazed across the silky fabric of the robe she was wearing. She slowly untied it, allowing it to fall to the sides, exposing a matching black lace lingerie set.

"Okay, I lied. Seeing you like *this* is the best thing I've seen in a while."

I reached for her playfully, ready to carry her to my bed and devour her, but she swatted me away.

"Dinner will be ready in a few minutes."

"Okay, but I already know what I want to eat," I teased, growling lowly in her ear.

"You better behave, or I won't give you any dessert." She picked up her spatula and shook it at me.

"Is the dessert you?" I asked, reaching for her again as she turned to face the stove.

"No. I made a pumpkin pie from scratch."

"I'd like to eat your pumpkin pie."

She looked over her shoulder and rolled her eyes, but it did nothing to stop the grin on her beautiful face.

"How was your day?" I asked, not wanting to distract her any more than I already had.

"It was nice. Calli had Dylan come pick me up for work this morning so I didn't have to be ready at two in the morning to catch a ride with her. It'll be nice to have my car fixed so I don't have to keep asking for rides. But it was busy at Cravings, which helped the day go by fast. Calli brought me hom—here, so we got to chat for a little bit on the way."

"I'm glad Calli was able to bring you *home*," I corrected. " I don't mind taking you and picking you up. We can look at our schedules and find something that works."

"I don't want you to be stuck in Whiskey Mountain earlier than you have to be. I can figure something out for now."

"It's not a problem, really. Plus, I'll be spending a whole lot more time there soon enough."

"Oh yeah? Why is that?" She turned off the stove and moved the pan to the trivet, giving me her full attention.

"My dad asked to meet with me today, and during our meeting, he let me know that he's retiring."

"Wow. Were you expecting that?"

"No," I said, shaking my head. "Not at all. I mean, I knew he would eventually, but I guess I just thought he had another ten years or so before he even started considering it."

"So, what does that mean for you? What was the meeting about?"

"My dad wanted to meet with me so he could offer me to take over the company."

Paisley's eyes widened in surprise as her mouth hung open.

"Oh my gosh! Maverick! What did you say?"

I grinned and lowered my head for a second before looking up and locking eyes with her.

"I said yes. I'll officially be the new owner of Thompson Mechanical on January 1st. Until then, I'll still be running my business, but I'll also be making trips to visit the businesses my dad works with in Whiskey Mountain. This way, everyone can get used to the change before it happens. Plus, it allows my dad to get through the holidays and wrap everything up that he needs to before he steps away. It just felt like a new year, a fresh start was the way to go."

"I'm so happy for you. That's incredible news! So does that mean you won't be traveling for work anymore since you'll be taking over the business in Whiskey Mountain?" She wrapped her arms around my neck and hugged me.

"That means I won't be traveling for work anymore. I'll be here permanently. Well, technically in Fallen Oaks, but I could be persuaded to move to Whiskey Mountain…"

"I happen to know of a place," she teased before my lips crashed down on hers.

Twenty-Seven

Paisley

The first few weeks of living with Maverick flew by without any issues. It was unsettling how easily we just fell into a routine and how uncomplicated things were. I had expected us to get tired of constantly being in each other's space, but it was never like that.

It was as if he could read what I needed without me having to ask for it. If I was feeling a bit off or grumpy, he would run me a bath and insist that I take some time to relax until I felt better. If I were craving something, he would either cook it or take me out to get it. If I just needed time to myself, he would work on something in a different room or go run errands to give me space.

I liked to think that I was doing the same for him, but I found early on that Maverick was never one to ask for anything or complain. He always had a smile on his face, and whenever I asked him if there was anything I could do for him, he would find a way to twist it around to see what *he* could do for *me*.

Thanksgiving had come and gone without the threat of another massive snowstorm they had predicted—which was nice. Thankfully, it wouldn't be bad if we got stuck together again since this time we would have the comfort of his house, but we also weren't stranded in the middle of nowhere waiting for someone to come rescue us.

We celebrated at Calli's house, where she cooked an elaborate meal. It was nice to see some of our friends, but I was more interested in checking on her mom to make sure she was doing okay. I'd spent so much of my time helping Calli care for her when we first moved to Whiskey Mountain that it felt weird not to be as involved anymore. Not only that, but her mom stepped in and raised me after I lost mine when I was little, so it felt a little like I wasn't being there for her like a daughter should.

Even though I was happy living with Maverick, I couldn't shake the feeling that something big was going to happen. A change neither of us would see coming.

"So, did you decide what you're going to get him?" Calli asked, nudging me with her elbow as I wiped down the counter. Our morning rush was over, but I was already too tired to face the lunch crowd that would be coming in soon.

"Get who what?"

I frowned as I tried to stifle a yawn. I hadn't slept well last night with the wind howling, keeping me awake.

"I was asking if you decided what to get Maverick for Christmas. It's only two weeks away, Paisley. You're going to run out of time."

"I haven't." I sighed heavily, jumping up to sit on the countertop, even though I knew she hated it when I did that. "I have everyone else done except him."

"Do you want me to ask Dylan and see if he has any ideas?"

"No, but thank you. I already feel like shit for not knowing what to get my boyfriend for Christmas. I would feel worse if I had to sink to asking his friend what to get him. I mean, I live with the guy. I should know what he wants."

"It's hard picking gifts for a partner when you're in a new relationship. I struggled with what to get Dylan." She shrugged as if we were in the same boat.

"Are you kidding me?" I tipped my head back and laughed. "Calli, you have at least twenty gifts for him under the tree. I think your problem was knowing when to stop," I teased.

"Maybe. But I'm a good gift giver. It just comes easily to me."

"Okay, then tell me what to get the guy who has everything and wants nothing. That can be your gift to me this year."

"I don't think so. I already got your gifts, and you're going to love them."

I pouted my bottom lip and made it quiver, hoping she would take pity on me.

"I don't know Maverick as well as you do, but from what I know about him, I would go along the lines of apparel. He's more than just a basic t-shirt and jeans guy, so maybe a nice button-down shirt or a scarf that would go with the leather jacket he loves wearing? Or maybe some new gloves? You could also get him some of the cologne he wears. He always smells so good."

"Why are you smelling my boyfriend?" I asked playfully, giving her a look as her cheeks flushed with embarrassment.

"I'm not! I mean, it's not like I'm going up to him and straight up sniffing him. I just notice it because it lingers in the air around him."

"Relax, I'm just teasing."

"Don't tell Dylan I said that his friend smells good. I'll never hear the end of it."

"Maybe you should get him a bottle of the same cologne since you like it so much. You can go around smelling your own man."

"I did. It's not the same."

My eyes bulged as I tried not to burst into laughter.

"What?" I snorted, lifting my hands to my mouth.

"I bought him the same cologne, but it doesn't smell the same on him as it does on Maverick. Don't you dare tell him that, though. I'll cut you…"

"Your secret is safe with me." I held my hands up in front of me.

"Thanks. But honestly, I think he's going to love whatever you get him. You could wrap a bow around yourself, and he would love it."

I knew she was just being sarcastic, but suddenly, I had an idea.

"You're a genius!" I hopped off the counter and grabbed my phone before heading to her office. I didn't need anyone looking over my shoulder or seeing what I was about to look up.

Twenty-Eight

Maverick

"Do you know her size?" the woman behind the glass counter asked as I held up a beautiful diamond ring and examined it.

"Unfortunately, I don't. I can find out, though."

"I think it's so romantic that you're going to propose on Christmas morning. It's not often that we get to hear the story of how someone is planning to do it."

"Can I be honest?" I asked, peering up at her. "I didn't know I was going to do this until about twenty minutes ago when I was walking past your shop to get to Spill The Beans. Something just clicked, and I knew I wanted to do this. You're the only one who knows about it, so I trust you won't say anything to anyone in town. We know how quickly news like this can travel in a small town…"

"Oh, of course. My lips are sealed. I won't say a word. And the good news is it's less than two weeks until Christmas, so you won't have to keep the secret too much longer. But I do worry about not knowing what size ring you'll need. If we don't have that size in stock, I would have to order it, and that would take—"

She stopped talking as I lifted my finger to stop her and held the phone to my ear.

"Cravings, how can I help you?"

"You're just the person I was looking for," I replied, pressing the phone closer to my ear to keep the saleswoman from overhearing my conversation. "I was hoping to ask you something without Paisley hearing."

"Sure, what's up?"

"Is there any way you can find out what size ring she wears?" I felt my jaw tighten as I asked, knowing that Calli would absolutely know that I was shopping for an engagement ring.

"Six."

"Six?"

"Yes, we will close at *six* on Friday, so if you'd like to come pick up your order for your dinner party, I'll be here to give it to you."

I frowned, wondering if she had missed what I was asking for.

"Sorry, she came up front, so I had to make something up," Calli said quickly, her voice drastically lower than a few minutes ago. "She wears a size six ring and prefers rose gold, however, if that's not an option, she'll love whatever you pick. Nothing big, gaudy, or flashy. She likes simple and dainty."

"Thanks, Calli."

"Anytime."

I was grinning like a fool as I hung up the phone and let out a heavy breath.

"Do you, by chance, have that in a size six?"

"It's your lucky day," the saleswoman said, her smile now matching mine. "There's one left."

After I finished up at the jewelry store, I rushed over to Spill The Beans for a latte before they closed. I was supposed to be meeting with clients today with my dad, but he was feeling under the weather so we rescheduled. Since my calendar was already cleared on my side, I decided to take the day to finish my holiday shopping since I had been struggling with what to get Paisley.

I knew her well enough by now to know what she would like, but every time I considered getting something, it felt like it wasn't good enough. I wanted her to know how much I loved her and needed her in my life, yet I couldn't find the perfect thing to convey that until now.

With the ring secure, I headed through the strip mall, finding a few other small gifts that I thought she would like.

By the time I was done, I was too tired to go home and cook, so I sent her a text message to see if she wanted to stay in town for dinner.

Me: Hey baby, do you want to do dinner in town?

Paisley: That's so funny; Calli literally just asked if we wanted to go to La Salsa with them tonight as your text came through.

Me: Sounds like fate.

Paisley: We don't have to go with them if you had something else in mind.

Me: Not at all. I'm just tired and didn't feel like going home to cook. We can go with them if that sounds good to you.

Paisley: I could totally get down with some tacos and queso tonight. Maybe a margarita since I got to be a passenger princess today.

Me: You can have five margaritas if you want.

Paisley: Is that because of that song?

Me: ???

Me: What song?

Paisley: You know, the one that's all over social media where she talks about the stuff she'll do based on how many margaritas she's had.

Me: I haven't heard it, but I might look it up now… you know, just for reference.

Paisley: Trust me, you don't need me to be filled with margaritas. You can have whatever you want.

Me: Well, in that case, maybe we should skip dinner and eat at home instead. Or in my truck. It doesn't matter where we are—I'll eat you anywhere.

Paisley: As tempting as that sounds, my heart—and stomach are settled on tacos.

Me: Fine, you can eat your tacos now, and I'll eat mine later.

Me: Do you want me to come pick you up, or are you going to ride over with Calli?

Paisley: I can ride over with her. Where are you at?

Me: I was finishing some shopping, so I'm actually right across the street from La Salsa.

Paisley: Perfect! We're wrapping up now and can head over if you want to go grab us a booth in the back.

Me: I'll see you soon.

Paisley: Love you.

Me: Love you more.

I tucked my phone back into my pocket and headed over to the restaurant.

It was busier than I had expected, especially for the middle of the week. But then again, it was close to all of the major stores in town, and everyone seemed to be rushing to get their shopping done.

By the time the girls got there, Dylan and I were already holding the booth everyone liked, and food had been ordered since we knew what they wanted. It was nice to feel as in sync with Paisley as Dylan was with Calli.

"I'm gonna run to the restroom real quick," Paisley said, getting up from the table and rushing off.

Once she was gone, Calli leaned in and locked eyes with me as she kept her voice low.

"Did you get it?"

I nodded, glancing briefly at Dylan to see if he had any idea what was going on. I looked around to make sure Paisley was still in the bathroom before pulling the ring out of my inside coat pocket and passing the box to Calli.

She looked over her shoulder to make sure it was clear before opening the box. A soft gasp escaped her lips as her eyes teared up. She leaned in to show Dylan, who smiled warmly at me before wrapping an arm around her shoulders.

"Oh my God, Maverick. She's going to love it. It's perfect." She quickly closed the box and passed it back to me before Paisley came back.

"Thank you. The moment I saw it, I knew it was the one."

"When are you going to do it?" Dylan asked.

"Christmas," I rushed out, shoving it back into my pocket as I spotted Paisley heading our way.

"I told him it would have to wait until next year for a job that big," I said a little too loudly, drawing the attention of those at nearby tables and earning a confused look from Calli and Dylan in the process.

"What did I miss?" Paisley asked, sitting down and looking around the table.

"Oh, nothing. I was just telling them that I had to push back a big project until next year. Things are just too busy right now with merging my dad's business and mine."

Before she could question anything, a scrawny kid came over with our food.

I sighed heavily, thankful for the distraction. There was nothing I wanted more than to marry Paisley and spend the rest of my life with her—but I was going to be a nervous wreck trying to keep this secret from her until Christmas.

Twenty-Nine

Paisley

"Are you sure about this?" I asked, suddenly doubting myself as I ran a hand across the thin fabric that was attempting to hide my stomach.

"Yes!! Now get your ass out here and show me how hot you look," Calli called, making sure I could hear her through the bathroom door I was hiding behind.

I had the wild idea to do sexy Christmas-themed boudoir photos for Maverick for Christmas but hadn't taken into consideration the time I would need to pull all of this together. Thankfully, Calli was entirely on board and agreed to not only take the photos for me but also had a great printer so we didn't have to have that awkward conversation trying to get them printed in town.

I took a deep breath in through my nose and released it slowly through my mouth, trying to calm my nerves. There was nothing to be this nervous about, yet it was like I was getting ready to walk down Main Street, strutting my stuff for everyone to see.

"I know we have the room for the entire day, but we're going to lose daylight if we don't get started soon."

"Okay, okay," I replied, opening the door. "I'm coming."

I walked into the room, thankful that we had gotten one on the top floor so no one could see in the windows that were completely open, letting in enough natural light to not need any other lights on.

"Holy. Shit."

Calli's jaw dropped open as her eyes widened and a smile started spreading across her face.

"You look amazing!"

"Thanks," I said nervously, still rubbing a hand across my stomach. "I was going for a naughty Mrs. Claus look."

"Umm, I think you nailed it."

I stepped in front of the floor-length mirror, taking in the red bodysuit I was wearing and the white fur that lined the long sleeves, the deep plunging neckline, and the bottom of the skirt that barely covered my ass. It was a corset style that laced up the front, putting my breasts on full display with just a hint of skin that showed between the laces. I wore the red thong that came with it, but for the most part, it was covered by the skirt.

I adjusted the Santa hat on my head, then pulled on the knee-high black stiletto boots I had brought to go with it.

"He's going to love this," Calli said, checking the settings on her camera as I applied red lipstick to finish the look.

"I really hope so."

Calli gave me a look that said I was being ridiculous, then guided me to where she wanted me. We did a handful of photos with me standing in front of the window or sitting on the tiny ledge as I spread my legs seductively. Part of me wondered if anyone could see me, and I couldn't deny the heat that was spreading through me at the thought that maybe they could.

I climbed onto the bed and got into the poses she asked for, along with a few of my own that just felt natural. It was better to have too many photos and not be able to use all of them than to not have enough. This was his main gift from me for our first Christmas together, and I didn't want to screw it up.

We spent a few hours doing photos with some wardrobe changes in between. Calli loved the Mrs. Claus outfit, but I found myself torn between the naughty elf get-up and the snow bunny one. It was more fun than I imagined it would be, especially after my nerves settled.

"Okay, this is the last one, and then we can stop and grab dinner," I said, coming out of the bathroom in a black leather lingerie set that was giving some serious dominatrix vibes. I knew this would probably be Maverick's favorite and wanted to make sure I did it right with some more risqué photos.

I climbed onto the bed and got onto my knees, making sure not to damage the white comforter with my heels as I spread my legs. My hair was pulled up into a high ponytail for this one, and my makeup darker with a dramatic smokey eye look. I felt more confident like this than I had in any of the other photos. I moved freely, getting into the positions I wanted as Calli snapped the photos, telling me how much she loved all of them.

Before we finished, I decided to do one last pose—just to be cheeky. I got down on all fours on the bed and angled myself so she could get the picture from behind. I knew Maverick loved my ass and that this picture would drive him crazy. To up the ante, I spread my legs, looked over my shoulder, and lowered my hand so my fingers were pushing the thin fabric of my thong to the side. My lips were exposed, but I knew I wanted to go all in with this, so I slowly slid one finger inside, knowing Calli wouldn't be bothered by any of it. Heck, I had helped her do something similar for Dylan a while back.

"He's going to go crazy over these," Calli said, getting the last picture so I could pull my hand away and fix my panties. "Let me get one more from the side."

She bent to take the picture, but I noticed an odd frown on her face as she looked at me through the viewfinder.

"What's wrong?" I asked, wondering if something had happened to the lingerie or if I had accidentally popped a titty out or something.

"Nothing," she rushed out, lowering the camera quickly. The look on her face confirmed she was lying.

"What is it?" I probed, suddenly feeling super self-conscious.

"It's nothing. I promise."

"Stop lying to me, Calli. You're my best friend, so act like it."

She rubbed her lips together and avoided looking at me as I climbed off the bed and stood in front of her. I raised my eyebrow, forcing the question again.

"I noticed a small bump and my mind just immediately got ahead of me before I could process what I was thinking."

"Small bump? Where?" I rushed over to the mirror, wondering what sort of skin abnormality she had seen that I wasn't aware of. Was it a pimple? Ingrown hair? A wart? Now my mind was spiraling out of control, wondering what she had seen that had freaked her out.

"Calli, where is it?" I asked, panic thick in my voice. "Where's the bump?" I turned quickly, my eyes scanning every inch of my body in the mirror as I desperately tried to find what she had seen.

"Here," she said softly, rubbing her hand over my lower stomach.

Her eyes lifted to mine in the mirror and it was at that moment that I knew.

<u>Thirty</u>

Paisley

"When was your last period?" Calli asked as we sat on the hotel bed, unwrapping the boxes of pregnancy tests she had run out to purchase.

"I don't know." My mind was racing a mile a minute, and all I could focus on right now was getting the stupid test sticks out of their packaging. Why was it so hard? Didn't they know most women would need to get to these in a hurry?

"Paisley, calm down. We don't even know if you're pregnant. I shouldn't have said anything. I just saw it, and I don't know… I guess I just thought maybe…"

"No, I'm glad you did. God knows I probably wouldn't even know until nine months later when I was having a kid on the toilet or something."

She reached over and grabbed my hands, stopping me from the panic attack I was about to have.

"Let's not freak out until we know for sure, okay?"

I nodded my head and took in a shaky breath. Maverick had checked in earlier to see how things were going, but he knew I was staying with Calli tonight, so he told me he would give us some time to ourselves. I was kinda thankful that I didn't have to worry about talking to him right now. We didn't need everyone freaking out until we knew for sure what was happening.

I got up and went into the bathroom to pee in one of the disposable cups we found in the room. I pulled the plastic off of it, sat down, and closed my eyes while I tried to get it together.

"You ready?" Calli asked from the room as I stared in the mirror after washing my hands.

"Yeah. Let's get this over with."

She joined me at the vanity and gave me a reassuring smile as she handed me a few sticks that had been removed from the packaging. We each took turns dipping them into the cup, then put the caps on and laid them on the plastic bag from the store. In three to five minutes, I would have answers and would know whether my life was about to change forever.

"We can sit down while we wait," she offered, gently leading me back to the bed.

"How long has it been since you guys got stuck together in that storm?"

"I don't know," I said with a heavy sigh, trying to remember. "That was at the beginning of November, I think? I was there to get those stupid gnomes for you so you could decorate for Thanksgiving."

"That's right. Okay. Let me check my calendar real quick."

I waited while she scrolled through her phone, doing some sort of period math in her head.

"And you don't remember the last time you had your period?"

I shook my head and tried to force my shoulders down from my ears.

"Okay, so that was about seven or eight weeks ago. And you guys did it while you were there, right?"

I nodded, trying to remember the details.

"Yeah, we spent one whole day doing it. It was a fuck-a-thon," I said with an awkward laugh while I chewed my nail.

"Okay, then," she replied with a little giggle. "I don't think we're going to have any questions about *how* this happened if those tests are positive. Did you guys use protection?"

"No."

"At all?"

"I'm on the pill," I said with a shrug. "It's supposed to work."

"Yeah, but Paisley, birth control pills are only like 99% effective. Did you have them with you while you were stranded?"

"Nope," I said, quickly realizing where this was going. "I missed a few days while we were stuck there."

"And then you moved in with him and have been fucking nonstop ever since?" she asked with a smirk.

"Yup."

"Well, then, I guess there's only one thing left to do."

"What's that?"

"Let's go check the test and see if you're knocked up."

She got up and extended her hand, but I refused to take it. I looked up at her, tears welling in my eyes as I shook my head.

"I can't do it. Can you please tell me?"

"Okay." She nodded her head, squeezed my hand, and then walked back to the bathroom.

I had no idea how long she was really gone because minutes felt like hours as my lungs burned trying to pull air through them.

"Calli, you're killing me," I whined, wringing my hands together nervously.

She came around the corner holding three tests in one hand while covering her mouth with the other.

I opened my mouth to speak, but the words refused to come out.

"Congratulations, you're gonna be a momma," she said, her voice breaking with emotion at the end.

****

"Are you sure we shouldn't order real food?" Calli asked, staring at my second bowl of banana split that we'd gotten with room service.

"No. I'm apparently eating for two, so that justifies having two bowls of ice cream," I countered, my nerves still shot.

"Yes, but I worry that you're going to crash soon from all of this sugar, and I'd like to have some protein ready before they close room service for the night. I don't want to have to call Dylan and have him bring us food, especially with you in this state," she teased, pointing to the chocolate syrup smeared across my cheek.

"I'm fine. Really. I mean, who wouldn't be? I just started dating someone who I got stuck with in a general store during the most bizarre blizzard in the history of blizzards, only to have my birth control fail and get knocked up. Not only that—but I'm getting fat early, so why not justify it with some freaking ice cream?" My voice was so high-pitched that it even scared me.

"Okay, I'm just gonna make a quick phone call," she said warily, grabbing her phone and stepping into the hallway.

"You better not be calling Mav—" I started before the sound of the door closing cut me off.

I knew I needed to tell him I was pregnant, but I wanted some time to process the news myself before I ran off and scared him, too. If she could spot a baby bump on me this early, it would be impossible for him to miss it. However, a quick Google search confirmed that I likely wasn't actually showing yet and that it was probably slight bloating—not that I was helping anything by eating all of this ice cream.

A few minutes later, Calli came back inside and sat on the bed as if nothing had happened. She grabbed the remote and started flipping through the channels on the TV without saying anything about who she had called or what was happening. I knew her well enough to know without a doubt that something was up.

"Are you seriously not going to tell me what you did?" I asked, finishing the last of the ice cream before setting the empty bowl on the nightstand between us.

"Nope."

"Why?"

"Because it's better that you don't know. You're already all twitchy as it is."

I frowned and stared at the side of her head, willing her to look at me.

"Stop it. I'm not going to tell you anything. But I do suggest you go wash your face. You still have chocolate on your chin."

I stuck my tongue out at her before getting up and relieving myself again before washing my face. By the time I got back to the bed, she was sitting there with her head down, focused on her phone.

"It should be here in a few minutes."

"What should?"

"Your care package."

I sat on the bed and took a deep breath, loving that I had someone here to help me through this right now. Not that I didn't have Maverick, but I wasn't in any condition to tell him right now. Not when I was still a mess and unable to wrap my head around how I felt.

A few minutes later, there was a soft knock on the door. Calli got up and opened it, my body immediately going into panic mode when I heard Dylan's voice. I wasn't sure if she had told him to bring Maverick with him and that was supposed to be my care package.

I couldn't hear what they were saying and sat rigidly on the edge of the bed as they talked quietly in the hallway. I was getting ready to get up and pace the room when I heard the door shut, and Calli walked toward me with two bags in her hands.

"Real food because you need it," she explained, waving the bag of takeout from La Salsa. "And a self-care package because you need it. But because we're doing self-care, I say we start with food because that's a priority right now. Plus, you don't let good tacos go bad."

I laughed and felt some of the tension release from my shoulders as I joined Calli at the small table in the corner of the room by the window. She unpacked the food and pulled out a few bottles of water that she set between us.

She passed a to-go box of chicken tacos my way, knowing my order perfectly. I grabbed a chip from the box in between us and dipped it into the salsa, closing my eyes as my stomach growled loudly. Calli laughed as she took her food out and set the bag on the floor behind her.

"Thank you for ordering dinner. Sorry I was being so difficult."

"It's not a problem at all. I'm just thankful you're eating something other than ice cream," she joked.

"Yeah, I might have to change my eating habits if I don't want to gain a bunch with this preg—"

The words died in my throat before I could get them out.

"It's all about balance. You can indulge in the sweet stuff, but just make sure you're eating plenty of healthy stuff, too—and lots of water. You'll want to make sure you limit how much caffeine you're drinking as well," she said before taking a bite of her food.

"You know so much about this," I commented without thinking. "I have no idea what I'm doing, and you seem to be a wealth of knowledge."

"I had Dylan stop and grab some stuff for you while he was out getting dinner," she said, ignoring my comment. "You'll want to start prenatal vitamins right away. I had him grab these ones since I like them."

She reached down, grabbed a bottle from the other bag, and passed it to me.

"Oh, thank you. That's so sweet of—"

I stopped and narrowed my eyes at her as she suddenly looked away from me.

"Calli?"

Slowly, she looked up at me, her eyes quickly giving her away.

"What do you mean these are the ones you like?"

She rubbed her lips together as she leaned back in the chair and thought about how to respond.

"The pill ones are hard to swallow for me and have a bad smell that makes me more nauseous. I like the gummy ones better and thought you might too."

I leaned forward and looked her in the eyes.

"Calli, you're pregnant?"

She nodded, lifting her hands to brush away the tears.

"Oh my God! Why didn't you say anything?"

I jumped up from my seat and pulled her up to hug her. I wrapped my arms around her, squeezing every emotion out of us, before stepping back and looking at her stomach.

"I just found out a few weeks ago. We were waiting until after our first doctor's appointment before telling anyone."

"I can't believe this. So we're going to be pregnant together?"

She nodded her head, tears sliding down her face.

"When is your appointment?"

"Next week. It's the day I have myself leaving early."

"Wow. This is so wild. Do you know how far along you are?"

"Not exactly, *but* I think I'm around ten or eleven weeks."

"How does Dylan feel about it?"

"He's already in love and keeps saying it's a girl," she said with a laugh. "I think me being pregnant is what led me to thinking you might be when I saw your little bump. Dylan is constantly checking to see if he can see one on me, so now I'm obsessively looking for it."

"That's so awesome. I'm so happy for you guys!" I gave her another squeeze before letting her go so we could finish our dinner. "He's going to be such a great dad."

"Maverick will be too," she said softly. "And I already know he's going to be just as excited as Dylan was when he found out. We won't say anything about you being pregnant until you tell him yourself. Just be sure to do it soon. You don't want him to miss out on being there for you, Paisley."

I nodded and popped a chip into my mouth, giving it some thought.

"I guess I ended up finding the perfect Christmas gift for him after all," I replied with a laugh. "I mean, that is if I can go five more days without telling him."

Thirty-One

Maverick

It had been the longest two weeks trying to keep the proposal from Paisley. I kept almost slipping up, calling her my wife and then having to play it off as some weird thing that couples that lived together did. She seemed distracted the past few days and didn't seem to pay it as much attention as the first few times I'd done it, but then again, she might have just gotten used to it. Or maybe it wasn't as easy to freak her out anymore after all.

I rolled over and pulled her close to me, inhaling the soft scent of her shampoo as she turned and faced me.

"Good morning," I greeted, giving her a few minutes to wake up.

"Good morning."

Her eyes were still closed but she looked more beautiful than ever.

"Merry Christmas."

"Merry Christmas," she replied as her eyes slowly fluttered open.

I didn't want to rush her, especially since we didn't have anything pressing to do until dinner this evening at Calli and Dylan's house. But I was so anxious to finally get to ask her to marry me that I felt like a kid standing in front of a candy shop, begging my parents for an early allowance.

"I know it's early," I said as calmly as I could. "But I want to give you your present."

"Okay, go for it," she said sleepily, her eyes fluttering closed again as she shifted and spread her legs. "I'll enjoy it. Promise."

"As romantic and tempting as that sounds, eating you out is not my gift to you. I have something that I *hope* you'll enjoy even more."

"Okay, okay. I'll get up. I have something I want to give you, too."

She seemed more tired than usual, which made me feel bad for pushing her to get up.

"How about I go make us some breakfast before we open anything? You can take your time getting up and around while I start a pot of coffee."

"No coffee for me. I'm not supposed to have caffeine."

I pulled my head back in confusion as she slowly climbed out of bed before suddenly stopping. It was as if she realized the words she said as she said them, frozen in place as her face turned white as a sheet.

"Why aren't you supposed to have caffeine?" I questioned, stepping closer to her.

She opened her mouth and then snapped it shut, clearly not ready to say whatever was trying to come out.

"Paisley…"

I didn't want to push her, but my mind was already racing with reasons why she couldn't have it.

"I umm. Well…"

"You're killing me here."

I stepped around the bed and stood in front of her, grabbing her hands and holding them in front of me.

"Paisley, what's going on?"

"I'm pregnant."

My body temperature spiked as my heart started racing with excitement.

"You're pregnant?" I asked in disbelief.

She nodded, her eyes clouded with tears as she tried to look away.

"Baby, what's wrong?"

I pulled her into me and wrapped her in a protective embrace.

"Nothing, I just do this now. I cry over everything," she sobbed, digging her head into my chest.

"Are you okay?"

"Yeah, just a little nervous to tell you. I had planned to do something for you as a gift to tell you the news, but I ran out of time."

"Paisley, you being pregnant is the best gift you could have ever given me."

My eyes traveled down her body to her stomach, where I placed my hand.

"Are you really okay with this?"

"Of course. Why wouldn't I be?"

"I don't know, Maverick." She sighed heavily, sitting on the edge of the bed and looking up at me. "We didn't plan any of this. We weren't trying to have a baby. All of this kind of just fell into our laps, and bam—now I'm knocked up with your child."

"True, we didn't plan any of this, but I also wouldn't have it any other way." I reached down and lifted her chin to look at me again as she tried to look away. "I told you that I want a life with you, Paisley. This has never been something temporary for me. I've wanted you from the start, and I wasn't kidding when

I told you that you were mine. Having a baby with you just strengthens the connection between us."

"Yeah, but we just started living together. Don't you feel like all of this is kind of rushed? I mean, call me crazy, but I thought I would be married and stuff before I started popping out babies."

I arched an eyebrow, wondering if she knew about me proposing.

"I mean—I wasn't saying you need to marry me because I'm carrying your child. That's not what I meant. I just always thought that *if* I had kids with someone, we would be—"

"Paisley," I said, interrupting her.

Her face was the cutest shade of red as she tried to avoid looking at me.

"This isn't how I was planning to do this," I muttered, walking over to the dresser and grabbing the ring box. "But if the time is right…"

I stood in front of her and smiled before dropping to one knee and opening the box to face her.

"I had this really romantic proposal planned," I explained with a laugh, shaking my head. "I was going to do it in front of the tree with the beautiful snowy background behind us. I even had a camera set up so I could get a picture of it."

"Oh my God!" she squealed, covering her eyes and dropping her head. "I'm ruining everything this morning!"

I reached over and grabbed her hands, forcing them down.

"You're not ruining anything. Just because this isn't going according to how I thought it would doesn't mean this isn't the perfect way to propose."

"You're just saying that to make me feel better."

"I'm not. But I do have something to ask you."

She took a deep breath and slowly released it as she looked down at the ring in my hand.

"Paisley, I love you more than I have ever loved anything. Being with you makes me feel like my life is complete, and I cannot imagine spending another day without you beside me. Would you do me the honor of marrying me and being my wife?"

Her bottom lip quivered as she looked from me to the ring and then back to me.

"Yes," she said, her voice shaky as she reached forward and wrapped her arms around my neck.

I stood up, taking her with me as I locked my lips over hers and kissed the heck out of her.

"You just made me the happiest man in the world," I exclaimed, refusing to let her go as I gently swung us in a circle. "My fiancée is having my baby!"

"I guess today is filled with lots of big things," she giggled.

"It sure is. And we're only a week away from you officially moving in with me."

"I think that was pretty much a done deal when you knocked me up. There's no way I'm doing all this by myself."

"I would never allow that to happen." I stopped swinging her and set her down, hoping I hadn't made her nauseous. I had no idea if she was experiencing any morning sickness, but I didn't want to make it worse if she was.

"You are my life, Paisley. You and this baby. There is not a single thing in the world that I wouldn't do for both of you. My only goal in life is to make sure you're happy and taken care of. I will be there for you every step of the way with this pregnancy. This is you and me together, baby. Nothing is going to stop us now."

"I love you, Maverick."

"I love you more."

Thirty-Two

Paisley

"You did not have to cook all of this for me," I said, sitting uncomfortably full at the table after devouring a four-course meal that Maverick made me for breakfast.

"It was my pleasure. Gotta feed you and my little squirt."

I scrunched my nose, not liking the nickname he was giving our unborn child. We had already been through muffin, nugget, bean, and peanut, none of which sounded right. It felt like we needed something other than *unborn child*, but we just hadn't found the right one yet.

"What's wrong with Squirt?" he asked, leaning over to load the dishwasher. "I think it's cute."

I popped a grape into my mouth and chewed, enjoying the view as his t-shirt stretched tightly over his muscular back.

"It reminds me of what *I* do and how you got me pregnant."

"Fair point."

He stood up and leaned against the counter, giving it some thought with his arms crossed over his chest.

"How about Cletus the Fetus?" he offered.

"Cletus? Do you want our kid to get bullied in kindergarten?" I got up and walked over to him, wrapping my arms around his waist.

"There's no way in hell that will happen. I'll take down the little snot licker before they have a chance."

"Easy there," I teased, running my hands down his chest. "There's no need for such violence. Give the kid a break; they can't even tie their shoes."

"True." He nodded his head as if this was an everyday kind of conversation to have. "What about Spawn?"

"No. I'm not referring to our baby as *spawn*."

He arched an eyebrow, questioning my veto.

"When I hear spawn, I think of demon spawn. No thanks." I shrugged my shoulders.

"Alright, I've got it," he said, rubbing his hands excitedly as I stepped to the side.

I tilted my head, waiting to hear the ridiculous nickname he would throw at me this time.

"Pumpkin."

As much as I wanted to hate it, I didn't. Maybe it was because the baby had been conceived in the fall, and I associated that with pumpkins, or maybe it was because I was craving pumpkin pie all the time. But something about it just fit.

"Pumpkin," I repeated, nodding my head in agreement. "I like it."

"Good. Then that's settled. Now let's go open presents. I got you something I think you're really going to like."

"Same," I said with a flirty smirk as I walked past him and headed to the living room.

****

"I want to say I have a favorite, but I love them all," Maverick said, flipping through the photos I had printed for him from the boudoir session I had done with Calli. I sat there nervously chewing my nails as I waited for him to get to the black leather dominatrix ones.

I could tell the moment he did because his fingers stopped moving, and his eyes darkened. He shifted uncomfortably on the floor beside me, tugging at the fabric of his joggers as he slowly flipped through them. The last picture was the one Calli got a close-up of me with my finger slipping inside my pussy.

"Let's go," he said gruffly, setting the pictures to the side and standing up.

"But we didn't finish," I objected with a laugh as he bent down and tossed me over his shoulder, carrying me back to the bedroom.

"Maverick," I squealed, loving the way his fingers gripped my body before gently setting me on the bed. "We weren't done opening gifts."

"The rest can wait—trust me." He wiggled his eyebrows before pulling his shirt over his head and tossing it to the floor. His beautifully sculpted body was one of my favorite sights, and suddenly, I didn't care about the rest of the presents we hadn't opened yet. He was about to give me the gift that kept on giving.

Thirty- Three

Maverick

"I'm going to be a dad," I announced proudly to my parents, pulling Paisley into my side as we sat on the couch at their house. We were celebrating Christmas with them on New Year's Eve because they had been out of town for the holiday. Since Paisley was pregnant, we didn't see the need to go to any big parties and stay up late to watch the ball drop. I was getting ready to start the new year with a fiancée and a baby on the way, and nothing could top that.

"Oh my goodness," my mother said, immediately wiping the tears from her eyes. "Congratulations! I'm so happy for you guys!"

"Congratulations! That's wonderful news," my father replied before standing up to pull me into a hug. "I'm proud of you, son."

"Thanks, Dad."

"I can't believe it," my mom said, smiling proudly at us. "First, we find out that you two are getting married, and now that we're going to be grandparents. There are so many exciting things happening in our family and I just love it. Have you guys set a date for the wedding?"

"Not yet," Paisley answered, looking up at me briefly. "I wanted to have a spring wedding, but I worry that whatever dress I pick now won't fit then. I'm not sure whether it's a good idea to try to plan a wedding while being pregnant since so much can change so quickly."

"We could always get married now," I offered. I didn't want to put her on the spot, but at the same time, I couldn't stop the nagging feeling deep inside of me saying that I should marry her now. It wasn't that I worried something would go wrong and she would change her mind; it was that I couldn't wait another minute to make her my wife and spend forever with her.

"Like as in on your parent's couch right now?" she teased.

"No," I replied with a laugh. "But we could do a winter wedding that would still be beautiful, Paisley. And you wouldn't have to wait as long, so whatever dress you pick now would likely still fit. We could do something like Valentine's Day—"

She scrunched her nose and shook her head, forcing me to chuckle.

"Or not. The point is that we don't have to wait that long to get married. We can plan a perfect wedding and do it soon. That way, you don't have to stress over all the what-ifs, and I get to call you my wife sooner."

Paisley pulled her shoulders back and stared off into the distance as she thought about it.

"How about January 14th? That gives us two weeks to get things situated. I don't need a big wedding with all the bells and whistles. I can find a dress and take care of the little things during my downtime at work. Calli can make the food for the reception, and I'm sure I can ask Maggie to make the cake."

"I can do the photos," Mom offered, leaning forward as she hung onto every word.

"And if you're interested, I have a friend who has a large ranch with a gorgeous rustic barn that you guys could get married in." My dad wrapped an arm around my mom's shoulders, both of them looking happier than I'd seen them in a while.

I loved that they were as excited as we were but that they weren't being pushy or trying to tell us what to do.

"We can talk over things later and let you guys know," I said, squeezing her hand reassuringly. I didn't want her to feel rushed into making a decision on everything right now, especially if she had other ideas for what she wanted. There was a lot happening all at once, and I didn't want to create any unnecessary stress for her right now.

"Sounds lovely, dear. And Paisley, if there's anything we can do for you during your pregnancy, please don't hesitate to let us know."

"Thank you. I appreciate that."

I leaned into the couch, allowing my body to relax, knowing that everything in life was finally going in the right direction.

****

By the time we got home from my parents' house, it was late, and Paisley had gone straight to bed. She had insisted that she would stay up so we could ring in the new year together, but I felt better that she was getting the rest that she and the baby needed.

It still felt incredibly weird to say that we were having a baby, but I couldn't be happier.

Never in a million years did I see myself getting married and having a baby with a woman I had only been dating for a few months, but that was exactly what was happening. Who were we to try to intervene when fate was involved?

I finished cleaning up the mess in the kitchen before heading up to bed when I noticed a missed call from Jackson. We had been chatting back and forth for a few weeks through text messages as he was slammed with the holidays—both at work and with his family.

I pressed the play button and listened as the voicemail started.

"Hey Maverick, sorry to call so late. We just wrapped up the end-of-year stuff we needed to get done, so I wanted to check in on our conversation. If your friend is still interested in a marketing position, please have her email her resume, and we'll

take a look at it. I'll be in the office on Monday, but you can send it to HR and they'll get started on it. Let me know if you have any questions."

My grin split across my face, knowing that there were more wonderful opportunities on the horizon. I couldn't wait for Paisley to wake up so I could tell her the good news.

Thirty-Four

Paisley

"What do you think about this one?" Calli asked, holding up a beautiful long-sleeved white dress with a sheer lace overlay.

My heart raced at the sight of it, admiring the beauty in the intricate details. I stepped forward, trying to see the price without letting her know.

As if already knowing what I was up to, she quickly covered the tag in her hand and cocked her head to the side as she pinned me with a look.

"Do you like it?" she pressed, still refusing to let go of the tag.

"I do…"

"But?"

"But you won't let me see how much it costs and I'm getting anxious about how expensive everything in here is," I whispered loudly to her without letting the sales lady by the register overhear us. "We're getting married and having a baby—both of which are already getting to be quite costly. I don't want to spend an absurd amount on a dress that I'm only going to wear once."

"Paisley, I say this with love—stop being a pain in the ass and just pick a dress."

I arched an eyebrow and placed a hand on my hip as I stared at her.

"It's not that easy."

"Yes, it is."

"I hate to break it to you, but I'm not just rolling in the dough. I don't have the luxury of buying whatever I want without having to worry about how much it costs."

Calli set the dress down and stepped in front of me, holding my hands in hers.

"I get that. And I wasn't going to say anything—because I was threatened not to—but you are already set up to have whatever dress in here you'd like. There's no cost to you. So literally all of them are free, Paisley. You just have to pick the one you want."

I shook my head, hoping it would dislodge the words that were stuck in my head.

"What are you talking about?"

"It's already been taken care of."

"How?"

"Your future in-laws made some arrangements. This is one of them. And since this is the best—and only," she whispered, "dress store in Whiskey Mountain, you have your pick. Whatever your heart desires."

My heart raced in my chest, beating wildly. It hadn't even been a full forty-eight hours since we announced our engagement to Maverick's parents and they were already moving mountains to make this work for us on such short notice.

"Can I still see how much it costs before I make a decision?" I asked.

I knew that it technically didn't matter to anyone else since I wasn't the one paying for it, but I wasn't going to take advantage of Maverick's parents' generosity. There was a big difference between the $200 dress I initially looked at compared to the $1500 dress I saw in the window before we walked in.

"No."

I frowned and tugged my lower lip between my teeth.

"Just follow your heart, Paisley. Which dress is calling your name?"

I sighed heavily, looking from the $200 one I had my mind set on to the one she was holding again. It was gorgeous, and it was what I imagined I would wear someday if I got married.

"That one." I pointed at it and felt my cheeks split into a grin as she smiled widely at me.

"Perfect. I'll take care of this, but while I'm doing that, it wouldn't hurt you to browse the bridesmaid dresses over there. I'll need some guidance on what you want me to wear since I'll be your maid of honor and all." She winked playfully but already knew she was going to be it.

I walked over and browsed the dresses on the rack, hating that I hadn't figured out any of the details for our wedding yet. Technically, it had only been a day since I agreed to marry Maverick in two weeks, but I was starting to reconsider moving so quickly with everything.

He had sent me out to do some shopping with Calli while he and Dylan took care of moving my stuff over to his house. Everyone was all hands on deck, ready to jump in and help however we needed, but I hated the feeling that I couldn't even stop for a few minutes to think about what I wanted. I needed to sit down and talk to Maverick, but I didn't want him to think that I was reconsidering marrying him. I wanted nothing more than to be his wife, but I didn't need the big wedding and stuff to make our marriage real.

I pushed a handful of dresses to the side, already ruling them out since they were sleeveless and short—not ideal for a winter wedding. There weren't a lot of options to choose from, and I wanted something that Calli would be comfortable in. We weren't having a big wedding, so I wasn't concerned with finding anyone else to be in it. Maverick had asked Dylan to be his best man, which worked well since Calli was my maid of honor.

I picked up a blush-colored dress that would look beautiful on Calli and checked the price tag. It wasn't as expensive as I had expected, but still, $120 for a dress she would only wear once was a bit much. I set it back on the rack and went to reach for another one when my phone rang. I pulled it out of my pocket and swiped my finger across the screen to answer it, not recognizing the phone number on the caller ID.

"Hello," I answered, tucking the phone between my ear and shoulder as I hung the dress up.

"Hi, may I please speak with Paisley?" a woman asked, her voice soft yet professional.

"Yes, this is she."

"Hi, Paisley. This is Bea, calling from Mason, Inc. We received your resume, and I wanted to touch base to see if we could set up a time for you to do an online interview."

"Oh my gosh, yes, hi!" I hated how high my voice squealed when I realized who I was speaking to. Maverick and I had talked about it after he got the voicemail from Jackson, and I sent in my resume right away, but it still surprised me to get her call. "That would be wonderful. Thank you."

"It's our pleasure. Mr. Mason mentioned that he wanted to schedule something as soon as possible as he has a position immediately available. Would you be available this afternoon at four pm?"

I glanced at my watch, noticing it was already after two. Calli and I had a few more errands we were planning to run, but I knew she would totally take a raincheck so I could do the interview.

"Yes. That sounds perfect."

"Wonderful. I will email you shortly with the details and the link so you can join the call. If you need anything in the meantime, please feel free to reach out to me."

"Thank you so much, Bea. I appreciate it."

"Not a problem. We'll see you at four."

I smiled as I hung up, feeling electricity in the air around me. Calli headed my way, her brows pulled in with curiosity as a garment bag hung over her arm.

"What's up?" she asked, tilting her head as she studied me.

"I just got off the phone with the company Maverick's friend works at—Mason, Inc. I have an interview today at four!"

"Oh my gosh! Paisley! That's amazing!"

"Thank you! Sorry, we'll have to wrap stuff up a little early."

"Don't be. We got the most important thing done today—finding you a dress."

"Thanks. I still can't believe his parents did that."

She smiled warmly and grabbed the dress I had been looking at before I took the call, hanging it over her arm on top of mine.

"What are you doing?" I asked, frowning as we headed toward the front door.

"Getting my dress."

My brow furrowed deeper, not understanding.

"I saw you looking at it, and you had this look in your eye. It's the one you get when you really love something. Then I saw you check the price and put it back, which confirmed that this is the right dress. So I'm getting it."

"Calli, you don't have to do that. We can find something less expensive," I said quietly through clenched teeth as I attempted to smile at the sales lady at the register.

"I don't *have* to do anything, Paisley. My best friend is getting married, and *this* is the dress I'm wearing to her wedding. Now stop fussing and let me have my joy."

"This is a beautiful dress," the saleswoman said, scanning the tag to ring it up. "Did you need shoes to go with it?"

"No, thank you. I already have some that will go perfectly," Calli answered.

I waited for Calli to finish paying, and then we walked out together, greeted by a cold rush of air.

"Do you have something to wear to your interview?" she asked, pressing the button to unlock her car.

"It's an online one," I said, not even thinking about what I should wear to it. "It's not an actual in-person one."

"No, but you still want to be dressed appropriately for it," she countered as we climbed in and got buckled. "We'll tackle the rest of the wedding stuff this week, but right now, we're going shopping for your new job."

"I don't even know that I'll get it." I laughed nervously. It wasn't like I had the experience they were looking for, so it was a long shot. Plus, I would be starting a new job pregnant and needing to take maternity leave before I even completed a year there—not that I had to disclose that information to them in the interview. But still, it felt wrong to lead them on and not let them know that I had some personal things that would be happening soon.

"You will get it because you're insanely talented and one of the best marketers I've ever met. You could sell free water and make a profit on it."

I rolled my eyes and laughed at her overly dramatic analogy.

"I don't want to go spend a bunch of money on clothes for a new job until I know for sure that I have it. Plus, I'll have to be smart about it since I'll have to transition to maternity clothes sooner rather than later."

"Well, how about we start with finding a new outfit for you to wear to the interview?" she offered.

"Deal. But can we *please* go to the thrift shop? It's giving me heartburn thinking about how much money we've spent already today."

"I think the heartburn *might* be from the six strips of bacon and four sausage links you had at breakfast, but yes, we can hit up Whiskey Savers. I was hoping to do some shopping there for maternity clothes, too, so we can multitask."

I leaned back in the passenger seat and wondered when things were going to feel calm again.

****

I sat up straight in front of the computer screen, adjusting the tank top Calli had convinced me to buy for the interview. It felt weird to be wearing a sleeveless shirt during the middle of winter, but it went perfectly with the beige pencil skirt that was also on sale. The shirt was a darker brown with a polka dot print that matched the color of the skirt and screamed professional compared to the clothes I typically wore.

The screen changed as Bea and Mr. Mason entered the call, their cameras turning on as my face popped up in a square alongside theirs.

"Hello, Paisley. Thank you for taking the time to meet with us today," Bea said warmly.

"Thank you so much for giving me the opportunity to interview for a position with Mason, Inc." I rubbed my hands nervously under the table as I struggled not to fidget or appear nervous. "It's an honor to be considered by such a prestigious company."

"The honor is ours," Mr. Mason said, clearing his throat.

I smiled and tried to breathe through the flush that was washing over my cheeks.

"We've reviewed your resume and reached out to a few of your previous employers," Bea said, getting straight to it. "Can you tell us a little more about your experience with Cravings?"

I nodded, hoping that I would be able to clearly articulate what I needed to since this was the closest job I had to actual advertising. I didn't want to stretch the truth about what I did for Calli, but I also didn't want to make Maverick look like an idiot for recommending someone who didn't have any real experience.

"Yes, um. Cravings is a restaurant that my best friend opened in Whiskey Mountain after moving to town to take care of her mother. I moved with her, not sure of what my role would be until after we got here." I cleared my throat and pinched the skin between my fingers to try to force myself to concentrate.

Mr. Mason's features changed suddenly, but I tried not to focus on that. If he were already unimpressed, then it would be pointless to continue with the interview. But I only had one chance to impress him, and I was determined not to waste it. I sat taller, pulled my shoulders back, and tried again.

"It was a big change moving from Miami to such a small town, but I quickly learned to navigate it. As I'm sure you saw on my resume, I worked as an executive assistant at a large advertising company in Miami. I already had some experience, just not directly in advertising."

They both nodded with Mr. Mason keeping his focus on me while Bea lowered her head and wrote something down on the notepad in front of her.

"When we got to Whiskey Mountain, I knew deep in my heart that I wanted to make my best friend's dream a reality. It was hard being new in town, but even harder trying to get a restaurant started from the ground up. Not only that, but the concept of her restaurant wasn't anything like what the locals were used to. It was a huge change, and she needed help getting started. I decided to take over the advertising for her, and before we knew it, her business skyrocketed."

I noticed a ghost of a smile on Mr. Mason's face as I continued talking.

"People were lining up before we opened, ready to be the first ones to see what would be on the menu that day. Calli, my best friend, changed it daily according to what her mother was craving that day. It was a fun twist that kept everyone interested and gave me an opportunity where to direct my marketing. Instead of just telling people that there was a new food place in town, I focused on why it was different and drove business through fear of missing out. No one knew when Calli would have something on the menu again, so there was this need to get it before it was gone. I created social media accounts for Cravings and constantly made teasers about what would be on the menu that day before we were open to drive interest. When people came into Cravings, I would have signs up asking them to follow us on social media for sneak peeks at what would be coming and to get exclusive deals. I made sure that there was a benefit for them coming into the restaurant, as well as having an online presence."

"That's quite creative," Mr. Mason said, nodding his head. "How is business going for Cravings now that it's been open for a while?"

"It's going very well. There's a line out the door constantly, and unfortunately for me, word of mouth has taken over as the new marketing tactic, so there's not as much of a need for marketing right now. I maintain the social media accounts and keep those active, which helps keep a steady line of traffic out the door. But honestly, I think Cravings would do just fine now that it's established, even without the social media presence. It's great to find new patrons, but that's kind of hard to focus on being in a small town when you don't get a lot of new people. The town regulars already know what to expect and are devoted customers by now."

"Have you guys thought about expanding due to the demand?"

I shook my head, feeling more relieved that I was getting in my element.

"No, I don't think that will ever be an option. Calli enjoys running her own business, but she's very dedicated to caring for her mother and doesn't wish to take on more than she can handle right now. Expanding the business would be both expensive and time-consuming, which would have a negative effect on her current business. If we were to expand and start a second one, there wouldn't be as high of demand since there would be more access to it, which would also make it harder to recoup the costs of adding a second location."

"Very well said," Mr. Mason commented. "I agree. I think her current business model is quite successful."

"Where do you see yourself now with the company, since you've stated that your role with marketing has more or less come to an end?" Bea asked, looking up from her notepad.

"Honestly, I'm not sure. I still help out there, but more so up front, working the register and taking over wherever Calli needs me. While I wish there were more of a need for marketing, I'm thankful that her business is doing so well not to need it."

They both nodded and exchanged a look that I had a hard time reading. I tried to ignore the negative thoughts running through my head about how I wasn't cut out for this.

Mr. Mason leaned forward and steepled his hands in front of him on his desk, looking down before lifting his eyes to meet mine.

"We have an opening for a marketing consultant that I think you would be a great candidate for," he said, sending a wave of shivers over my skin. "One of the hardest aspects of marketing is thinking outside of the box, but you've proved you're very capable of doing just that. You took a business from the ground up and got it to the point it can stand on its own without needing any additional marketing. That's a feat in itself and speaks volumes to your abilities."

I breathed in deeply, letting the air out slowly through my mouth as I tried to calm myself.

"If you're interested in moving forward, I would like to schedule an interview with our New York office as soon as possible. We're looking to fill that position as quickly as possible and have it narrowed down to a handful of candidates. Most of the interviews are taking place tomorrow; however, I can add you to the schedule for Wednesday if that works better for your schedule," Bea offered.

"New York?" I blurted out, trying to keep the shock off of my face.

"Yes. This position would be for our New York location. Would that be a problem?"

I pressed my lips together to keep from blurting out a response that I wouldn't be able to take back.

"Um, no. Not at all," I lied, wringing my hands together in my lap.

"Wonderful." Bea smiled and wrote something else down before turning to her computer and staring at the screen. Her hand moved over the mouse as she clicked it rapidly, then stopped and looked at me. "We can do tomorrow at three thirty or Wednesday at ten AM. Do either of those work for you?"

"Wednesday would be great," I replied, feeling a sheen of sweat cover my skin as I thought about how to navigate all of this.

"Perfect. I've got you down for Wednesday at ten. I'll send over the details in an email, however, please reach out if you need anything in the meantime."

"Thank you."

"It was a pleasure meeting with you, Paisley." Mr. Mason smiled and then his camera turned off, ending the call.

I pushed away from the table, staring at the blank screen as I wondered what I had just gotten myself into.

Thirty- Five

Maverick

Paisley was acting differently after she finished her interview, which made me hesitant to ask her how it went. I was excited for her and knew that Jackson would likely give her a chance because of our friendship, but I didn't expect him to just give her a job. At the same time, I also didn't want to accept that he was possibly a dick to her because then I would have to kick his ass. Nobody messed with my girl or hurt her feelings—not on my watch.

I started on dinner, giving her time to herself until she was ready to talk. I had learned enough about Paisley to know when she needed space and when to push her. Now wasn't the time for pushing. If anything, now was the time to pamper and take care of her however she needed.

The food was just about done by the time she came into the kitchen, wearing her favorite loose pajamas.

"Dinner is almost ready," I said, leaning in to kiss her cheek.

She smiled, but it didn't last longer than a few seconds. It was killing me to know that she was upset about something but not what it was.

I worked on taking the lasagna out of the oven and finished the garlic bread while Paisley sat down at the table and fidgeted with the glass of water I had poured for her. I tried to keep my mood light and not focus on the dread that was threatening to take over me as I worried about what was going on.

I served each of us and then set the plates on the table, taking a seat across from her.

"It smells delicious. Thank you for cooking," she said softly, cutting into the lasagna with her fork.

"My pleasure."

I wanted to add that it was a celebratory dinner, but given that I didn't know how the interview went, I didn't want to stick my foot in my mouth. The tension in the air between us was thick, nearly suffocating me.

We ate in silence for a few minutes, neither of us bothering to look at each other. I didn't want her to see the worry on my face, nor did I want to stress her out further than she already was.

"I can't do this," she blurted out, letting her fork fall to the plate.

I set mine down and gripped the sides of the table, preparing myself for whatever she was about to say. My heart raced, palms sweating as I waited for her to break my heart in some way or another.

"I'm sorry," she continued, wiping the tears that started rolling down her face.

"You don't have to apologize for anything, Paisley," I said softly, reaching over and placing my hand over hers. I had no idea what she couldn't do anymore, but I knew for certain that I wasn't letting her go.

"Yes, I do. I can't do all of this, Maverick." She pulled her hand away and threw them in the air. "It's all too much. The wedding. A baby. The interviews. New York. I can't deal with all of this at once."

"What are you talking about? What's in New York?"

"The job I'm interviewing for with Mason, Inc. They asked me to continue with the interview process, but the position would be at their New York office."

I leaned back in my chair, suddenly understanding what the problem was.

"I can't do this, Maverick. There are too many decisions that I'm supposed to make without having any time to think through them. Between planning the wedding and having a baby—that's overwhelming enough. To add on a possible new job that's thousands of miles away—it's just too much. I can't do this right now."

"What are you saying, Paisley."

She looked down at the table as her tears continued rolling down her face. I knew what was coming, but that didn't help soften the blow once she started speaking.

"I want to take a break. I can't marry you right now, Maverick. I need time to think about what I want and what all of this means."

Thirty- Six

Paisley

The hurt look on Maverick's face was worse than anything I had ever seen before in my life, and it was because I knew that *I* was the reason it was there. *I* had hurt him.

"I'm sorry," I apologized, hoping he would hear the sincerity in my voice with the words I spoke. "I'm not trying to hurt you. I just need a moment to figure things out and try to catch my breath. I can't *breathe* right now, Maverick. I'm suffocating and don't know how to fix any of this."

He worked his jaw back and forth as he continued his grip on the side of the table. I could see his knuckles turning white as he struggled to control himself.

"What is that you want, Paisley? If you could have the perfect life, what would it look like?"

"That's not a fair question," I objected, frustrated that he couldn't understand.

"Yes, it is. You know what you want. Deep in your heart, you know what you want. I'm asking you to tell me what that is. In a perfect world, what would yours look like?"

I sat back in my chair, unsure of how to answer him.

"It would be me and you. Our baby." I swallowed hard, trying to work up the courage to say the rest. "But at the same time, I want a career. I want to have it all. Being a mom and happily married to the love of my life while also having a career that I love. A job that is meaningful and brings me the same joy that you do. But I can't have both, Maverick. And it kills me that this is all happening at the same time because I don't want to have to pick. I know we didn't plan to have a baby, and I don't know that we would still be getting married if I wasn't pregnant. It's just like the timing is all wrong."

"I had your ring before I ever knew you were pregnant," he said softly, looking up at me as his grip on the table softened. "I knew I wanted to marry you before you told me you were pregnant. Our engagement had nothing to do with you getting knocked up, Paisley."

"I know," I said with a heavy sigh. "But still, this is all happening and I have a once-in-a-lifetime chance at my dream job, yet I can't take it."

"Why not?"

"How in the world do you think I could?" I asked, laughing in disbelief at his delusion. "We live here, Maverick. You're taking over your dad's business. Everything is set up here, I can't just up and move to New York because I have a chance to work for Mason, Inc."

He pushed away from the table and paced the space in front of the island for a few as he ran a hand through his hair.

"We'll move to New York," he said matter-of-factly.

"What?" My brows pulled together as I stood up and blocked his path so he would stop pacing. "What in the world are you talking about?"

"I'll move to New York with you. We'll get married when and how you want—if you still want to marry me. We'll raise our baby in the city."

"Maverick, it's not that easy. You can't just up and move your entire life for me."

"Yes, I can. Paisley, life isn't worth living without you. You give me something to live for, so if your happiness comes from taking a job in New York, then you can bet your ass I will make that happen."

I shook my head, feeling dizzy from how fast things were moving again.

"What about your business? What about taking over your dad's business? You already got everything settled with that. You can't just walk away."

"Sure I can. I have cousins who can take over. It'll still stay in the family."

"Maverick," I said softly, reaching for him. "You can't do this."

"I can and I will. I wasn't lying when I told you that *you* are my life, Paisley. We do this together. If this is what you want, I'm fully on board."

I pulled in a deep breath and slowly exhaled it.

"I don't even know if I'll get the job," I said shakily.

"Either way, my only goal in life is to make you happy. You tell me what you want and need, and I'll make it happen. If you want to put off getting married for a while, that's fine, too. I don't want to cause any unnecessary stress for you, Paisley."

"I appreciate that. I'm sorry I freaked out. It's just a lot all at once, and I feel like I'm drowning under the weight of all the decisions I'm supposed to make."

He grabbed me gently, pulling me into his arms where he held me. I breathed in his soft scent, allowing it to calm my senses the way it always did.

"I still want to marry you," I said softly. "I picked a dress today and everything."

"I can't wait to see it. But Paisley, trust me when I say that I will wait as long as you need me to."

"Thank you." I leaned closer to him and listened to his heartbeat.

"When do you find out about the job?" he asked softly, releasing his hold on me as he guided me back to my seat so we could eat dinner.

"I have a second interview on Wednesday with the New York office. Bea, the HR manager, sent me an email with the information for it, as well as to confirm that they would make a decision by Friday. They're trying to fill the position quickly."

"Well, it sounds like the one today went well if you're moving on to the next round."

"It did," I said, taking a bite of my bread and nodding. "They were both very nice, and I felt excited about the possibility of working with them when they talked about the company and the current projects they're working on."

"I bet you'll get it," he said, winking before taking a drink of water. "Life in New York is going to be fun."

"We don't have to rush into anything yet," I replied softly. "Let's see how the next interview goes before we start making any big plans."

Thirty-Seven

Maverick

I was waiting on pins and needles for a call from Paisley once I knew her interview would be over. It had been over an hour since it started, but I had no idea how long it should take.

"Have you heard anything?" Calli asked, coming to check on me as I sat impatiently in a booth, poking at the food I hadn't bothered to eat yet. I had spent the day running errands in town, including finally meeting up with Mr. Crawford to settle what I owed from when Paisley and I stayed there.

"Not yet." I let my head fall back, wishing I could somehow have Paisley call me with an update.

Just then, the door to Cravings opened, and she walked in.

Seeing her in another one of those tight skirts made my body temperature skyrocket as I tried not to get turned on by how sexy she looked. Now wasn't the time nor the place, but still, there was something incredibly sexy about a plain black skirt that hugged her curves just right, mixed with a somewhat sheer shirt that showed her bra.

"Hey," I said, getting up and rushing over to her. "How did it go?"

She smiled at me and then at Calli, who joined us.

"It went well," she replied with a smile as she exhaled heavily. "I got the job."

"What? That's amazing!" I grabbed her and spun her around, trying my best not to make her nauseous, but I couldn't contain my excitement. "I thought they weren't deciding until Friday?"

I stopped moving and set her back down, allowing her a moment to fix her shirt that I had accidentally pulled loose from the skinny belt wrapped around her waist.

"They were, but said that they knew I was right for the job so they offered it to me on the spot at the end of the interview."

"Congratulations! That's amazing!" Calli said cheerfully.

"Yes, congratulations, my love. I'm so proud of you."

"Thank you, but I turned it down."

Calli and I stepped back at the same time, both of our jaws dropping.

"What do you mean you turned it down?" I asked, my brows pinched together.

"I thanked them for the opportunity but told them my life is in Whiskey Mountain."

"Paisley," I said, struggling to get my words out. "I told you, I will go wherever you go."

"I know, but it's not just that. I don't want to rush off to something new and exciting without giving my all to what I already have here. My life is here, Maverick. In Whiskey Mountain. My best friend is here. My *mom* is here. I can't just walk away from that, especially when I think about what all you would be walking away from for me. It just didn't feel right, so I turned it down."

I sat down at the table, unsure how to process all of this.

"Are you sure that's what you want?" Calli asked softly as they both sat down and joined me.

"It is. I gave it a lot of thought and considered all options. While it would be nice to have a job doing something I love, I would rather do something that makes me happy. And that's being here with you guys. I want to be a mom and have our babies grow up together. I don't want to be miles away, only talking to each other on FaceTime when we get the chance."

"We can make things work," I offered softly, not wanting her to give up so easily.

"Things already work," she countered, covering my hand with hers. "Don't you see that? We have everything we need right here. While the job sounded amazing, I would miss out on what truly makes me happy by going after it."

"But, Paisley…"

"No, Maverick. You have always told me that life is about finding something to live for, and I found that. I found you. You're willing to go the extra mile to make my dreams come true, but they already have."

"I'm going to get back up there since we're getting a line, but we'll talk later," Calli said, excusing herself from the table.

"Are you sure about this?" I asked, squeezing her hand gently. "I don't want you to give up on something you wanted so badly."

"I'm more than sure about it. I think I knew all along what I wanted, I was just overwhelmed with too many decisions and got freaked out. It was like I had a sudden sense of clarity when they offered me the job and I've never felt more certain about anything in my life. I know what I want, and it's you and this baby. Our life together. Here. Forever."

"Okay," I said softly, nodding my head in agreement. "Well, I guess I'll have some calls to make then."

"Why's that?"

"Well, I was being proactive with us moving to New York, so I already started talking to my dad about selling the business to my cousin. I also talked to a realtor who is getting ready to list the house."

Her eyebrows shot up to her forehead.

"Maverick!"

"I was fully on board with moving, Paisley. I wanted you to know that by being a team player and getting stuff done. I worried that if I dragged my feet even a little, you would worry that I wasn't serious about it."

"I can't believe you did that!"

"It's okay. I can talk to my dad and tell him not to do anything. I'll make a call real quick before the agent makes the listing. It's all easy to take care of."

She smiled and shook her head at me.

"What are you doing with the rest of your day?" I asked, pushing my plate to her so she could eat.

She picked up a chip and popped it into her mouth.

"I'm going to run some errands."

"Yeah? What kind?"

"The wedding planning kind."

She smiled widely, making my heart flutter.

Thirty-Eight

Paisley

"Are you ready?" Calli asked, fixing my veil as I looked at myself in the full-length mirror.

"I am."

"You look beautiful," Mom said, pulling me into a tight hug. I was happy that she was having a good day, even if she might not remember any of it later. She and Calli were the closest thing I had to family, so it meant a lot to me that they were there with me on my special day. But still, there was a sadness pulling inside my chest that my real mother never got to see this moment since she passed when I was little.

"Thank you." I leaned in and gently kissed her cheek.

"Alright, ladies, it's show time," Dylan said, popping into the doorway and smiling at us. "I'll walk Mom to her seat, then come back for Calli."

I nodded, feeling butterflies swarm in my stomach as I took one last look in the mirror. Calli stood next to me, lifting her cell phone to get a selfie of us on my wedding day.

"No crying," I warned, noticing the tears in her eyes.

"You either."

"Deal," I sniffled, gently wiping at mine to keep from smearing my makeup.

I walked over to get a tissue, thankful I had a few minutes to get myself together. Dylan came for Calli a few minutes later, leaving me to myself.

I didn't have anyone to walk me down the aisle, but it didn't bother me. It was a small wedding, and I was more than comfortable walking by myself. It wasn't about having someone to give me away as much as it was about having someone who was waiting to spend their life with me.

The music started playing, my cue to head out. I admired the effort and attention to detail that Maverick's family had made in decorating the barn for the wedding. I had given them some color swatches that I liked that matched the bouquets and Calli's dress, and they handled the rest. From the flowers lining the blush-colored runner to the soft lights strung across the wooden beams, it was perfect and romantic.

My head was down as I focused on not tripping over my own two feet, but when I looked up, I found the most incredibly gorgeous man smiling at me. I felt my cheeks split as I smiled back, walking faster to get to him.

"You look incredible," he said softly as I finally reached him, neither of us able to keep our hands off each other.

"Thank you. So do you."

He smiled and leaned in to kiss me before the officiant cleared his throat to remind us of his presence.

I giggled and looked away from Maverick before I got myself in trouble.

"Ladies and gentlemen, we are gathered here today to join Paisley Brooks and Maverick Thompson in holy matrimony. Every one of us has a deep longing to love and be loved; however, your marriage today is a public affirmation of the bonding that has already begun. Today is a day of celebration. We celebrate the love the two of you hold in your hearts as you embark upon the journey to share the rest of your lives together. If anyone has any objections, speak now, or forever hold your peace."

The room was silent as Maverick and I looked at each other, knowing no one would have any reason to object.

"Paisley and Maverick have written their own vows, which they will now read to each other."

I smiled as Maverick nodded for me to go first. I had mine memorized, but when I looked at him, I couldn't remember a single thing I had written down.

"I love you," I said with more certainty than anything before. "I'm head over heels, absolutely in love with you, Maverick. I can't promise to be the perfect wife, but I do promise to always try my best. I will love you unconditionally and will always do everything in my power to make you happy. We might fight and disagree, but I will always be on your side. Your demons will be my demons, and we'll conquer them together. I want nothing more than to be your wife and bring you the same joy that you bring to my life. I love you more than words will ever be able to express."

"I love you too, Paisley," he said softly with a grin.

"Oh—and I won't cheat on you, nor will I hold you responsible for the stuff you do in my dreams," I added, feeling self-conscious when I heard people chuckling. "For the most part. You have done some messed up stuff in my dreams."

"I promise to do my best to stop messing up in your dreams," he replied with a sneaky grin, saying it loud enough for me to hear but not everyone else.

"Paisley, I love you more than I love anything. You are my world, and I will live the rest of my life making sure you have everything you want and need. I will never take you for granted or forsake you. I will always respect and honor you, making sure that you feel safe, loved, and secure in our marriage. I will be the best husband and father I can be and will do my best to learn along the way. My life is devoted to loving you and making sure you know how much you mean to me. I promise to take care of you and to do everything in my power to make you happy."

"You're going to be a wonderful dad," I agreed, squeezing his hands.

The officiant looked between us, making sure we were done before he continued.

"Do you, Paisley, take Maverick to be your lawfully wedded husband? To live together in matrimony, to love, comfort, honor, and keep him in sickness and health, from this day forward, as long as you both shall live?"

"I do."

"Do you, Maverick, take Paisley to be your lawfully wedded wife? To live together in matrimony, to love, comfort, honor, and keep her in sickness and health, from this day forward, as long as you both shall live?"

"I do."

"I now pronounce you man and wife. You may kiss your bride."

Everyone clapped and cheered as Maverick wrapped his arm around my waist and lowered his mouth to mine, placing the most tender kiss against my lips.

I wanted nothing more than to take my husband back to our room and celebrate our wedding, but we still had to get through the reception. I giggled as he deepened the kiss, pushing him away gently before things could get too out of hand.

"You're officially Mrs. Thompson," he said, his voice low in my ear.

"And I couldn't be happier."

I stepped away as we turned and faced our audience, happy faces greeting us as they stood with tears in their eyes and continued to cheer for us.

"Let's get this party started," Maverick said, leading me down the aisle as rice was tossed in the air, falling lightly around us.

Thirty-Nine

Maverick

I held my wife tightly as we danced our first dance, followed by the next ten. I wasn't ready or willing to give her up, even when my father asked to cut in and have a dance with the bride.

The reception was going smoothly, with Calli knocking it out of the park with the food and Paisley constantly having a smile on her face. My mom had done a great job with capturing plenty of pictures until I had to tell her to stop so she could enjoy herself. Everyone had gone out of their way to ensure everything was perfect, even with the last-minute planning.

I was standing in line at the bar for a glass of water when I felt someone's hand on my shoulder. I turned slightly, expecting it to be my dad or Dylan, but was surprised to see Jackson standing there.

"What? No fucking way," I said, turning around and clapping my arm around him in a hug. "What are you doing here?"

"We would have been here sooner, but the weather got bad on the way up. Sorry to miss the ceremony, but hopefully we aren't too late for the reception."

"Not at all. I'm glad you made it."

"I wouldn't miss it for the world."

I chuckled and shook my head, wondering what could have changed the hard exterior I used to know. The old Jackson that I went to school with would never have stepped away from work long enough to maintain a friendship, let alone drive hours to come to a friend's wedding he hadn't seen in years. But then a beautiful woman stepped out from beside him, and everything made sense.

"Thank you for coming. It's really great to see you."

"Thank you for the invite. We can't wait to meet your beautiful bride," the woman said as Jackson reached back and wrapped his arm around her waist, pulling her into his side.

"This is Emily. Emily, this is Maverick."

"Nice to meet you," I said, extending my hand to shake hers. "Paisley is right over—"

I turned to look for her when I felt her hand wrap around me as she snuck up behind me.

"Right here," she said happily, tucking herself into my side.

"It's nice to officially meet you," Jackson said, shaking her hand. "Congratulations."

"Thank you."

I took a moment to allow the happiness to overflow as Emily and Paisley introduced themselves to each other.

"We won't keep you guys. We just wanted to say hi," Emily said, starting to pull Jackson away.

"Before we go, I did want to give you a wedding gift," Jackson said, stopping her as he handed me a card.

"Thank you. We appreciate it." I lowered my head in thanks.

"It's our pleasure. But if I'm being honest, I do have a selfish reason for being here."

"Oh yeah? What's that?" I cocked my head to the side and studied him.

"I came to offer Paisley a job."

She gasped softly beside me as she leaned in to hear him.

"I understand how hard it would be to move to New York when your life is clearly in Whiskey Mountain. I don't blame you for not wanting to start over when everything is already established here. So, I did some thinking and figured out a way to make things work for everyone."

"Okay," Paisley said, her voice uncertain.

"I have been very intrigued by how you managed to get a business off the ground so quickly and realized that we have an opportunity to continue that success, but on a small-town level. After doing some research, I found that there aren't any advertising companies here in Whiskey Mountain, which is where I come in."

We all took a deep breath and waited for him to continue before letting it out.

"I would like to set up business in Whiskey Mountain, and in doing so, I would like you to lead our branch here. Since this is a new initiative, I don't have an office for you to report to, but I thought we could start with a remote position. You could work from home or wherever you're most comfortable working. I'll pay for any operating expenses you need to get started and send down one of our IT techs to get you set up in our systems. You'll handle the local business here and report to Sugarplum Falls once a quarter for administrative meetings when needed. The salary can be negotiated, but if you're interested, I would like to officially offer you the position."

I stepped back, gently pushing Paisley forward so she could talk to Jackson.

"I don't know what to say," she whispered, shaking her head. "This feels like a dream."

"I can assure you it's not," I said with a laugh, resting my hand on her shoulder.

"I believe we could work well together and that starting a branch in Whiskey Mountain could be very profitable," Jackson assured her. "It would be my honor to bring you on board and have you take charge of this."

"Well, in that case, I accept."

Jackson smiled and accepted the hug she offered before leading Emily away to give Paisley and me a moment.

"Congratulations," I said, pulling her into a tight hug. "I'm so proud of you."

"I can't believe it. It's so surreal."

"Good things happen to those who deserve it. And you, my love, deserve all the best."

"So do you, my *husband*."

"Say it again," I urged, lowering my mouth to her neck and nibbling the area below her ear that drove her crazy.

"Husband."

"God, I can't wait to fuck you and have you scream that for the whole world to hear."

"What are you waiting for? Let's get this wedding night started."

She giggled as I picked her up, tossed her over my shoulder, and carried her through the barn and out the doors. Tonight was the first night of the rest of our lives, and I was determined to make sure my *wife* had everything she could ever ask for.

735

Something To Love
Whiskey Mountain Bonus Short Story

Samantha Baca

Copyright © 2024 by Samantha Baca

Cover Design: Oh So Novel

740

One

Maggie

Ask Mags,

It's been over thirty minutes since I've seen my wife, and I'm going out of my mind. She insists she's busy baking for Thanksgiving, but I can't help thinking about how she must be avoiding me. And as if that isn't bad enough, there's this voice in my head shouting negative things and infiltrating my thoughts. Please assure me that it's not as bad as I think.

Sincerely,

Horny and afraid

I closed my laptop and chuckled as I got up and grabbed a muffin from the cooling rack. We had only been in the new house for a few months, but I loved the enormous kitchen area and that I had so much room to spread out and bake. There was a large room toward the back of the house that Owen was using as his office now that he was working from home, and Leroy and Pablo were thriving in their designated living area. It was like we were one big, happy family.

"You're being a bit dramatic this morning," I said, handing Owen a banana nut muffin as I sat one butt cheek on the edge of his desk.

"Banana nut?" he questioned, one eyebrow raised as he peeled the liner back and took a bite.

I nodded, chewing my lower lip as I watched his tongue sweep out to grab a crumb before it fell. We'd been together for a while now, but something as simple as that still got my heart racing and blood rushing through my body.

"I think we both know my stamina is perfectly fine," he says softly. "But thank you, this is delicious."

"You're a nut. Crazy nut," Pablo squeaked from his cage in the corner.

"Has he been harassing you all morning?"

"Yeah. I tried making a phone call to check on the status of a deal I'm working on, and he wouldn't stop cussing. I had to pretend my connection was bad because of the weather and hang up."

"Cocksucker. You're a cocksucker. Lick my balls."

"Maybe it's just a sign that you shouldn't be trying to work on *Thanksgiving*."

"Anyway," Owen said, clearing his throat and ignoring Pablo's outburst. "How did the baking go?"

He was always working, even if he refused to admit it.

"It went well. I *love* that kitchen. I was able to get all of the pies baked to take to Calli's tonight, as well as some for Spill The Beans. It was quite the productive morning."

"Then I guess that means you finally have time for me," he teased, pulling me down onto his lap as he nipped at my neck.

"We're supposed to be at Calli's in an hour," I said softly, allowing him to kiss me in the spot that drove me crazy right below my ear.

"Lucky for you, I drive fast, which means we have an extra fifteen minutes to spare. And I just so happen to know a good way to spend it."

Before I could say anything, he stood up and carried me in his arms as he walked down the hall to our bedroom.

"You know that I actually love quickies. Fuck me hard and fast," I replied as he tossed me on the bed.

We were already stripping off our clothes, knowing that neither of us was willing to waste a single second if it meant we got to have our fill of the other before spending the day with our friends.

"Tonight I'll eat you like a full Thanksgiving feast, but for now, you're just gonna have to take this hard cock in your tight little pussy."

I tossed the last of my clothes to the floor and rolled over, popping up on my hands and knees as I heard him groan from behind. This was my favorite position because I loved how deep he could get while I fingered myself to get off. While he loved it because he got to play with my ass while he pounded into me from behind.

"Look at you, already wet and ready for me," he growled as he climbed up behind me and lined himself up at my entrance.

"Always." I looked at him over my shoulder and smiled. "Now fuck me."

It felt weird not waiting for him to grab a condom and slide it on, but we'd both talked and apparently caught baby fever because we were officially trying. This also meant we were having sex *every* chance we got, including after closing at Spill The Beans. Those were some fun times and I would never look at the table I always worked at the same again.

I felt his finger slide inside me first, spreading my wetness before he slowly pushed his cock inside. Despite us having constant sex, he was still well-endowed and my body needed a few seconds to adjust to his size every single time.

"Ahhh," I cried out, gripping the pillow beneath me as he filled me. "Fuck, you feel so good. I love your huge cock and can't wait to suck it when we get home."

"While I would love that, baby, I don't want you swallowing our future kids again," he teased as he gripped my hips and started thrusting.

I pushed my ass up higher, allowing him to penetrate me deeper. My clit was already tingling and ready, but I didn't want to come until he was close.

I bounced against him, loving the way he felt.

"Later, I'm going to fuck this ass," he said, gently rubbing his finger around my asshole.

"If I can't swallow our kids, you can't release them in my ass."

"Fair enough. I guess we'll just have to play for a while tonight and get you impregnated before the fun stuff happens."

He pulled out and slammed into me harder, making me cry out from how good it felt.

"How long do you think we have to stay there?" I asked, already wanting to skip it so we could stay home and do this instead.

"At least until after lunch. Probably through pie. Then we can come home, and I'll fuck you the way you need to be fucked." His hand reached down and began rubbing my clit. "I'll fuck you so hard you won't be able to stand for days, Maggie. My cum will be dripping down your thighs, just like it was when I fucked you before Spill The Beans opened. Remember that? You had to stand there, taking orders while my cum ran down your thighs. Or how about the time I sent you a picture of my cock while I was at work, and you fingered yourself beneath the table so no one would see you."

His words were doing exactly what they were supposed to, sending me right over the edge as my pussy convulsed and spasmed around his cock. A few seconds later, he gripped my hips as he released his load deep inside of me.

Two

Calli

"Alright, the turkey is roasting in the oven; the bread is resting. What else do I need to do?" I asked, more to myself than to Dylan, who was leaning against the counter and looking ready to devour me.

"Nothing. You've done everything you need to—except me."

"Stop it," I whispered with a giggle while swatting his arm with the towel. "We don't have time for that today. We're hosting Thanksgiving, and everyone will be here in an hour."

"Relax, baby. Everything is going to go just fine. Remember, we agreed to do this as a potluck, so you didn't have to worry about as much today. Maggie is bringing the pies. Ramona is bringing mashed potatoes and green bean casserole. Paisley and Maverick are bringing sweet potato casserole and stuffing. Everything is handled."

"Why do I feel so nervous about this?" I asked, standing in front of him as he ran his hands up and down my arms to comfort me.

"Because it's your first time hosting as a mom?" he offered, nodding to the monitor that was sitting on the island, the sound turned all the way up so I didn't miss it if the baby woke up.

"Maybe. I don't know. Something just feels different. I can't put my finger on it, but it's like I can feel this big change in the air."

"Don't forget that the doctor said it's normal to feel a little off still. Your body went through a lot bringing a tiny human into this world. Give it some time to rest and heal while also allowing your mind to do the same."

I looked around the kitchen, doing mental inventory again.

"Are you sure there's nothing else I need to do?"

"Well, I've got *one* thing if you're up for it."

The corners of my lips turned up into a smile as I hugged him tighter.

"Where's Mom?"

"Across the street with Rita and the girls. She's helping make stuff for dinner tonight."

"So, is she not doing lunch here with us?"

"She is. She said she'll eat light at lunch so she can save room for dinner with the girls."

I grinned wider, loving that my mom had such a beautiful group of friends to brighten her days.

"And Amelia is asleep, which means…"

"Which means I get to start being thankful for my smoking hot wife, who I'm about to devour."

He lifted me by the waist and set me down on the island, which I had, thankfully, just finished wiping down. His eyes locked onto mine as he slowly pushed the fabric of my dress up, kneeling in between my legs.

"Dylan," I panted, closing my eyes and leaning back on my hands as his tongue swiped down my slit.

He didn't say anything as he gripped my thighs and held me in place while his mouth worked its magic.

Having a baby had changed a lot between us, especially how often we got to have sex. We loved being parents, and I enjoyed spending time with Amelia, but I also missed the special time Dylan and I used to share. Even though we didn't get to fuck as often as we used to, he took every opportunity to please me that he could, always making sure I knew how much he loved and worshipped my body—especially post-baby.

I gripped the back of his head and held it in place as he sucked my clit, teasing it mercilessly before bringing me to climax. I cried out, thankful no one could hear me, as waves of pleasure washed over me.

He stood up and wiped his mouth with his fingers while giving me a devilish grin.

"That was amazing, Dylan." I sighed heavily, already feeling more relaxed. "Now it's my turn to return the favor."

He leaned in and kissed my forehead before helping me off the island.

"While I would love that, we don't have much time before people start arriving. If you want to go clean up, I'll watch the turkey."

I felt my face fall with disappointment, but knew he was right. Plus, we chose to do Thanksgiving lunch instead of dinner so everyone could call it a night early. Again, another thing that changed with having a baby.

Three

Ramona

"Have you seen my Cool Ranch Doritos?" I yelled, hoping Preston could hear me as I rummaged through the cabinet, frowning when I couldn't find them.

"No, I haven't seen *our* Cool Ranch Doritos."

I turned around and glared at him, one hand on my hip.

"You know I don't play around when it comes to my chips, Preston."

"I understand, *Ramona*. But I didn't eat them. Are you sure you didn't leave them by the bed again?"

"No," I said with a heavy sigh. "I already looked there."

"Well, is there something else you want to snack on instead?"

"No." I lowered my head in defeat, feeling his arms wrap around me as he pulled me into his chest.

"You need to eat before you get hangry. We have about an hour before we have to leave. I can make you something real quick if you want."

"Does it include Cool Ranch Doritos?" I asked, looking up at him with sad puppy eyes.

"No. But you can either eat what I make you, or we can go to the bedroom, and I can try to fix this attitude of yours in there."

"What if we make me a sandwich *and* go to the bedroom? We can multitask," I offered, grinning up at him.

"You're such a princess," he said, sighing as he shook his head.

Then, without any warning, he lifted me, tossed me over his shoulder, and stormed out of the kitchen.

"Wait! You forgot my sandwich!" I yelled, laughing as his hand reached up and slapped my ass. "Preston, I'm hungry!"

"Me too. But lucky for you, there's still a sandwich from last night in the mini-fridge, so you can eat that while I eat you."

I laughed, loving how much of a genius he was for putting a mini fridge in our new bedroom. He knew how easily I got hangry and made sure I always had options since I was a constant snacker.

He set me down on the bed, then reached into the fridge to pull out the sandwich wrapped in foil. I grabbed it out of his hands like a little raccoon and opened it, ready to eat.

"I was thinking," I said around a mouthful of bread, lunch meat, and cheese. "Maybe I can eat this while I ride you? We don't have a ton of time before we go, and I still have to finish the mashed potatoes and green bean casserole. We can both get off and still have time before we have to leave."

"I love it when you talk dirty to me," he teased, pulling his shirt over his head and tossing it to the side.

I took a big bite of my sandwich and chewed while stripping off my clothes, leaving the thin, black lace thong that he loved so much on.

He climbed onto the bed, resting his back against the padded headboard while I got myself situated. Instead of facing him, I decided to do reverse cowgirl, knowing how much he would love to watch himself slide in and out of me without having to watch me eat.

I lined him up at my entrance, then looked over my shoulder to wink at him as I slowly slid down his already rock-hard cock. I closed my eyes and tossed my head back as I adjusted to the sensation of being spread tightly around him. His fingers firmly gripped my hips, holding me in place as he adjusted as well.

"Fuck, baby," he growled, reaching forward and pulling the string of my thong before snapping it against my skin. "This is so fucking sexy."

I leaned forward slightly as I began riding him, lifting myself up and then slamming down on his cock. I could feel him getting harder as my juices coated him, helping him to glide easily inside my pussy.

I took another bite of the sandwich, then set it on the bed as I started bouncing, loving the way he held onto me as if he was about to lose control.

His hands reached around to my breasts, holding the weight of them as his fingers brushed lightly against my nipples.

"You ride my cock so good, baby," he murmured, pulling me against his chest as one hand slid down to rub my clit while the other continued its torture on my breasts.

"I love your cock. It's so long and thick. Makes me want to come just thinking about it."

"Maybe I'll fuck you on the way home tonight. Pull over on the side of the road and let the whole world know how thankful I am for this pussy."

I closed my eyes as I pictured it—which was easy, given how many times we'd done exactly that. Preston knew how turned I got having sex in public places and made it his mission to make sure we always had somewhere new to try.

"I'll press these tits against the window as I fuck you from behind. That way, everyone who drives by will know how good you're getting fucked. Someone might even stop and jerk off, Ramona. They might get so fucking turned on watching you get fucked that they watch us while touching themselves."

That right there was the key to detonating the bomb inside of me.

"Fuck!" I cried out, my hips bucking against him as he rubbed my clit harder, sending waves of pleasure rocking over me as I climaxed.

"That's my dirty girl," he teased, playfully nipping my ear before shifting me on his cock and thrusting up from beneath me. Within seconds, I felt the warm ropes of cum as they shot inside of me.

Four

Paisley

"Maverick, if you don't stop," I warned, gripping the sheets beneath me.

"What? You'll squirt?" he offered with a knowing smirk. "Trust me, I'm fully aware of what I'm doing, Paisley."

"We don't have time to clean up the mess. I still have to go make the stuffing and finish the sweet potato casserole. If we're late, Calli will kill us."

"We're not going to be late. The twins are still napping. I can help with the food. Now, will you stop talking and let me make you come?"

His finger slid in deeper, turning slightly so he could do that come hither thing that always made me squirt. I closed my eyes and gripped the sheets, knowing I was close.

"I fucking love your tits, Paisley," he said as he leaned in to pull a puckered nipple into his mouth while continuing to finger me. "I might just keep you pregnant so I can have them like this all the time."

"You also love fucking my tits," I added, smiling as I thought about last night when he did exactly that.

"Fuck yeah, I do. They're perfect. So heavy and full. My dick wants to slide between them again."

"We have time," I offered, my body stiffening as I felt the tingle start up my spine. "Fuck," I hissed, knowing I would be coming any second.

Maverick continued to apply pressure to my g-spot as he sucked my nipple harder, sending me over the edge.

"Oh my God!" I cried out, trying to keep my voice down to keep from waking the babies. I panted heavily as I felt waves of pleasure, my body immediately relaxing. He pulled his mouth away, chewing his lower lip as he glanced down at the mess I made.

"Perfection," he replied. "Such perfection."

A satisfied breath passed softly through my lips as I stared up at the most incredibly gorgeous man.

"Now for the good part," I said, pressing my breasts together as I sat on the edge of the bed and waited for him to stand in front of me.

He grinned down at me, brushing a finger tenderly across my cheek. Then he lined his cock up between my breasts and fucked them the way I knew would get him off in seconds. He wasn't the only one who loved the recent changes to them.

Once we were done and cleaned up, I headed into the kitchen to finish getting the food ready before we went to Calli's. I knew it was a big step for her to allow everyone to help out by doing Thanksgiving as a potluck, but I wanted to make sure she could trust us to make it as perfect as she would have if she cooked everything herself.

I prepped most of the food this morning so I wouldn't have to do as much at Calli's house, just in case her oven was full. The goal was for everyone to take their dishes hot and ready to eat, which meant I needed to time everything perfectly.

Just as I was getting ready to heat up the stuffing, I heard one of the twins start to cry. I sighed and tried to calm myself before I got stressed with the overwhelming pressure to get food made while taking care of the babies. It had been a rough adjustment, but Maverick had been there every step of the way for me. Between the new job, getting married, buying a new house, and now having twins, it was a lot. But he never complained, and I found that he always seemed to know what I needed before I had to ask for help.

He came into the kitchen, holding Wyatt against his chest as I covered the baking dish with foil and popped it into the oven.

"Hey, my sweet boy," I said softly, tilting my head to look at my son as he laid his head on his dad's chest. "Are you hungry?"

"I think that's why he got up," Maverick said. "He was pretty fussy this morning and didn't take much of his bottle before he fell asleep."

"Poor baby. I can sit and nurse him for a few," I offered, looking back at the food I needed to finish.

"I can give him a bottle if you want to finish what you're doing."

"Okay," I said, nodding. "I pumped a little while ago, so there's fresh milk in the fridge."

He smiled and got what he needed while I refocused on what I needed to get done. We worked well together as a team, which was nice given how quickly our little family was growing.

Five

Calli

"They're here," I called to Dylan as I balanced Amelia on my hip and stirred the pot of gravy on the stove.

"I'm on it," he called, rushing to the door while I felt another wave of nerves come over me.

I turned the stove off and moved the gravy to a trivet as I shifted Amelia to the other hip. The turkey was already carved and in a warmer, while the dinner rolls were already in bowls on the table that my mom had helped me set when she got home a little while ago.

Everything was coming together as it should, but I still felt worried something terrible would happen. My doctor said that it was normal to feel this way for a little while, but I was starting to grow concerned with how long it was lasting and how I felt like I couldn't stop worrying all the time.

I headed into the living room, smiling when I saw Paisley and Maverick had arrived and were unloading their twins from their car seats. It had been a shock when Paisley and I found out we were pregnant at the same time, but it was also the best thing that could have happened to us. Our friendship had always been close, but this experience bonded us even further. Not only that, but my mom absolutely loved being a grandma to three new babies.

"Hey, happy Thanksgiving," Paisley said, adjusting the swaddle blanket she was wrapping around a sleeping baby.

"Happy Thanksgiving to you, too," I replied, checking to see who she had. "Happy Thanksgiving, Wyatt."

"He's finally out," she said with a heavy sigh. "He's been a little fussy today. How are you doing, Miss Amelia?" She reached over and gently pinched her cheeks, making Amelia smile.

"She's good so far. Took a long nap, so I hope that keeps her from getting cranky while everyone is here."

"Babies aren't cranky, my love," Dylan reminded me as he slid an arm around my waist and kissed my neck. "They're just unable to tell us what they need."

He took Amelia from me and bounced her on his hip as Maverick came over.

"Happy Thanksgiving. How's Julia doing today? Ready for her first Thanksgiving?"

"As ready as she'll ever be," he said with a laugh. "Thanks for hosting today, Calli. The turkey smells amazing."

"Thank you guys for helping out with the food. I know I struggle to ask for help, but I do appreciate it."

"No problem." He turned to Paisley and offered her the baby, something that seemed so easy and seamless for them now that they'd had a few months to practice. "If you've got the babies, I'll go grab the food."

She nodded and kissed both of their heads, bouncing gently to keep Wyatt asleep.

"Here, let me take Julia," I offered, reaching for her.

Paisley handed her over just as Dylan came over, ready to hand me Amelia.

"Ummm, hold on," I said, trying to figure out how I was going to hold both.

"I've got her," my mom said, wiggling her fingers at Dylan as she waited for her grandbaby.

I smiled at my mom, feeling relieved. She was having an amazing day, which made my heart soar.

A few minutes later, Maggie, Owen, Ramona, and Preston showed up, and the house was filled with the beautiful sound of friendship and laughter.

<u>Six</u>

Paisley

I tried not to gag as the green bean casserole passed in front of me. Maverick was quick to move it away from me, but not before Calli noticed and eyed me suspiciously.

I had Julia snuggled against me in a baby carrier as she slept on my chest while Maverick had Wyatt strapped to his. They were both too little to sit in a highchair and seemed more tired today than usual. Calli was holding Amelia, even though Dylan had offered to take her several times so she could enjoy her food without having to fight the baby who kept trying to grab her fork. They were all still too young for real food, but that didn't stop Amelia from trying. She was going to be a foodie, just like her mama.

"Everything is delicious. Thank you again for hosting, Calli," Maggie said, smiling from the other end of the table.

"It's my pleasure. Thank you all for your contributions. Everything is delicious. Even the green bean casserole."

I felt her eyes on me as she said it, though no one else seemed to notice.

My palms began sweating as I sat under her watchful eye, wondering if now was the time to tell them. I glanced up at Maverick, who had been watching the whole thing. He nodded and gave my thigh a gentle squeeze under the table.

"I'm surprised you didn't get any," Calli continued, her eyes locked on me. "I thought it was your favorite."

I rubbed my lips together and set my fork down before looking up at her.

"It used to be."

"Used to be? As in, you don't like this one?"

I saw Ramona look at me from the corner of my eye, her face immediately scowling. Shit, the last person I wanted to piss off right now was Ramona. It wasn't like I thought to bring a bag of Cool Ranch Doritos with me.

"As in, I currently don't like green beans."

I pinned Calli with a look, hoping she would back off. Something was off with her, and I didn't know what. It wasn't like her to act like this or to be so aggressive. But until I could get her alone and talk to her, I had no choice but to come clean.

"That's so weird. You've *always* liked green beans. You're the one who says it's not Thanksgiving unless there's green bean casserole."

"Yeah, well, apparently, *this* baby doesn't like them."

Calli's eyes widened as silence fell around us. I turned to glance at Maverick, catching the smirk on his face as he lifted his fork and took a bite of green bean casserole.

"*This* baby?" Calli questioned, her voice changing.

"We're expecting again." I pulled my shoulders back, took a deep breath, and patted Julia's bottom to get her back to sleep.

"Wow. I umm… I didn't know you guys were trying already." Calli shook her head as if trying to make things make sense.

"We weren't. We knew that we wanted to have more kids in the future, but I guess the future is now." I shrugged, not knowing what else to say.

"Congratulations," Maggie said, followed by Owen.

I smiled politely at them, still wondering what was up with my best friend.

"Congratulations," Ramona said, smiling, though I wasn't sure how genuine it was after the whole declining her food fiasco. "I'm happy to hear that it's not just my cooking you don't like. Hopefully the mashed potatoes are to your liking."

"Stop it," Preston said, intending to keep his voice low, but we all heard it, given how silent it was around the table. "I told you we would stop for chips on the way home if I can find a store that's open. You don't need to take it out on everyone else."

"Why didn't you say anything?" Calli asked, her brows pulled together. "Why wait until I question it at dinner?"

"Because we just found out, for one. Two, I wanted some time to process the news before we started telling everyone. Three, I didn't want to jinx anything before I could get to the doctor and make sure everything was fine."

"I see." She rubbed her lips together as everyone started eating again. The tension was thick, and I knew everyone felt it.

"What is the actual problem, Calli?" I asked, my tone causing Maverick to flinch beside me.

"I don't have a problem. I guess I just thought we were close enough you would tell me something was going on, but I guess not."

"It's been TWO days since I took a test, Calli. Did you expect me to call you from the bathroom and tell you before I even told my husband?"

"I don't know what I expected!" she shouted, startling everyone. "Nothing is what I expected. Being a mother isn't what I expected. Being stuck at home on maternity leave and not being able to do the one thing I love isn't what I expected. Feeling like a prisoner in a body I don't recognize anymore is not what I expected!"

She pushed her chair back, handed Amelia to Dylan, and then stormed out of the kitchen.

I lowered my head and took a deep breath, knowing I needed to go talk to her. I unstrapped Julia from my chest and handed her to Maggie when she generously offered to hold her. I walked down the hallway and stopped outside the bathroom door in the master bedroom.

"Hey, it's me," I said, knocking. "Please open the door."

Slowly the door opened, and I found her with tears running down her face.

"Calli, talk to me. What's going on?"

I stepped inside and closed the door behind me to ensure we had privacy.

"I don't know." She tipped her head back in frustration as she let out a heavy sigh. "I just can't shake this feeling that something bad is going to happen, and I feel like I'm constantly waiting for things to go back to normal. But they never do. And then I find out in a roundabout way that you're pregnant, and it just made me feel even more alone than I already am."

She sat on the edge of the bathtub and brushed her tears away with the palms of her hands.

"Oh, honey. I'm so sorry. I wasn't trying to keep it from you. We literally just found out. I haven't even had a chance to schedule a doctor's appointment, but I swear, you were going to be the first person I told besides Maverick. I wasn't trying to leave you out on purpose."

"I know. This is all so stupid," she said, sniffling. "I'm making a fool of myself in front of everyone on Thanksgiving because I can't keep it together anymore. I've officially turned into the crazy mom who doesn't stop crying."

"No, you're not. You're the tired mom who is learning how to be a mom," I said softly, squeezing her hand as I sat next to her. "You're the mom who is trying to figure out who she is now because everything has changed. Our whole lives basically turned upside down, and now we're just waiting to see where the pieces fall."

"Yeah, but you and Maverick seem like you have it all figured out."

"Trust me—we don't. I cried last night because he ate the last cookie. There was a brand-new pack in the cabinet, but I cried because he ate the last one in that pack. It was stupid, and I don't know why I did it, but I was convinced he didn't love me anymore. Clearly, if he did, he would have saved *that* cookie."

"Okay, maybe I don't feel so bad," she replied with a soft laugh.

"You definitely should not feel bad, Calli. You're an incredible mother, and Amelia is so lucky to have you. Dylan absolutely adores you. And your customers can't wait for you to come back to Cravings. It might feel super hard now, but it will get easier. Things will start fitting into place, and a new puzzle will be complete."

"Maybe…"

"Not maybe," I corrected, shaking my head. "Things will absolutely get better, Calli. And I'm sorry I haven't been around as much as I should. Postpartum depression has gotten to me a little bit, too. It's okay to talk to your doctor if you don't feel like it's getting better and to lean on your friends and family. We're here for you and will always be your support team. I know we're both going back to work soon, but I promise I'll be around more often. Plus, our babies love each other, so it'll be fun watching them grow up together like we did."

She inhaled deeply and slowly let it out.

"Thanks for talking with me. I'm sorry I'm such a hot mess."

"Don't be. We'll be hot messes together."

I stood up and extended my hand to help her.

"I do have a question," she said as I reached for the doorknob to open it.

"What's up?"

"What kind of cookie was it?"

"One of those super soft chocolate chip ones."

She closed her eyes as if it pained her.

"Yeah, I would have cried over it, too," she admitted.

"He went out and bought three more packs and promised never to eat the last of them again," I said, laughing as I realized how silly it sounded.

<u>Seven</u>

Maggie

"This pumpkin pie is amazing," Paisley said around a mouthful, nearly moaning as she shoved another bite into her mouth.

"Thank you. I'm glad you like it."

"Like it? I think she's ready to divorce me and marry the pie instead," Maverick joked, watching her take another bite. "At least we know what this baby likes."

I felt my stomach flutter as I thought about how eventful the day had been already. It was fun being around the babies and watching their parents as they learned to navigate each new step, but I couldn't help but wonder what that would look like for me and Owen.

"Well, I'll be sure to keep extra stocked for when you need your fix," I assured her with a wink. "And plenty of apple crumble muffins for you, Calli."

"Oh my gosh, I could totally go for one of those right now," she said with a sigh. "But I'll gladly take this pie instead. I swear, Maggie, you really outdid yourself on these pies. From now on, we're going to keep the potluck thing going now that I know you all can cook like this."

"I don't mind at all. Plus, it's nice to split the work up so it's not too overwhelming for just one person. This really was such a relaxing, easy-going day. I could use a lot more of those."

"Are you saying you don't enjoy chasing Leroy around the house, trying to get your panties back?" Ramona asked, grinning ear to ear.

"Ah, my sweet, confused Leroy. No matter what we do, he *still* finds a way to get to my underwear. I've even started buying all black, hoping he would stop because they didn't look like food, but no. He's obsessed with eating fabric. He's lucky I love him."

"How are things going with Dreamland?" Calli asked Ramona as she took another bite of apple pie.

"So busy! I actually had to turn a few people down recently because we are booked solid for the next three months."

"Any thoughts of expanding and building a second location?" Owen asked.

"No, not at the moment. Things are so hectic that I haven't even had a chance to do inventory or keep up with the story, let alone try to put together a business plan for another location."

"If you do, you could always branch out to Sugarplum Falls," Paisley offered. "I've been a few times for work, and I just love it there. Maverick and I are taking the twins up there this year to see Santa and the reindeer. I guess Christmas is a huge thing up there and the whole town decorates and everything!"

"That sounds amazing. I would love to see that sometime."

"Why don't we plan a trip to go this year?" Owen offered, pulling me tight against his side.

"No, I couldn't do that. While it would be great to visit, I couldn't miss Christmas here with all of you guys. Plus, it would be the babies' first Christmas. I want to be here for that."

"I would be on board with spending Christmas in Sugarplum Falls," Ramona said, looking at Preston.

"My family is in Fallen Oaks, but I bet I could convince them to spend a week in a winter wonderland. We know how much my mom loves Christmas and those cheesy movies about it."

"I mean, Maverick and I are already planning to be there, so that just leaves you guys," Paisley said, turning to Calli. "Want to run away to Sugarplum Falls with us for Christmas? You, Dylan, Amelia, and Mom?"

"I don't know. What do you guys think?" Calli asked, looking from her mom to Dylan.

"I'm in," Dylan said, smiling at Calli.

"I would love to go," her mom said happily.

"Well then, I guess that's settled. We'll plan a group trip to Sugarplum Falls," Owen announced to everyone at the table before turning to face me. "And I plan to get you good and knocked up while we're out there."

****

Are you looking for more small-town romance? Be sure to check out the Beaumont Creek series and get ready for some smoking-hot firefighters!

Just One Time (Beaumont Creek Book 1)

https://books2read.com/u/3G52zK

Wanna hang out and chat books? Come find me in my Facebook reader group!

Samantha Baca's Smutties:

https://www.facebook.com/groups/2945710968775398/

Other Books By Samantha

The Haven Brook Series
(small-town romantic suspense):

'Til Death Do Us Part (Haven Brook Book 1)

https://books2read.com/u/m2RJNR

The Cradle Will Fall (Haven Brook Book 2)

https://books2read.com/u/b6O0QE

The Ties That Bind (Haven Brook Book 3)

https://books2read.com/u/mqgoz8

A Very Haven Christmas (Haven Brook Book 4- Novella)

https://books2read.com/u/mvqGjj

Three Strikes, You're Gone (Haven Brook Book 5)

https://books2read.com/u/mvqL2z

The Dark Shadows Trilogy
(romantic suspense)

Five Steps Ahead (Dark Shadows Book 1)

https://books2read.com/u/38Q0gO

Ten Seconds Too Late (Dark Shadows Book 2)

https://books2read.com/u/3JRgVB

Against The Clock (Dark Shadows Book 3)

https://books2read.com/u/m2YwoR

The Stone Creek Series
(small-town- novellas)

Chocolate Covered Mistletoe (Stone Creek Book 1)

https://books2read.com/u/3LRk9N

Candy Coated Promises (Stone Creek Book 2)

https://books2read.com/u/mldP5Y

Pumpkin Spiced Possibilities (Stone Creek Book 3)

https://books2read.com/u/bojdwV

Beaumont Creek Series
(small town)

Just One Time (Beaumont Creek Book 1)

https://books2read.com/u/3G52zK

Second Chances (Beaumont Creek Book 2)

https://books2read.com/u/4Aj6Z0

Third Time's The Charm (Beaumont Creek Book 3)

https://books2read.com/u/b5lEyG

Four-ever Single (Beaumont Creek Book 4)

https://books2read.com/u/4j5jMX

Fifth Wheel (Beaumont Creek Book 5)

https://books2read.com/u/4XwKwa

Whiskey Mountain Series
(small-town- novellas)

Something To Talk About

https://books2read.com/u/4X62ag

Something To Think About

https://books2read.com/u/3GWAan

Something To Believe In

https://books2read.com/u/3yVzgB

Something To Live For

https://books2read.com/u/mllEOP

Sugarplum Falls Series
(Holiday Novellas- can be read as standalone)

Blame It On The Mistletoe
https://books2read.com/u/bw1rqe
Blame It On The Eggnog
https://books2read.com/u/38PPY6
Blame It On The Candy Canes
https://books2read.com/u/31DNo7
Blame It On The Blizzard
https://books2read.com/u/b6z6XE
Blame It On The Reindeer
https://books2read.com/u/baLAG6
Blame It On The Carols
https://books2read.com/u/me8E9z
Blame It On The Lattes
https://books2read.com/u/mB1E2A
Blame It On The Secret Santa
https://books2read.com/u/mY9dGY

Standalone Books

One Last Wish

https://books2read.com/u/mqg7D9

Finding Love In Apartment 2C (novella)

https://books2read.com/u/bze9aZ

Cocky Counsel: A Hero Club Novel

https://books2read.com/u/31Kzkn

All Is Fair In Food And War (novella)

https://books2read.com/u/bp8qjX

Holiday Books (novellas)

Snow Place To Go

https://books2read.com/u/4A560N

A Very Merry Kissmas

https://books2read.com/u/bPDgy7

A Christmas Wish

https://books2read.com/u/4EKXpE

Holiday Hijinks

https://books2read.com/u/4DP6Ze

About the Author

Samantha lives in the southwest with her husband and two small children after abandoning her childhood dream of living in a cabin in Colorado when she found that she couldn't afford to live there and was deathly allergic to the woods. When she's not writing, she's usually spouting off sarcastic remarks while drinking wine out of a coffee mug to look like a functional adult while chasing down her toddlers. She enjoys spending time with her family, watching reruns of Friends, and the 24/7 flow of coffee that can be found in her veins. Be sure to follow her on social media for updates on what she's working on.

You can find her here:

Facebook: https://www.facebook.com/AuthorSamanthaBaca

Instagram: https://instagram.com/author_samantha_baca

Goodreads: http://www.goodreads.com/authorsamanthabaca

Facebook Reader Group:

https://www.facebook.com/groups/2945710968775398/

Webpage: https://authorsamanthabaca.wordpress.com

Newsletter: http://eepurl.com/g0NcSj